Summer Club

A Novel

Katherine Dean Mazerov

outskirts
press

To Bob and Zach
For your love and support and not so gently pushing the real-job idea

And

Stanley, Gracie, and Stella
The brains behind the operation

At the end of May, in cities and suburbs across Middle America, a seasonal rite occurs with the annual opening of the Summer Club. For three months, from Memorial Day to Labor Day, people who normally don't spend time together join in an intense season of partying, swimming, lounging, tennis-playing, and camaraderie. They drink together, barbecue together, compete against each other, and cheer on their kids. They complain, gossip, and have affairs. It all ends with a grand fling on Labor Day. Then the pool is drained, the chairs are stacked, and the gates are locked. Summer is over.

Summer Club

The big black SUV slowed to a stop next to the small fishing pier that jutted out over the river. Two men got out and walked toward the back of the car. The moonlight was dimmed by heavy cloud cover — a good omen. The darkness was punctuated with a flame as one of the men lit a cigarette. The other clicked his key ring to open the trunk. Together, they lifted a large bag out of the vehicle and carried it to the end of the pier. It was heavy; at least 170 pounds. They set the bag down on the edge of the pier then, on their hands and knees, slowly edged it into the river. It lay on the surface for just a moment, then sank beneath the inky black water. The men quickly returned to the car and sped off.

JUNE

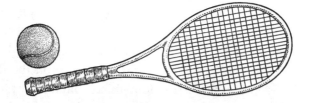

A Box of Troubles

THERE IT was again. *Click.* A click disrupting the comforting hum of the ceiling fan. White noise interrupted. As Lydia watched the silhouette of the blades rotating above her, she calculated the irritating blip was occurring about every seventeen seconds. A project for Bill. She looked over at her slumbering husband, his head barely visible above the bedcovers and the snoring from earlier in the night reduced to a soft gurgle. Stacie, the family dog, was curled up on the floor breathing deeply and evenly. It was early, four-thirty, but a faint pink light was peeking through the shade. Soon, the birds would start chirping and Stacie would awaken to begin her morning ritual of rolling around on the floor and making her moaning-growling sound, punctuated by shrill barks and whines, until someone got up.

Lydia had been awake for at least an hour. She wasn't tired and knew she would not go back to sleep. Four hours of sleep these days was good. So, she lay there thinking about the past weekend and the day that was ahead of her. The weeks ahead of her. The months. Summer had always been her favorite season. She loved the warm weather, the relaxed pace, the long days, a weekend getaway, playing tennis, planting flowers, a family vacation, hosting their annual summer party. But this year there would be no relaxation, no getaway, hardly any tennis, no vacation, maybe not even any flowers. And definitely no party. How, she wondered, had she gotten herself into this mess?

Actually, she knew the answer to that question. The truth was, Lydia Phillips was still trying to fill the void left over from her working days as a reporter, and later an assistant city editor, at the local newspaper, the *Beacon-News*. Ten years ago, after the paper had been purchased by a private equity group, she had taken a buyout. The plan was to stay home and focus on her then-four-year-old fraternal twins, Geoff and Andy, leaving the bread-winning to Bill, a CPA who also happened to be a fabulous cook. They'd met at Penn State and spent many a night engaged in pretty awesome sex in Bill's studio apartment on the second floor of a rickety Victorian near campus. Boozy brunches with herbed frittatas and syrup-drenched French toast and decadent, sauce-laden dinners with multiple bottles of wine and lots of chocolate completed the package. Lydia didn't have to think twice when Bill popped the question. As he built his practice, she worked her way up the ladder at the newspaper. Then came the twins.

She didn't miss the long hours and the never-ending budget cuts while the paper continued to shrink in size and the staff was reduced in multiple rounds of layoffs as digitization continued to change the traditional journalistic paradigm. All while the owners raked in profits for their investors.

Yet Lydia, who found day-to-day cooking and other household tasks tedious, did miss the fast-paced, adrenaline-rush deadline environment of the newsroom, particularly her salad days as a police reporter. Later, she'd been assigned the City Hall beat and then moved to the City Desk, supervising the police and court reporters. So, she channeled her energy into the twins' activities—volunteering in the classroom, joining the school PTA, chairing an extracurricular reading program. She also donated countless hours at Meadow Glen Swim and Tennis Club, conveniently located four doors down the street from their home in Jorgentown, a middle-to-upper-middle-class suburb in the Midwest. A type-A personality and slender, with short blonde hair and freckles, Lydia was not a serious athlete but had always been active, exercising routinely, and was a decent tennis player.

Lately, she'd enjoyed taking on the challenge of volunteer leadership positions, treating them like a paid job. So dedicated was she at tirelessly embracing non-paying positions, that people continually asked her to join their boards and committees. This had begun to rankle Bill, who was pushing her to pursue something that would bring some revenue into the household, especially with college for the boys only four years away. The twins, now fourteen and about to enter high school, also agreed that Mom needed to get a "real job." Even Stacie got annoyed and barked when Lydia was on the phone for more than twenty minutes—which she was all the time, it seemed.

But after taking on the volunteer job of junior tennis chair at Meadow Glen—growing the program to record numbers—Lydia was nominated, and subsequently elected, as the club's board president. Bill, who'd strongly advised her to step down from the board, was furious, the twins embarrassed. Lydia had assured them that this would be her last stint on the volunteer circuit. Now, after several months of planning and organizing, the club had officially opened for the season with the annual Memorial Day weekend festivities.

Certain that all her hard work over the winter would ensure a smooth season, Lydia was dismayed when the opening weekend had been bumpy. There was massive complaining about everything from the snack bar offerings to the temperature of the pool. The directories were late. The tennis players were fighting. The unruly Murphy boys had already christened the playground, peeing all over the slide in front of a horrified father and his little daughter. Twice, the pool had been closed for several hours due to toddler potty accidents. Stacie, who frequented the club more than some members, had joined in the opening weekend festivities, once coming within inches of devouring a duckling belonging to the ducks that had made Meadow Glen their nesting ground for the past three years.

Stacie began to stir and whine, putting a sudden end to Lydia's reflections. A clear signal to get up and start what would be a busy day. It was five-fifteen. She would check her e-mail, log into the online Suggestion Box that had been added to the club's website, and then take a run—more for her mental well-being than to stay in shape. Later, she would get to work on the agenda for the upcoming board meeting.

"Come on, little girl," Lydia said to Stacie, as she went downstairs. She started the coffee and went into her office, a bright, peach-colored room with botanical print Roman shades, a hardwood floor with an oriental rug, and a very cushy club chair. The room was a mess as usual, with papers strewn all over the floor and the desk covered in Post-it notes, bills, and stacks of yellow legal tablets.

She opened her e-mail. Surprisingly, there were only a few. She had expected an onslaught. This was good! Stacie padded into the office, wagging her tail and whining and carrying her favorite toy: a beloved pink bunny with fraying ears and a hole where the squeaker had been. Pink, as the toy was affectionately called by the family, was Stacie's constant companion. A golden lab/beagle-and-whatever mix, the four-year-old dog had hit the jackpot when the Phillips family adopted her from a shelter. Now, three years later, she pretty much ruled the household, her good nature masking the fact that she was extremely spoiled and demanding. Lydia got up, gave her a treat, and opened the pet door, which was just big enough for the dog's seventy-pound body to squeeze through. She poured herself a cup of coffee, logged on to the Meadow Glen website, then hit the Suggestion Box link.

Oh. My God! The list was loading, loading, and still loading. This was not good. Several minutes later, the download was finally complete. Lydia could feel the heat rising from her chest into her neck and face. Her stomach twisted into that familiar knot of anxiety, and her hands became clammy. The list was overwhelming. In an effort to delay the inevitable, Lydia first took a moment to count. There were eighty-seven "suggestions" in the box. *Eighty-seven.* Just then, Stacie came back in looking for her reward for venturing outside. Her big feet were wet and slightly muddy, and her long, golden-brown coat was damp from running through the bushes.

Welcoming the distraction, Lydia went to the treat jar and cleaned off Stacie's paws, then buried her head in the dog's thick fur, lovingly caressing her ears and rubbing her chest. "What would I do without you?" she said. "You are the best stress reliever in the world." She poured another cup of coffee and considered mixing a Bloody Mary, but quickly reasoned it was probably a little too early.

Whose stupid idea was this damn Suggestion Box? she wondered, then remembered it was her stupid idea to have a way for members to participate in the betterment of Meadow Glen by offering constructive suggestions. Sadly, most were only interested in complaining or finding a way to get more for less money. Over the past nine months, Lydia had identified what she now considered to be a universal truism: people actually enjoy complaining and find it cathartic to engage in vitriolic exchanges about mostly trivial matters. God forbid an issue would be resolved, thus robbing the complainants of this rich form of entertainment. Of course, the perpetual whiners would always find something else to carp about.

Perspective, she thought. *Let's keep this in perspective. This is a summer club; we're not curing cancer here.*

MEADOW GLEN was a rundown, clapboard swim and tennis club built in the early 1970s. Despite its location on a lovely shaded street at the edge of an upscale neighborhood, five miles from a posh country club, the facility was an eyesore with its faded, peeling paint and overgrown junipers. The property, including a long, ranch-style clubhouse, took up a full square block and had an ugly patched asphalt parking lot on one side. A squeaky iron gate served as the official entrance on one end of the building, while two service gates were located on the opposite end near the boiler room and toolshed. There were six tennis courts, two of which had large, stubborn cracks due to the expanding clay-rich soil that lay beneath them. The pool was heated by an aging boiler that had been patched and jury-rigged through the years by overzealous and meddling board members. The bathrooms smelled because the toilets backed up routinely.

The twenty-five-meter pool also had a tiny, but constant, leak onto the street behind the club, a problem that had gone on for so long no one really noticed it anymore. It had just become part of the rustic charm of Meadow Glen Swim and Tennis Club.

Unlike the other local summer clubs, Meadow Glen had been through a series of economic setbacks ever since half the members had resigned fifteen years earlier when the board issued a special assessment to resurface the pool. After the initiation fee and dues had been reduced to a ridiculously low price, the membership had gradually grown back, and the club was on the cusp of turning around. Both the initiation fee and the dues had been raised back up, bringing in some cash flow for improvements. Last year, the club had built a new baby pool, complete with a fountain and colorful red, blue, and yellow tiles, and added a slide at the deep end of the main pool. Still, the swim team remained small and fledgling. The adult and junior tennis teams, while growing, were at the bottom of the standings. The club had been further weakened by a revolving door of managers, swim coaches, and tennis pros, who would leave after a year or two, run out by micro-managing board members.

What the club did have was a snack bar that was beloved by the members—a junk food emporium filled with candy, corn dogs, fruity ice drinks, soda pop, ice cream bars, snow cones, chips, and popcorn, the kernels of which frequently clogged the pool filter. The Sugar Shack, as it was lovingly called, was very important to the mothers of Meadow Glen, absolving them from having to pack a lunch so their children could happily fill their faces with lots of sugar and fat.

Despite its problems, Meadow Glen year after year provided residents of the neighborhood and surrounding area an affordable place to go in the summer.

It was now six, and the sun was rising. Lydia began going through the list of suggestions, soon realizing there were so many she needed to create categories since many addressed the same issue.

From the swim team mothers: How about selling Starbucks in the snack bar during early morning swim practice? *We've tried that in the past, and there wasn't enough demand to cover the cost of staffing during those hours,*

Lydia thought. The snack bar only was open from 11:30 a.m. to 7 p.m.

It would be great if we could get some gluten-free pastries in the Sugar Shack. *Please!*

At least twenty were complaints about the pool being too cold. This one worried Lydia. That boiler was on its last legs, and this may not be a fixable problem. She would have to speak with Pete, the club manager.

The list went on:

The tennis courts are dirty.

Can we have a mom-and-tot swim program?

The guards don't know the names of my kids.

Please open the club before 11 a.m. It's not fair that the swim team hogs the pool in the morning.

You ran out of food for the Memorial Day BBQ.

My two-year-old cut her foot on the playground.

Why can't we have glass on the pool deck? I don't like wine in a box, or tequila in plastic. *Because if glass breaks in or near the pool it's a safety hazard. Worst case, we have to close the pool, drain it, clean it out, and refill and reheat it. Costs a lot of money and takes several days.*

Why did we install lights on the tennis courts, when there are other needs that are more pressing? Will the members be assessed to pay for the lawsuit?

The lawsuit. Now, there was a sore subject. Lydia's stomach tightened up again remembering the day she had received the thick packet from Peters Hart Holmes and Hoskins, a downtown law firm. For years, Meadow Glen had been at odds with the neighborhood Homeowners Association about installing lights on the club's six tennis courts. The HOA covenants, written when the neighborhood and the club were being developed, explicitly prohibited lights on the courts. But tennis court lighting technology had come a long way in forty-five years. In addition, the lights could be programmed to automatically turn on at dusk and turn off at a specified time. They were designed in such a way as to only shine downward, onto the courts, minimizing their impact on the surrounding homes now shielded from the club by decades of tree growth.

Emboldened with those seemingly logical arguments, the elite tennis players had last summer finally worn down the club's board of directors to allow lights only on Courts 1 and 2. Over the off-season, the board had taken $20,000 from the capital improvement budget and advanced another $30,000 from the line of credit to have the lights installed. The ultimate goal was to install lights on all the courts and update lighting throughout the club grounds, replacing the existing, barely functional lighting system rigged with dated wiring that no longer met code. For years, only the floodlights on the patio and one light near the deep end of the pool had operated. By updating the lighting on both the courts and the club grounds, security would be enhanced to at least deter what had become an annoying teenage rite of summer: nighttime pool jumping.

But two months ago, Claire Hoskins, a tax attorney and partner in the prestigious law practice and whose property abutted the club grounds, filed a lawsuit. No, the suit maintained, the board could not simply install the lights. The HOA bylaws would have to be changed by a two-thirds vote of the neighborhood. Despite being a member of Meadow Glen, Claire, a heavy-set, pugnacious litigator who rarely lost a legal contest, was not about to cave on this issue. She had embarked on a vicious campaign rivaling the gun lobby to get rid of the lights, even though they were not visible from her yard.

Disruptive and potentially expensive, the lawsuit had put a crimp in the board's plans to paint the exterior of the clubhouse and landscape the front. The members were furious and adjacent residents were complaining.

Lydia pushed the lawsuit out of her mind as she continued reading the list of "suggestions."

The dues are too high.

The tennis clinics are too expensive.

There was gum on the pool deck and it ruined my flip-flops. Can the club reimburse me?

Why does the pool have to be shut down when somebody poops?

Keep your damn dog out of the pool.

This one was aimed directly at Lydia. Ever since she had followed Geoff and Andy to the club one day last year, Stacie had made it her second home. Anytime she was bored or left alone, Stacie, who loved the water, would simply jump the fence, lope down the street, and brazenly dash through the front gate of the club, wreaking havoc on whatever activity was going on. Twice she had made an appearance during opening weekend. The first had been early Sunday morning when the ducks were in the pool, their line of ducklings behind them learning to swim. From his office, Pete heard the squawking as Stacie, in the pool, was about to snag one of the ducklings while the mother duck dive-bombed her. Pete jumped into the pool in the nick of time and grabbed the startled dog.

The second episode occurred on Memorial Day at the busiest time of the afternoon when Stacie flew into the baby pool, knocking over several toddlers as their irritated mothers tried to shoo her away. She then snatched a bag of Goldfish snack crackers from a frightened three-year-old whose guttural scream could be heard as far away as the parking lot. Lydia was mortified, but amazed and thankful no one was hurt. Stacie spent the rest of the day inside the house, with her dog door closed.

It took Lydia over an hour to read through the list. By then, Bill and the kids were up. It was the last week of school, which was a good thing. That would give the board and Pete more time to work out the bugs before next weekend when the pool would be crowded with out-of-school kids and the summer programs—hopefully—up and running at full participation.

She took a break from her desk to feed Stacie and see Geoff and Andy off to school. The boys looked nothing alike—Andy was fair-haired with wavy reddish blond hair while Geoff had straight dark brown hair and a more olive complexion—and were as different as night and day. Andy was studious and quiet, a saver and a reader, while Geoff was outgoing and social, more of a risk-taker. Both were decent athletes, although not superstars.

"Last week of school, guys," she said. "Try to pay attention."

"Whatever," Andy responded.

She touched base with Bill, a six-foot-three tennis player with dark, graying wavy hair, nearly black eyes, and high cheekbones, whose game had been sidelined by a knee replacement in November. He'd played in the Memorial Day round-robin doubles tournament but would not be playing any league matches this season. Between that and her commitments to the club, his summer had been reduced to tending his vegetable and herb gardens, the only part of the yard receiving any attention over the spring. *At least we'll eat well.*

"Morning," Bill said. "You were up early. You got some sleep, I hope."

"Yes, but only about four or five hours. You slept like a log." Her good sense convinced her not to vent to him about the Suggestion Box. He likely would not be very sympathetic, leaving her with, "Well, I'm sure you'll figure it out." Code for, "I warned you not to do this!" Or, his standard "How bad can it be?" *How bad is there.*

She did, however, mention the click in the ceiling fan.

"Probably just need to redistribute the weights," he said. "Shouldn't be a big deal." Code for: "I'm not going to get to it anytime soon."

"Will you be late tonight?" she asked, pouring Bill a cup of coffee.

"No, shouldn't be too bad. I want to work in the garden; then I'll figure something out for dinner. We've got some leftovers and vegetables. Risotto?"

"Sounds great. I'll throw together a salad. I know I don't need to say it, but thanks for keeping us all very well fed," she said, giving him an affectionate kiss.

"You know it's a labor of love."

With everyone gone, Lydia went back to the computer. It was almost eleven by the time she finished going through the suggestions list and responded to the issues she could. She made notes for those that would go to the Tennis and Swim chairs, head of Operations, and other appropriate board members for them to respond. *I'm delegating,* she thought, proud of herself for recognizing she could not take on all the responsibility.

Lydia remembered she had planned to take a run. But by now it was too hot and humid to exercise outside. *Damnit!* Starving, she fixed herself a tuna sandwich and took a shower. She stretched out on the couch, figuring she would go over to the club later that afternoon to talk to Pete about the pool temperature. The cheerful family room, anchored by a large stone fireplace, looked out onto a spacious wooden deck with a porch swing, tables, comfortable chairs, and a mostly empty array of flower boxes and pots that Lydia was still trying to plant. She and Bill had put a lot of hard work and money into improving their two-story Tudor home over the past fifteen years, upgrading every room in the house and re-landscaping both front and back yards. The spacious kitchen was equipped with high-end appliances, including a large designer gas range with five burners and two ovens. Her birthday gift to Bill five years ago. The most recent addition was a climate-controlled wine cellar, complete with a mural depicting the Tuscan hills they had visited before the twins were born.

She picked up her iPad and logged on to the *Beacon-News* website, scanning the top stories before turning to the local news section. She began to read a story about a missing businessman, then dozed off. The jolting ring of her cell phone awakened her an hour later. Stacie had jumped the fence and was at the club again. This time in the Sugar Shack.

Night Visitor

IT WAS one a.m. Pete Merrick, wrench in hand, was on his hands and knees in the boiler room, squinting at the temperature dial. He had heard the complaining about the pool temperature over Memorial Day weekend and had experienced it firsthand when he swam a few laps. The temperature was perfect for him, but he knew it would not be acceptable to most of the members, especially mothers with young children, who enjoyed the pool for playing and dipping not hardcore swimming. Unable to sleep, he'd returned to the club just after midnight to see if he could correct the problem. He was sure the dial had been set at eighty-three degrees over the weekend. Now it was at seventy-nine degrees, the same reading the pool thermometer was showing. What had caused the drop?

Pete stood up and surveyed the chaos of equipment in the boiler room, located at the far end of the clubhouse. By modern-day standards, the boiler was ancient, a strange configuration of pieces and parts, each one needing to be manually adjusted daily. Most clubs had updated their systems with streamlined, computerized models that held temperature levels precisely as set and required little or no hands-on maintenance. Fortunately, Pete had figured out the Meadow Glen system quickly and mastered the controls. Now, the boiler was running better than it had in years.

A Princeton graduate who had been captain of the university's swim team, Pete had gone on to the University of Chicago for his MBA then joined a prestigious Wall Street investment firm, becoming a successful portfolio manager. He took early retirement at forty-five, walking away with millions. Now, to fulfill the passion he'd initially planned to pursue, he taught AP economics and calculus at nearby Roosevelt High School, one of the premier public schools in the country. For the past five years, he also had coached the girls' swim team at the school, taking a program that had been mediocre at best to one of the top-ranked in the state. This year, the team had taken first place at the state swim meet.

Both Pete and his wife Shelly had grown up in the Midwest and had been thrilled to come back to be closer to family. They purchased a home in one of the area's toniest neighborhoods, and Shelly, an interior designer, opened her own firm. Their two daughters, Tess and Chloe, were in middle school and high school at the time. Chloe was now a senior at Stanford, and Tess had just finished her freshman year at Tufts University in Boston.

Quite sure of himself, Pete was in his mid-fifties, lanky with a medium build, a full head of graying reddish-brown hair, and a ruddy complexion. He had a great sense of humor and an affable, easygoing nature about him that belied the brilliance and drive that had propelled him in the world of high-powered finance.

This was his third summer as manager at Meadow Glen. He liked the atmosphere and the unique challenges of running a summer club—a far cry from the rigor of Wall Street. He believed he could help turn the place around, raising it to the level of the other summer clubs in the area that had enjoyed the consistency of capable, long-time managers.

Pete knew he was good at his job. He was not afraid to try new things and he liked being in charge. Through his teaching and coaching jobs at the high school, he was able to recruit top students and swimmers as lifeguards and coaches. With their help, he had built the swim lesson program up from virtually nothing and created a fun, relaxing ambiance at the club. He knew most of the members by name and listened to what they had to say. He was great at giving tours to prospective members, personally bringing in ten new families this year alone. It was Pete who two years ago had suggested the club update the aging baby pool to attract young families. Last summer, thirty families, all with children under age five, had joined the club. By all measures, he had brought his success from Wall Street to Meadow Glen.

Crouched down in the dimly lit boiler room, Pete was startled by the familiar creaking noise of an iron gate. He listened for a moment, then heard what sounded like a gate closing. There were two gates to access the restricted back area of the club. One was a narrow iron gate that could be opened only with a key. The other was a sliding wooden gate, secured with a combination lock, that was used for deliveries and moving the trash dumpster and equipment in and out of the club.

Standing, his knees cracking as they shifted to a new position, he flung open the slightly ajar boiler room door and looked outside, waiting for his eyes to adjust. It was quite dark, although a streetlight cast some illumination onto a small concrete space that was full of equipment, broken umbrella stands, and buckets of pool chemicals.

This was not the first time Pete had been interrupted by noises at the club in the middle of the night. To get the club open for the season, he frequently worked well into the wee hours during the month of May before school let out for the summer. Several times he'd heard what sounded like the iron gate closing. One night, he was certain he heard footsteps, but found no evidence of anyone being there. Except for a still-smoldering cigarette butt near the dumpster.

Unsettled at what appeared to be yet another incident, he went around the corner to his office to get a flashlight. As he came back, he heard the screech of tires in the street. He grabbed an overturned bucket next to the fence and stood on it in time to see the taillights of a car speeding away. He got down and shined the flashlight around the area.

Both gates were closed, but the iron gate was unlocked. *Someone with a key had opened this gate and left in a hurry,* he thought. On the concrete next to the iron gate were several wet spots. *What…?* After a more careful study, Pete was able to distinguish them as two sets of footprints, probably sneakers or running shoes. He remembered the sprinklers along the club perimeter had been on earlier that night. Looking down at the footsteps, Pete became troubled. As far as he could tell, nothing had been disturbed or taken. But someone had been inside the club grounds, in a place where no one had any business being.

In the Weeds

LYDIA SAT down at her cluttered desk to compose the agenda for tomorrow's board meeting. The house was quiet. Geoff had gone over to the pool for afternoon swim practice and Andy was getting ready for baseball practice. Stacie, stretched out on the couch in the basement, was snoring loudly. Lydia jotted down the main subjects for discussion:

> Review of Opening Weekend
> Committee Reports: Swim, Tennis, Operations, Social
> Snack Bar
> Suggestions distributed to the appropriate committee chairs
> Lawsuit/Petition status
> Keys

This last one was primarily for informational purposes. Lydia had decided last year that she wanted to re-key the club, and Pete had agreed. There were dozens of keys floating around that previous board members had failed to turn in—either because they had lost them, forgot they still had them, or wanted to hang on to that small entitlement of being able to access the club whenever they wanted. Lydia assumed the latter was the biggest category. How many times had retired board members used the pool for late-night soirees? Or told the manager they would "lock up" if he would let them stay past closing? Last summer, two former board members had been caught skinny-dipping with some of the lifeguards. Before the pool opened this year, several people had "inaugurated" the season with a midnight cocktail party. In his first two years as manager, Pete several times had caught members late at night in the boiler room, tools and beer in hand, tinkering with the controls and adjusting the pump settings.

These offenders saw no problem using the club surreptitiously. "What's wrong with a little off-hours fun?" one former board member had argued after being chastised. "Why not let us keep our keys as a legacy, a thank-you for our service? We aren't hurting anything."

No, Lydia was adamant about getting the key problem under control. "It's dangerous without a lifeguard on duty with drinking going on, creating an insurance liability," she had responded. "Trash has been left in and around the pool, and we can't run the risk of any broken glass."

New keys would be issued to the staff and to board members who needed to access the club off-hours, such as the Swim, Tennis, Operations, and Social chairs, president, and vice president. Pete had already scheduled a locksmith to come out. He planned to order a small number of keys, each engraved with DO NOT DUPLICATE. While not legally binding, the words would at least make it a little harder for the keys to be copied.

Lydia finalized the agenda and e-mailed it out to the board. They would meet at the picnic tables at the far end of the pool, seven p.m. She picked up her keys, hollered to Andy to get in the car, and checked one last time that the dog door was closed. After dropping Andy off at the baseball field she drove back home and put on her favorite pair of Capri pants, happy to see they still fit.

Clouds had moved in, and it had become cooler in the last hour. She walked the short distance to the club. It was four-thirty. School had been out for more than an hour so Pete would be there as the club would be getting crowded for the evening.

Entering the club, Lydia was pleased to see things operating smoothly. Despite the cloud cover, people were playing tennis and lounging by the pool. On Court 2, Brad Stovall was hitting balls to his eight-year-old son, Tad—a ritual that would play out for hours nearly every day until the club closed for the season. Lydia didn't know anyone who had ever actually spoken to Brad, Tad, or Brad's wife, who rarely made an appearance. *That kid is going to be on the circuit someday,* she thought.

The main club entrance took her alongside Courts 1 and 2. Overlooking these tennis courts were three raised rows of rusted metal bleachers that were always too hot to sit on as they baked under the sun all day. The board had planned to replace them and put up an awning, but the lawsuit had put that project on hold as well. Grant Rogers, the tennis pro, was giving a semi-private lesson to two blonde women on Court 1 while some teenagers hit balls on the back courts.

Grant was, Lydia guessed, in his mid-thirties and a relatively good instructor who was in his third year at the club. His best feature was his looks—six-foot-two with dark hair, piercing blue eyes, and a captivating smile—which could be why the number of female players had grown by more than 30 percent. But beneath that charismatic exterior, Grant had a dark side, a terrible temper due in part to the fact that he was disorganized and an inept administrator. The tennis office was a mess, full of boxes of tennis balls, a device for stringing rackets, and dusty shelves displaying tennis awards from years past. His desk was barely visible under the stacks of papers and sign-up sheets that he failed to attend to. In the past, checks often had been lost or gone uncashed, and clinic rosters had rarely matched actual attendance. Last year, the board had finally instituted a system whereby members signed up for lessons, clinics, and league play through the Tennis committee, looping Grant out of the financial and administrative aspect of the job altogether.

Grant was also ambitious and political, and he was obsessed with winning. After figuring out who was who among the tennis players, he had embarked on what he called a "new beginning" for Meadow Glen Tennis, starting with the USTA league teams. This spring, he and some of the high-ranked players had joined forces in a process that one member likened to a sorority rush. Teams that had been together for years were separated into A teams and B teams to make them more competitive. Team practices were mandatory, and players who did not sign up—and pay—for the practices would only get on a team as a substitute, meaning they were more likely to watch the matches than play.

For the women, especially, the reorganization had been hurtful; friendships were strained, splitting up long-time partners who played together for social connections as much as tennis. Lydia understood the rationale behind the reorganization but recognized this was also a cultural change that would be very disruptive. She wasn't sure this was the best move right now. However, preoccupied with more pressing matters at the club, she had put this one on the back burner and was relieved to have had a legitimate reason to sign up only as a substitute this year.

Opposite the bleachers was the Sugar Shack, which also served as the check-in point for members and guests. The area included the front section with counters, the soda fountain, popcorn maker, and the FunFro machine that provided thick iced drinks in raspberry, orange, and strawberry flavors. Behind that area was the kitchen with a microwave oven and a freezer and two refrigerators where food was stored. A back room housed various supplies, napkins, plastic utensils and paper plates, containers of syrup, and equipment with a tangle of tubes and wires that ran through the ceiling to feed the soda and FunFro machines in the front.

Adjacent to the kitchen was an old, dark storage room that had been converted into an office of sorts with a desk, locker, and an old overstuffed couch undoubtedly infested with bugs and mice droppings.

Lydia smelled microwave popcorn and the sweet syrup of snow cones. Then she caught a whiff of something else — marijuana, which was forbidden at Meadow Glen. That could mean only one thing: Jules was here.

Jules Maguire was an aging hippie and would-be artist who had begged to run the Sugar Shack again this year. She was constantly in court over her ex-husband's failure to pay the $3,000 monthly maintenance that had been mandated as part of their messy divorce settlement. Complications following a series of knee surgeries had put Jules in constant pain. Her drug of choice was marijuana, which she smoked and ingested frequently. Jules, who had been active in the women's movement and anti-Vietnam War demonstrations at UC Berkeley in the 1970s, had been at the vanguard of petition drives to legalize medical marijuana, which had been approved by the state legislature three years ago. Last year, voters had approved legalization of recreational marijuana, but cultivation of large-scale plants was limited to licensed retail marijuana establishments. Individuals could have six plants, only three of them mature plants, in an enclosed, locked space for their personal use. It was no secret that Jules, who still had a "Vote to Legalize MMJ" bumper sticker on her rusted-out Volvo station wagon, liberally self-medicated with her own supply of pot. She swore she didn't smoke at the club, yet there was always a faint aroma emanating from the Shack.

The Maguires had joined the club years ago when their children were babies. Both were extremely bright. Ed, a psychologist, had been a college professor with a successful private practice, while Jules, who held a master's degree in art history, dabbled in painting. They had been one of the most popular couples at the club, holding board positions and organizing parties. Their four kids had participated in the swim team and junior tennis programs. All had gone on to top-notch colleges and grad schools, pursuing PhDs in such erudite subjects as English literature and Asian studies.

Jules, who had always been considered a bit avant-garde, had once been a striking woman with beautiful skin and thick, long brown hair. Now she was stick-thin with a leathered complexion. Her hair was still long but was now a frizzy gray mess that hung with no shape around her face. Lydia's efforts to get her to pull her hair back when she was working in the Shack had failed. Since the operation didn't involve actual cooking it wasn't mandatory, but Lydia was sure that strands of Jules's gray locks had landed in more than one corn dog.

"Hello, Jules," Lydia said brightly. Jules, standing on a stool, looked over her shoulder, half a candy bar sticking out of her mouth. Her eyes were red and dilated. She was wearing a dirty yellow T-shirt with *Cal* written in blue cursive, referring to her alma mater. Jules was putting the finishing touches on her new mural above the snack bar. *Sugar Shack* was scrawled in big red letters amidst colorful drawings of ice-cream cones, pool drinks, hot dogs, lounge chairs, and umbrella tables.

"Hi," she mumbled, her mouth full. "Good news. The directories are here."

That *was* good news. One problem Lydia could cross off the list. "Great. Did you find the labels I left in that red folder under the counter? And we need to put up a sign." Labels for the directories had been printed to keep track of who had received their one allotted copy. Inevitably, there were always members who took more than one copy, meaning others didn't get theirs. This year's budget didn't allow for families to receive more than one directory.

"Yes, the kids are sticking them on now. I told them to check people's names off when they pick up their copy." The "kids" in this case were a group of thirteen- and fourteen-year-olds, all children of members, who worked in the Shack, checking in members and guests and waiting on them as they lined up to purchase candy, drinks, and snacks. Lydia had always felt that hiring children of members was a risky policy as it created a natural conflict of interest. Indeed, there had been instances in the past when a Sugar Shack employee had been reprimanded or let go, causing friction with the parents. The fact that there were always more applicants than positions made the hiring process especially touchy.

Both Geoff and Andy had lobbied hard to work in the Sugar Shack, but Lydia and Bill had been united in their opposition, especially given Lydia's position as board president. This had caused a huge family fight with the resolution that the boys each would receive extra allowance for the summer and iPads. In other words, Bill and Lydia were subsidizing them to *not* work in the snack bar.

"Be sure to tell the staff to give directories only to adults," Lydia said. "By the way, Jules. I know we've discussed this before, about your smoking marijuana at the club."

"Lydia, I've told you I don't smoke it here," Jules said, refusing to make eye contact. A sure sign she was lying, Lydia speculated. Jules put on her sunglasses.

"Then why am I constantly smelling pot, always in the vicinity of the snack bar?"

"I don't know. I'm sure it's not coming from me."

"Well, if the smell continues, we're going to have to determine where it's coming from." Lydia was irritated that Jules didn't seem at all phased by this pronouncement.

Lydia moved on, just in time to see a young child drop his snow cone on the patio. Syrup splattered everywhere and the child immediately burst into tears. *Great. Here come the bees,* she thought, showing no compassion for the sobbing toddler. By late July, after multiple spills of Sugar Shack fare, bees and wasps would infiltrate Meadow Glen with a vengeance. Last summer the club had paid a lot of money to have several huge hives — on the patio and in the awnings of the tennis court water stations — removed with an ecofriendly bee vacuum. Two kids had been hospitalized due to bee stings. Both Pete and Grant kept large supplies of bee and wasp spray in their offices and used them liberally. Lydia hoped the club could avoid the need for another round of pest control this season.

The bee problem was one of several reasons she and others had pushed so hard to get rid of the Sugar Shack, which lost money due to the extra staffing needed and required a health department permit. But two years ago, after the board had drastically reduced the food offerings and replaced the soda fountain with vending machines, the members complained vehemently and even circulated a petition, BRING BACK THE SHACK. *Oh well,* Lydia thought. *This is what the members want, and I have bigger fish to fry anyway.*

"Hey, kids, can one of you please come over here and clean up this snow cone mess?" she called out to the snack bar workers.

By now, the mother had arrived on the scene to comfort her distraught child. "Can he get another one?" she asked.

"Sure, no problem," Lydia responded tersely.

Pete was in his office, on the phone ordering chemicals for the pool. He waved for Lydia to come in. About thirty kids were swimming laps as head coach Alex Taylor and assistant coach Bridget Martin walked along the side of the pool, watching the kids' strokes and correcting them when appropriate. Lydia recognized the back of Geoff's head as he swam the breaststroke, his favorite.

Alex was in his second year as coach. A nice kid, about twenty-five, he emanated little emotion or enthusiasm. Tall with short blond hair and wire glasses, he was somewhat aloof and tended to pay attention to only the more talented swimmers, something that irked a number of parents who wanted him to push their kids harder to qualify for the summer league and state swim meets. Bridget, a junior in college who had worked at Meadow Glen for years as a guard and coach, primarily coached the eight-and-under group. She was beloved by the kids and their parents.

Alex had been recruited by Lawrence Haskell, the Swim chair and meet announcer who also ran a Masters Swimming program three days a week at six a.m. for serious adult swimmers. It was really Lawrence, who referred to himself as Lawrence C. Haskell the Third, who ran the show, directing Alex every step of the way. A retired Army captain, Lawrence was a hardcore swimmer, and for the past four years had coached swimming at a regional college. He was a firm believer that rigid discipline and grueling practices were the ways to motivate kids. This was his third stint on the board in twelve years, and his second year as Swim chair. Alex had been one of his top college swimmers. Lawrence, who was thin and short, but very muscular, and had a crew cut, had been married once. Word was his wife left him after three months.

When he wasn't in the water, Lawrence was often sitting at a table on the far side of the pool drinking beer while he pored over the kids' swim times. Lydia marveled that he didn't have a huge beer belly. He did, however, have several distasteful tattoos on his arms and legs—a scantily clad, voluptuous blonde holding a semi-automatic gun and a machete-wielding pirate, among others. At the insistence of the board, he did his best to conceal them with long shorts or fatigues and long-sleeve T-shirts when he was in contact with the kids.

As Alex and Bridget walked up and down one side of the pool, Lawrence, wearing a U.S. Army baseball cap, long-sleeved shirt, and sweat pants, stood at one end, letting out a shrill whistle as each swimmer made the turn, a way of spurring them to swim faster. Swim team competition would begin next week, but the first home meet wasn't until the last week of June. As the announcer for all the home meets, Lawrence started every event by firing a starter pistol rather than using the conventional sound system that the other clubs used. His insistence at using the pistol had been raised at league meetings by parents and coaches who felt the practice was archaic and set a bad example.

Lydia went into Pete's office, a small, dark space with papers everywhere, and moved a first-aid kit off a dirty plastic chair.

"Sorry about the mess," he said. "I haven't had much of a chance to get things organized in here yet."

After exchanging a few pleasantries, Lydia told him about the eighty-seven "suggestions" she had culled through earlier in the week. "I think we may have a problem—" she started.

"Let me guess," Pete interrupted. "The pool temperature."

"Yes." She felt relieved that Pete was already aware of the situation.

"Yeah, I noticed the water was cool yesterday, which is odd because I had set it for eighty-three degrees the day before. When I checked it last night, it was down to seventy-nine degrees. I was here until well after midnight trying to figure it out."

"I'm worried this may be the end of the boiler," Lydia said. "We know we're on borrowed time with it. Do you think it's about to go out for good?"

"That could be the case, but I don't think so. It almost looks like the dial was reset. It could be a faulty thermostat, which is not a big deal. I may need to have someone come out and look at it."

"Okay, well I guess just monitor it. People are complaining."

"It's fine now," Pete said. "We're at eighty-three degrees."

Lydia felt a huge wave of solace wash over her. "That's good. Maybe it was just a fluke."

"Yeah, I'll keep an eye on it," Pete said. "By the way, I think we had a visitor late last night."

"Pool jumpers this early in the season?" she suggested, referring to the teenagers who jump the fence at night, swim, drink beer, and occasionally throw furniture into the pool. It was a problem that plagued every summer club in the area, a rite of summer. It usually started in late June when the weather was starting to get hot. By mid-July, the novelty had pretty much worn off.

"No, pool jumpers are only interested in the pool. This was someone in the back, by the boiler room. I heard the gate close." Pete then explained what had happened the night before, along with the other apparent trespassing occurrences. "I can't figure out why anyone would want to be in that area. It's just pool chemicals and equipment. I suppose it could have been an old board member wanting to mess with the boiler, or maybe someone trying to steal chemicals."

"That's odd." Lydia thought for a moment. "I guess all you can do is make sure the gates and boiler room are locked." Then she remembered the other thing she wanted to discuss with Pete. "On that note, are we still on for re-keying the club?"

"Yeah, I have a locksmith coming in a couple of weeks."

"Good. I'm going to announce it at the board meeting and explain that only some board members will be receiving new keys. I don't think everyone on the board needs one."

"I agree. I'll make a list of the staff who'll need new keys."

"Thanks for getting on that and keep me posted on the temperature situation. See you at the meeting."

LYDIA DECIDED to take a walk before going home. Rounding the corner to the back side of the club, she saw the tiny stream of water trickling down Franklin Street from somewhere deep within the pool. Try as he might, Pete had been unable to determine the source of the leak, most likely a cracked underground pipe. Every morning he or the assistant manager would have to fill the pool, replacing the few gallons of water that had been lost the day before. Seeing the water disturbed her, but Lydia dismissed it as one of those "back-burner" problems she didn't need to deal with. She continued down the street and saw her good friend Susan Adams working in the garden.

"Hey," Lydia called out. "That looks therapeutic."

Susan stood up, a big smile on her face. "I was about to quit and have a glass of wine. Come on in. I'm unwinding from a horrible day at work."

They sat down in the bright red Adirondack chairs on the beautiful terrace, where colorful pots were filled with an assortment of flowers that Susan, who had an incredible green thumb, had planted. The music of Chris Botti floated from inside the house. Lydia took a sip of wine and listened to Susan rant about the frustrations and latest goings-on in her job as chief marketing officer for a large homebuilder. Lydia listened sympathetically but in awe of Susan's high-level position and six-figure salary.

Lydia and Susan had been friends for years. Susan's husband, Joe, and Bill walked together every Sunday morning; their kids, Nick and Lauren, were in school with the Phillips boys. The families had spent many hours together at the club, barbecuing nearly every Sunday night during the summer. The two women often traded stories about their lives, each of them envious of the other. After regaling Lydia with stories from her day, Susan asked, "How are things at the club?"

Lydia went through the litany of complaints she had received and her concerns about the pool and Jules and the snack bar. "It's just one thing after another. There will never be closure. People really only care about themselves, not the club in general. It's very disheartening, and I feel very overwhelmed. I think I'm finally ready to take Bill's advice. When this summer is over, I'm retiring from volunteer work. I am going to reinvent myself with a new career that actually pays me for all this brain damage. Anyway, we still on for the Literary Society?"

The Summer Literary Society was one of Meadow Glen's most popular events of the season, a ladies' night out featuring Ginnie Kistler, a local librarian, who presented all the hot new summer reads while sixty-some women sipped wine and snacked on hors d'oeuvres. Susan, Lydia, and a few other women had conceived the idea one night about eight years ago during a late-night session of wine-drinking. The group originally had gotten together to come up with several recommended new summer reads and then follow up with a book exchange. But the women had become so engrossed in chatting and drinking, they never got it off the ground. "We're just a bunch of Summer Lovin' Sloshes," Susan had said.

The following year, the SLS group met again and this time they did launch a summer book exchange, kicked off with a ladies' night at the club where Ginnie would present her summer reading picks. Realizing they needed a more respectable name, they decided to keep the acronym but officially rename the group the Summer Literary Society. Susan had remained the chief organizer and contacted Ginnie every year. Several of the members continued to meet during the summer and into the fall to discuss the books they'd read.

"Absolutely. Ginnie is thrilled to come again, and I will be there front and center. It's a week from next Tuesday, right?" Susan pulled out her iPhone.

"Yes. Let's plan on sitting together." Lydia stood up to leave. "I've got to get home. Thanks for the wine and for letting me vent. If the weather is nice, maybe we can have dinner at the club Sunday."

"We're always up for that." Susan turned on the hose to water the plants flowering in the pots. "We'll talk this weekend."

Lydia retraced her steps along the back of the club. She passed Claire

Hoskins' two-story red brick colonial with its meticulously manicured lawn that abutted the club. She wondered why the woman was even still living there. Claire was technically a widow, although her marriage had been considered a sham. It was common knowledge that her husband had died of a massive heart attack while having sex with his mistress in a downtown hotel. There were no children; however, Cliff Hoskins had left his wife a sizable fortune. His large stock portfolio reportedly had been worth millions at the time of his death.

She continued walking around the corner past the main entrance of the club. As she approached her house, she noticed a piece of trash in a tuft of crabgrass. It was a business card with the name Darrell Baker on it. His name rang a vague bell, but Lydia couldn't recall where she'd heard it. She stuck the card in the back pocket of her Capri pants, intending to toss it when she got home.

Keys to the Kingdom

THE BRAND-NEW silver BMW sports car pulled slowly into the lot. Warren Reinhart, the club treasurer, precisely angled the car to take up two parking spaces, minimizing the chance of it being dinged. Dressed in a dark blue Armani suit, button-down blue striped shirt with a white collar, red silk tie, gold cuff links, and shiny Cole Haan shoes, he emerged carefully from the car and stood gazing at it for a moment, unaware of Lydia's approach.

"Nice car," she said. Lydia thought it strange he hadn't changed into shorts and a short-sleeved shirt for the picnic table meeting. She handed Warren two leather money pouches. One contained cash and checks from members for swimming and tennis programs and general invoices. The other bulged with the weekend's take from the Sugar Shack.

"Thanks. Just picked it up today," he said, his chest puffed out in a show of self-importance. Warren owned a real estate investment firm, WLR Real Estate Ventures, which had a portfolio of three dozen or so commercial strip centers and small shopping developments throughout the South and Midwest. The firm sought out older, often rundown centers in gentrifying neighborhoods, paid for with investor money. The investors received disbursements from the rental income. Warren's firm would make enough improvements to raise the rent and achieve full occupancy. Then, once the market was deemed healthy enough, he would sell the property at a significant profit, with the proceeds distributed to the investors—minus Warren's generous cut. At least that's how Bill had explained it.

An extreme right-wing conservative, Warren was obsessed with money and status. He and his wife, Celia, had donated lots of money to many ultra-conservative causes and were frequently pictured in the newspaper attending benefit galas. Lydia found Warren to be obnoxious and somewhat slimy, both in his appearance and demeanor. Several years ago, he had been sued for racial discrimination at one of his properties; the case had reportedly settled. A slight, unattractive man with a pale, angular face and a huge nose accentuated by the wire-rim glasses that perched on it, he lately had taken to dyeing his hair a brassy yellow color to cover up the encroaching gray and growing it long to conceal a bald spot. Last year, he and Celia had purchased a multimillion-dollar mansion in one of the wealthier suburbs, although they still owned a rental property in the neighborhood near Meadow Glen.

Warren nitpicked and questioned nearly every decision and expenditure that came before the board, except when they involved exterior improvements. Because the club was such an eyesore, he tended to support showy capital expenditures that ultimately would add value to the neighborhood — and his rental property.

Lydia wondered why he was even still on the board, since last summer he had joined the nearby country club, which was much fancier and had a golf course ranked among the top 200 in the country. He claimed he was keeping his membership at Meadow Glen so his two children could enjoy summers at the club with their school friends. Most believed it was so Celia could spend her time at the country club while the family's nanny supervised the kids at Meadow Glen.

Lydia and Warren, who was now engrossed in text-messaging, found the most remote corner of the club where two picnic tables had been set up. A few board members and Pete had already gathered. Meetings were BYOB, with one board member assigned snack duty. Tonight, Mary Cramer, the Membership chair, had brought chips and guacamole and a cheese and fruit platter. Several members were already sipping on beer or wine or some other libation. Amanda Wilson, the Social chair, had a steel shaker of martinis and two plastic glasses, which she was sharing with Rex Simons, head of Tennis Operations. The temperature was close to eighty degrees, with the high humidity making the air thick and still. Everyone was dressed in shorts and T-shirts or tank tops, making Warren look like a fool in his expensive shirt and suit that were now becoming drenched in sweat.

After passing out the suggestions she had culled through earlier in the week to the appropriate committee members, Lydia called the meeting to order with a discussion of the opening weekend. Several people raised the issue of the pool temperature, which Pete said he was working on.

Warren, who hadn't set foot in the club the entire Memorial Day weekend, abruptly jumped in. "Well, what's the problem? These people aren't paying twelve hundred dollars a summer to freeze." He shot Pete a glaring look.

Warren felt no need to hide his contempt for the manager. He resented Pete's Ivy League education, his seemingly easy and early success, and the fact that he had been able to retire young with a huge nest egg and do what he wanted. Warren, who did not hold an advanced degree, had dabbled in both residential and commercial real estate, working for some local real estate companies before launching his own firm. WLR Real Estate had had a few ups and downs before taking off.

"I'm monitoring it closely," Pete responded, explaining what he had determined so far. "Worst-case scenario, we have to replace the thermostat."

"What will that cost?" Warren asked.

Before Pete could respond, Lawrence Haskell chimed in. "Keeping the pool temperature lower will save money, and our competitive swimmers will get better times. The Masters swimmers also need it cooler. Plus, as the outdoor temperature heats up, we can rely less and less on the boiler," he said, pausing to take a swig from a can of beer Lydia had never heard of. Lawrence usually brought a six-pack or two of some exotic IPA to the meetings, managing to down most of them before the meeting was adjourned. He never shared. "You know, I practically rebuilt that boiler," he added.

Lydia remembered that Pete had had several run-ins with Lawrence during his first summer as manager over how to operate the archaic boiler system.

"That's ridiculous," Warren responded. "Most of our members don't care about competitive swimming. Our manager should be able to fix this. That's why we have a manager. We spent fifteen hundred dollars for him to become a certified pool operator and we need to get our money's worth out of that."

Pete nodded. "I hear what you're saying, and I will do my best to get this resolved."

Lydia quickly moved on to the next agenda item: committee reports.

Amanda stood, martini in hand. About five-foot-four, with long, wavy brown hair and a huge amount of makeup, she was wearing a short black skirt, open-toed black heels, and a tight white tank top that accentuated her perfect, artificially sculpted breasts. She wore multiple bracelets on each arm and a flashy gold necklace. A divorcee who planned the club parties, Amanda loved to "cocktail" on the pool deck while her two young sons had the run of the club. Since her nasty divorce from her stockbroker husband two years ago, she had slept with several club members and was now rumored to be having an affair with Rex, whose wife, Bonnie, was an oil geologist. Thanks to a resurgence in oil prices over the past six months, Bonnie was of late spending most of her time in such far-flung places as North Dakota and West Texas as her employer began aggressive drilling campaigns and ramped up production.

"We've got all our events scheduled and on the master calendar," she began, her voice shrill and grating. "We will have extended pool hours on Sundays and Wednesdays in June and July and three family events—a Mexican fiesta, Hawaiian luau, and a pasta night. All but two Saturday nights are booked for private events, mostly graduation parties. The remaining Saturdays have been reserved for the adults-only Steak and Karaoke Night on June twenty-six and the Lobster Boil in August. Attendees will bring a side dish or dessert—and of course it's BYOB." The club did not have a liquor license, so members who wanted to drink alcohol had to bring it in. The club could not serve or sell it.

"Sounds fantastic," said Rex, ogling Amanda. "You've done a great job."

Jules's arrival interrupted the meeting. "I thought the meeting started at seven-thirty."

"No, seven, Jules. Since you're here, this would be a good time to bring up the Sugar Shack. Any issues we need to address?" Lydia knew she would have nothing substantive to contribute.

"We were swamped over Memorial Day. I had to make a candy run on Sunday and I've already made another one this week. I'm picking up more corn dogs and popcorn tomorrow. Some of the women are asking for salads and coffee drinks in the morning."

Lydia hoped she had at least put the coffee issue to rest.

"How much money did you take in?" Warren asked.

Jules stared at him, glassy-eyed. "Oh, I don't know. I have no idea. Am I supposed to keep track of that?" After last year's failed experiment to allow charge accounts—which Jules had badly bungled—the club had returned to a strictly cash policy.

"Yes, that's what it means to be a manager." Not surprisingly, Warren did not have a high opinion of Jules.

"I'll help you with the finances," Pete offered.

Next came the Operations report, with Bud Wright noting that he had scheduled a plumbing firm to come in once a month to snake the toilets and drains in both bathrooms to keep them running freely.

"Again, that's something the staff should be doing," Warren interjected. "Why do we need to pay a damn plumber to ream out the toilets when
we have a manager and an assistant manager to do that?"

"This job requires—" Bud started to explain.

"Don't give me some bullshit excuse," Warren interrupted. "We're
spending money all over the place here. We can't afford this."

"It's already been budgeted." Bud was becoming agitated. "Pete has
his hands full with managing the pool. He is not a plumber."

"Bud is correct. Plumbing is not in Pete's contract," Lydia echoed,
wanting to end this discussion. "Pete was not hired to be the resident
plumber. He was hired to manage the club and the pool."

"Then I'd say we need to revisit that contract," Warren snapped.

Lydia took back control of the meeting. "Long-Range Planning?"

George Bishop, a well-known local architect, had formed a committee that was devising a five-year plan for capital improvements. "It comes
down to the money and how many new initiation fees we take in each
year," he said. "Of course, everything is on hold now because of the lawsuit. We aren't able to make any needed improvements this year because
of that, so those will be pushed to next year."

"We also talked about paying down the line of credit," Warren reminded him. "We have a fiduciary responsibility to get this club out of
debt."

Ignoring the comment, Lydia knew Warren was being contrary, attempting to demonstrate what he perceived to be his vast knowledge of
finance and assert his authority.

Tennis was next, with Liz Driver, who coordinated and registered
the adult league players, giving what amounted to a defense of the new
system for organizing the league teams. Tall and slender, with medium-
length blonde hair, Liz always exhibited an impassive expression, almost
a poker face, but when she smiled her face lit up and changed completely.
She also had the uncanny ability to make what on the surface seemed like
a compliment but was really a nasty dig.

A year after her divorce, Liz had taken up with a well-off physician.
They were supposedly engaged but were holding off getting married until
the kids turned eighteen so she could continue to collect child support and
maintenance.

Liz was a 3.5 rated player and extremely competitive, a trait she had
passed on to her son, Max, who was number two on Roosevelt High's

highly ranked tennis team and was also working at Meadow Glen this summer as an assistant tennis pro. Liz was president of the Court Club, the tennis team's parent booster club at Roosevelt. Geoff was planning on going out for the team, meaning Lydia would be dealing with Liz well beyond the summer.

"The teams are up and running, although things have been a bit rocky with the new system," she acknowledged. "I understand that some members are very upset about the teams being reorganized into ability levels. I've gotten a lot of calls on it. But look, this is what Grant wants and if we're ever going to be competitive, we need to do this. People just need to get over it."

This was Liz's second year as tennis coordinator. Several seasons ago, she had embarrassed herself and Meadow Glen when she opted to play as a non-member on another summer club team that was more competitive — which meant she ended up playing against what should have been her own team. Lydia remembered her phone ringing off the hook that year with people calling to complain. This was Liz's way of resolving the issue.

"But this isn't who we are." Mary Cramer, a 3.0 tennis player, was visibly upset. For years, Mary had been the Tennis coordinator, recruiting a lot of new players, but took over Membership after a contentious season last year. A social worker at a nearby hospital, she was one of the nicest, most decent people at Meadow Glen. "Everybody here wants to have fun, not have to compete in some dog-eat-dog environment. It's changed the whole atmosphere on the courts," she went on, making a case to return the teams to the old system. Lydia assumed she was one of the players who had been bumped down to a B team.

"Let's just see how it goes," an unsympathetic Liz responded. "Meanwhile, the Juniors program is filling up. Max has some great ideas. They're going to have two tiers: one for the more competitive players, and another for the kids who just want to have fun." She looked directly at Lydia: "That would be a great fit for Geoff." Feeling the sting, Lydia bit her tongue.

Warren, clearly bored by the discussion, looked at his watch. "Anything else?"

"Well, of course the 4.0 Men have not paid their fees," Liz said.

"Then tell them they can't play," Warren responded. "No pay, no play. One time and they'll learn."

That was easier said than done. The 4.0 Men's Team, which included the top players at the club, routinely failed to pay their team fees on time despite constant reminding. As of last summer, it was Bill's group. After years of taking clinics and playing three or four times a week, Bill had finally risen to 4.0 status in the USTA rankings, only to receive a lukewarm reception by the arrogant Meadow Glen team, which was not very patient with new players. Between his bad knee and competing at a higher level, Bill had had a tough season, winning just two matches.

Since it was such an elite group, Meadow Glen's highest-ranking team knew it had the upper hand, with the full blessing of Grant. Usually the Tennis chair was still collecting the league fees in October. They ultimately paid, but never with any apologies. Another reason Lydia was thankful Bill wasn't playing this year.

The agenda moved to Membership, with Mary reporting that the club had taken in fifteen new members so far and had five spots left before it could start a waitlist. That was good news.

"But I do have a situation that may be a bit awkward," she continued. "We have a member who is switching from single status to family. Of course that happens all the time, but it turns out this man is gay. He and his partner have two kids and have registered the older one for swim team."

For what seemed like an eternity, no one spoke.

Then, "No!" Warren sharply broke the silence. "That is an absolute NO. This is a violation of the bylaws, and we can't have this. I don't want my ki—"

"You don't want your kids what, Warren? Are you afraid they'll catch something?" Bud's face was reddening.

"This is a family club," Warren yelled back. "We can't have this. Pretty soon we'll have a reputation as the gay club, and these people will come out in droves."

The heated discussion continued for at least twenty minutes with various board members referring to the club bylaws and trying to define the meaning of family. The bylaws merely designated two categories of members: Single or Married Couple with no children, and Family. Warren, banging his fists on the table, sweat pouring down his face, remained adamant that the gay couple should be kicked out.

Lawrence and Liz agreed. "Warren's right. This opens up a whole can of worms," a sneering Lawrence, now on his fourth beer, said. "Here I am trying to build up the swim team, and now I'm going to have this headwind to deal with. We don't need this right now. Look at all the problems this has caused in the military. If this were a normal unmarried couple it would be a no-brainer to deny membership."

"What's a 'normal' couple?" Lydia asked, staring directly at Lawrence.

"You know, a man and a woman," he said. Lydia recognized he had made a legitimate argument in pointing out that unmarried couples were not a membership category. But she also knew that Lawrence's comment was more about his political and social views than a bylaw technicality.

Most board members wanted to leave the issue alone. Mary, already feeling the sting of exclusivity over the tennis team situation, felt the club should welcome the couple with open arms.

"We'll need to have Mike look at this and see what our options are legally," Lydia said. "We will have to determine if our bylaws are behind the times on this issue and need to be rewritten. So, we need to table this discussion for now." Mike Patterson was the vice president and next in line to be president. He was also an attorney whose free counsel had saved the club on more than one occasion.

"This is a difficult situation," Mike acknowledged. "Technically, our bylaws may prohibit this, but perhaps we need to recognize that social mores are changing and we need to adapt."

"Exactly my point," Warren said. "This is the problem with our country. We're losing our traditional values and American culture to this anything-goes mentality."

"It's getting late, and we have other matters to discuss," Lydia said, hoping to end the discussion and diffuse the situation.

"I agree," Mike echoed. "Let's move on. Lawrence, do you have a report?"

"You bet. We have seventy swimmers, including seventeen new swimmers," he said, opening his fifth beer. "Our first home meet is in about three weeks, and we're hoping to have at least fifteen qualify for the state competition in late July. We may schedule two-a-day practices after school is out to get them up to speed."

Rolling her eyes, Lydia knew Geoff and most of the other kids would balk at that idea. This was summer club, not a military school swim team, for God's sake. Lawrence still had a lot to learn in his role. *Summer is for fun, and he's trying to turn the swim team into the Olympics.*

Next on the agenda was Rex, head of Tennis Operations, who had been charged with addressing two main problems: the tennis gates and the lawsuit. Outgoing, an avid tennis player and golfer, and a heavy social drinker, Rex was an account manager at a downtown ad agency. He loved nothing better than schmoozing people over drinks or on the golf course. He had brought millions of dollars in client fees to the agency through his vast network of contacts.

There were two sets of gates for the tennis courts. Two outer gates connected the courts to the parking lot, while the inside gates provided access to the club grounds from the courts. The outer tennis gates had become a security and liability problem because they provided easy access for non-members to come into Meadow Glen when the inside gates between the courts and the pool and grounds were unlocked.

A few years ago, the board had installed a system permanently locking the outer gates. The gates could be opened only with a magnetic card key, one assigned to each member household. Members could conveniently use their card keys to get onto and off the courts to play tennis when the club was closed or during the off-season. The problem was that thunderstorms frequently tripped the system, rendering the card keys unusable and requiring the mechanism to be reset. On more than one occasion, tennis players had been trapped inside the club in a downpour, unable to get out after the front gate had been locked by the manager on duty.

"I've had a couple of people out to look at the gates, and there's not a whole lot we can do short of installing a new system with a backup to avoid the tripping problem. That will be quite expensive, at least twelve thousand dollars," Rex explained.

"Oh for God's sake," Warren snapped. "We don't have the money to fix this. The gates are going to have to be locked all the time, and either the manager or the assistant is going to have to stay late when necessary to let the nighttime tennis players out."

Lydia looked over at Pete, who was calmly making notes. She wondered how he was taking Warren's relentless badgering.

"Well, let's see what transpires during the season and go from there," Rex offered.

"I agree," Lydia said, grasping that this was going to be a summer-long issue. "In the meantime, let's alert the nighttime tennis players and tell them to make sure the gates are working before Pete or the manager on duty locks the front gate. Worst-case scenario, if a board member needs to come down and unlock the main gate, then that's what we'll do."

"No, the manag—" Warren started in yet again.

"We need to move on to the more pressing issue of the lawsuit and petition," Lydia interrupted him.

"I have the petitions here, and we've already collected sixty signatures from neighborhood residents in favor of changing the HOA bylaws to allow installation of the tennis court lights and enhance the lighting around the club grounds," Rex announced. "We have three hundred residences in the neighborhood HOA, and we need a two-thirds majority. That translates to at least two hundred votes in favor." Rex handed the papers to Mike.

"I assume you've reviewed with your committee how these forms are to be completed?" Mike asked. Only the legal homeowner could sign the petition with his or her printed name, signature, and address. The property's lot and filing number also had to be included.

Although slightly worried about the technicalities of the process and the fact that a lot of work still needed to be done, Lydia was confident Rex ultimately would deliver enough signatures. Put against Claire's bulldog approach and negativity, he would win, hands down. In addition, of the three hundred residents more than one hundred were members of Meadow Glen.

"I thought this would be a good opportunity to collect some signatures from the few board members who haven't signed yet." Rex pulled out a master list. "Bud, this says you're the sole owner of your property. Can you sign tonight?"

"Sure." Bud took the petition with the lots and filing numbers already filled in and, with Mike looking over his shoulder, scrawled his signature and clearly printed his name in the designated spaces. "That was painless."

"Now Warren, you haven't signed," Rex said. "You still own your rental house in the neighborhood, right?"

"I'm not signing." He shifted his eyes downward as the board members stared at him in silence.

"What do you mean you're *not* signing, Warren? I—" Lydia started.

"I said I'm not signing. I've got a lot going on with my business right now, and I don't need to be in the middle of a lawsuit."

Lydia wondered if his company was in trouble again, then remembered the country club and the new BMW. It didn't make sense. "Warren, you *are* involved. You're an officer of the board, and the club is being sued. And, in fact, you originally voted for the tennis court lights."

"Look, Warren, we have Directors and Operators insurance that covers us, so—" Rex began the sales pitch.

"I am not signing," he responded defiantly. "I never should have voted for those stupid lights. I mistakenly trusted that the Tennis committee had done their homework and taken care of this properly. Turns out, it was very badly handled, and now I don't want my name in any way connected to this issue. My business has a lot of visibility, and I need to keep a low profile."

Lydia felt the heat rising to her face. She was livid.

"Then Warren, perhaps you should consider resigning your position," she said.

"Absolutely not," he retorted. "I have done a great job as treasurer and I've played a huge role in bringing this club into the black. Besides, we should be focusing on making exterior improvements. We could have repainted the building and put in new landscaping for a fraction of what these damn lights cost—and what this lawsuit is going to cost us. Now that the club is open, for me to bring someone else up to speed on the various accounts would take more time than doing it myself."

That was a lame argument, Lydia realized. At Warren's urging, the board had hired a bookkeeping firm in his office building to actually cut the checks, prepare the monthly financials, and make deposits at the bank. Lydia collected the bills and money and either gave them to Warren at meetings or left them in Pete's office, where Warren picked them up each week. Warren simply delivered pouches of invoices and money collected from the Sugar Shack, swim and tennis lessons, swim team, tennis league registrations, and social events to the firm on his way into work.

"Well, to say I'm disappointed would be an understatement," Lydia said. "I feel you have let the board and the club down. You gave us no indication last month that you would have a problem with this, and you should have. Plus, since you've joined the country club, I find myself wondering why you haven't dropped your Meadow Glen membership."

Warren's face reddened, but he didn't back down. "I can afford to belong to this club and the country club. It's nobody's business what clubs I belong to and whether I sign this thing or not. I've got bigger things than this place going on right now." His voice had risen to a high pitch.

"Okay Warren, do you have financials for us?" Mike abruptly broke the tension by moving on with the agenda.

"Yes. These are not complete as they don't reflect all the income we have taken in so far." Warren opened a file folder with a stack of financial reports and passed out copies of the May balance sheet and profit and loss statement. "While these reports show we're technically running at a loss, once we account for the unrecorded income we should be back in the black."

No one said anything, for which Lydia was grateful. It was now after ten-thirty, and she was suddenly very tired. There was only one more issue to discuss — the keys.

"Moving on, I need to let you all know that, as I mentioned earlier this year, we are going to re-key the club. Pete has scheduled a locksmith to come out and change all the locks. The staff, the Swim, Tennis, Social, and Operations chairs, Mike, and I will be receiving new keys. Pete is also changing the code on lockbox on the front gate. He will notify the lawn people and others who make necessary deliveries so they can access the spare key to get inside the grounds. Retiring board members will turn in their keys on Labor Day or sooner."

"Hold on." Warren raised his hand. "Are you saying that some board members won't have keys to the club?"

"That's right. Only board members who have occasion to access the club during off-hours. We're doing this for security reasons. There are probably dozens of unaccounted-for Meadow Glen keys floating around out there, and that's a problem."

"So am I getting a key?" Warren asked defensively.

"No." Still seething about the petition, Lydia liked that she was in control of this issue. She then referenced the incident of the strange "visitor" earlier in the week, and signaled Pete to relate the story.

"It was probably just some kids wanting to drink beer and skinny-dip," Warren said.

"No, I don't think so." Pete was looking directly at Warren. "Not this early in the season. Also, pool jumpers do just that — they jump the fence and then into the pool. They would have no interest in accessing the club by way of the service entrance or hanging out near the boiler room. That's not their M.O. Plus, the back gate was unlocked. Which means the intruder had a key."

"Well whatever the case, the problem of trespassers is your problem, Pete," Warren responded. "That's why we pay you thousands of dollars. That should have no bearing on how and to whom we distribute keys." He was ranting now. "All board members should have keys. I am an officer of the board and I should have a key. I want a key. There's no debate here."

The discussion continued for another fifteen minutes. Only Mike said he did not feel it necessary to carry a key. Lydia, who now had a raging headache, couldn't believe it. In her mind, she was back at Geoff and Andy's preschool trying to reason with a bunch of screaming two-year-olds. Apparently for these board members, a key was a coveted badge of privilege that gave them unlimited access to Meadow Glen whether or not it was necessary. It seemed having a key elevated them to the category of uber-member. Finally she relented, more because of her headache than a desire to make everyone happy.

"Fine. Every board member who wants one will be given a key at the next board meeting—unless you absolutely need one beforehand for a specific reason. But we are having a limited number made, so you will have to turn them in at the end of your terms. Also, again, Pete is changing the code on the lockbox and will give that code only to people who use the lockbox on a regular basis. Even I won't know what the lockbox code is. I am not backing down on that. Is there any other new business?"

Thankfully, no one answered. They had gotten what they wanted. The meeting was adjourned. A still-angry Warren picked up his papers and briefcase and stormed out of the club.

As she walked out with Pete, Lydia asked, "How do you take that crap from Warren? I mean, he attacks you every chance he gets. How come you never take him on?"

"I have a personal rule. Never argue with an idiot."

Dream On

THE ROLLING, lavender-covered hills seemed to go on forever under a cloudless blue sky. The air was rich with an intoxicating mix of thyme, basil, rosemary. *Provence. Are we in Provence?* Lydia struggled to hang on to the reverie of a trip they had taken five years ago. Finally opening her eyes, she realized the dream was at least partially true. Bill was cooking! *Thank God I have a husband who's a foodie.*

The memory of that amazing vacation was abruptly pushed aside by the unpleasant reflections of the previous night's contentious board meeting. It was close to midnight by the time she'd walked in the door. Bill was still up.

"That was a long one," he remarked.

"Yes, and it got worse the longer it went." Lydia popped three Advil and briefly told him about Warren's reaction to the gay couple, his temper tantrum over the keys, and refusal to sign the petition.

"Well, I guess I can understand his position on the petition," Bill said. "Did you see the paper today?"

"No Bill, I don't have time to read the paper anymore," Lydia replied, fatigue evident in her voice.

"There was a story on the front of the business section. Warren's firm has purchased the Eastside Shopping Center for thirty million dollars. I imagine Warren wants to keep his image squeaky clean now that he's going to need permits and government approvals to upgrade the place."

Beyond the immediate impact of Warren not signing the petition, Lydia hadn't much cared about this latest move in his business dealings. Her head was still throbbing, and she was exhausted. She went to bed and dozed off but slept fitfully, finally falling into a deep sleep just before dawn.

The next morning, Bill decided to let her sleep while he fed Stacie and got the boys off for their last day of school. Geoff and Andy would be spending the day at an amusement park with the rest of the eighth grade to mark their continuation. At first, Lydia had been disappointed there was no ceremony, then realized it was a blessing in disguise as she didn't have time for it anyway. *Besides, what does continuation even mean?*

Lydia glanced at the clock. It was going on ten o'clock! She jumped out of bed almost falling over Stacie, who had returned to the bedroom for a morning nap. It had been years since she'd slept this late. She threw on a pair of shorts and a golf shirt and followed Stacie and Pink to the kitchen.

"Thank you," she said to Bill, pouring a cup of coffee and eyeing the spread of food he had put on the table. "This looks amazing."

"I didn't have much going on this morning, so thought I'd stick around and cook your favorite breakfast," he said, sliding an omelet out of the pan. "You need to keep your strength up." A drooling Stacie waited patiently for her own special helping.

Between mouthfuls of the gruyere cheese-filled omelet with tomatoes and fresh herbs from Bill's garden, crepes dripping with butter and powdered sugar, and a bowl of plump strawberries, blueberries, and raspberries, Lydia recounted the events of the board meeting in more detail. "The good news is, I've only got a few more to go."

She helped Bill clean up the kitchen, then planted a long kiss on his mouth. "You've figured out that a way to a woman's heart is putting food on the table," she said. "This breakfast is the best thing that's happened to me all week!"

"I know. Why do you think I love to cook for you so much?" Bill said, walking out the door.

As he pulled out of the driveway, Lydia settled herself in her office and got to work on her first blast e-mail of the season to Meadow Glen members. Ron Gutierrez, an at-large board member and web designer, had donated his time to develop the club's website several years ago. Each year, for almost nothing, he updated the site and added features. This year, it had been the Suggestion Box. Last year, he'd set up a system whereby members who provided their e-mail addresses could receive online notifications about upcoming events and announcements.

First, she typed out what she wanted to say to the members.

Thanks for helping make the opening weekend a huge success.

**Swim lessons and junior team tennis start June 9;
look for sign-up sheets on the website or at the club.**

We apologize about the pool temperature. We are monitoring the situation closely to resolve the problem. Thanks for your patience!

Upcoming events: Summer Literary Society; Steak and Karaoke Night; Sundays are family grill nights.

Reminder: If you have children under age 3 and/or not potty trained, please be sure they are wearing swim diapers. Accidents force us to close the pool.

Then, carefully following the directions Ron had given her, Lydia went through the steps to access the website. A text box came up. Lydia pasted in the information, then clicked Send. The box disappeared. The action gave her a sense of power and accomplishment. She sat back with a sigh of relief, then noticed the Suggestion Box link. After the previous onslaught, she had avoided looking at the box again. Now, as much as she dreaded it, Lydia decided to check it before the weekend hit. She closed her eyes and clicked the link. Five suggestions came up. *Not too bad.*

Much to her relief, there was nothing about the pool temperature. Again, the swim team mothers asked for Starbucks coffee in the mornings. There were a few comments about kids throwing rocks on the playground. The last one, however, annoyed her:

What about installing a clay tennis court?

Lydia knew that was a collective request from the notorious 4.0 Men's Team, who had been raising the issue of the clay court for years. Bill, who would love to play on clay, especially since his knee surgery, had known better than to join the chorus and thankfully kept his mouth shut. The issue had always been dismissed as frivolous, impractical, and too expensive. Which it was. *What a bunch of elitists,* she thought. *Join a country club that doesn't have a leaky pool.*

A clay court would need to be maintained—routinely watered and brushed or rolled after it was played on, something Lydia knew would be almost impossible to manage at a facility already overwhelmed with maintenance challenges. This was the same group that had spearheaded the tennis court lights. The group that couldn't pay their league fees on time. The club had spent a fortune installing those lights and was now facing a potentially expensive legal battle over them. No, it would be a long time before Meadow Glen would spend big bucks on anything related to tennis.

She would forward the item on to Rex and the Tennis Operations committee, confident that by the time anyone addressed it, her term would be over and she would never again have to concern herself with such a ridiculous suggestion. Lydia felt pleased that she was beginning to pick her battles and not get completely rattled over pie-in-the-sky notions that people insisted on pushing.

Maybe. Her cell phone was vibrating.

"Hello?" Lydia didn't recognize the number.

"Mrs. Lydia Phillips?" a man asked curtly.

"Yes, this is Lydia."

"Hello, Mrs. Phillips. This is Colin Stewart. I don't know if you know who I am, but I'm a member of Meadow Glen—"

"Yes, of course. How are you, Colin?" *Why the formality?*

Colin Stewart was Scottish, a retired oil and gas engineer who had joined the club a few years back with his wife, Jillian. Picturing his short gray hair and black eyes, Lydia figured him to be in his mid-seventies. She and Bill had met the couple last summer at one of the club parties. They had found him to be quite interesting and knowledgeable about a number of subjects but as the evening and his alcohol intake wore on, they realized he was a boorish, egomaniacal know-it-all.

"I'm calling about the upcoming book event. The Summer Literary Society. Why is this for women only? Do you consider men too stupid to pick up a book and read?" Colin's rude, sarcastic tone was sharpened by his clipped accent.

"Of course not, Colin." Lydia was dumbfounded. "Uh, I think, uh... this is a Meadow Glen tradition, Colin, a chance for the women members to come together for a fun night of fellowship and sharing. Most of the book titles will be ones that appeal primarily to women."

"Then perhaps you should expand the subject matter. I pay dues for both my wife and me, and now I'm being excluded from something I would very much like to attend. I feel this is discriminatory."

Lydia took a moment to collect herself. "Colin, I can assure you there was never any intention to discriminate against men. As I said, this is a long-standing tradition, an event for women members to get together. Just like the group of men that gets together every Sunday morning to play tennis."

"I don't play tennis. I read. This is wrong and I am personally offended."

Lydia thought a minute, then offered: "You know, if you would like to come, I'm sure no one will mind."

"Fine. I'll wear something appropriate to blend in so no one will be offended by my presence." He disconnected abruptly, without saying goodbye.

Unbelievable, Lydia thought. *I guess this is what happens when you don't have enough to do.* Then she felt a twinge in her stomach. *Is this what's going to happen to me when I quit all my volunteering? Call people and complain about things that don't matter?*

She put the nagging thought out of her mind and called her friend Susan Adams at work. "You're not going to believe this," she said, recounting the story of Colin's phone call.

Susan laughed raucously. "Bring him on. It'll liven the place up."

"So, let's make a plan for Sunday night," Lydia said. As they had done for years, the two families would take a picnic up to the club and grill burgers and brats, steak, chicken, or some kind of fish.

"You got it. We're on. I'll bring vegetables and hors d'oeuvres. And wine, of course."

"I'll bring a salad and Bill will bring burgers and something for dessert. And yes, definitely wine. See you around five-thirty."

Manhattans and Mahjong

L YDIA AND Bill arrived at the club just after five o'clock on Sunday with a picnic basket of food, including her German potato salad and his gourmet hamburgers and key lime pie. The temperature had hit a humid eighty-five degrees earlier in the day, but cloud cover brought it down to a pleasant seventy-eight. The boys were already there hanging out with friends. Lydia had a swimsuit on under her clothes. This would be her first time in the pool this year. She and Bill walked past the parking lot, which was full to the point that cars were double-parked, blocking the thoroughfare. Lydia suspected that would irk some people but decided to let it go. If people couldn't get out, they would have to come back into the club and ask around until they found the person who was blocking them.

Pleased to see that the club was being used, Lydia recalled a time when Meadow Glen on a Sunday evening was like a ghost town. Four of the six tennis courts were full, a mixed doubles tennis social underway. Brad and Tad Stovall were hitting balls on Court 2. Kids were lined up at the Sugar Shack as Jules, in sunglasses, and two teenagers took orders. The operation looked chaotic, Lydia observed. People already had the grills going, and a group of women had taken over two tables to play Mahjong. In the far corner, four older men — Frank Fair, Al Flood, Bob Mackie, and Sean O'Brien — all of them widowers, were engaged in their regular Sunday afternoon poker game as they shared a platter of snacks and a bowl of Bridge Mix. And drinks. A metal thermos, usually filled with Manhattans, Old-Fashioneds, or some other fancy cocktail, was positioned in the middle of the table next to a pile of cash. Lydia presumed there was plenty more to drink in the large cooler next to the table.

The men, dubbed the Silver Foxes, had been getting together for years at the club for their regular game. Longtime members, they all had served on the board in an earlier Meadow Glen era. Rumor had it that they occasionally let themselves into the club at night to swim in the nude, drink, and smoke cigars, probably because at least one of them still had a key.

Not for long, Lydia mused. *In a couple of weeks the locks get changed.*

The pool, however, was not crowded. It didn't take Lydia long to learn why: once again, the temperature had dropped. Several people approached her to complain. "We brought guests, potential members, up here to swim and have a barbecue and now nobody wants to even get in the pool," an unhappy member whined. Lydia cringed as she looked for Pete. Then she remembered this was his night off. Assistant manager Sam Hutchinson was on duty. She walked over to the office.

"Hi, Sam. I guess we have another problem with the pool temperature. Does Pete know what's going on?" This was Sam's second year at Meadow Glen. Lanky with dark hair pulled back in a ponytail and a beard, he had been one of Pete's star math students and had been accepted to Cal Poly. Lydia didn't know him well, but he seemed responsible enough.

"Yeah, I did call Pete. I checked the dial in the boiler room, and it was set at seventy-nine degrees, which is odd because this morning it was at eighty-three. Pete thinks there may be some kind of malfunction. I noticed around four o'clock that we had a problem, but it will take several hours for the temp to come back up."

Sam's laid-back manner did not give Lydia a lot of confidence; she wanted someone to exhibit her own sense of urgency. "Yes, we definitely have a problem," she said, her heart sinking. She was puzzled that the pool apparently had been fine for several days and now the problem had come back on the busiest night of the week.

She made her way to the table on the grass that the boys had staked out earlier in the afternoon. Even they were grumbling. "Geez, Mom, the pool is freezing," Andy complained. "Can we just go home?"

"No, we're not leaving!" she snapped, recognizing she was taking out her irritation on them. "We'll have a nice dinner with the Adamses, and you guys can hang out, play some cards or something. We won't be here that long."

With Andy was a dark-haired, wiry boy Lydia had never seen before. "And who might this be?" she asked.

"This is Chip," Andy said. "He's new."

"Welcome to Meadow Glen. Have you met some other kids your age?"

"Yeah, I joined the swim team and I've been playing tennis. I'm a really good athlete."

"Wonderful," she said, somewhat taken aback by his bravado. "That should keep you busy this summer."

Lydia laid out a tablecloth as Bill opened a bottle of wine. Susan, Joe, and their kids arrived with a tray of deviled eggs, a cheese platter of brie, camembert, and English cheddar, and vegetables in olive oil for grilling.

"Madame President," Joe acknowledged Lydia with a dramatic bow. He loved to needle her about her title.

"You'll only be able to say that for another couple of months," Lydia responded. "By the way, do *not* say anything to me about the pool temperature."

Bill filled them in as he poured some wine, and all four raised their plastic wineglasses in a toast. "To summer," he said. "And good friends."

Hal and Arleen Schneider, who were at the next table, raised their glasses as well. Both were real estate brokers, and Hal was a master on the grill. He and Arleen had two daughters who had raised the bar significantly for the swim team, breaking records and usually taking first or second place in their events. They were a great family and lots of fun. "Give me your meat and I'll throw it on with our stuff. We're grilling some salmon, and we've got plenty to share," Hal offered.

"The pool *is* a little chilly." Arleen was not complaining, Lydia understood, but was just giving her a heads-up—not knowing she already was aware.

While the six of them chatted, a series of loud whistles came from the far end of the pool. "Attention, everyone," shouted Lawrence in full boot camp regalia—Army fatigues, a long-sleeve white T-shirt, and baseball cap. "We're going to have a mock swim meet featuring some of our top swimmers versus our Masters swimmers." As Lawrence scanned the crowd for swim team "volunteers," Geoff dove under the table. The Schneider girls had been recruited, as had several other teenagers on the team. The coach, Alex Taylor, was nowhere in sight. This was Lawrence's show.

The swimmers stood on the diving blocks waiting for Lawrence to start the event. "Swimmers, take your mark." He fired off his starter pistol, startling people. Six swimmers, three teenagers and three adults, dove into the pool for a fifty-meter freestyle. The drill was repeated for the other strokes—breast, back, and butterfly. Then there were two relays. Next, a second group competed. Each event was signaled by the loud bang from Lawrence's pistol, followed by wails from babies and toddlers throughout the grounds.

As Lydia was happily reflecting that the mock meet had mitigated the temperature situation a bit, Lawrence suddenly fired off his gun several times. A young boy had jumped into the deep end of the pool, seemingly unaware of what was going on. "Clear the pool, please. Clear the pool." Lydia looked over at Hal and Arleen and couldn't help but laugh.

"This must be Fort Bragg West," Arleen said.

The Masters swimmers fared far better than the teenagers in the competition. "We'll repeat this exercise at the end of the season and see how much you kids have improved," Lawrence announced.

Lydia wondered on what authority he had hijacked the pool on a busy Sunday night. Watching him, Lydia suddenly realized how much Lawrence relished this role of being what amounted to a commando, giving orders, firing off his pistol, always being in charge, always in the spotlight.

As the smell of gunpowder dissipated, Lydia, Bill, and the others enjoyed catching up on everyone's activities, and Joe opened another bottle of wine. The kids were playing cards. A few people had decided to brave the pool now that Lawrence had wrapped up his exhibition. The food smelled wonderful, and every few minutes Hal would check the grill and rotate the meat. He liked to cook slowly. Lydia began to relax.

Within minutes, however, she heard a commotion coming from the Sugar Shack. A woman she didn't recognize was speaking to Jules in a raised voice and trying to make a call on her cell phone. Several people had gathered to watch. Lydia started to get up when she saw Sam head for the snack bar. *Let him handle it*, she told herself. After a brief conversation, Sam looked around, spotted Lydia, and began walking in her direction. Lydia felt her stomach knot up. This didn't look good.

"We seem to have a situation." Sam seemed unsure what to do. Beyond balancing the pool chemicals and rotating the lifeguards, he didn't have much experience with the people side of club management. "That woman over there, she says her car was stolen from the parking lot. She wants to call the police." Lydia followed Sam back over to the snack bar.

"Hello, I'm Lydia Phillips, club president. And you are?" she asked, extending her hand to the woman. "Can you tell me what's going on?"

"I'm Lillian Bergan. I'm a longtime club member, and I've been here all afternoon playing Mahjong. I went out to the parking lot and my car was gone."

Lydia guessed the woman to be around eighty. She recognized the name from the member roster but had never met her. "Are you sure it was in the lot? People sometimes forget that they've had to park around the corner when the parking lot is full."

"Oh, no. I parked in the lot. I took the last space, right next to the fence."

Lydia froze. *Was hers one of the cars that had been double-parked?* "Uh, when you say next to the fence, do you mean parallel to it?" Lydia was now picturing the **NO PARKING Violators Will Be Towed** sign that hung on the fence. However, no one's car had actually ever been towed to her knowledge.

"Yes, I think so. The lot was very crowded." Lillian was now close to tears.

"Let's go out to the lot." Lydia figured that if she was going to have to tell this woman that her car had been towed, it would be helpful to show her the sign first. The two of them walked out. "Can you show me exactly where your car was parked?"

"Right here." She pointed to the fence. "Oh, I didn't see that NO PARKING sign before. It must have been covered up."

"No, I don't think it was covered up. I think you just didn't see it. The problem is, by parking here you blocked the thoroughfare." Lydia suddenly felt a wave of sympathy for the woman.

"Are you suggesting my car was towed?"

"That's certainly possible. I think —"

"Oh no." Lillian was crying now, and noticeably angry. "This is an outrage. I am a charter member of this club. There were other cars parked along the fence."

Lydia had no doubt that other cars were parked there and understood how Lillian could have been confused and parked in the NO PARKING zone. Just then, Lawrence came around the corner on the way to his truck. "What seems to be the trouble, ladies? Lawrence C. Haskell the Third," he said, extending his hand to Lillian. "I'm a board member here."

"This is Lillian, and I'm afraid her car has been towed," Lydia explained. "It was parked right—"

"Oh yeah, it was towed all right." Lawrence looked smug and triumphant. "Lady, you were illegally parked, blocking traffic. I'm the one who called the towing company and had your car and three others towed. Can't you read?" he said caustically, pointing to the sign.

Lydia was shocked. "Lawrence, why did you do that? Did you even attempt to ask around to see who owned the car? This could have been handled in a much more civil manner. Plus, you should have reported it to

Sam, the manager on duty, rather than take matters into your own hands."

Showing no sign of backing down, he squared off to face Lydia. "Excuse me, Lydia. I'm a board member, and I don't have time to go through the club asking who is illegally parked. Any idiot can see that parking here is illegal, and if they don't get that there's a sign posted for them to read. This has been going on for years, and we've just ignored it. This is how people learn." Lawrence, spit flying from his mouth, was shouting now. He turned to Lillian. "Here's a tip, lady. It's Delgado Towing, and I hope you're carrying a lot of cash or you won't be getting your car out anytime soon." He stormed over to his truck, gunning it as he drove out of the lot.

Lydia guided the now sobbing Lillian back into the club. While the woman called her daughter, Lydia looked up the number for Delgado Towing. Yes, they had the car. It would be $500 to get it out. Cash. Lillian had $45 in her wallet. Her daughter was coming over with another $75. Lydia took $100 from the snack bar cash register. She went back over to the table where Bill, Joe, and Susan and the Schneiders were talking, oblivious to what had been going on for the last fifteen minutes.

"Okay, does anybody have any cash?" Lydia explained what had happened. "If we can pull together enough so Lillian can get her car out, then I'll just get a check from her." Together, they came up with another $230, bringing the running total to $450. Lydia looked at Andy, who she knew had a stash in his room.

"Mom." He rolled his eyes.

"Andy, please don't whine. I'll pay you back tomorrow. Please just run home and get fifty dollars."

Andy returned just as Lillian's daughter arrived. Lydia exchanged the cash for a check.

"My mother helped build this club," the daughter said, her voice shaking with anger. "For her to be treated this way is unthinkable. It was an honest mistake. You should be ashamed of yourselves."

"I'm terribly sorry this happened." Lydia realized that nothing she said would placate the woman. Lawrence, in his narrow-minded, militaristic way technically had been right, but this was a swim club, not the Pentagon. Now Lawrence was nowhere to be found, and here she stood taking the flak for trying to help.

No good deed goes unpunished, Lydia thought, as she watched Lillian and her daughter walk out the gate, Lillian still in tears.

Lydia returned to the table and plopped down in her seat, feeling exhausted by what had just taken place. She sat back, closed her eyes, and took a series of deep breaths, taking in the smell of suntan lotion and food cooking on the grills. It conjured up memories of many summers past. Shadows were beginning to fall across the pool. It was six forty-five. They had another hour and fifteen minutes before closing.

Lydia stood up and poured herself another glass of wine. "I come up for a pleasant dinner with friends, and it's one problem after another," she said, taking a long sip. "And it's not even the middle of June."

"Hang in there, Madame President, we've got your back," Joe said, holding up his glass in a toast. Lydia couldn't help but laugh. Bill, Susan, Hal, and Arleen raised their glasses as well.

Then Geoff approached the table. "Mom, can Chip have dinner with us?"

"Sure, honey. As long as it's okay with his parents."

"Oh, it's fine," Chip said, clearly excited about the prospect.

Dinner was fabulous. Susan's crispy grilled vegetables proved the perfect complement to the potato salad and Bill's burgers, seasoned with a rub of brown sugar, Worcestershire sauce, and pepper, and topped with caramelized onions and avocado slices on toasted buns. Chip managed to wolf down two burgers and a large helping of salad.

"Wow, you've got a healthy appetite," Lydia said, cutting slices of key lime pie. The creamy yet tart filling and the sweet, crunchy crust came together in a silky, comforting combination.

Another glass of wine and the angst from earlier in the evening was a distant memory.

Blue Sedan

PETE PEERED out the front window of his sprawling brick-and-stucco home. It was four a.m. — still dark, but the row of streetlights provided ample light for him to see more than a block down the street in either direction. He and Shelly had purchased the property seven years earlier, razing a 1970s ranch and replacing it with what was now a showplace designed by Shelly. Inside, a vaulted entryway led into a great room, with an expansive state-of-the-art kitchen and a formal dining room off to the left. A den and office were located in a wing beyond the kitchen. Four bedrooms were located to the right of the entryway. The great room opened onto a large flagstone terrace with a fire pit, large pots of flowers, and comfortable furniture.

Pete had gotten virtually no sleep. Yesterday had been his day off, but when Sam called about the pool temperature, any attempt at trying to relax was foiled. Now that school was out, Pete planned to go to the club early this morning to tackle the problem. He had already decided to set up an aggressive monitoring schedule, checking the temperature gauge every hour.

But the pool was not the foremost problem on Pete's mind. As he looked down the street, he thought back to when the car, a dark blue sedan with shaded windows, had first appeared. Early May, he figured, was when he had first seen it parked a couple of doors down from his house. He thought nothing of it at first. But after about ten days, the car's presence began to make Pete feel nervous. The vehicle was there at various times, sometimes early in the morning before he left for school, sometimes in the evenings when he returned. He couldn't recall seeing the car at school, although he thought that once it may have followed him there.

His initial thought was that it was Tess's ex-boyfriend, who had not taken their breakup over winter vacation very well. The two had dated junior and senior years in high school and swore they would keep the romance going after Tess went off to Tufts and Randy headed for USC. But when the two reconnected at Christmas, a rift was apparent. It was Tess who'd suggested they call it off but remain friends. Randy, however, had been hurt and angry at being jilted. He texted Tess constantly and drove by the house several times a day. He posted unpleasant things about her on Facebook. Now that school was out, Pete wondered if this was Randy watching the house, driving a different car. He eventually rejected that theory after calculating that while the blue sedan had been around for at least a month, Tess only had been home two weeks for summer vacation. And why would Randy follow Pete to school?

Pete's uneasiness had spiked last week after the unsettling late-night incident at the club when he'd heard the screeching tires of a car leaving hurriedly. He quickly dismissed it as a just a coincidence, chastising himself for being paranoid. It was probably a former board member with a key who'd been nosing around and left the back gate unlocked in his haste to get away, he reasoned. But the continued presence of the car was making Pete nervous. Maybe the driver was someone out to harass him. An angry student? Pete tried to recall who he'd given Ds and Fs to last semester.

A few times, he had started to approach the parked car, attempting to speak with the driver or see the license plate. But the car would always speed away before he could get close enough.

He called the police but there seemed to be little they could do—except grill Pete with a barrage of questions. "Has the car been parked in front of your house for more than seventy-two hours? How do you know they're watching you and not waiting for someone? Have you been threatened? Have you been receiving harassing phone calls? It *is* a public street." At Pete's insistence, the police had put on some extra patrols, but the car was never there when the police passed through. Pete had considered hiring a private investigator, but that would involve telling Shelly, which he was not prepared to do. Not yet. *Funny,* he thought. *I spent all those years on Wall Street handling billions of dollars of investments and never felt threatened. I move here and feel like I'm on someone's hit list.*

As the first light of dawn appeared, he opened the front door and stepped onto the porch. Nothing. No blue sedan. He sighed a deep breath of relief just as a car turned the corner. Pete ducked back inside the house; it was *The Wall Street Journal* being delivered. He laughed nervously as he ventured out onto the walkway and picked up the paper. Now wide awake, he decided he would shower and go on over to the club.

It was five forty-five by the time Pete pulled into the parking lot. He recognized Lawrence's truck, remembering that the Masters swimmers began their workout at six. The front gate was open. Lawrence had put the lane lines in the pool and posted the morning's workout for the swimmers on a large whiteboard. But Lawrence was nowhere in sight. Pete unlocked his office, cleared off the desk, and turned on his laptop. Among the day's tasks was the guard schedule for the next two weeks. Seeing that the pool was down the normal three inches, he turned on the hose and began filling it by the steps at the shallow end. It would not interfere with the swimmers. The pool water felt warm. *That's a good sign.*

He headed back to the boiler room and was disturbed at seeing the door was ajar. Muttering that he would have to mention this to Sam, Pete suddenly heard something from inside the boiler room. The light was on. His heart pounding, he slowly pushed open the door and was startled to see a man, flashlight in hand, down on his hands and knees in front of the boiler.

"What the hell?" Pete stood with his hands on his hips as a surprised Lawrence fell backward. "Lawrence, what are you doing? You don't have any authority to be in here. And what the fuck is going on?" As Pete's eyes adjusted to the dim light, he became aware that Lawrence was tampering with the temperature settings on the boiler.

Lawrence, wearing a tight-fitting black Speedo bulging with his well-endowed masculinity, stood up tall and faced Pete. The provocative tattoos covered his shoulders and upper arms.

"Actually, Pete," he said defiantly, "I do have a right to be in here. I'm a board member and I practically rebuilt this boiler. I am the only person at this club who really understands how this boiler works. This pool is too hot. You're wasting energy, and it's not good for the boiler or the swimmers. I'm simply adjusting the temperature."

"So *you're* the problem." Pete had caught him red-handed. "You're the one responsible for all the complaints. You've been sneaking in here and moving that gauge. Well, the game is over, pal. This stops right now. This pool is not just for competitive swimming; it's for everyone. And as manager, a big part of my job is to make sure the members enjoy their time here. And the overwhelming majority of them want a pool that is warm and comfortable. Now step away from that boiler. Right now! I'll have to inform the board of this, and unless they want to deal with complaints all summer long, I imagine you run the risk of losing your seat."

"This isn't over," Lawrence said angrily. Outranked, he moved toward the door and spat, "I can save this club hundreds of dollars in utility bills by keeping the temperature lower. The members will get used to it, trust me. Now get out of my way. I have a class to teach." As he attempted to exit, Pete blocked him. Pete was at least three inches taller than Lawrence, but he knew Lawrence was extremely fit and schooled in martial arts. He wondered how he would fare in a physical fight with him.

"Hold on. I suppose you're the one who was back here in the middle of the night last Tuesday. You had come up to mess with the gauge and when you realized I was in here you bolted."

Lawrence stared at him. "No, I'm afraid not. I was playing poker that night until two in the morning. And I've got people who can vouch for me. Now as I said, get out of my way." He threw open the door and marched out.

Pete looked at the gauge. Seventy-nine degrees. As he reset it to eighty-three, he felt a mix of emotions. On the one hand, he was happy and relieved that the temperature problem had been solved. On the other, Lawrence's apparent alibi had dashed his hopes of resolving the issue of last week's strange intrusion, leaving him with the nagging question of why someone with a key had accessed this area in the middle of the night. That, coupled with his worries about the blue sedan, made him feel anxious and out of sorts.

Pete dismissed the thought and returned to his office. Later, he called Lydia and told her the good news of catching Lawrence in the act. "Our temperature woes are over."

"That's great, but how are we going to keep him out of there?" Lydia asked.

"Easy. When the locksmith comes, I'll have him cut two sets of keys—a master and a separate one for the boiler room. That no one but I will have."

"Brilliant!"

Court Case

YDIA STRETCHED out on the lounge chair. After the rocky Memorial Day weekend and subsequent flurry of activity to get the programs up and running, the past week had been relatively quiet. A respite from the chaos. The club was beginning to fill up with kids and mothers tending to babies in strollers or supervising toddlers in the baby pool. Lydia counted six pregnant women. Group swim lessons were underway in the shallow end of the pool. Predictably, Brad and Tad Stovall were on Court 2. Jimmy Buffett's "Margaritaville" was playing on the sound system that Pete had hooked up to his iPad. Most of the members seemed to like the music, which typically ranged from jazz to new age or sometimes country, most of it coming from Pete's private collection of playlists.

Assistant manager Sam Hutchinson had taken it upon himself to add some of his own selections, mostly rap and other millennial-friendly music. This had prompted complaints, notably from the women tennis players who were furious that the music was being played too loudly during their morning matches. Last week, Nancy Brown, dressed in a crisp green and white tennis dress and white visor, had come running up from the courts to order Sam to turn off a Drake album while her smirking partner Liz Driver watched from the court. "You listen to me," she'd screamed, waving her spindly finger in his face. "I don't *ever* want to hear that music played here again. Do you understand? It is totally inappropriate. In fact, we don't want *any* music played during our tennis matches." Sam, who never seemed to emote much, had promptly and calmly turned off the music.

Daytime tennis matches started at nine o'clock. Nancy, ever the perfectionist, arrived every day at eight to practice her groundstrokes on the backboard.

As it turned out, Lydia had played a match that morning, substituting for someone on the 3.0 Ladies' A Team who was sick. Her partner was

Jennifer Murphy, a loud woman with a sharp New Jersey accent. Jennifer, who had long brown hair pulled back in a ponytail, refused to wear the dark green and white tennis outfit the rest of the team wore, opting instead for her standard tennis attire—a tight white sports bra and a navy-blue tennis skirt. During the match, Jennifer's breasts bounced up and down while her diamond tennis necklace dangled in her cleavage. Lydia feared the breasts would pop out at any moment.

As she had done in the past, Jennifer brought her three boys, Johnnie, Jason, and Justin, all under age eight, to the club to entertain themselves on the playground during the match, a full two hours before the club officially opened for the day. This was against the rules as there was no one on duty to supervise them, even though the swim team was practicing. The boys played quietly for about ten minutes then began throwing pebbles onto the court closest to the playground. Finally, Lydia stopped the match while the players switched sides and asked Jennifer to intervene.

"Oh, they're fine," she replied, clearly perturbed that Lydia had raised the issue. "You know, boys will be boys. Where are the lifeguards? Can't they watch them? That's what we pay dues for, isn't it?"

"Jennifer, the lifeguards don't come in until eleven. That's why we don't like kids playing in here before then. Those pebbles are going to damage the court. Plus, they're dangerous and very distracting to the players. A ball could bounce erratically. Please tell them to stop."

"Oh, give me a break! They're not hurting anything." Then, three-year-old Justin burst into tears and came running over to his mother. Jason had hit him in the head with a tennis ball. "That's a felony, Jason. That's a felony. Cut it out or I'm telling Daddy when he gets home. Justin, go back and play on the slide." Jennifer's husband, Bob, was equally difficult, especially on the tennis court.

Lydia and Jennifer won the first set, 6-4, thanks in part to Jennifer's questionable line calls. After Jennifer called one clearly good shot as out, Lydia challenged her out loud. "Are you sure about that?" as their opponents angrily approached the net.

"It was out. It's my call and I saw it. It was out by a good two inches." Jennifer gave Lydia an angry look. Lydia then glanced over at Grant, the tennis pro, and Liz, who were watching the match. Neither said a thing. *They want to win this match as much as Jennifer does even if it means cheating.*

Lydia and Jennifer lost the second set, 6-3, to some degree a reflection of Lydia being increasingly distracted by the Murphy boys. She missed several shots she should have made and double-faulted three times. This irritated Jennifer, who began correcting Lydia and telling her where to stand even though, Lydia noticed, she was making her own share of unforced errors. The second set loss prompted a tiebreaker to decide the match. By then, the unruly behavior of the boys had escalated.

The oldest, Johnnie, had found a pool noodle in the lost-and-found barrel and was walking around the pool deck hitting the bushes and knocking petals off the flowers. Lawrence, who was helping Alex coach the swim team, grabbed the noodle out of Johnnie's hand and made him sit in a chair. The child screamed for his mother, who left the court in the middle of the tiebreaker and engaged in a loud shouting match with Lawrence. Then Lydia saw Pete rush over to the playground and grab five-year-old Jason by the arm as he was peeing on the slide. Jennifer paid no attention to the scene unfolding on the playground and returned to the court.

Lydia and Jennifer eventually lost the tiebreaker and the match. At that, Jennifer threw her racket into the fence. "Fuck it," she said, glaring at Lydia and storming off the court. "God, I hope I never have to play with you again." *The feeling's mutual,* Lydia thought. *You are just a cheating bitch.* Embarrassed, Lydia apologized profusely to their opponents and invited them to stay for coffee, juice, and pastries with the rest of the team. The group was joined by Liz who, as the Tennis chair, felt entitled to partake of the spread. "You know Lydia, there are still some openings on the B team, and I'm sure with some clinics you could improve your game," she said, smiling.

"Thank you, Liz," Lydia responded as diplomatically as possible. "I think my plate is full enough this year."

NOW, AS she relaxed in her lounge chair decompressing from her stressful morning, Lydia reached into the picnic basket and pulled out a thermos of iced tea. She'd decided that since she was going to be at the club early, she would pack a picnic for herself and the boys, who usually spent at least the middle part of the day at the club with friends. Geoff had a tennis clinic at one and Andy didn't have to be at baseball practice until four. She had gotten up early, made ham and cheese sandwiches, and added a fruit salad, carrot and celery sticks, chips, and brownies. Lydia knew her days of having lunch with the boys at the pool were numbered. Hanging out with Mom wouldn't cut it for two soon-to-be high school freshmen. Two years from now they would be sixteen and driving, with summer jobs.

The boys knew better than to suggest they buy their lunch at the Sugar Shack. Ever since Andy had carelessly dumped an iced FunFro drink in the garage four years ago, Lydia had refused to purchase anything for them at the snack bar. She thought back to that hundred-degree day in the middle of July. She had opened the door from the house to the garage, dismayed to see greenish liquid flowing out from under the car. Assuming it was antifreeze or transmission fluid, she called the Audi dealer who advised her to have the car towed. But as the tow truck was pulling into the driveway, Lydia noticed the same fluid trickling from the bottom of the trash can. Investigating further, she discovered the cup her son had thrown away had slipped between the plastic liner and the trash can itself, which had a crack in the bottom. What Lydia had thought was fluid from the car was really the slimy, greenish remnants of the iced drink oozing from the trash can across the garage floor. "I will never buy you guys anything again from that snack bar," she had lectured the boys. It took Andy three months to pay back the fifty-nine dollars for the tow truck to show up.

It was just before noon. Both boys were in the pool. She knew they would have to get out at twelve-fifteen for Adult Swim, the fifteen-minute time period each hour when everyone under age eighteen had to exit the pool and allow adults to swim laps. This provided a few minutes of calm, a break from the splashing and screaming and a time for adults to swim in peace. The kids didn't mind; most hit the Sugar Shack and loaded up on ice cream, candy, chips, and popcorn. Lydia figured she would eat lunch with the boys and use her free afternoon to catch up on her reading and get to work on a tan. *I should at least be able to accomplish that this summer,* she reasoned. There would be plenty of opportunities over the season to show off her tan with the sundress she had purchased on their fall break trip to Mexico.

Lydia felt a splash of cold water. Geoff and Andy, dripping, were standing above her, having just gotten out of the pool. A shivering Chip stood behind them. "Hi, Mom. Can we eat now? And can Chip have lunch with us?" Geoff asked. Lydia guessed her son and Chip were probably famished from their earlier ninety-minute swim practice and subsequent horsing around in the pool.

"Yes, of course," she said, looking around for a parent.

"Thanks, Mrs. P," as Chip had taken to calling her.

Geoff opened the basket and all three boys began wolfing down the sandwiches. A long whistle sounded and one of the guards yelled, "Adult Swim." Thirty seconds later, Lydia was startled to hear some loud, high-pitched shrieks coming from across the pool. She looked up and saw a group of girls she guessed to be around age seven or so screaming and running away from a large man as he lowered himself into the single lane that had been designated for lap swimming.

Fred Lyons was a widower, a charter member of the club whose sole reason for belonging to Meadow Glen was to swim laps every day around lunchtime. Lydia had met him but didn't know him well. Quiet and aloof, he never interacted with other members or attended social events. He was rumored to be CIA. About six-foot-four, with a stomach that bulged over his lime green swim trunks, Fred had a very fair complexion with freckles and thinning red hair. He wore white, tight-fitting goggles and a white cap, and had plastered his nose, mouth, and forehead with zinc oxide. He wore black fins on his feet. As he entered the water, Lydia could see how the sight of him could be frightening to young children.

He's grotesque. He looks like a big white whale, Lydia thought as she watched him slowly swim down the lane and back, repeating the process six or seven times until the whistle signaled the end of Adult Swim. Fred then got out of the pool and sunned himself in a lounge chair. Forty-five minutes later, Lydia again heard the loud shrieking as Fred entered the pool and duplicated the ritual. Then he dried off, put on a terrycloth robe, and left.

By then, some clouds were passing over, blocking the sun. The air remained hot, however. Lydia pulled out her iPad to read the newspaper. Scanning the lifestyle section, she noticed a photo of Warren and Celia Reinhart at a symphony benefit. Celia was wearing what looked like an expensive designer gown; Warren, all smiles, was in a tuxedo.

Then she turned to the business section and saw an article about WLR Real Estate Ventures and Warren's plan to make over Eastside. There was a photo of Warren standing in front of the rundown shopping center. *Oh no, he's going to be on such an ego trip.* Lydia read on and cringed at the thought of the next board meeting.

Eastside was a small strip center that once had been a popular shopping destination but had fallen on hard times as the population moved south and west. Many of the retail establishments had closed, leaving only a Goodwill outlet, a small grocery, and a laundromat. A gas station was on the corner. The block had become a destination for loiterers and drug activity.

The article quoted Warren saying he was devising a plan to spruce up Eastside's buildings, re-landscape the area in front, install lighting, and attract restaurants and businesses that would appeal to the gentrifying neighborhood. "Eastside has enjoyed a long, successful history in this area, but has not kept up with the times. We want to turn this retail center around and make it the jewel of the neighborhood, a place where folks feel safe and want to gather. We want to bring it back to where it was in its heyday."

Then sell it off and make a ton of money, Lydia reflected cynically. She thought about Warren and his new BMW, remembering his obsession with money. *And yet, he clings to his volunteer seat on the Meadow Glen Board.*

Her musings were interrupted by a series of loud whistles and Pete's voice over the loudspeaker to clear the pool. Lydia assumed he had seen lightning until she heard the second half of the announcement. "The pool will be closed for at least four hours for a chemical adjustment." Lydia knew what that meant. A young child had had an "accident" in the pool — again. She stood and walked over to the edge of the pool. There it was. Two brown, Tootsie Roll-looking objects floating near the steps in the shallow end. She quickly turned her back to avoid being recognized.

"Great, Mom." Andy and a friend came over to their table. "Why can't you do anything about these kids who poop in the pool? Can't you fine them or something?"

"It's difficult to determine who is doing it, let alone punish them." Lydia felt Andy's frustration as they packed up their things. Andy headed home and Geoff went to change for his tennis clinic, the first of the season.

Lydia decided to stay awhile and watch Geoff play tennis. She pulled a chair out on the grass as thirty or so teenagers gathered on the courts. Grant and his two assistants, Max Driver and Amy Blankenship, a college student who was working her fourth summer at Meadow Glen, divided the kids into groups and fed balls to them. Then they had the kids play out some points, worked on serving, and set up some mini-doubles games. Geoff's winter tennis had made a difference; he was much improved over last year. Chip, on the other hand, was struggling. It was obvious he had never played before as he whiffed most of the balls Amy fed to him. Still, Lydia could tell he was naturally coordinated.

Geoff decided to stay beyond the clinic to get a game going with Chip and some other kids. Lydia picked up the picnic basket to go home and take a shower before driving Andy to baseball practice. As she walked down the block, she saw a dark sedan parked across the street from the club. The car had dark tinted glass but, because of the heat, the back window was rolled down. She was able to discern what looked like two men in long-sleeve, button-down shirts in the front seat, one talking and the other texting on their respective cell phones. *They must be really hot,* she thought.

He's Got Legs

THE FOLLOWING evening Lydia walked into the club, a bottle of Cabernet in hand, and ran into Susan. They were forty-five minutes early, in time to see the guards still hosing down the patio from the day's spills of snow cones, ice cream, and popcorn. A few people were in the pool. Some men were warming up on Courts 1 and 2 for their six o'clock league matches. While the players typically gathered on the porch for beer and snacks after their matches, tonight they would have to relinquish their space for the Summer Literary Society.

If Susan had been the inspiration for the annual event, Amanda was clearly in charge of logistics and decorating the patio, now adorned with tiny white lights. Dressed in a short white skirt and matching low-cut top accented with a pink boa, Amanda had rented small tables for four and purchased new tablecloths in a variety of bright colors. Each table had a candle and a stack of festive paper plates with matching napkins. A buffet table held an assortment of brie and other cheeses, French bread, fruit, and small quiches. Amanda, wineglass in hand, sat at a table near the gate collecting five dollars from each participant.

Liz arrived wearing an expensive sundress and high-heeled sandals. Eyeing Lydia she blithely remarked, "You are the only sensibly dressed person here!" Lydia started to thank her then, taking stock of the shorts, polo shirt, and flip-flops she had on, realized the comment was another one of Liz's snarky slams.

Lydia and Susan staked out a table in front and were joined by Arleen Schneider and Mary Cramer. When the librarian, Ginnie Kistler, arrived Susan went out to help bring in the books. Soon, the patio was nearly full, and Ginnie had assembled an inviting display of the summer reads she would spend the next two hours discussing.

Lydia was engaged in a lively conversation with Arleen when, out of the corner of her eye, she spotted Claire Hoskins with a friend. Dressed in red slacks and a loose, black sequined top that masked her large girth and nearly matched her dyed black hair, Claire scanned the crowd and let her gaze rest on Lydia. Smiling, she approached the table and asked in a syrupy sweet voice, "Hello there, ladies. How are we all doing this lovely evening?" Claire was wearing a pin that showed a lightbulb with a slash through it.

"Hello Claire, how are you?" Lydia said, looking around for a way out of conversing with this woman she loathed.

"Couldn't be better," she said, filling a plastic cup with red wine. "How's your summer going?"

Lydia bristled at the question. Claire was well aware of the turmoil she had created with her lawsuit.

"Things are going very well. As far as the club goes, I think we're going to ha—"

Suddenly, the distraction that Lydia was hoping for materialized, saving her from continuing the uncomfortable exchange. She heard Amanda's high-pitched voice. "No, I'm sorry, this is for women only. This is a Meadow Glen tradition. I'm afraid you'll have to leave." As Lydia began to grasp what was taking place, Susan, not even trying to conceal a laugh, ran over to their table. "Your boyfriend's here."

Lydia went over to the check-in table to see Amanda standing face-to-face with Colin Stewart, who was dressed in a hideous white tank top tight enough to reveal his nipples, a plaid green and black kilt that exposed two skinny legs covered with thick black hair, black crew socks, and tan wing-tip shoes. His wife Jillian, obviously embarrassed, stood next to him holding two cans of Guinness. Lydia took a deep breath, suppressing a laugh at Colin's ridiculous outfit. She recognized the situation was so bizarre that she had to keep her sense of humor.

"This man doesn't understand that this is a ladies-only night." Amanda appeared distraught and confused.

"Amanda—" Lydia started to explain when Colin interrupted her.

"Ah, Mrs. Phillips," he said in his thick Scottish brogue. "As I indicated, I have come appropriately dressed to fit in with the ladies. Per our conversation, would you please order this shrill woman to allow my wife and me entrance to the evening's program?"

"Yes, of course, Colin. Please, find some seats and help yourselves to some food," Lydia offered, turning to explain the situation to Amanda, now visibly upset that her soiree had been tarnished.

The only seats left were two at Claire Hoskins' table. *Good.*

As Susan approached the microphone preparing to introduce Ginnie, Claire immediately stood up and broke in with a big smile and her most cloying voice. "Excuse me, Susan. Before we begin, I would like to briefly call everyone's attention to an important issue we are facing as a club and a community. As many of you know, last year the Meadow Glen board decided to violate the Homeowners Association covenants by—"

"Wait a minute, Claire." Lydia was shaking she was so angry. *Another problem to deal with.* Susan and Ginnie remained standing, both perplexed by what was unfolding. "I don't think this is an appropriate time to—"

"Oh, I think it's perfectly appropriate," Claire interrupted, beaming. "We know that Rex Simons has been up here passing around his petition in favor of the tennis court lights. I'm simply asking for equal time to give the members present a chance to hear both sides of the issue so they can make an informed decision." She then went on to deliver an impassioned, albeit rehearsed, spiel about the precedent of breaking rules, the tyranny of the minority, the nuisance the lights would cause for the neighbors, the cost, and all her other reasons for opposing the petition.

"If anyone would like to sign *my* petition, I have one here." Finally, she was finishing up. Amanda was in tears at this point.

"I will be happy to sign it." Colin raised his hand and stood up. "This was an outrageous expense that only benefits a few of the members. The lights are quite unsightly."

"Wonderful!" Claire rushed back to her table and pulled out her petition.

Who do you think is going to pay for the removal of these lights, assuming it gets to that? Lydia thought, realizing that Claire and the oppositional Colin were natural allies.

"I think we can get started now." Susan seized the moment of opportunity. She introduced Ginnie, who thoroughly entertained the group with her rich and insightful reviews of the more than twenty books she had on display. Afterward, everyone, now feeling the buzz of the wine, clapped enthusiastically and signed up to purchase the books they wanted.

Lydia did not purchase any books. She couldn't remember the titles and did not hear any of the evening's discussion. Preoccupied and still seething from Claire's rude seizure of the microphone, she had left the table, gone to the far side of the pool, and called Rex at home, urging him to step up his efforts to get the neighborhood behind his petition drive. This was going to be a more difficult fight than they had anticipated.

Guns and Doughnuts

T HE LIGHT to the right of the front gate was just bright enough to see the lock. Lawrence slid his key, the new one Lydia had given him the night before, into the lock. He turned it easily then swung open the gate, quickly closing it. He flipped on the patio lights as he made his way to the pool area. It was four a.m. Lawrence could see the outline of two tents where the swimmers would gather and relax between events. One was Meadow Glen's green-striped tent that he, the coaches, and some of the parents had assembled the night before. The fraying canvas had been patched and re-stitched multiple times. The other, a brand-new blue tent with white piping, belonged to Southland, the opposing team and the toughest in the league. The team's coaches had come over the night before to set it up.

A long table had been positioned along the back of the covered patio. By six-thirty, the table would be outfitted with a printer and six laptop computers for officially entering the times for every swimmer. Cables from each computer stretched along the far side of the pool, each one attached to a touch pad in each lane. When a swimmer touched the pad at the end of his or her event, the time would automatically be transmitted to the corresponding laptop. Backup timers, mostly parent volunteers with stopwatches, stood at the end of each lane to manually record the times in case the touch pad failed for some reason.

Lawrence felt exhilarated for today's meet, the first home meet of the season. He also was anxious, hoping the team would perform better than at the previous two away meets after instructing the coaches to push the kids harder at practice. Lawrence had been up most of the night re-checking the entries for each swimmer and going over and over the heating lineups. Typically, it was the job of the coaches to do this each week, but Lawrence told Alex he would handle it. Alex was more than happy to oblige. He knew the obsessive Lawrence loved being in control. The meet start was seven-thirty, but swimmers would begin arriving for warm-ups by six.

That gave Lawrence a good two hours to test the PA system, turn on the laptops and printer, double-check that the starting blocks were completely bolted down, and replenish the pool water that had drained the day before onto Franklin Street. It also would give the pool enough time to cool down. Lawrence knew that Pete would not be in until noon at the earliest, meaning he would be able to lower the pool temperature then reset it back to eighty-three degrees before Pete arrived.

Lawrence grabbed his flashlight and walked back to the boiler room, positioning his new key to the lock. It wasn't going in. He bent down and shined the flashlight directly onto the lock. But no matter which way he tried to insert it, the key wouldn't go. After a good thirty seconds of fiddling with the lock, it dawned on him: Pete had put the boiler room on a separate key! *That asshole. He's locked me out.* Lawrence threw his flashlight against the door, smashing it into several pieces. *That guy has way too much power around here,* he thought as he stormed back to the pool. *Warren's right. We need to revisit his contract big-time. Or fire him. I should be the manager here anyway.*

He sat down at one of the picnic tables on the lighted patio with his Starbucks and a pastry, an indulgence he treated himself to on meet days. He plugged in his and Alex's laptops and booted them up. He went through the computer entries for each swimmer one last time and checked them against the event cards with each swimmer's name and the individual or relay event he or she would be swimming. The cards would be given to the swimmers in the heating area. They, in turn, would give them to the volunteer timers before the event. The timers would manually record the swimmers' times on the cards, then give the cards to a runner who would take them over to the computer table where volunteers there would compare them against the computerized times. There were rarely any discrepancies; Lawrence prided himself on running a perfect meet.

The sun was beginning to rise now. It would be a scorcher of a day. Lawrence stripped down to his Speedo, did a series of stretches, and dove into the pool. He swam a medley of the four strokes: butterfly, backstroke, breaststroke, and freestyle. The exercise felt good, but the water temperature irritated him. It was already too warm, and by ten it would be hot, not a good situation for competitive swimming. After a quick towel dry, Lawrence donned his usual long-sleeve T-shirt and sweatpants to hide his tattoos. At five forty-five, he opened the front gate for the soon-to-be-arriving coaches and swimmers.

By six-fifteen, the club was full of kids, most of them from Southland. Coaches Alex and Bridget had arrived and were walking along the pool, timing several swimmers. Lawrence tried to do a tally of who from Meadow Glen was there, and who was not. Swimmers who had not shown up on time to practice would be reprimanded, and letters sent home to their parents. He glared at the Meadow Glen kids as they straggled into the club with their backpacks and sleeping bags, many of them wearing pajama bottoms and looking quite disheveled. *They've just gotten out of bed,* he realized. *Which means they haven't eaten anything!* Lawrence had lectured them the day before about proper nutrition before a meet. Lots of protein and carbs; no dairy.

Under the covered patio, several swim team moms were setting up the bake sale which, over the course of the four-hour-plus meet, would bring in several hundred dollars that benefitted the team. Already out of sorts, Lawrence strode over to the table and angrily surveyed the fare: doughnuts, sweet rolls, bagels, muffins, candy, bags of chips. "What the hell? This isn't what we should be selling here. We've talked about this. I want fruit, nuts, protein bars, hard-boiled eggs, Gatorade and water."

"Lawrence, those items just don't sell." Kathy Stark, who had been running the swim team bake sale for at least ten years, was a tiny bundle of energy and very sure of herself. Two of her five kids were still on the swim team. Lawrence did not intimidate her. "We're bringing in breakfast burritos, which have a lot of protein, and I'm sure we'll have bananas."

"Damnit! This is why our team has such a hard time competing. We don't take this seriously. Are you aware that I'm a board member?"

"Yes Lawrence, everybody knows you're a board member. As far as the food, I honestly don't think it matters. You know, the kids from Southland will be buying too, so they're all eating the same crap. Plus, a lot of this is consumed by the parents."

"Oh hell." Lawrence stormed off to his own small white tent, where he would hold court for the next several hours and where the PA system had been set up. Lawrence would use it to announce each event, instruct swimmers to take their marks, and make necessary announcements. The system had a buzzer and a light to officially start each event, but Lawrence preferred the attention-getting starter pistol. He would use the buzzer only to make announcements or to signal a false start.

It was now seven-fifteen. Lawrence turned on the PA system. "Testing. Testing." Then he sounded the buzzer signaling coaches from both teams to assemble in his tent. "Gentlemen! And ladies," he added with exaggerated deference. "Welcome to Meadow Glen. I am Lawrence C. Haskell the Third, Meadow Glen Board member and chairman of the Swim program. A few announcements before we begin. We will follow the state rules governing swim meets, which I'm sure you all know." He was pacing back and forth, eyeing each person to punctuate his message. "There will be no tolerance of false starts. Two false starts, and I will DQ that swimmer from the event. Am I clear? We will abide by the rulings of two lane judges, who will disqualify any swimmer not performing the stroke correctly or making an illegal turn or touch at the end." He paused, scanning each coach's face with a challenging glare. "I want all swimmers to assemble in the heating area when their event is called. Swimmers will have five minutes to be in their seats for a head count by the heating area coordinator. Any swimmer not in his or her seat at the appropriate time will be DQd. Understood?"

The coaches, most of whom had endured Lawrence's egomaniacal ritual for years, said nothing, turned, and left. Even the most competitive summer clubs weren't this dogmatic.

Next, the volunteer timers were instructed to come to Lawrence's tent to collect their stopwatches and test them to make sure they were working properly. "Does anyone here not know how to use a stopwatch?" Lawrence asked, a condescending sneer on his face. "Push the button in the middle to start and stop the time. Then, hold down the button to clear it. Let's everyone do that now." After several seconds he asked, "Any problems?" No one answered. "Okay then. Let's get the first shift to the lanes." Timers worked in two shifts: 7:30 to 9:30 a.m. and 9:30 to 11:30 a.m., or whenever the meet ended.

Seeing his watch tick down the final minute before seven-thirty, Lawrence turned on the PA system, which was connected to speakers throughout the grounds. "Good morning, swimmers, coaches, and parents. Welcome to Meadow Glen. I am Lawrence C. Haskell the Third, your starter and meet coordinator for today," he announced. "At this time, I would like to call all swimmers for the four-hundred-meter freestyle to the heating area. Repeat. All four-hundred-meter swimmers, please report to heating. You have five minutes to be in your seats."

It was showtime.

As Lawrence prepared to launch what he was certain would be a well-orchestrated meet, chaos ruled throughout the club grounds. Moms, coffee in hand, looked around for chairs and gossiped with friends while their kids, listening to music on headphones, reclined on lounge chairs in their tents, wolfing down doughnuts and candy as they waited to be called for their events.

BY THE TIME Lydia arrived at the club, the meet had been going on for more than twenty minutes. She had gotten Geoff up for practice, taken Stacie for a walk, and made certain the dog door was closed. She left a note for Andy and her still-sleeping husband. "Do NOT let Stacie out!" she scrawled in bold black letters on a piece of white paper. Stacie running loose at Meadow Glen during a swim meet would be nothing short of a disaster.

Lawrence had just called the age eight-and-under medley relay teams to the starting blocks. Lydia looked around for Geoff and saw him in the tent playing poker. It would be another forty-five minutes before his first event. Coffee in hand, she went over to the patio and surveyed the bake sale table.

"Hi, Lydia. Don't worry, I saved you one." Kathy Stark handed her a glazed doughnut wrapped in a napkin, a treat Lydia allowed herself on swim meet days. She noticed the untouched bowl of bananas and stacks of raisin boxes.

"Thanks, Kathy! Gotta have my sugar rush to get me through the morning." Lydia paid her the seventy-five cents, then scoped out a table in the shade to catch up on the news on her iPad and relax before she had to stand in the blazing sun for her nine-thirty timing shift. Not five minutes later, she noticed two girls and a woman in a big white hat rushing into the club. It was Ernestine Knutsen-Askeland, without a doubt the most self-absorbed and demanding member of Meadow Glen, and her daughters, who were just now showing up for the meet. Claudia, who was a year ahead of the Phillips boys in school, and twelve-year-old Gwen were both, in Ernestine's words, "highly gifted."

Oh boy, they're in trouble, Lydia thought, unable to suppress a smile. On the other hand, she considered, Alex and Lawrence may not even bother to reprimand them. The girls, by far the worst swimmers on the team, rarely attended practice and did no swimming over the winter to get themselves in shape. The same was true for tennis. Ernestine always signed them up, but they participated infrequently and made little effort. Both Alex and

Grant had gone around and around with Ernestine trying to make her understand that it was the girls' lack of commitment, not the coaching, that caused their continued poor performance. Undaunted, Ernestine always pushed back, insisting the coaches devote more time to her daughters.

Lydia settled in with her coffee and doughnut and thought back to last year's annual membership meeting on Labor Day when Ernestine had hijacked the microphone with her litany of issues and complaints that ranged from the inappropriateness of the July Fourth adult beer dive, to allowing pool toys, which she claimed were being used as weapons. Ernestine was a trust-funder, supposedly from a long line of blue bloods, who spoke with a put-on New England accent even though she'd grown up in Omaha. She had gone to a private school in California, majoring in philosophy, and had never held a job. She had lots of ideas but never volunteered for anything. Her husband, Randall, was a psychiatrist. They rarely set foot in the club, as neither of them played tennis or used the pool. They made a point of avoiding the club socials primarily because of the high level of drinking.

Once at a neighborhood gathering, a slightly inebriated Bill had found himself trapped in a conversation with Ernestine trying to explain the pronunciation of her last name to a confused couple. "It's Ka-noot-sen-As-ke-land," she sounded out.

"Or, you could just say 'Hyphen,'" Bill had quipped, as a shocked Ernestine scowled at him. From that point on, Bill referred to them as the Hyphens and Lydia often found herself struggling to recall their actual surname.

Lydia recalled in more detail how Ernestine had spent nearly an hour presenting her list of concerns to the board last year. She wanted healthy food in the Sugar Shack, a buddy system to help her daughters and children who were new to the club get to know more kids, a ban on hard liquor at the club, a ban on pool noodles, and an ice machine that members could access free of charge. Another issue was what she had called the "overuse" of e-mails. "I suggest we have a monthly newsletter that is mailed out to the members so we can see what is going on at the club. My girls have missed several swim team and tennis parties because we didn't know about them."

Ernestine had only shut up after a board member suggested she be the one to put together the newsletter.

Lydia had just opened her iPad when she was interrupted by the all-too-familiar faux highbrow accent. "Yoohoo, Lydia. How ahrr you?"

There, standing a few feet from the table was Ernestine, still wearing the large hat she likely had put on to hide her disheveled reddish blonde hair. She was garbed in a frumpy designer navy-blue shift and worn down Ferragamo flats—a look Lydia characterized as "old-money rumpled."

Lydia desperately tried to think of a way to escape, knowing she didn't have one. "Hi, Ernestine. How have you been? How was your winter?"

"Oh, hectic as always. Claudia is at the top of the class at Roosevelt, even taking all honors classes. We'll see how this year goes. We may have to move her to Vickers Hall to ensure she's challenged enough. Roosevelt is fine for average students, but I'm not sure it's a good fit for Claudia. Gwen had a wonderful year at Hartsall Academy."

In fact, Roosevelt was a top-notch school that offered a broad assortment of challenging honors and AP classes. Lydia had heard through the grapevine that Claudia wasn't quite the brain Ernestine touted. The girl was known as a nasty, spoiled brat who cried when she didn't get her way. If she received any grade below a B-plus, Ernestine and Randall would complain to the teacher, or to the principal if necessary, to have the grade changed. In one case, they had brought in an attorney. It was easier to give the child all A's than contend with Ernestine and Randall.

Lydia thought about her own kids. At Roosevelt High and the feeder middle and elementary schools, a burgeoning population of highly competitive parents seemed to see every accomplishment, however ordinary, as evidence of genius. Got an A on a spelling test: gifted. Scored a goal in soccer: an athletic prodigy. Performed in a piano recital: highly talented. Except for her boys. Above average and well-rounded, but not exactly what Lydia would classify as gifted, a trait she had always associated with a six-month-old arranging shapes and colors in the crib. Or doing math story problems in kindergarten. "Is it something in the water?" she had asked at a PTA meeting, seeking an explanation for the disproportionate number of students being placed in the gifted and talented program. The question was met with angry stares from parents.

"Lydia!" Ernestine's raised voice snapped Lydia back into the moment. "I've been meaning to call you," she said, sitting down at the table and pulling *The New York Times* out of her bag.

Oh no. Here it comes. Lydia looked at her watch and realized Ernestine was going to hold her captive for at least the next thirty minutes.

"Lydia, if I may be frank, these coaches are very unrealistic and demanding. I received a letter from Alex chiding us because the girls had been to only one practice," Ernestine said, launching what amounted to a diatribe in a dramatically hushed voice. "The letter indicated they couldn't remain on the team if they didn't start attending practice regularly. Both girls are upset because they aren't swimming in the relays this morning."

Relays netted the most points in a meet, and Lawrence and Alex slotted the stronger swimmers in those events. Lydia also knew that Alex, no doubt at Lawrence's urging, would likely use the girls' poor practice attendance as justification for kicking them off the team, something she had never seen happen at Meadow Glen.

While she didn't necessarily agree with the approach, Lydia surprised herself by taking the side of the coaches. "Ernestine, they're trying to build up the program, and if the girls want to be a part of the team they need to make the commitment. It's not fair to the other kids who are getting up early every morning to make the seven o'clock practice."

"Lydia, swim team for us is simply an activity to balance out the girls' summer, not the be-all and end-all it is for these other people. My girls are going to get ahead on their academics, not athletics. The fact is, seven in the morning is an ungodly hour to expect these children to get out of bed and engage in a vigorous workout. Studies have shown that adolescents and teenagers perform much better when they are allowed to sleep in. We should push the practices and meets to nine. It would be better for everyone. Last night, Claudia was up past midnight reading *The Catcher in the Rye*. This is one of the challenges I deal with having two exceptionally bright children who would spend every waking hour with their heads in a book if I let them. The practice and meet times are just very difficult for me to work with."

"Ernestine, we can't start that late." Lydia didn't know whether to laugh at the ridiculousness of her suggestions or slap her. "That would mean the pool would be tied up until noon and virtually unusable for other members of the club. As for the meets, we have to start this early to avoid the heat in the middle of the day. It gets too hot for these kids. And, I don't think we could convince the other clubs to change the time anyway."

"Well, this is very difficult for us, and I think we need to have a sit-down with these coaches. They don't seem to grasp that my girls are not average children and need special consideration."

Claudia approached the table to ask her mother for help putting on her swim cap. "Here's another problem, Lydia." Ernestine was winding Claudia's long, stringy dark hair into a tiny bun. "These swimsuits don't fit properly. She must have tried on three different sizes and none of them worked. This style is too big on top."

Lydia eyed Claudia's skin-and-bones physique. She looked like a third-world refugee, the dark green and black suit hanging loosely on her bony shoulders while the bottom sagged. "An e-mail went out inviting parents to a meeting to provide input on the suits in terms of color, style ev —"

"Lydia, I didn't see that e-mail. I don't do e-mail on a regular basis. I would much rather speak to someone on the phone. I just don't sit at my desk all day reading e-mails."

Lydia started to speak, then remembered Pete's mantra: *Never argue with an idiot.*

Lawrence's booming voice called Geoff's event. "Ernestine, Geoff is swimming. I need to watch." With that, she picked up her bag and ran to the other side of the pool to cheer him on.

Bad Timing

IT WAS HOT enough to fry an egg as the unforgiving sun beat directly onto the concrete pool deck. Lydia and Arleen had been timing for more than hour. Occasionally, the bake sale volunteers would come through with trays of water and lemonade. To avoid becoming dehydrated, Lydia had consumed a large amount of water over the past twenty-four hours. She also had repeatedly applied sunblock throughout the morning. She had to admit that Lawrence ran an efficient meet, but there had been several false starts that slowed things down. Lydia and Arleen passed the time by chatting about everything from Bill's latest marinade recipe to the best-seller mystery Arleen was reading.

The meet had advanced to the hundred-meter breaststroke. Erica Broadhurst, thirteen, handed Lydia her pink event card. "Hi Erica, how are you? You going to set a new record today?"

Erica was one of Meadow Glen's star swimmers, who already held four records at the club. Her mother Betsy had been a champion swimmer in college and was one of five participants in Lawrence's Masters Swimming program. She also took every opportunity to get in the pool with Erica and privately coach her. Swimming was going to be Erica's ticket to a top-notch college—and a top-notch scholarship.

"Maybe. But I'm in a new age group this year and swimming a hundred meters, so it might be hard." Erica nervously glanced over to her mother, a tense, thin woman whose hair was pulled back in a long, blonde braid. Betsy had two stopwatches around her neck. She was gesturing the proper technique to Erica, reminding her to pull her arms and breathe properly.

"Swimmers, take your mark." As the girls leaned forward, Lawrence fired the starter pistol. Erica exploded into the pool. Alex, Betsy, and Lawrence all stood on the side, their stopwatches running, screaming at Erica, who was in third place at the first turn. She continued pacing herself then picked up her speed in the last half length, finishing a close second.

Lydia stopped her watch at 1:25.10 seconds, exactly what Arleen had recorded. As Erica got out of the pool, Betsy rushed over to their lane, an area technically off-limits to parents. "What was her time? What was her time?" Arleen showed her the card. "No. That's not right. I had 1:24.91. Your time is wrong."

"What does the computer say?" Arleen was disgusted. "That woman is psycho," she mumbled as Betsy sprinted for the computer table. Half a minute later, Betsy's shrill voice could be heard arguing with volunteers at the computer table. "No. It's wrong. This isn't right. I know she finished in under 1:25."

Betsy then ran back over to Alex, who shrugged his shoulders. "NO! I know my time is right. I know how to time these events."

By then, Lawrence had joined the conversation. Betsy was sobbing, making a complete spectacle of things. Lydia looked for Erica but couldn't spot her in the chaos. She most certainly had returned to the tent, trying to hide from the embarrassing scene her mother was making.

Finally, Lawrence put up his hands to signal that the argument was over. Betsy stormed off toward the tent. Lydia cringed, recalling how in the past she had witnessed several of Betsy's volatile outbursts to Erica, berating the girl for not swimming faster, starting better, turning more efficiently. She considered Betsy's behavior to border on abuse.

Susan, the runner for this shift, approached and took Erica's card from Arleen. "Wouldn't be a Meadow Glen swim meet without some parent drama from Betsy Broadhurst," she quipped. "And just when you thought it couldn't get any worse, check out the meltdown in Lane six."

Arleen and Lydia glanced over to see last-place Claudia Knutsen-Askeland being DQd for an illegal turn. As Ernestine attempted to console the sobbing girl, she looked angrily over at Lydia.

By noon, the meet had finally come to the last event—the freestyle relays. Seeing that Chip was on the first relay team, Lydia smiled and said, "Swim fast and have fun."

"Thanks Mrs. P," Chip said, handing her his card as he climbed onto the diving block. As the first relay team member touched the pad, Chip belly-flopped into the pool and took off, his arms and legs flailing in a primitive freestyle. *He barely knows how to swim,* she realized. *Why is Lawrence even allowing him on the team?* She soon found out. Despite the poor stroke, his hands slapping the water, the kid was amazingly fast. The team finished a respectable third.

Lydia glanced over at Geoff, who was in the heating area waiting for the final relay in his age group. He had already qualified for the League Meet and was close to the state qualifying time in the individual medley. He would be fine.

When is this going to be over? I'm getting too old for this, she thought, as Hal Schneider made his way over to Arleen and Lydia's lane. He was wearing what looked like a small backpack with a Thermos, with tubes protruding from each side. "Care for a little spritz?" Hal sprayed one of the tubes into Arleen's mouth. Lydia then opened her mouth and felt the refreshing spray of something very cold and tart with a familiar flavor. Margaritas!

"Thanks, Hal. I needed that."

Suddenly, Lawrence's voice boomed over the PA system. "Lydia Phillips, please come to the starter's tent." She quickly turned to Lawrence, searching for why he might be summoning her, trying to imagine what crisis needed her attention right now. Considering that the tent was only a few feet from where she stood, Lydia wondered why Lawrence simply hadn't walked over and asked her to come to the tent. Then she remembered how much he liked hearing the sound of his voice over the loudspeaker. As she walked to the tent, Lydia spied someone in a designer suit. Warren. As usual, he looked ridiculously out of place.

Why is he here now? she wondered, recalling she had seen his kids earlier in the day. Only the nanny seemed to be around.

"Yes Lawrence, what is it?"

"Warren needs to speak with you," he said dismissively, then ordered the swimmers to take their marks for the next event.

"What? Why?"

"I came to collect my new key, Lydia." Warren was now in the tent, iPhone in hand, sweat dripping from his forehead and his glasses fogging up. He looked tired and anxious.

"What? Are you kidding me? I'm timing right now, Warren. And I don't have the new keys with me anyway. Why are you asking for it now? This is extremely inconvenient, not to mention inappropriate."

"When will you be finished here?" Warren pressed, ignoring her response.

"I don't know, in another thirty or forty minutes. Anyway Warren, I am not going to give you a key today. Lawrence and Amanda were given keys yesterday because they need to access the club during off-hours.

All the other board members will receive their keys at the July meeting." Lydia turned and walked back to the lane, having missed the entire relay. "Hope your stopwatch didn't malfunction," she said to Arleen.

It was twelve forty-five when Lydia left the club. A party rental company was unloading white tables and folding chairs, tablecloths, silverware, and china for tomorrow's Steak and Karaoke Night. She saw Pete as he came in, but he was preoccupied and only said a quick hello. Alex and an agitated Lawrence were conferencing, although Lawrence was doing all the talking and gesturing dramatically. It was no surprise that Meadow Glen had lost the meet, but apparently the loss was worse than the coaches had anticipated.

As she walked home, she recognized Warren's fancy BMW sports car parked in front of her house. *I don't believe this. He couldn't care less about watching his kids compete in a swim meet, yet he's obsessed with his stupid key.*

Warren had been watching for Lydia from his rearview mirror and got out as she approached. "I need my key now," he demanded. "I'm going out of town and I want it before I leave."

"No, Warren. As I explained to you, the rest of the keys will be distributed at the July board meeting. Besides, I have only one extra key, and that's for the lockbox. Pete has the others and he's not distributing them until the meeting. By the way, I have the latest batch of money and bills."

"Then give me *your* key," he said, ignoring Lydia's mention of the receipts and invoices that needed to be delivered to the bookkeeping firm.

"What? No, I'm not going to give you my key. You'll have to wait like everyone else."

"Oh bullshit," he said, angrily flinging open his car door. "You just don't want to hand over the key. This is a control thing. I waited around all morning to get this, and now I'm late getting out of town for the weekend."

"Chill out, Warren. You'll get your key. What's the rush? It's not like you spend a lot of time hanging around the club," she called out as Warren slammed the car door and sped down the street.

As she walked to the curb to check the mailbox, Lydia heard a car engine start followed by the screech of tires a few doors down the street. She turned to see a car make a quick U-turn, then head off in the direction of Warren. *Those damn teenagers*, she thought, shielding her eyes from the sun in an attempt to see whose car it was. She recognized it as the dark blue sedan that had been parked across from the club several days earlier. But by the time she went back into the house, it was long gone from her mind.

Let Them Eat Clafoutis

THE DAY BEGAN well enough. Lydia had gotten up early, taken a run, and then tackled some much-needed gardening, her thoughts frequently drifting to the previous day and Warren's strange obsession with the key. *What a rude, self-centered nut job he is.* Bill had gone to an early tennis clinic, then come back to make his dessert for Steak and Karaoke Night—a French clafoutis comprised of a simple, but rich, batter, blueberries and raspberries, and flecks of chocolate sprinkled throughout, then baked to a golden brown. They ate lunch together on the deck. Later, the family went to Andy's baseball game, taking separate cars so Lydia could go to the grocery to get, among other things, two steaks to grill that night.

Watching the game, Lydia felt strangely relaxed. The club had been open about a month and, despite minor problems and complaints, things were rolling along amazingly well. And she was holding her own. A few nights earlier, while once again lying in bed listening to the ceiling fan—*click...click...click*—she'd had what amounted to an epiphany about her expectations for the summer. She'd started out with high hopes to make this a wonderful and memorable season for Meadow Glen, an accomplishment she would be proud of. But as the weeks wore on, Lydia came to understand she had three main goals: get through the Fourth of July without a major meltdown or crisis at the club, renew Pete's contract, and fend off the lawsuit. *Just hang in there. I can't make things perfect here, and I can't make all the members happy,* she'd mused. *In two months it will all be over, and people will go on with their lives. It won't matter.* The past two nights she'd slept better than she had in months.

Lydia had made a point not to go over to the club and check up on Amanda's decorating and preparations for the party, a Meadow Glen tradition. Steak and Karaoke Night had been going on for so long that it was practically on autopilot. The logistics were simple: everyone brought their own steaks to grill and either an appetizer, salad, or dessert based on the first initial of the member's last name. Four couples had agreed to handle the grilling and cleanup. Amanda had done the promotion, collecting fifty dollars from each couple to purchase the potatoes and cover the cost of renting the tables, linens, silverware, and plates. She was also in charge of the decorations and an ice-breaker game during the cocktail hour.

That evening, Susan and Joe came by for a drink. Then the four of them headed over to the club with their steaks, respective dishes, and three bottles of wine to share. Seventy people had signed up for the event, the best turnout in years, which Lydia chose to see as a barometer of how people were feeling about their summer at Meadow Glen.

"Is Stacie in?" Lydia, wearing her new green and yellow sundress and a pair of heeled white sandals, grabbed Bill's arm.

"Yep. She's in," he said reassuringly. "She's up on Andy's bed." Both boys were spending the night at friends' houses.

The patio was beautiful; Amanda had done a great job. Little white lights twinkled on the bushes and trees. Tables of four and six had been set with black-and-white checkered tablecloths and napkins. Each table had a centerpiece of flowers and a candle. A long buffet table with a white tablecloth was covered with an enticing spread of hors d'oeuvres and salads. People were chatting while soft jazz played in the background. Lydia felt relaxed and elated as she and Susan staked out a table for four.

The usual crowd was there—many of them the older tennis players who had been members for fifteen or more years. For some, it was their first club social of the season, and they were visiting with people they hadn't seen since the previous summer. There were a few swim team parents and two or three new members. Lydia and Bill knew most everyone since both played tennis and Geoff was involved in the youth swim and tennis programs. Lydia was happy to see that Claire Hoskins was nowhere in sight.

She and Bill reintroduced themselves to some new members they had met on opening weekend at a new member social and orientation. Since many of them were young with small children, the conversations pretty much centered on the baby pool. One recalled the incident of Stacie diving into the baby pool on Memorial Day, for which Lydia apologized. "She thinks she deserves the same perks as any other toddler." The woman was not amused.

Amanda was dressed in a tight green-and-hot-pink strapless dress with a gold choker and matching earrings. Her hair was piled on top of her head, and she wore bright green spike-heeled sandals. The outfit co-ordinated well with the margarita in her hand. She tapped her glass to get everyone's attention. "Good evening, everyone. Welcome to Meadow Glen's twentieth annual Steak and Karaoke Night. We're going to play a little game now to make sure everyone is feeling comfortable and loose." A few people snickered as Rex, standing to one side, gazed longingly at Amanda.

"I'm going to give everyone a sticker with the name of a celebrity on it. Please have your spouse or a friend place it on your back so you can't see the name. Your job is to ask people—preferably someone you don't know or don't know very well—for clues so you can guess who you are."

The game was a Steak Night institution and, even though it was old, it was always fun. Bill slapped a tag on Lydia's back, and she reciprocated. They wandered from person to person, seeking clues and seizing the opportunity to chat with old and new friends. After fifteen minutes of asking questions like, "Is this person younger than fifty? Female or male? An actress? A musician? Caucasian? African-American?" Lydia guessed herself to be Janet Jackson. Bill was George Bush, Joe was Michael Douglas, and Susan was Meryl Streep. It didn't take long for the relaxed and friendly ambiance to set in as everyone continued to munch on hors d'oeuvres and sip their drinks.

There were two men at the party Lydia didn't recognize, nor could she figure out who they were with. She looked around and made a mental note of all the women who were there and was able to match them to their spouses or, in the case of Amanda, a "friend"—meaning Rex. But not these two.

During the game, Amanda and her committee had pushed the appetizers to one end of the buffet table to make room for more salads, baked potatoes, and desserts, and lit all the candles. She tapped her glass again. "Everyone, we're going to start grilling. We have four grills going. The one on the left is for last names starting with A to F; next G to L; then M through R; and on the right, S to Z. Please grab your steaks and go to your designated grill and tell the griller how you would like your steak cooked. And please feel free to take your cocktails with you."

By now, Sam Hutchinson had arrived to serve as the on-duty lifeguard in case someone chose to take a "dip" in the pool, and also help with cleanup.

"Okay, we need to coordinate this so our steaks go on when your steaks are on so we can eat together," Joe said, pouring Lydia a glass of wine while Bill and Susan went to get the plates. "Bill and I will take the steaks over while you two hold the table. And don't drink all the wine!"

"Sounds like a plan to me. No promises on the wine, though." Lydia was thankful for the opportunity to sit down and relax with Susan.

She glanced over to the far end of the patio and saw the two unfamiliar men open a cooler and take out their steaks. As they walked over to the grill, they began holding hands. Then it hit her. *This is the gay couple! This should be interesting.* She was relieved that Warren and Lawrence were not among the guests, although Liz and her boyfriend were there. Liz had been quite vocal in her opposition to allowing the couple to keep their membership. Lydia wondered who the two men were sitting with.

When Susan sat down, Lydia pointed out the couple to her, then recounted Warren's reaction and the lengthy discussion that had ensued at the board meeting.

"Oh for God's sake, that's ridiculous." Susan poured herself a glass of wine. "Who cares? I think it's pretty brave of them to show up tonight with this crowd. I had a conversation with one of them, Roger, during the icebreaker. He's hilarious. A nice guy. This should not be an issue."

"Oh, I agree." Lydia almost felt guilty for bringing it up and perceived a need to explain herself. "It's just there are people at this club who have a real problem with it. And while I don't have a problem with it, the fact that these guys are being open and visible — which is fine — could bring the issue to a head. And I'm hoping to dodge that bullet this summer. I'm try —"

Their conversation was interrupted abruptly by a loud commotion over by the grills followed by a series of shrieks and screams.

Now what? Lydia turned toward the grills, becoming distraught at the chaos that seemed to be unfolding. Then a wave of nausea came over her. *Stacie!* There she was, gallivanting around on the grass with a huge T-bone steak in her mouth. The dog had broken several plates, and Lydia could see three steaks on the cement under the grills, a result of Stacie jumping up to grab what she could.

"Oh my God!" Lydia gasped as Susan began laughing loudly at the spectacle.

Then she saw Bill, Sam right behind him, sprint over to the playground area where Stacie was happily chomping on the steak. Each time he got close to catching her, she ran away with the steak in her mouth, enjoying her favorite game of chase. Finally, as Sam blocked her in a corner with a makeshift fence of lounge chairs, Bill was able to grab the dog by the collar and pull her over to the table. "Go get the leash," he ordered Lydia.

"I thought you said she was in." Lydia was furious.

"She was. She was on Andy's bed." Bill's tone was short and matter-of-fact; he was not happy.

"When I said 'in,' I meant was her dog door closed. You know the problems we've been having with her jumping the fence and coming over here."

Bill, realizing he had not paid attention to that detail, shifted the focus from himself to the crisis at hand. "Lydia, is this really the time to discuss the meaning of 'in'? We've got an immediate situation to deal with here. Go get the goddamned leash, please."

Lydia stormed off, so angry she was on the verge of tears. *Damnit, why is it always 80 percent with him?* she wondered, recalling that he still had not fixed the ceiling fan. Stumbling in her high-heeled sandals, she took them off and broke into a jog until she got to the front door, at which point she realized she had no key. She debated whether to go back and get the key from Bill but decided to try another way. She went around the side of the house to the back door. Sure enough, the dog door was open. Crouching down on her hands and knees, she angled her upper body through the door and was able to reach up to the knob and unlock the door from the inside. By now, her new sundress was streaked with dirt, the residue from Stacie's paws. She didn't care. She opened the door, then immediately closed the dog door. *Knowing Bill, he'll forget to do that when he brings Stacie home, and within thirty minutes she'll be back inside the club devouring the dessert table.*

Suddenly, Lydia froze. She heard something that sounded like footsteps in the upstairs hallway where the floor always creaked. *Is someone in the house?* Then she heard the front door close. Shaking, she grabbed the leash and rushed out the back door to the front of the house in time to hear, but not see, a vehicle speeding away.

BY THE TIME Lydia returned with the leash, Stacie had calmed down, oblivious to the havoc she had wreaked. Bill, still firmly holding onto the dog's collar, was surrounded by four or five people. Rex Simons was writing something on a pad of paper. "Okay, so we lost two filets, a T-bone, and one New York strip," he said, attempting to take charge of the situation and diffuse it as best he could.

"Nancy and Ed, since you had the two filets, why don't you take Lydia's and mine. They're next to the grill over there," Bill said. "Lydia, please go to the store and get a T-bone, a New York strip, and something for us. I'll take Stacie home." Lydia could tell Bill was still angry because he refused to make eye contact with her. He grabbed the leash, put it on Stacie, and started toward the front gate.

"Well, our steaks were organic; we got them at Whole Foods." Nancy Brown, impeccably dressed in a pink and green Lilly Pulitzer dress and matching pink sandals, her striking white hair pulled back into a severe bun, was clearly miffed. "But I guess these will be fine." She put the two thick steaks on a plate, which she promptly handed to one of the grillers.

Catching up with her irate husband, Lydia said, "Bill, I think someone was in the house. I heard footsteps upstairs when I was getting the leash and then I heard the front door close. I think we should call the police."

"Oh, great," Bill responded sarcastically. "Call 911, and I'll see what I can find out. Joe, want to keep me company?"

"Sure. Let's go."

Lydia made the phone call, then remembered she still needed to replace the steaks that Stacie had ruined. It took her less than five minutes to get to the grocery store where the specialty meat counter was by now quite sparse. Fortunately, the store had enough to replace the meat—except Lydia's and Bill's. She purchased a New York strip, a T-bone, and two chicken breasts.

By the time she returned to the club, most of the guests were eating their dinner while music continued to play in the background. She handed the steaks and chicken to one of the grillers, then ran back home where a police car was parked. An officer was questioning Bill while his partner looked around the house, now lit up from top to bottom.

"There was definitely someone in the house," Bill said. "They jimmied the lock on the side door. But it looks like they didn't take anything. The computers are fine. TVs, cameras, electronics all there. I checked your jewelry box, but you might want to take a closer look."

"That's odd. Why would someone break into a house and not take anything?" Lydia tried to think of something they could have been after.

"My guess is, you arrived just in time, ma'am," one of the officers said. "But definitely continue checking to see if something's been taken. You'll need to get your door fixed, and I would recommend changing the locks as well."

Finally, Lydia and Bill returned to the club where their now overdone chicken breasts were resting on the grill. They sat at the end of a table of six and ate in silence. As they finished dinner, Susan came over to their table. "Hey, sorry about the seats," she whispered in Lydia's ear. "Liz and her boyfriend came over while we were grilling our steaks and since I didn't know when you'd be back, I really couldn't get rid of them. Why don't you two come over to our house later for an after-dinner drink."

"I'll let Bill make that call," Lydia said.

As darkness set in, Rex and Amanda and one of her committee members set up the microphone for karaoke. Several people had signed up, and now were lining up to perform. Bill had always participated in the past, usually singing Paul Simon songs. But not this year. Lydia found a lounge chair at the pool and listened to the music in an effort to decompress from the miserable evening.

Then, Bill approached. "I accepted a drink invitation from Joe and Susan."

"Okay with me."

Bill appeared to have calmed down, pleased that his clafoutis had been one of the more popular desserts. He put the remaining bottle of wine and glasses into the picnic basket and retrieved his empty clafoutis dish from the buffet table.

Sitting on Joe and Susan's terrace was wonderful. Diana Krall, Steve Wynwood, and the music of other artists played softly in the background. The night was star-studded, and the terrace was illuminated by an array of candles. Lydia relaxed a little, the horror of Stacie's romp subsiding. Bill and Joe spent most of the evening talking with each other as Susan and Lydia listened to the music.

They got home around eleven-thirty. Lydia followed Stacie outside and sat down on the deck. Bill joined her and suddenly went into a rant, complaining about Meadow Glen and how he wished they'd never joined the club in the first place. "Now, with you taking on this ridiculous job as volunteer president, this is turning out to be the worst summer of our lives."

"Bill, you were fine before Stacie jumped the fence and disrupted the party, and that has nothing to do with me being president."

They argued until Bill finally went to bed. Lydia stayed up for a while and was joined by a contrite Stacie—carrying Pink as perhaps a peace offering. She gently rubbed the dog's ears. "What am I going to do with you, Stacie? You're such a bad girl. But I still love you," she said, looking into the dog's big brown eyes.

Lydia tossed and turned most of the night, her thoughts going from Bill, to the events of the disastrous night at the club, to the break-in. *What would have happened if I'd actually confronted the burglars? Did they have a gun? What if they'd had the run of the house for several hours? Or, God forbid, Stacie had been home? Would they have hurt her?* She reached down and stroked the side of the sleeping dog.

At six-thirty, her cell phone rang.

Hidden Treasure

A S THE END of June approached, the rocky opening weekend was a distant memory. Yes, there were problems and complaints, with members often bypassing the website's Suggestion Box and going straight to Lydia or Pete. No matter how smoothly things went, somebody was always unhappy about something — like the Murphy boys continuing to pee on the playground and throw rocks on the tennis courts.

For the most part, though, things were going relatively well. And the weather was cooperating. There had been a few evening thunderstorms, but the days had been mostly clear and sunny. By noon every day, the grounds were full of people playing tennis and enjoying the pool. Now that the pool temperature problem had been resolved, the water stayed at a comfortable eighty-three degrees.

Fred Lyons arrived promptly at noon every day to sunbathe and swim his laps. The ducks, with their growing ducklings in tow, appeared in the pool early every morning. Brad spent hours on the court feeding balls to eight-year-old Tad, occasionally stopping to give him direction and pointers.

The club had hosted the first — and hardest — of three swim meets, and in a month swim team would be almost over for the summer. The swim lesson program had taken in record sign-ups, as had the tennis programs for both adults and kids. There had been two Friday night tennis socials. Every morning at eight, a perfectly coiffed Nancy Brown arrived to practice her ground strokes on the backboard.

Pete was generally pleased, but he remained worried. He continued to see the blue sedan on his block and, more recently, near the club. The first time had been mid-June, directly across the street from the main entrance. Then, on his way to the club one morning, he saw it again in front of the house next to Lydia's. The sedan sightings, along with the unresolved and strange trespassing incidents at the club early in the season, had convinced Pete that someone was targeting him. But who?

Pete had wracked his brain trying to figure out what he'd done or who he had been in contact with that might prompt someone to stake him out. He'd even set up a grid on an Excel program to chronicle his daily routine for the last year, along with special events and parties where he had interacted with people.

That had involved checking back to the calendar on his phone and accessing Shelly's calendar, which she frequently left open on her laptop.

He listed school meetings, parent conferences, parties, dinner engagements with friends, golf games, dealings with people at Meadow Glen, problem students, over-involved parents. He tried to recall phone conversations he'd had with old colleagues from Wall Street. Despite the thorough research, he'd come up with nothing that triggered anything obvious. Yet, he was convinced someone was watching him.

Now, as he sat in bed with his laptop at four a.m. on the last Sunday of June, Pete made the decision to hire a private investigator, something he knew nothing about, and tell Shelly and the girls. *I'll tell them tonight,* he decided. *Who knows, maybe one of them will have a reasonable explanation for what's going on.*

Relieved he'd made a plan to confront the problem, Pete got up and took a shower. He made a pot of coffee and turned on the small television in the kitchen. At five, he heard the newspaper hit the front porch. In what had become a morning ritual, Pete slowly opened the front door and peeked around the frame. He took a step onto the porch and glanced up and down the street. No cars. Thankful, but tired, he went back to the kitchen and prepared himself an omelet, bacon, and toast. Then he was out the door, headed for Meadow Glen.

Pete had taken the early shift, as Sam had been on duty for Steak Night. He was confident the assistant manager had overseen the basic cleanup the night before, but there was always some trash left behind and no doubt the bathrooms would need a once-over. The plumbers were scheduled to come in later in the week to snake the toilets and floor drains. He hoped Jules would take care of any additional kitchen cleanup, although there was a good chance he would have to send the lifeguards in to help at some point as Jules was not exactly a clean freak.

When he entered the grounds, Pete could smell the remnants of baked potatoes and grilled meat. The rented tables had been stacked against the patio wall alongside several boxes containing dirty table linens, plates, and silverware that would be picked up tomorrow.

Pete decided to tackle the worst job first: the bathrooms. He scrubbed the toilets and sinks, then mopped the floors. Satisfied at the result, he grabbed a scraper and cleaned the residue of meat from the grills. Then he turned his attention to the service area, where three large trash bags were piled next to the dumpster. He glanced over at the boiler room door. It was locked. He would need to spend the next hour or so attending to the pool, vacuuming it, cleaning popcorn kernels from the filter, checking the chemicals, and replenishing the water that had leaked out since yesterday.

As he tossed the last two bags, he noticed the dumpster was flush against the fence, which made it impossible to move. Pete had instructed Sam to keep the dumpster a good two feet from the fence so they could easily maneuver it out the gate on Thursday nights for Friday trash day. With the trash from the swim meet and Steak Night, plus the usual waste from what would be a busy Sunday night and week at the club, he needed to remedy this situation before the dumpster became too heavy to maneuver at all.

Pete tried to pull and push, but the large metal container wouldn't budge. Something was catching on the bottom of the bin. He grabbed a flashlight and looked underneath and saw an object wedged under one of the wheels. *Damnit, Sam. Probably wasn't paying attention when he rolled the dumpster back in Friday morning,* Pete thought. He retrieved a long pole and tried to push the obstacle out. No luck. But he could tell that whatever it was, it was soft.

He pushed his back against the dumpster and, after several good pushes, was able to rock it back and forth. A few more tries and the dumpster finally rolled off whatever it was that had been caught. By now, he was sweating, his shirt was filthy, and his knuckles were scraped and bleeding.

What the hell? How in God's name did this thing get so catawampus? Pete stepped back and looked at the dumpster. Whatever had been lodged under the wheel was no longer in the way, but the bin was still awkwardly positioned up against the fence. He would have to try to pull it out a few inches at a time, alternating sides. With each pull, the dumpster moved an inch or less. Finally, Pete managed to pull the dumpster out about six inches from the fence. Now, he could easily roll the container out another foot.

Exhausted and sore from the laborious ordeal and disgusted that Sam apparently had left the dumpster in such an unmovable position, Pete went into the men's bathroom to clean his face and wash his hands. He needed a clean shirt; Shelly or one of the girls could bring one up later.

Then he remembered the object that had been lodged under the dumpster. He went to the back again and found it in the space he'd created between the bin and the fence. It was a black satchel of some kind, the size of a backpack or duffel bag.

Pete picked up the object, fully expecting to toss it into the dumpster, but hesitated when he felt something inside. He opened it. After seeing what the bag contained, he dropped it to the ground. His hands shaking, he reached for his phone and called Lydia.

Sex, Money — and Maybe Drugs

L YDIA STOOD at the kitchen counter waiting for the coffee to finish brewing. Dawn was just breaking so it was still cool. Bill had gone back to sleep after being awakened by the phone and muffled conversation. She had already been awake when her cell phone rang, listening to the ceiling fan clicks that seemed to be louder and more frequent than even a week ago. She was almost relieved to have an excuse to get up and start a new day. Stacie, thrilled at the prospect of an early breakfast, followed her downstairs, wolfed down her food, then bolted back upstairs with Pink to nestle herself next to Bill.

It was about a week before the Fourth of July, a date when temperatures, tension, and tempers always seemed to reach their peak, a sort of breaking point for the season. Five years ago, a manager had walked off the job on July third in the midst of a boiler breakdown and ever since, everyone held their breath until the holiday was over.

Fourth of July came early this year, I guess, she thought, watching the black coffee stream into the carafe. While the debacle of the previous night still weighed heavily on Lydia's mind, it paled by comparison to what Pete had intimated in his phone call. "We've got a problem. Need you to come over ASAP," was what he'd said. *It's got to be the boiler*, she thought. Now, as Lydia poured the extra-strong coffee into a Thermos, she once again made a vow that this indeed would be her last tour of duty as a volunteer.

After entering the club, Lydia immediately went over to the pool and put her toe in the water. It was surprisingly warm. *Doesn't seem like a boiler problem*, she thought, taking a generous sip of coffee.

Then she turned her attention to Pete who was slumped in a chair, filthy and covered in sweat. Realizing she had never seen him look so deflated, she became alarmed. "What's happened? What is it?"

"In here." Pete got up and led Lydia into his office. He handed her the bag. "Take a look."

Lydia slowly opened the bag and was perplexed to see several bundles of cash. She picked one up and thumbed through it, becoming increasingly unnerved. "Oh my God, is this real? There must be thousands of dollars here."

"Fifty," Pete said. "Fifty thousand dollars is what I counted. And my guess is, it's real. This isn't someone's lost lunch money. This is big bucks that should be in a bank vault. This is serious."

Lydia counted ten bundles of cash, each one containing what looked like $5,000 in $100 bills. "Where did you find this? This isn't club money, is it?" She quickly realized the stupidity of her question.

"No, of course not. I keep that money in a plastic grocery bag in the safe," Pete said, then told her about his ordeal with the dumpster and finding the satchel underneath. "I have no idea how the money got there. You don't just misplace a black bag with fifty thousand dollars under a dumpster."

"Are you saying someone deliberately put it there?"

Pete shrugged. "I guess so. But if someone left it there, they're going to want it back."

"What should we do? Call the police?" *Hold on*, Lydia thought before Pete could answer. As a former newspaper editor, she knew that calling the police would make this a matter of public record, triggering publicity. She imagined the *Beacon's* police reporter, Vern Livingston, getting wind of this over his police scanner. "$50,000 in Cash Recovered at Local Swim Club," the headline would read, giving the members yet another issue to complain about.

"I think we may need to consult a lawyer," Pete said, recovering his composure a bit. "We need some legal advice on what to do with this. Anyway, I've got to get the pool ready." He suddenly jumped up and went to turn on the hose. "Let me get things started here, and I'll call Sam and ask him to come in early to manage the club so we can figure out what to do. Let's put the money in the safe in my office."

"Okay, I'll call Mike Patterson." Lydia grabbed her phone and found the number for the board VP and attorney. It was now going on eight, not too terribly early to call someone on a Sunday morning. But Lydia decided to hold off for another thirty minutes.

To burn off her own anxiety, Lydia began arranging lounge chairs. While Pete filled and vacuumed the pool and cleaned out the filter, she watered the plants, hosed off the patio, and straightened the picnic tables and benches. Soon, the grounds were back to normal, and there was no evidence that a party had taken place the night before.

Confident that it was late enough to contact Mike, she placed the call. "Mike? Sorry to bother you on a Sunday morning, but we've got a situation here at the club that's a little unusual. We could use your legal advice."

"Sure. What's going on? Somebody fall into the pool last night?"

"It's a little more complicated than that. You'll see when you get here."

"Sure. I need to get dressed. See you in thirty, okay?"

STANDING IN Pete's office, Lydia, Pete, and Mike stared at the pile of cash that was now scattered on the floor. Pete recounted to Mike how he'd found the bag lodged under the wheel of the trash dumpster. "So, what do we do with this?" he asked. "It obviously belongs to someone, but we don't know where to return it."

"Technically, it's found money but yes, it certainly belongs to someone," Mike said. "We can assume it's stolen but we can't be certain about that. I suppose this could be the take from a drug deal and somebody hid it here planning to come back for it. Or a robbery. But why stash the money here?"

As Pete's thoughts turned to the blue sedan, Lydia's mind went to the one person at Meadow Glen who she knew was involved with drugs. *Jules!* Though Jules had long been strictly a medicinal pot user, Lydia wondered if she had gotten in too deep and was buying and selling the stuff — or dealing cocaine or methamphetamines.

"It's Jules. It has to be," Lydia blurted abruptly. "I've been suspecting her of using pot at the club, but now I'm thinking she's using this place as a front to run a little drug trafficking operation. She definitely needs the money. No wonder she begged to manage the Sugar Shack again. It's a perfect cover!"

Her mind continued racing. *Could Meadow Glen be held liable for Jules being a dope dealer? Would the club's D&O insurance even cover this? Could the board be dragged into any criminal proceedings?*

"I guess that's a possibility, but we need to be careful how we handle this. We don't want to jump to conclusions," Mike cautioned. He had pulled a legal pad out of his briefcase and was making notes.

"Who else could it be?" Lydia insisted. "Who else would be able to stash a wad of cash under the trash bin?"

"Like I said, that's a possibility. But we can't just go and accuse her of this. We can ask her some questions but unless we have some proof or evidence, we have nothing. The money could have been left there by anyone."

"The bigger question is, what do we do with the money?" a frustrated Pete asked again. "I personally think we should just call the police and be done with it."

"That could be problematic," Lydia said, explaining her concerns about media attention. "What if we run a blast e-mail notifying the members and staff that we found some money and are holding it for the rightful owner to claim? That would force whoever did this to come forward. The person would have to identify the bag, where it was found, and the amount of money in it."

Yet even as she uttered the words, Lydia could hear the voice of her father, arguably the most morally upright and ethical person she had ever known, chiding her. *That isn't right, Lydia. The right thing to do is call the police. When you do the right thing, everything always works out in the end.*

"The blast e-mail idea isn't bad," Mike said. "Maybe that will at least buy us some time to determine if the money came from someone inside the club. A member or an employee."

"If we're going to suspect Jules or someone else on the staff, maybe we should check out the kitchen for any evidence of drugs — or more money, for that matter," Pete said, looking at his watch. The guards and Sugar Shack crew would arrive soon. He also remembered he had not heard back from Sam.

Lydia and Mike followed Pete into the snack bar. The kitchen had been given a cursory cleaning, but the floor needed mopping and the counters were still dirty and cluttered with bowls and plates people had left from the night before. The three of them searched the front check-in area and kitchen, opening drawers and cabinets. Then they moved into the back area and rummaged through the items on the shelves. Nothing.

Off to the side was a locked door — Jules's office and rest area for the guards when they were on break. "This is where she would keep the stuff," Lydia said, slowly turning the key, expecting to find a room full of drug paraphernalia.

Instead, they found a lumpy blanket on the flea-bitten couch that was — moving? And a soft moaning sound coming from the same area.

As Pete flicked on the light switch to get a better look, a man suddenly jumped up from the couch and attempted, without success, to cover his naked body with a pillow. A woman screamed and raised her head, then quickly dove under the ratty blanket. But too late to avoid being identified. It was Sam and Amy Blankenship, the assistant tennis pro.

The Sugar Shack had become the *Love Shack*.

Stirring the Pot

I
T HAD been two days since Pete discovered the $50,000. Thinking back to that fateful day, Lydia found the events to be surreal. First, Pete deployed Sam to take his shift as manager on duty, something that was not difficult given the circumstances in which the assistant manager had been found. Mortified, Sam and Amy had quickly put on their clothes; Amy left hurriedly in tears.

"Since you're already here, you can finish cleaning up the kitchen and get the club open. I've got another matter to attend to," Pete said, attempting to evoke a stern demeanor. Lydia detected the hint of a smile. A bit of welcome comic relief.

Then Mike, Pete, and Lydia went over to Mike's house to discuss the situation. "I need a day or two to think about how we should move forward as far as sending out the blast e-mail to the members and talking to Jules," Mike said. "Meanwhile, let's put the money in the safety deposit box at the bank."

The rest of the day was a blur as Lydia, after telling Bill what Pete had found, attempted to carry on as if nothing unusual had happened. "Wow, I've got to admit that's pretty bizarre," Bill said, marinating two large steaks and a medley of vegetables—asparagus, peppers, leeks, and tomatoes—for their regular Sunday night dinner at the club with the Adamses and the Schneiders. "But don't you think you should call the police? Someone is going to want that money back, and if they find out you have it..." His voice trailed off.

"Calling the police will trigger an investigation and publicity, which we don't need right now," she answered. "Who knows? There could be a very logical explanation for this. Maybe it's money somebody is hiding in a divorce settlement. Or a surprise for a birthday."

"Are you listening to yourself?" Bill challenged her. "You don't put a bag of fifty thousand dollars under a dumpster to surprise someone on their birthday."

Lydia waved her hand to signal an end to the discussion and went upstairs to take a shower. At the barbecue that evening, she had a difficult time making conversation and didn't have much of an appetite. Monday morning, she took the money to the bank. That night, Mike called. "Go ahead and set up a meeting with you, Pete, Jules, and myself for tomorrow," he advised.

———————————

LYDIA'S EARLY-MORNING call had awakened Jules, who wasn't due at the club until eleven. During the ten-minute drive, Mike laid out the game plan. "We need to be extremely careful and not accuse her of anything. We want to make it clear that we're just letting her know about the matter and ask her if she's seen anything suspicious at the club or has any idea who might have dropped the money. I'm pretty good at reading people when they're lying. If I think she's going down that road, then we'll have to determine if we need to call the police. We need to take this real slow. I'll do the talking."

Lydia felt good knowing that Mike was taking charge of the meeting. Jules's house, a small 1970s brick ranch, was located at the end of a cul-de-sac in the west end of the neighborhood. She'd moved into the place after her divorce, and it was a far cry from the spacious, upscale home she and her ex had shared while raising their kids. As they pulled up, Lydia was struck by the home's rundown condition. The brown trim paint was peeling, and a piece of the rain gutter hung down on one side. The yard was full of mowed green and brown weeds. She suspected that the only time the grass got watered was when it rained. Two rusted metal chairs were on the front porch.

Lydia rang the doorbell. "Just a minute," Jules called out. After what seemed an eternity, but was only about a minute, Jules opened the door. She was wearing a frayed gray bathrobe over a pair of red sweatpants, and her hair was pulled up on top of her head. Her eyes were glassy and bloodshot. She was holding a cup of coffee.

"Come on in. Sorry about the mess. I had some friends over for dinner last night. Anyone want coffee?"

Lydia considered it for a moment, then changed her mind when she saw the condition of the kitchen: dirty dishes and pots and pans were piled in the sink, the counters were filthy with food that had not been wiped up, and the floor was sticky. A box of cat litter was on the floor next to the stove. A large tan cat meowed loudly and rubbed against Lydia's leg. The house stank of marijuana, incense, stale food, and cat urine. Lydia now understood why the woman always smelled of marijuana. The stuff was permeating her skin, hair, and clothing every day.

"No thanks, Jules. We're not going to stay long. We need to talk to you about an issue that has come up at the club," Lydia said, looking over at Mike who then assumed the leadership role.

"Is there a place where we can all sit down?" Mike glanced into the adjacent family room, which was cluttered but seemed relatively clean. "Why don't we go in here. It looks like there are enough chairs."

The bright room featured an entire wall of windows that looked out onto the unkempt backyard. A cracked slab of cement ran under the windows. However, Lydia noticed that Jules had attempted to counter the effect with some flowerpots and a row of large green, overgrown bushes that provided a strange contrast to the dry brown weeds that covered most of the area. Then it dawned on her. *These are marijuana plants. She's growing marijuana! A lot of it. If nothing else, we can nail her for running an illegal pot operation!* Lydia's mind was going a mile a minute as she sat down. She sensed that Pete had noticed the illegal plants, but Mike showed no sign of recognizing them.

On the far wall of the family room was a large bookshelf that contained probably fifty brightly colored ceramic pots and jars, some with corks, apparently the products of Jules's potting wheel, which was in the corner.

Noticing Lydia looking at the wall, Jules announced proudly, "Those are my pot-pots. This is what I do when I'm not at work. I make pot-pots."

"Why do you call them pot-pots?" Pete asked.

"Because they're for stashing marijuana. They're pots for pot. I make them every summer and give them away as Christmas presents—with a little extra surprise inside. Most of my friends have health or pain issues that are treatable with marijuana, and they look forward to my pot-pots filled with my homegrown supply." She motioned to the plants in the backyard. Mike appeared dumbfounded by Jules's openness about her use and manufacture of the substance. Lydia realized he had never had a conversation with Jules about her passionate views on the subject.

"Jules, we've had a rather strange issue come up at the club, and we're hoping you might be able to help us determine what is going on," Mike began. "Early Sunday morning, Pete found a large sum of money in a small black case that was lodged underneath the dumpster. We're going to have to deal with this in some fashion, but we wanted to talk with you first since you are at the club a lot and see most of the people coming and going. We're wondering if you saw anybody with a black bag or have seen any unusual activity, particularly in the back near the toolshed and dumpster."

Jules stared at Mike for a good five seconds. "How much money are we talking about?"

"I'd rather not say at this point, but it's not a small amount. We're hoping to resolve this internally, without calling the police." Mike, Lydia, and Pete looked closely at Jules to study her reaction to that statement.

"Well, I don't know," Jules said. Lydia anticipated she would avert her eyes, a sure sign of lying, but she didn't. "I mean, I never go into the back area. I'm usually in the kitchen when I'm there. And usually the kids man the check-in desk, so I don't see people going in and out that much. As far as the money, I give the day's take to Pete or Sam when I close up, and it's generally only about a hundred or two hundred dollars. I don't think any of the kids are stealing. I mean, they're good kids."

"Do any of your friends come up to the club to see you for any reason?" Mike was pushing the envelope with his question.

"What do you mean by that?" Jules's face turned red; she seemed offended at his implication that something inappropriate was going on. "Are you suggesting that someone I know left some money in an area of the club that's off-limits?"

"No, we're not implying anything," Mike responded, realizing he had struck a nerve. "It's just that for someone to leave a sum of money this large is very troubling. We will probably speak with other staff members about it; you're the first though. The money is separated into bundles, which is somewhat intriguing. We're concerned it might be connected with criminal activity. Again, we want to try to resolve it internally. Otherwise, we'll have to call the police, and they may want to question everyone on the staff. Certainly, board members could be questioned. This could be serious."

Jules thought a moment. "Apparently, I'm first in line of your suspects," she said defensively. "I don't know what to tell you. It's very strange. I have no idea who would be carrying around a bunch of cash and leave it at the club."

"We think it may have been dropped back there, and then gotten stuck under the dumpster," Mike said, watching Jules carefully. "My concern is that someone is using the club as a drop-off point for some kind of criminal activity, like drug-dealing."

She widened her eyes but kept them fixated on Mike. Then she turned to Lydia. "You think I'm dealing drugs!" she said, her voice rising in anger.

"We aren't accusing you of anything Jules," Lydia said, realizing the woman was insightful enough to see what was happening. "We j—"

"I'm not stupid, Lydia. I know where this is going. Yes, I use marijuana for medicinal purposes. I use it every day. It helps the pain in my neck and knee. But I'm not a drug dealer. I grow my own supply for myself and give some away to friends. I know I'm growing more than the legal limit, but it's not hurting anyone. If you want to bust me for that, fine. I know you think I use pot at the club, but I don't. I don't know anything about your damn money. I'll take a lie detector test. You can check the bag for my fingerprints. I don't know anything about this. How dare you come into my home and question me like this!"

Jules was furious, but Lydia also thought she seemed close to tears. "Jules, you're an important part of Meadow Glen. Please don't jump to conclusions," she said.

"Calm down, Jules," Mike added, rising from his chair. "We're not accusing you of any wrongdoing. We're just trying to figure this out. I think we've talked enough for today. Jules, I'm sorry we interrupted your morning. If you see or hear anything that might provide some clues as to where the money came from, please let us know. Again, I'm sorry for disturbing you. We'll be going now."

Back in the car, Mike started up the engine, made a U-turn in the cul-de-sac, and drove about a block before pulling over. He turned off the engine and said, "Jules may be a crazy, eccentric pothead, but she's not lying. I don't believe she had anything to do with this."

"I agree. So, what do we do now?" Pete looked exhausted and worried.

"We go to the next step," Mike replied. "Lydia, go ahead and send out the blast e-mail. Be as vague and general as possible about what we've found. We'll see what happens."

BY THE TIME Lydia got home, it was after noon. With the July Fourth holiday approaching, Bill had taken the week off and spent the morning working in the garden and playing catch with Andy.

As Lydia put down her purse, Geoff walked into the kitchen but stopped suddenly. "Whoa, who's been smoking weed? Mom? Are you kidding me?" He came nearer to Lydia and began sniffing loudly.

"Stop it Geoff," she said, batting him away. "Don't be ridiculous."

"Actually, you do reek a little," Bill said, grinning. "I think your trip to Jules's place may have gotten under your skin, so to speak."

"Oh my God." She ran upstairs, took a long, hot shower, scrubbed her skin and washed her hair twice, then threw her clothes into the washing machine.

"Much better," Bill said, sniffing Lydia's hair.

That evening, she composed a paragraph that she uploaded to the club website.

To the members: Some money was found recently on the club grounds. If you believe this money is yours, please contact Club Manager Pete Merrick or Board President Lydia Phillips to identify the amount so it can be returned to you in a timely fashion.

July

True Confessions

JULY ARRIVED hot and sticky, and as the busy holiday weekend loomed, Lydia and Pete were consumed with the issue of the found money. The Fourth of July was one of the biggest events of the summer. This year, it paled in comparison to what had occurred over the past several days.

Pete cracked open the shutters and peeked out into the predawn sky illuminated by pink-rimmed clouds. Reflecting on the previous evening, the conversation with Shelly about the blue sedan and the strange goings-on at the club had not been as difficult as he'd anticipated. Both girls had been out on dates, meaning he and Shelly were home alone. Pete grilled some steaks while Shelly prepared a salad and roasted potatoes. He chose a good California Pinot Noir, one he'd had in the wine cellar for four years.

Dinner on the candlelit terrace was relaxing as they updated each other on their day and talked about the girls. Then Pete dropped the bomb. "I need to talk to you about something." Words he reserved for only the most serious of issues. Pete noticed Shelly tensing up, but then was surprised by her response: "Does this have anything to do with why you've been so distracted these last few weeks?"

Pete looked at her sheepishly. "It shows?"

"We've been married for more than twenty years. Don't you think I can tell when something is bothering you?"

Pete felt foolish. "Yeah, you're right. You do know me well. So here goes. For the last several weeks, a blue sedan has been tracking me. It's not exactly following me, but it's often parked outside the house or down the street, usually early in the morning. And whenever I start to approach the car, it speeds off. I've also seen it near the club a few times. But there's more."

Shelly listened intently as he proceeded to list the series of events that had happened at the club. The times back in May when he'd heard noises while working late at night. The strange midnight visitor outside the boiler room after Memorial Day.

"Then a few days ago, I found fifty thousand dollars under the dumpster at the club," he continued, telling her the story of discovering the money, the meeting with Jules, and Lydia's blast e-mail to the membership.

"What? Pete, this sounds serious," Shelly said, her eyes widening with alarm. "It seems to me this is something for the police."

"As far as the car goes, the cops tell me there's nothing they can do about it. They say the car has a right to be on the street, and I haven't been hassled or threatened in any way. They did put an extra patrol on for a few nights, but the sedan didn't show up so nothing happened. As for the money, Lydia wants to avoid calling the police because of the potential publicity. If no one from the staff or membership claims it, then we'll have to report it," he said, opening another bottle of wine.

"Shelly, I've gone over this in my head dozens of times, and when I combine the issue of the car with what's been going on at the club, my gut tells me something's not right. I just feel like somehow all this stuff is connected. I've been over and over practically everything we've done for the past year. I've combed through my class rosters from school, wondering if some pissed-off student is targeting me. I just don't know. Something's not right." Pete poured himself a big glass of wine.

"Why didn't you tell me about this earlier?" Shelly was gentle in her reproach.

"I didn't want to worry you. I was hoping the sedan would go away and things at the club would settle down. But things have only escalated, and the sedan hasn't gone away. I saw it again a few days ago near the club. I started to approach it and, as usual, it turned around and sped off. So, I know I'm being watched."

"What do you want to do?"

"I think hire a private investigator. Someone who can track these guys without their knowing it. Get a license plate number and find out who the hell it is."

"I think that's a good idea. Should we tell the girls?"

"No, let's hold off a bit. I've decided it's best not to worry them at this point. Let's see where this goes. I don't think they're in any danger or anything. If somebody were going to do something like break into the house, they'd have done it by now. Whatever is going on, I'm the target."

"Yes, it sure sounds that way. This is all very upsetting. I love you and I know you wouldn't be feeling this way if you didn't have a good reason."

Shelly put her arms around him. "Go ahead and hire the investigator. Just make sure it's a good one. I'm willing to fork out some money for this."

Satisfied they had resolved the matter for the time being, she finished her wine and stood. "I've got a long day tomorrow, so I'm going to go to bed and try to get at least *some* sleep. Glad you told me what's going on. Keep me in the loop on this. And please, *please* be careful." She kissed him good night. "Don't stay up too late."

In fact, Pete did stay up late. Telling Shelly had been a relief, and he felt encouraged they had agreed on a plan. The wine gave him a strange buzz, and his mind darted from one thought to another. He plopped down on a lounge chair and finally drifted off, only to be awakened by the sprinkler system at one a.m. He stumbled up to bed and fell into a deep sleep, waking before the sun rose.

Now, as he looked out the window, he saw that the street was clear. No blue sedan. *Must be their day off*, he thought, going out to retrieve the paper. He went into the den and Googled private investigators on his iPad; there were several listed. He wrote down the names and numbers of those who had been in business for more than ten years, with the intent of contacting them later that day.

Realizing he was starving, he brewed some coffee and fixed himself a hearty breakfast of scrambled eggs with cheese and diced tomatoes, bacon, toast, and potatoes left over from last night's dinner. The intense sun signaled it was going to be a long, hot day.

And, he had a hangover.

LATER THAT morning, Pete ran into Lydia at the club. "Hey, do you have a minute?"

"Sure, what's up?" she asked, walking with him into the office.

"I need to talk to you about something that's been occurring over the past several weeks that has me a little concerned."

Lydia felt a surge of adrenaline as her interest piqued. "You mean to tell me there's more going on besides the fifty thousand dollars?"

"Well, I don't know quite how to say this, so I'll just say it. I think someone's been surveilling me, and I think it might have something to do with the crazy things that have been happening around here lately."

"Oh my God. Are you kidding?"

"I wish I were. Maybe I'm being paranoid, but I've gone over this in

my head a million times." Pete proceeded to tell Lydia how he'd first noticed a car hanging around in early May and how sightings of the car began increasing just after Memorial Day, around the time of the strange
night "visit" from the intruder back by the boiler room.

"Two to three mornings a week, there's been this car with tinted windows sitting outside my house. And every time I try to get close enough to
talk to the people inside or get a license plate number, the car speeds off.
It's been creeping me out. I mean, why would anybody want to keep an
eye on me? I'm a high school math teacher and a summer club manager,
for God's sake."

As she listened to Pete recount the events of the last few weeks — the
continued sightings of the car, the bag full of cash — Lydia found herself
feeling that all-too-familiar unease rising from her stomach up into her
throat. *A car with tinted windows. Have I seen a car like that?* Her head was
spinning. It seemed like she had seen such a car, but she couldn't place
where or when. And the harder she tried to remember, the less focused
her mind became.

"...And so last night I finally told Shelly everything, and she and I
agreed to hire a private investigator to put our minds at ease and hopefully get to the bottom of all this. I feel like if these guys were going to rob
us, they'd have tried it by now, don't you think? Lydia? You there?"

"Yes...sure," Lydia said, her mind jumping from her vexing thoughts
back to the conversation. She realized she hadn't heard the last several
words of what Pete had said. "I was just thinking. Yes, you definitely have
reason to be concerned, and you did the right thing telling Shelly."

Looking at Pete, she added, "You know, I feel like I've seen a car with
shaded windows too, but I can't remember where. There are cars with
shaded windows everywhere these days, right? What exactly did the car
look like?"

"It's a dark blue sedan, maybe a Honda or a Hyundai, nothing memorable. An average car. But I'll tell you, every time I see a dark blue car, my
heart jumps. Do you think I'm crazy?"

"No, not at all. This sounds very odd, and in light of all the weird stuff
that's been going on I think you're wise to have someone check it out. Do
keep me posted."

"Will do. I'm going to call some PIs later this afternoon. Glad to get
this off my chest."

Walking home, Lydia started to cross the street. Suddenly she stopped at the curb, right at the spot where last month she'd seen a dark blue sedan with tinted windows and two men inside. The same car that had sped away, screeching past her house after Warren left. The day before her house was broken into.

She turned around, ran back into the club, and rounded the snack bar for the office. "Pete," she said, pausing to catch her breath. "I just remembered something."

Deep Diving

THREE THINGS. As explained in Bill's theory of threes. Almost anyone can deal with one crisis. And most people can handle two crises. But for the vast majority, having three crises amounts to three legs falling off the stool. Most people crack. And on this hot and muggy Fourth of July morning, that was indeed how Lydia felt as she woke before dawn from another fitful night, dreading the day that lay ahead.

Three things, Lydia thought as she listened to the ceiling fan. *Still clicking!*

First, there was the day-in, day-out grind and stress of the club. The complaints about the staff, Ernestine's continued whining about the swim team rules, spilled soda, popcorn clogging up the pool filter, poop in the pool at least once a week, the tennis court light petition campaign that seemed to have lost momentum. Lydia stopped herself from adding more to the list.

Then, there was the situation with the found money, which was nowhere near a resolution.

Finally, there was the matter of the blue sedan. After Pete had shared his suspicions about the car, Lydia realized he was describing the same vehicle she had seen twice near her own house, including the day before the break-in. "Why didn't I pay attention to that car when I saw it?" she'd chided herself out loud. "Obviously, the person or persons were checking out my house to do a hit."

"Don't beat yourself up. You've got a lot going on," Pete had reassured her, then expressing his own frustration at not remembering the dates he had seen the car. "I've got to start documenting these sightings."

Lydia had told Bill about the car, but he'd dismissed her concerns as overreacting. "It was probably someone picking up their kids at the club," he'd suggested.

"Two men in long-sleeve shirts sitting in a hot car waiting to pick up their kids? I don't think so Bill," Lydia had said testily. She wondered if he secretly was worried about the car but didn't want to let on so she wouldn't worry.

She looked over at Bill who was sleeping like baby, seemingly unconcerned about anything.

Three things. So, I guess I'm hanging by a thread.

Yet, as she lay in bed mulling over these strange affairs, Lydia recalled another truism: it's always the little things that ultimately break you. And today, it was the click in the ceiling fan that was putting her over the edge. The click was not only still there but had gotten worse — now it was clicking every fourteen seconds, up from seventeen. She kicked Bill, disrupting his snoring.

In the shadows, Lydia saw Stacie's head pop up. *Well, at least some things are right with the world,* she thought as she rolled out of bed. She put on her slippers and went downstairs, Stacie happily following with Pink in her mouth.

Lydia was well into her third cup of coffee when Bill came down. He was dressed in his tennis whites to play in the July Fourth social. "Sure you don't want to play?" he asked. "They can always work in extra people." The social was a round-robin doubles format. With the club's six courts, twenty-four people could be playing at a time. Grant organized the event, having each group play eight games before changing up the pairing. It was usually a lot of fun — depending on who you were paired with and who your opponents were. Grant typically started by putting spouses together, then mixed it up. Some spouses played together better than others. There were always three or four singles who could be worked into the mix.

"No thanks. I'm tired and I've got a lot on my mind. I don't think I could focus very well," Lydia said. She and Bill played pretty well together, although Bill, who was quite competitive, occasionally got annoyed if they were losing and would reprimand Lydia if she missed a shot. Playing in the social had the potential of making an already tense day worse.

Bill once again launched into a tirade about Meadow Glen and how her job as president was ruining their summer and their lives. "I begged you not to do this," he said. "You are so distracted by all this shit at the club that you're not paying attention to our family and this household or having any fun at all. We haven't sat down to a family dinner at home for weeks. This is turning out to be a miserable summer for all of us."

Lydia acknowledged she couldn't argue. "I know, Bill. I'm sorry. I really am. If I'd had any idea that things were going to turn out this way, I never would have done this. I knew the ins and outs of the club would be challenging, but we've had all these extraordinary events occur, and that has made it much worse. In two months I'll be done, and we'll have our lives back."

Bill seemed somewhat placated, so Lydia continued. "I'll be over around ten to make sure things are running okay for the barbecue and games, but can you please find a table for us? There are some towels on top of the dryer. You can just throw them on a table to reserve it. By the way, the click in the ceiling fan is getting worse."

"Yeah, I'll fix it when I have time," he said, grabbing the towels and hastily walking out the garage. *This is your slow season; now is when you have time.*

Fourth of July was by far the biggest day at the club. By eleven o'clock, when the pool officially opened, people were lined up at the gate to get in early and stake out tables, chairs, and lounges. Last year, there had been a huge brouhaha between two families, each claiming a table near the diving board. Pete had brought over a second table to satisfy both warring families, one of whom didn't renew their membership.

As she gazed out the kitchen window watching Stacie chase a squirrel, Lydia laid out her survival plan for the day. *First off, no computer. I'm not checking my e-mail or the website. If there's a problem, I'll deal with it at the club or tomorrow. It's all about getting through the day.*

The barbecue would kick off at eleven-thirty with caterer Peaches and Panache prepping the lunch. Drinks would be sold at the snack bar. Jules and the crew would be swamped. Some people preferred to bring in their own food and grill it themselves, which was fine.

The activities would start after lunch with games for the kids. The penny dive, where invariably at least one mother would dump a handful of pennies at a strategic place in the pool to ensure her child wouldn't come out empty-handed. The noodle race. The relays. Then the family relays. And finally, the adults-only beer dive, which always drew a large crowd—and criticism from Ernestine, who thought the event was totally inappropriate for a family environment. By mid-afternoon, a fair number of people were feeling no pain.

Lydia had already decided she would leave after the games ended. Geoff and Andy would probably stay until the club closed. Then, the four of them would head downtown for the baseball game and fireworks. Lydia was looking forward to getting out of the neighborhood and away from the club for a night. She wrote a note for her slumbering sons and brought Stacie in—checking twice to make sure her door was closed.

By the time Lydia arrived at the club, the tennis round-robin was in full swing. Play had stopped on Court 1 as Ed and Nancy Brown and Jennifer and Bob Murphy were engaged in what looked like a heated debate over a point. None of them looked very happy. To see Nancy in her fresh white tennis outfit with navy trim and matching navy visor arguing with Jennifer, wearing the ubiquitous sports bra, was comical.

"That ball was wide," she heard Nancy say.

"No, it was definitely on the line," Jennifer insisted. "You were on the baseline and I was standing at the net and had a clear view of it. It was definitely on the line."

Thank God I'm not involved in that exchange.

As she walked behind the bleachers, she saw an older man ahead of her dressed in tennis whites and a hat, carrying a tennis bag. But rather than stopping at the tennis courts, he kept going toward the pool, then made a quick beeline for the coveted corner table next to the baby pool fence. *Sean O'Brien! He disguised himself as a tennis player so he could get here early and snag the table,* Lydia realized. She saw him open the tennis bag and, slyly looking around to see if anyone was watching, pull out two decks of cards and snacks for the poker games that he and his buddies would spend the afternoon playing. *Unbelievable!*

In the Sugar Shack, Jules and three teenagers were getting ready to open. Pete was vacuuming the pool while Sam was hosing off deck chairs. The ducks were finishing their morning swim.

Her eyes hidden behind sunglasses, Jules turned her back as she spied Lydia. The two hadn't spoken since the contentious visit to Jules's house several days earlier. The smell of pot emanating from the snack bar had not abated, however.

Lydia walked past Jules and headed straight for the pool, easily spotting the table where Bill had put their towels. "Hey," she greeted Pete. "Any new developments on what we talked about the other day?"

"No, nothing to report. I left messages with a few PIs, but they haven't gotten back to me. I suppose it's the holiday and all. But I haven't seen the sedan for three days now. So that's good news."

"I haven't seen it either. But I can't stop thinking about it. Bill thinks I'm being paranoid."

Suddenly, Pete grabbed the hose and bolted for the playground where all three Murphy boys stood at the top of the slide, peeing all over it. "Hey, I've told you guys not to do that," he said. "Now, come over here and sit down on this bench until your parents are finished playing tennis."

With that, Justin started to cry loudly. Hearing her wailing son, Jennifer ran off the tennis court. "What's wrong, sweetie?"

"That mean man made me get off the playground."

"They were peeing on the slide, all three of them," Pete said. "Jennifer, we can't have them doing this. I'll have to take this to the board if you can't get these kids under control."

"Oh, don't be ridiculous. They're boys. This is what boys do. I'm sure you did it when you were a kid. God, you people are a bunch of freaks." Jennifer gave Lydia a dirty look.

Thankfully, Lydia was distracted by Amanda's high-pitched voice barking orders at the people from Peaches and Panache who had arrived to prepare a barbecue lunch of burgers, brats, hot dogs, potato salad, fruit salad, chips, and cookies. Amanda was garbed in a very skimpy pink and white bikini, covered by a flimsy white top, and high-heeled white sandals, and was dripping in bracelets and necklaces. Lydia noticed that Rex, who was on the tennis court, had stopped his game to watch her.

"We'll line up the picnic tables here for plates, salads, chips, desserts, and condiments. People can get their burgers over at the grills." Turning, she said, "Oh Lydia, I was hoping to see you. I tried calling you. Can you help me collect the money for lunch?" It was more a command than a request.

"Sure, I guess. But I thought you had that covered, Amanda."

"I thought I did too, but the two women I recruited decided at the last minute to go out of town. I know you've done this before. And you always do such a great job."

The last comment irked Lydia. The job didn't require any talent, just time, and Amanda's patronizing way of enticing Lydia into helping was insulting. "I'll help you because it needs to get done, Amanda, not because I'm good at it."

A crowd of people rushed past them, sprinting for the pool. The gates had opened. At the head of the line was Bob Mackie pulling a cooler on wheels, most certainly full of cocktails for an afternoon of poker. Seeing that his buddy Sean O'Brien had successfully secured the group's usual table, he signaled the thumbs-up sign and hurried over to set up the bar.

LYDIA AND Amanda sat at a card table near the snack bar to sell the lunch tickets. An easel listing the menu and prices was positioned next to them: $7.50 for adults, $5 for kids under ten. A PB&J lunch was offered for $3.50 for kids six and under. A long line formed, snaking back to the playground.

While the offerings seemed clear and reasonable, they were anything but.

"My daughter is twelve, but can she have a PB&J meal?" one mother pleaded.

"We need to keep enough on hand for the little ones," a smiling Amanda said with forced sweetness. "Why don't you check back around twelve-thirty."

"But we all want to have lunch together," the woman whined.

"I understand, but we have to stick to the rules."

The woman stormed off.

"Nicely done." Lydia patted Amanda on the shoulder. Underneath that sultry exterior she was no pushover.

"These prices are outrageous," another woman complained, rifling through her wallet for enough money to pay for her family of five. "Every time I turn around, I'm being asked to pay for something. What's the point of paying dues?"

Lydia said nothing, waiting for Amanda to respond. "The dues are to pay the staff to keep the pool and the club running," she said. "You know, you can always bring in your own picnic."

"I have a job," she retorted. "I don't have the kind of time you non-working women have." The woman threw her money on the table and snatched five tickets. *I'll happily trade jobs with you,* Lydia thought.

The line moved along. Next up were two men with a young boy and a small child in a stroller. One of the men put his arm around the other, identifying them as the gay couple.

Seeing the uncomfortable look on Amanda's face, Lydia stood up and extended her hand. "Hello, I'm Lydia Phillips, board president. We've met once or twice but again, welcome to Meadow Glen."

"Hello, I'm Vince Albright and this is my partner, Roger Morey. Yes, I met you on opening day when your dog jumped into the baby pool."

"I'm trying to repress that memory."

"Oh, no harm done," Roger chimed in. "We just got a puppy, so we understand."

"And who is this young man?" Lydia smiled at what looked to be a boy around age seven.

"This is Kevin," Roger said. "He's a little on the shy side, but he sure loves the pool, especially now that he can go off the diving board. His swimming ability has really improved since he joined the swim team."

Lydia nervously looked around for Lawrence. Thankfully, he was over by the pool in full camouflage regalia, gathering equipment and prizes for the games he would oversee using his starter pistol and whistle.

"How is Kevin enjoying the swim team?"

"It's okay," Roger said. "As I said, he's pretty shy and he's obviously not as good a swimmer as most of the other kids. But he loves Bridget, the eight-and-under coach. We'll see how it goes."

"Well, enjoy your day. Hopefully, you can find a table and get situated. We'll be having lots of games later on," she said, handing Vince the lunch tickets.

She also was glad to see that Warren and his family were nowhere in sight. Most likely, they were at the country club where a fancy bash culminating with fireworks was underway. Lydia again wondered why on earth Warren was keeping his Meadow Glen membership and clinging to his volunteer job as treasurer. *Surely, he has his hands full with all his real estate deals.*

Just then, Bill came off the tennis court. Lydia handed him their lunch tickets. "You might want to give the boys a call to see if they're up," she suggested. By now, Brad Stovall had snagged Court 2 and was already hitting balls to Tad.

As the lunch line diminished, Amanda took down the card table and handed the money bag and remaining tickets to one of the teenagers working in the snack bar. They were down to the last twenty burgers and a few brats and hotdogs. The PB&J meals had sold out, so she erased that from the menu. "If people still want to buy lunch, here are the tickets. Put the money in the bag, and when the tickets are gone take down the easel."

"Okay." The boy, who Lydia guessed to be around fourteen, looked confused.

She went off to find Bill, observing an argument underway on the pool deck: two men, both mildly drunk, playing tug-of-war with a chair. "We staked this table out right at eleven," said one. "This is my stuff."

"I don't want your damn table," the other said. "You aren't using this chair, and I need it. You can't just hoard chairs."

Lydia walked on to let them work it out.

Geoff and Andy had finally shown up, piled their plates, and joined Lydia and Bill at the table, next to the Schneiders. Hal was grilling chicken that smelled wonderful.

"Great day," Arleen said. "You couldn't have asked for better weather. Nothing's worse than a rainy Fourth of July."

Lydia had to agree, wishing she could take credit for the cloudless blue sky but thankful she didn't have to endure a hundred wet, angry club members and dozens of soggy burgers. She relaxed a little. The day was rolling, and people seemed to be having a great time. *Isn't this the way it's supposed to be?* As Bill visited with Hal and Arleen, Lydia put her feet up on a chair and surveyed the scene, sitting up to take a closer look at the poker table. All four men were there, munching on their own sandwiches and snacks and sipping what looked like Bloody Marys and margaritas from plastic cups. But there was a fifth, small-framed person huddled next to Frank Fair, looking at his cards and stuffing his face with Bridge Mix.

Chip! Are you kidding me? The kid has charmed his way into the old guys' poker game!

She turned to Geoff and asked, "What's Chip's last name?"

"I dunno. Morrison or something like that."

"He's sitting with those old men over there playing poker."

"Yeah, he's really good at cards, and he knows a lot of games. He's teaching us to play poker in the swim team tent."

"Have you ever met his parents?"

"Excuse me." Their conversation was abruptly interrupted by an unfamiliar voice. Bill tapped Lydia on the shoulder to get her attention. She turned to see a man, his hairy stomach hanging over his swim trunks and gold chains dangling on his chest, standing beside a grill he had rolled next to their table. He wore a yarmulke.

Lydia stood up from her chair to face the man, trying to place who he was. "Hello, can I do something for you?"

"I hope so. I'm Marvin Goldfarb. We've got a problem. Someone has used the kosher grill."

The kosher grill. Lydia thought a moment. Then she remembered that last year some of the Jewish members had pooled their money and purchased a grill that was to be used for kosher food only. They stored it with the pool equipment in the back near the boiler room.

"What?" Lydia was confused. "How do you know that?" She struggled to grasp the issue.

Goldfarb, visibly angry, stepped aside and pointed to the grill. "Look at it."

Lydia stared at the grill, searching for some understanding of the problem — beyond the fact that it had not been cleaned recently.

"There's cheese all over it," Goldfarb blurted out. He then opened the top of the grill to reveal the full extent of the situation. The grate was covered in cheese and hunks of meat.

"Oh, I see now." Lydia put her hand over her mouth. "I am so sorry. Do you know when or how this happened?"

"No. Someone obviously saw the grill back there and just took it. The club is going to have to replace this, you know. And now we're obviously going to have to buy a padlock for it, and the club will have to pay for that, too."

"Yes, of course," Lydia said. "Go buy a suitable replacement and a good lock and send the receipt to me." Her thoughts jumped to Warren, who would be the one to sign the reimbursement check. He would go ballistic.

"Fine. We'll get it this week. But what are we supposed to do today?"

"We've got plenty of chicken if you'd like some," Hal offered.

The man stared at him for a moment and replied, "No thank you." He turned around and strode off.

Lydia repositioned herself in her chair and pulled out a magazine. *We may get through this day yet.* The games were underway now. Lawrence was firing off his pistol and loudly explaining the rules. Bill, the boys, and Chip competed as a team in the wet T-shirt relay. After each leg of the relay, the finishing swimmer had to remove the wet shirt and give it to the next swimmer to don, not an easy feat. Even though they came in next to last, Bill's mood seemed to have improved. Then, another interruption.

"Hi, Lydia. Is there going to be a lane reserved for lap swimming?"

Lydia looked up to see Betsy Broadhurst staring at her from under a big straw hat, two stopwatches around her neck. Erica stood behind her.

"What? I guess so, maybe later. Why? We're doing the games now."

"I see that, but Erica needs to practice her breaststroke. You need to understand that not everyone at the club wants to play games."

Lydia's eyes shifted to a chagrined Erica.

"I'm sure we can designate a lap lane when the games are finished. Check with Pete or Sam." She opened her magazine and Betsy and Erica moved on.

As Sam cleared the pool for the beer dive, Lydia counted at least fifty people congregated near the diving board. The throng included Rex with his arm around Amanda. They appeared to be making no secret of their summer fling.

"On your mark, get set, go!" Sam shouted, then blew the whistle. He was filling in for Lawrence, who had stripped down to his Speedo, baring his hideous tattoos and crouching in a dive position. The crowd jumped into the pool in unison. Several immediately went to the bottom to grab the beer cans. Lawrence emerged with four in his hands and managed to get to the side and start a stockpile before diving back down. *What an ass,* Lydia thought. In less than ten minutes, the event was over. Lydia noticed there were several who had made a good score, including Rex, who was enjoying one on the side of the pool.

Then Lydia saw Betsy approaching Sam to ask him about the lap lane. Sam dutifully set aside a lane by clipping a rope the length of the pool. Within a few minutes, Erica was practicing her breaststroke while her mother coached her along the side of the pool.

As people began packing up their things to leave, Fred Lyons sat in a chair slathering zinc oxide on his nose, waiting for Erica to clear the lap lane for Adult Swim. Lydia stared at him, both fascinated and repulsed by his white largesse.

"Ready to go?" Bill approached and plunked two beer cans on the table.

"I didn't know you were going to do the beer dive," Lydia remarked.

"Well, I figured the least I can get out of this summer are a couple of free beers." He grabbed his towel and headed for the bathroom.

Mildly stung by his words, Lydia put on her sandals to make the trek home and get ready for the baseball game and fireworks. As she walked by the tennis courts, she once again saw Brad hitting balls to Tad. *Does that kid ever get a break from these drills?*

That evening, she and Bill had a cocktail on the patio while the boys showered. Both made an effort to put the earlier tension aside before they all went downtown. The four of them had a great time at the game, and the fireworks were fabulous.

Lydia slept like a rock.

Chasing the Money

THE HOLIDAY weekend had come and gone—a milestone in what had become a challenging summer. Lydia and Pete both felt a significant hurdle was now behind them. There had been no crisis over the holiday—no bathroom backups or equipment malfunctions in the Sugar Shack, no need to close the pool for accidents or broken glass, no cars towed, no safety incidents. Just the usual carping about the usual problems: the perpetual cracks in the tennis courts, the price of the catered lunch, the fact that members could not use credit cards for the snack bar. Add to that, the cheese-covered kosher grill. Issues that seemed insignificant in the face of the mysterious bag of money and the blue sedan. *Two months to go; I can do this*, Lydia thought.

She pushed the Send button to e-mail the agenda out to the board members for tonight's meeting. There would be the committee reports and a financial report. The new keys would be distributed. Amanda would update everyone on the remaining social events. But Lydia knew the main topic of discussion would be what to do about the $50,000.

Since sending out the blast e-mail to the membership, she had received no less than twenty-five responses from people claiming to have lost money at the club—everything from thirty cents to twenty dollars. People had gone to great lengths to describe where their money had been lost or left and offered theories as to what had happened to it. One member accused a guard of stealing. A mother claimed her eight-year-old had lost ten dollars and insisted they be reimbursed. But no one was able to identify the correct amount, the black case, or specify the location where the money had been discovered.

Several board members also had called to inquire about the matter. Lydia was careful not to say anything specific, explaining it would be discussed at the board meeting. Warren, however, had been particularly relentless in wanting to know the details, including where the money was being held. When Lydia explained it was in a "secure location," he berated her. "That's not the way to deal with this, Lydia. I'm the treasurer, and I should be handling this."

The meeting began promptly at seven at the far end of the pool. The skies were cloudy, but the air was dripping with humidity too thick to allow even the slightest breeze. It was stifling. Lawrence, who had snack duty, arrived in a skin-tight T-shirt and shorts with two six-packs of beer and two bags of chips and bean dip. *Nice.*

In deference to the weather, Warren had traded his usual designer suit and tie for an expensive polo shirt, linen shorts, and a pair of loafers with no socks. He looked very preppy, which Lydia assumed was the objective.

Lydia had specifically omitted the Sugar Shack from the agenda and told Jules she didn't have to attend the meeting. Jules had been at the club every day as scheduled, but the two women hadn't had a conversation since the awkward encounter at Jules's home.

"Okay, everyone, let's get—"

"I'd like to jump to old business," Warren interrupted. "I want my damn key. You said you would have them tonight."

"Yes, Warren, I have your key," Lydia said, pulling out a typed list of board members with their term expiration years, which she passed around the table. "Everybody, please sign next to your name to receive your key. When your term is up, you'll need to turn the key back in. You all got that?"

"Fine," Warren responded, scribbling his signature on the sheet and attaching the key to his key ring. He sat back in his chair and began texting.

"Since we're on the subject of old business, that gay couple was here with their two kids on the Fourth of July," Lawrence broke in, taking a long swill from a can of beer. "What are we doing about *that*?"

"Good point," Warren said. "We need to nip this in bud before it ruins our reputation. We're shirking our responsibility here."

"Well, given what has gone on over the past few weeks, we've had other issues that I think we can all agree take priority over that one," Lydia said.

"Absolutely the case," Mike Patterson added. "We've got bigger fish to fry right now."

"That's bullshit. What are we doing here, folks?" Lawrence protested. "The cat's out of the bag now, and we're gonna be getting a lot of complaints. Just what we don't need. And that kid of theirs is one of the worst swimmers on the team."

"What else is new, Lawrence?" Lydia responded. "Welcome to my world. The members aren't happy unless they have something to complain about, so let them complain."

Amazingly, that seemed to end the discussion.

Lawrence, Liz, Bud, Amanda, and Mary presented brief reports. Twenty-five swimmers had qualified for the State meet, tennis program registration was at an all-time high, and the toilets had been successfully snaked. There were now twelve people on the membership wait list. Lydia was ecstatic that at least some things were going well.

Rex then launched into his report on the status of the tennis court light petition. "We've got one hundred and thirty-five signatures, so we're more than halfway home. We still need to hit the south and west sides of the neighborhood. Right now, we're targeting non-member households. I'm going to suggest that we hold two or three 'guest days' and invite these folks to come in for a day to swim. Maybe late July or August, when things slow down a bit."

"No, absolutely not. We can't do that," Warren interjected. "This club is for paying members to use. This isn't a public pool. I am totally against that." Warren had been sullen through most of the meeting and now was agitated. Lydia knew this outburst was a warm-up to what would come later.

"Clubs do this all the time as a marketing gesture and for community goodwill," Rex responded. Fortunately, no one else said anything so the discussion died.

"I know we're all anxious to get to the new business item on the agenda," Lydia said, feeling the heat rising into her neck and face as she anticipated the discussion that was about to ensue. "At this point, I'm going to turn the meeting over to Mike, who will update everyone on what has happened."

Mike gave a brief overview of the events that had occurred since the money was discovered, officially informing the board of the amount—$50,000. Several gasped at hearing the figure. He did not bring up the meeting with Jules. "Troubling as this is, technically this is found money on private property. However, I feel we have an ethical obligation to try to determine whose money it is and how it ended up here. As you know, Lydia sent a blast e-mail about the money out to the membership, but to date no one has been able to correctly identify it. That nobody inside or outside the club has realistically claimed it is frankly quite bizarre."

Pete jumped into the discussion. "The fact that the money was left in an area of the club that for all intents and purposes is off-limits to the membership is as concerning as the amount. And the fact that it was wedged under the dumpster makes me think it may have been deliberately dropped in that area. And that opens up a whole list of possibilities, not the least of which is that the money is connected to a crime."

"And it shows we've got a security problem," said Warren. "The fact that someone, somehow was able to hide that kind of cash in the back is the real problem. And frankly, Pete, the buck for that stops with you."

"Ditto on that." Lawrence belched loudly as he opened his third can of beer.

"People, don't even go there," said Mike in a rare display of anger. "Anybody walking down the street can jump the fence or throw something over the fence. That is way beyond Pete's control."

Undaunted, Warren abruptly shifted the discussion. "The bigger issue is, where's the money now?" he asked, his face dripping with sweat and bright red. "At the very least, we should put it somewhere that is secure and where it can earn some interest. I propose you give it to me to put in a money market or investment account."

"No, we've put it in our safety deposit box at the bank," Mike responded.

"That's just stupid," Warren shouted. "I'm the treasurer, damnit. This is my responsibility. I should be handling this."

Ignoring the outburst, Bud asked, "Given the concerns about criminal activity, shouldn't we notify the police?"

"I agree," Liz echoed. "This could very likely be money that is connected to a crime, and we need to rid ourselves of it as soon as possible. We should contact the police immediately."

"Yes, I think we're nearing the point where we're going to have to notify the authorities about the money," Mike responded. "I had hoped we could resolve this internally, and I'm surprised nobody has claimed it. That makes me think it's connected to something illegal, and therefore I think we should report it. I have a contact at the police station who I'm sure would try to keep this under the radar as a favor to me. But you all need to understand that this could bring some unwanted publicity to the club. Once we report it, it's a matter of public record."

"This is absurd," Warren said, slamming his fist on the table. "Mike, you just explained that this is money found on private property. Since we can't determine whose money it is, I believe it's technically and legally ours now. If we give it to the police, it will just sit in a safe collecting dust with all the other money and property they hoard. I can invest the money so it will grow and benefit the club."

Despite that impassioned argument, everyone but Warren voted to turn the money over to the police.

Enraged, Warren stood up. "This is a terrible mistake," he yelled. "I am livid about this. You people don't know what the hell you're doing." He gathered up his papers and stormed out.

"I'd say this meeting's over," Lydia said, rising. "I'll keep you all informed via e-mail as things develop."

THE FOLLOWING day, Lydia retrieved the money from the safety deposit box. Then, she, Mike, and Pete went to the police station to meet with Mike's contact, a lieutenant who seemed very low-key about the matter, giving them the impression that finding large sums of money is not all that uncommon. After taking a statement from Pete, he stood up and thanked them. The entire process took less than an hour.

"Wow. That was a big nothing burger," Pete said. "I'm pissed I lost so much sleep over this thing."

Lydia, too, was relieved, especially since the officer said he would be as discreet as possible and not turn the report over to the department's PR person. "Hopefully, we can dodge this bullet altogether and get on with the rest of season," she said. "After everything that's happened, how bad can it be?"

The Ides of July

T O MARK the season's halfway point, Lydia headed over to the club with a picnic basket of sandwiches, fruit, chips, and what was left of the blueberry pie Bill had made the previous Sunday. Her plan was to park herself in a lounge chair, maybe swim a few laps, work on her tan, and lose herself in a *Maisie Dobbs* mystery. Geoff and Chip, who had become a fixture at the Phillips house, had come home from swim practice at eight-thirty, scarfed down some cereal and muffins, and then both crawled back into bed. After double-checking that the dog door was closed, she left all three boys asleep with Stacie and Pink positioned at the top of the stairs. She knew the kids would be over eventually to, if nothing else, eat lunch. Chip seemed to have a bottomless stomach, and he and Geoff had an afternoon tennis clinic.

The novelty of being at the club was waning, and both Geoff and Andy were reverting to video games and Facebook postings. At least Andy was reading a book. Since her "job" at the club had robbed the family of their annual summer weekend getaway, Lydia couldn't exactly jump on them for being couch potatoes. Nor did she have the energy. Besides, in just four weeks they would begin their high school freshman year. She would make up for this crummy summer next year, she rationalized.

Lydia tried to go to the pool at least twice a week to lie in the sun for an hour, then move to a shady corner where she could hide behind her sunglasses to read and observe what had become a predictable rhythm. Today was no different. Grant was running his tennis clinics, taking time to give a private lesson to a female beginner — which was more about flirting than teaching; Fred Lyons arrived for his midday swim; Brad and Tad were hitting tennis balls on Court 2; some women were playing Mahjong; the ducks, with their growing ducklings in a row, now marched along the perimeter of the grounds; the baby pool was full of toddlers; the inevitable splat of a snow cone hit the patio.

Betsy Broadhurst was aggressively coaching Erica on the breaststroke and freestyle to boost her times for the upcoming championship meets. Chip was at the club from dawn to dusk, it seemed, and had become a regular at the Sunday afternoon poker game with the old men. And of course the faint, yet distinctive, odor of marijuana wafted across the grounds from the Sugar Shack.

Two Wednesday night family events — a Mexican Fiesta and Hawaiian Luau, both catered by Peaches and Panache — had gone well, although a few members had complained about the price for what they got.

Swim team was two-thirds over, and Lawrence was ramping up preparations for the League Meet, pushing the team harder than ever. The fact that the club still had not won a dual meet galled him to no end. He also remained furious at being denied access to the boiler room, thus unable to lower the pool temperature for his Masters Swimming program. He was not shy about repeatedly voicing his displeasure.

Rex was slowly getting the tennis court light petitions signed, but Lydia wasn't sure where things stood. She made a mental note to call him later.

It had been more than a week since she, Mike, and Pete had turned in the $50,000. So far, nothing had come of it — no calls from the police or the media — which Lydia considered a blessing. The same day they'd turned in the money, Lydia stopped to tell Jules that the matter was in the hands of the authorities and that there probably would be no investigation.

"Thank you for telling me," a glassy-eyed Jules, wearing a ratty red T-shirt splattered with mustard, had replied icily.

"And just to bring this to closure, Jules, no one suspects you of having anything to do with the money. So, you can relax and enjoy the rest of your summer. Just forget about it."

"Thanks. What about all the marijuana plants in my yard? You're not going to bust me for that?"

"Nope, not interested in what you do on your own property. I don't think it's a good idea, but that's your problem, not the club's. I've got bigger issues to deal with than your weed empire."

"It's not an empire, Lydia, and it's not hurting anyone," Jules had argued. "I'm not making any money from it. This provides a continual and cheap way for me and my friends to get through the day without being in pain. Buying marijuana on the legal market is really expensive."

"I understand that, Jules, but you're running an illegal pot-growing operation with all those big plants. Anyway, I don't think we need to keep debating the point," Lydia had said, ending the conversation.

NOW, COMFORTABLY settled in her lounge chair with a big cup of iced tea, Lydia mulled over all the events that had happened, starting even before Memorial Day: the late-night incidents at the club; the break-in at her own house; the blue sedan sightings; the money.

The arrival of Geoff, Andy, and Chip interrupted her train of thought. She watched as Chip dug into the picnic basket for a sandwich, then pulled out a deck of cards and began instructing Geoff and Andy on some version of poker. *The kid practically lives here. Where are his parents?*

Later, with Andy in the pool and Geoff and Chip at their tennis clinic, she drifted off to sleep but was awakened by Sam, who had kept his distance since being caught in the act with Amy. "Excuse me," he said loudly.

Lydia sat up with a start, trying to orient where she was. "What is it?"

"We've got a little problem in the Sugar Shack. The FunFro machine broke, and it's leaking all over the kitchen and starting to seep onto the patio. We were able to shut it off, but we've got quite a mess to clean up. I'm covering for Pete but didn't want to make any decisions without talking to you first. Jules thinks it must have broken sometime this morning, but she didn't notice anything until about thirty minutes ago. There's syrup all over the kitchen."

"Oh no," Lydia groaned, stretching to get the nap out of her system before walking over to investigate the situation. "I was hoping we could get through the summer without something like this happening." Indeed, the iced drink machine was still dripping thick globs of orange, blue, and red high-fructose corn syrup. The sticky mess had spilled onto the patio and club entryway, and was slowly, but surely, oozing down the steps under the tennis bleachers and onto Court 1 as the temperature crept up past ninety degrees.

A barefoot Jules, her stringy gray hair practically covering her face, was in the kitchen futilely trying to soak up the goop with a filthy rag mop while Sam and the guards began hosing down the patio and area under the bleachers. Grant fumed when he saw the mess encroaching onto the tennis court and began venting a blue streak at Lydia as he saw her approach.

"You gotta be kidding me," he said, his face red with anger. "This could not have happened on a worse day. I've got adult and junior clinics scheduled all afternoon and six courts of league matches tonight. That damn snack bar is a menace."

Lydia agreed, but now was not the time to have that discussion. "Okay, get the kids off the courts, cancel all the clinics, and contact the team captain and tell him he's going to have to make other arrangements for at least one of the matches." A tall order for the disorganized, procrastinating tennis pro. He started to protest, but Lydia turned her attention to the patio.

"Sam, please call a disaster relief company and get them out here ASAP," she yelled, running over to her iPad to send out a blast e-mail. "Then, get everyone out of here. And post a sign at the entrance saying the club is closed the rest of the day. And call Pete. And tell Jules to stop mopping and get the damn FunFro people out here to fix their damn machine."

By five o'clock, the disaster relief company was finally gone after spending two hours sucking up the gunk with a special vacuum. However, a sticky residue remained. Pete had come right over, and he, Sam, and the guards continued hosing down the tennis court, kitchen, and patio. The area would require repeated washing. Or, a good rainstorm.

Not to be left out of the excitement, Stacie had made an appearance, galloping through the muck and lapping up the sugary sweet liquid. *Damnit.* Lydia's efforts to catch her failed until the exhausted dog finally collapsed in a shaded corner and proceeded to repeatedly retch. As Lydia held Stacie's head, Pete hosed her down as best he could. Her paws would be orange and purple for weeks.

"How did Stacie get out?" Lydia demanded of the boys, who had been observing the fiasco from the top of the playscape.

"Um, I think Chip was playing with her in the backyard," Andy said in a hushed voice.

"Oh, that's just great. Why can't you guys take any responsibility for making sure Stacie is securely in the house when we're over here?"

Grant, dressed in his tennis whites, had watched the entire cleanup effort from his office, which fortunately had been spared. The sickening smell of sugar permeated the entire club. Jules was in the back with the FunFro rep, who said the machine was beyond repair but couldn't schedule the replacement until next week.

"Good," muttered Lydia as she ran back to her lounge chair, Stacie at her heels. Her iPad was already blowing up with text messages and e-mails from members irate that the club would be closed on a hot evening. *A whole week without FunFro will be wonderful.* She didn't care how many complaints were lodged. She glanced toward the pool and saw that the boys were now in the deep end tossing a plastic football. Stacie seemed to

have recovered from her vomiting episode and was running around looking for the ducks.

"Hey, you guys, get out of the pool," she yelled. "The club is closed.
Andy, please go get Stacie's leash and get her home. Put her in the laundry
room with plenty of water. And make sure that dog door is closed."

The one piece of good news was that Pete had learned from the insurance company that the cleanup would in fact be covered after meeting the
five-hundred-dollar deductible.

With the boys and Stacie home and the cleanup crew gone, Lydia composed herself to send out another, apologetic blast e-mail, further explaining what had happened. By the time she walked in the door, Geoff and
Chip were playing cards and Andy was engrossed in *Lord of the Flies*. After
spending a few minutes calming down the bewildered Stacie, stroking her
head and stomach, Lydia called out, "Chip, is your mom or someone coming to pick you up?"

"My mom usually comes around eight to get me at the club, but I guess
I won't be there tonight. I can call her on my cell phone."

Eight? So she leaves him there all day long? "Tell you what, we'll give you
a ride home," Lydia said, welcoming the opportunity to check out Chip's
parental situation for herself. "Come on, guys. Let's go."

Chip's house was a long, mid-century ranch about three miles away.
The open garage revealed a red convertible sportscar as Lydia pulled into
the driveway. All four of them got out of the car, but Chip ran through the
garage and into the house. Moments later, the front door opened. A tall, attractive, but stern-looking, woman with long dark hair — dressed in shorts
and a sleeveless top and holding a glass of wine — stepped onto the porch.

"Hi, I'm Lydia Phillips, and this is Geoff and Andy. We've certainly
enjoyed meeting Chip this summer. Unfortunately, there was an equipment malfunction at the club, and we had to close early. So, we wanted to
make sure Chip got home."

"Thanks, appreciate it. I'm Deni Morales."

"I'm so glad you're home. I had assumed that since I've never seen you
at Meadow Glen, you probably work full time."

"No, I'm home most of the day except when I'm shopping or out for
lunch. I just drop Chip off at the club so he can swim and play tennis and
hang out. He loves the Sugar Shack."

"Oh." Lydia thought a minute. "Well, it's fine to drop him off for specific activities, which is what most parents of kids his age do, but leaving

him there all day is really not a good idea. I'm the board president. The club can't be responsible for unsupervised kids all day long. He is certainly welcome to come to our house — "

"Where in the bylaws does it say that?" Deni's cold, dark eyes bored into Lydia's.

"Uh, gosh. Well, I'd need to take a look — "

"Actually, my husband and I checked. There's nothing in the bylaws that addresses that issue. It only mentions parents leaving babies and young children unattended. So, I'm perfectly fine to drop off Chip," she said brightly, but in a steel-sharp voice.

Lydia was speechless. Finally, she collected herself to say, "Hmm. I guess that's something the board will have to look into. Nice meeting you." She turned around to leave, signaling Geoff and Andy to follow.

No one said a word on the short drive home. "Bill," she called out as she walked into the house. "We're going out for dinner tonight. And drinks."

And pray for some rain.

When it Rains, it Pours

MIRACULOUSLY, the rain did come two days later. In torrents. The onslaught began with a powerful bolt of lightning that struck the tennis court lock system, leaving the men in a nighttime league match stranded inside the club grounds. Around eight o'clock, Lydia received the frantic call from Grant to come over and unlock the main gate so the men could get out.

Arriving, she found more than a dozen soaked and angry tennis players, one of them attempting to scale the fifteen-foot chain-link fence. *Oh my God, he's going to get electrocuted.*

"Those damn gates have never worked right," Grant yelled. "There's gotta be a better system than this. You know—"

"Grant, I suggest you shut up and try to get that fool off the fence before he's toast," Lydia retorted. "By the way, where's *your* key? You could have handled this yourself you know."

"Uh, it's in my car," he replied sheepishly.

"Oh great," she said, glaring at him with no attempt to hide the sarcasm. "Get everybody out of here." A few minutes later, the fence-climber safely down, the crisis was over, and Lydia was back home peeling the clothes off her soaked body.

It rained for six days, saturating yards and washing away for good the sweet, syrupy residue left on the patio and tennis courts by the broken FunFro machine. The rains also caused the river and streams to rise. The fire department was even putting out sandbags in the event the water rose above the banks, something that had not occurred for more than ten years. Lydia was ecstatic. Not only would the courts and patio get a good washing, but the club would be closed—basically a vacation for her, Pete, and the staff! Now she could focus on the one big issue that still needed resolution: the tennis court lights.

Lydia contacted Rex, who reported he had 150 signatures—an improvement but still a way to go.

She also called Mike Patterson about Chip Morales, explaining she had taken time to review the bylaws and found that, indeed, Deni was correct. There was nothing specifically prohibiting parents from leaving their kids unattended all day at the club. The directory showed that Denise and Mitchell Morales had one child, Chip, and had joined the club this year. A Google search of Mitchell Morales revealed that he was a bank vice president.

"That's one more reason we need to review the bylaws," Mike said. "Remember, we still need to come to some resolution on the definition of 'family' when it comes to gay and cohabitating couples. We will need to tackle this over the winter."

Sounds good to me, Lydia thought. *I'll be long gone by then.*

The respite also gave her time to get some things done around the house. The first order of business was a big, colorful sign for the door to the garage. **STACIE IN? DOG DOOR IN?** Anyone going out the garage — the primary way the family exited the house — would see the sign and, hopefully, remember to make sure Stacie was inside. With the dog door closed.

For the first time in months, the family sat down to a normal dinner. Since Bill was not terribly busy at the office, he took the opportunity to prepare several nights of gourmet meals that a professional chef would have been proud to serve. They dined on beef bourguignon with a rich red wine sauce and carrots and onions from his vegetable garden. He fixed linguini and clams over homemade pasta, with a buttery sauce of tomatoes, basil, and oregano. He roasted a chicken with fennel and vegetables and made a decadent chocolate torte, homemade vanilla bean ice cream, and peach cobbler.

Lydia wasn't sure if it was Bill's cooking or the fact that her phone wasn't ringing off the hook with Meadow Glen issues and complaints that made the dinners taste so good. She ended up gaining two pounds.

She cleaned up her office, looked at the boys' schedules for the first semester, and read the newspapers, including the *Wall Street Journal* and the *Beacon-News,* every day. She and Bill went to a movie one night and binge-watched the most recent season of *The Great British Baking Show.* They even had sex. A long night of passion to the sound of soothing, gentle rain and an afternoon quickie in the wine cellar. Things were almost back to normal, and Bill was in a great mood.

Lydia also cleaned out her closet and sorted through the pile of clothes that had accumulated over the past two months. At the bottom, was a pair of Capri pants she had been looking for, remembering the last time she'd worn them was early in the summer when it was still relatively cool. As she reached for a hanger, she sensed something fall out of the back pocket. A business card. She recalled picking up the card one day on her way home from the club. **DLB Commercial Property Management. Darrell Baker.** She stared at it a moment, then tossed it in the trash.

Later that night, the lead story on the eleven o'clock news was about a body that had washed up from the swelling river. The man was identified as a commercial property manager who had been missing since Memorial Day.

His name was Darrell Baker.

The Big Dig

A FTER HEARING the news report, Lydia sat stupefied staring at the TV. Then, she sifted through the trash and found the business card she had tossed only hours earlier: **DLB Commercial Property Management, Darrell Baker, owner. Since 1989.** It listed only a phone number, and a post office box as the address. "Oh my God, I'm starting to freak out," she said to Bill. "Surely, it can't be a coincidence that I found his card a few doors away."

"Maybe. Maybe not," he tried to reassure her. "I know you're upset, and with the bag of money and all the other crap that's been going on around here, it is a little alarming. But let's not jump to conclusions. Take a deep breath. Where exactly did you find that card?"

Lydia struggled to remember. "I don't know, somewhere down the street between here and the club. It looked like a piece of trash so I figured I would be a good citizen and pick it up. I put it in my pocket and forgot about it. Then just today, I found it and threw it away. This is all so eerie. I'm worried that somehow this is connected to the money we found. Maybe this guy was involved in some shady deal, tried to hide the money, and got caught. And then ended up in the river."

"Well, if that's the case you can forget about it. You'll never hear from him or have to worry about him coming back to find the money. End of story. Don't let your imagination blow this out of proportion. Strange things happen sometimes."

Not completely satisfied with that reasoning, Lydia went to bed where she tossed and turned all night, prompting Bill to go to the guest room. A delighted Stacie then jumped up and snuggled next to her. Lydia was comforted listening to the dog's deep, contented breathing. At the crack of dawn, after about an hour of sleep, she finally got up, fed Stacie, and made a strong pot of coffee. By now the rains had stopped, and she knew Pete was probably at the club getting it ready to open.

Lydia studied the business card, then opened her iPad to the

Beacon-News to find Vern Livingston's story about Darrell Baker's body washing up in the river, which gave more details than what had been on the TV news. He was sixty-three and a long-time resident of Maywood, a suburb west of the city. *Nowhere near this neighborhood.* A blurry photo showed a man looking younger than his reported age with darkish hair, glasses, and freckles. The story said he had received a head injury, but that an autopsy would be conducted to try to determine actual cause of death. He'd owned his firm for more than thirty years. He left a wife, Marge, and two sons. Marge had reported him missing the day after Memorial Day, suggesting he'd seemed unusually distracted and anxious and had come home late at night on several occasions — not typical behavior. *Memorial Day.*

Lydia Googled Darrell Baker, eventually finding an address: 6402 Versailles Drive. She wrote it down knowing she would not be able to resist at least doing a nosy reporter's drive-by. She found a rudimentary website for DLB Property Management listing a few commercial properties he managed. The phone number was the same as on the business card. She called the number and got a recording: *You've reached Darrell at DLB Property Management. Please leave a message and I will get back to you before close of business.* She also found the original *Beacon* story she now recalled reading back in early June, reporting that Darrell had gone missing.

She went upstairs to take a shower. The boys were enjoying their last sleep-in before the improving weather got them back on schedule, especially Geoff who would have to be at swim practice the next morning. After several days of missed practices — and one more dual meet, only a week left until the League Meet, and ten days until the State Meet at the end of July — Lawrence would be pushing the kids harder than ever. Geoff would not be happy. The least of her problems.

When Lydia came back downstairs, a tired-looking Bill was sitting at the table reading the newspaper. "I assume you saw the story on that Baker guy," he said. "Wonder if the head injury was caused by hitting his head or if he was thumped by someone, then dumped in the river."

"That's a big question," Lydia replied. "We'll have to wait for the investigation."

"Listen, don't obsess over this," Bill said, wrapping his arms around her. "Nothing bad is going to happen."

"I'm trying not to," she said unconvincingly. "I'm actually going to the club. Can you rouse the boys before you leave?"

"Sure. How about grilled salmon for dinner?"

"Sounds great," she said, although the dinner menu was the furthest thing from her mind. She kissed him goodbye, adding, "Thanks for keeping the home fires burning."

Thinking about Bill's advice, Lydia felt a wave of calm wash over her as she breathed in the warm, damp air and watched the sun rise on her way to the club. A few puddles remained on the courts, but Grant was holding a tennis clinic with Jennifer Murphy and some other women. Fortunately, there was no sign of Jennifer's bratty boys. Lydia waved, but both Grant and Jennifer avoided making eye contact with her. *They can't stand me; oh well.*

She saw that Pete was already hard at work. But instead of getting the deck in order and replenishing the water for what undoubtedly would be a busy day, he was standing in the middle of the pool pushing chairs and lounges toward the shallow end. A grill was floating in the middle. *Pool jumpers.*

Lydia bent down by the steps so Pete could hand her the plastic furniture.

"Thanks. I was hoping we had dodged this problem this year. But, compared to some of the other problems we've been having this is a no-brainer."

"Are we okay to open on time?"

"Yeah, we should be fine. But they had a good time trashing the place. This grill won't be usable for a while. I've already picked up all the beer cans. How was your week off?"

"Wonderful—until last night." She told Pete about Darrell Baker's body being recovered and the strange coincidence of finding his business card near the club around the time he went missing. "So, now we've got midnight visitors at the club, a break-in at my house, a bag full of fifty thousand dollars, a car with shaded windows lurking around here and your house, and the business card of a dead guy who may have been in the area around Memorial Day."

"Yeah, I saw the news story on TV last night, but of course didn't think much of it. It is pretty crazy that you found the guy's business card. By the way, I hired a PI last week to try to track that blue sedan, but after three nights of watching my house he hasn't turned up a thing. The good news is, I haven't seen the car lately. Whoever it is probably knows I'm on to him and is laying low."

"That *is* good news," she said. "I haven't seen the car, either. Maybe that's one problem we can cross off our list."

Lydia surveyed the grounds. The grass was soggy, the tennis courts were dotted with puddles, and the pool vacuum was hard at work removing debris from a week of storms, along with some popcorn kernels. Her kids were in bed, and not much would be going on at the club, at least until the afternoon. A good day for an adventure.

"I've got some things to do, errands to run, so I'm going to take off," she told Pete. "I'll have my cell." She ran back home, nearly getting clipped by a red Miata convertible careening into the parking lot. The car stopped to let Chip out, then quickly took off. Deni Morales didn't see Lydia waving to signal that there was no swim practice and the club was closed until eleven. *The woman was probably going crazy with the kid home for six days.*

"Morning, Mrs. P," Chip said.

"Hey, Chip. The club is closed, so why don't you come home with me."

Lydia settled Chip in front of the TV with some sweet rolls and milk. Bill was still reading the paper. "Now Chip, please do not take Stacie outside to play," she cautioned him. "Just watch TV until the boys get up."

She checked in briefly with Bill and told him she would be back in a couple of hours—and to keep an eye on Chip. Then, she closed Stacie's door, got into her car, plugged 6402 Versailles Drive into her GPS, and backed out of the driveway.

———

IT TOOK about forty minutes to reach Maywood, an older, middle-class neighborhood with tree-lined streets. As Lydia turned onto Versailles Drive, she felt the familiar rush she used to experience in her early days as a police reporter going to the scene of a crime. The street was empty, save for a pickup truck and a black SUV.

Number 6402 was at the end of the block. The modest but neat ranch house was set back from the sidewalk with mature trees on either side of the walkway and potted geraniums flanking the front door. Lydia got out of the car, her heart racing. It had been a long time since she'd gone digging around for a story, but back then she'd had the credibility of the newspaper behind her. This time, she was on her own.

She walked gingerly up the walkway and rang the doorbell. Before long, the door opened to reveal a short, sixty-something woman with medium-length bleached blonde hair wearing a robe and holding a cup of coffee. The woman clearly had once been quite attractive, but now looked tired and worn. Her eyes were red.

"Hello, Mrs. Baker?" Lydia asked.

"Yes, can I help you?"

"My name is Lydia Phillips. I live over in Jorgentown. I heard the news about your husband, and want to tell you how very sorry I—"

"What do you want?" the woman—Marge—demanded.

"Oh, yes. I'm sorry." Lydia picked up the pace of her speech before Marge could slam the door in her face. "Several weeks ago, I found your husband's business card near my house. I put it in my pocket and forgot about it. I found it yesterday when I was cleaning out my closet, and then I heard about Mr. Baker's body being recovered in the river." Lydia pulled the card from her purse to show the woman.

"Darrell had clients all over the metro area," she responded sharply.

"Oh, I'm sure he did. It's just that there are no commercial real estate properties near my house. I used to be a reporter and editor at the *Beacon*, and usually coincidences like this are somewhat questionable. And apparently there is an investigation under—"

"The police have been here twice asking about Darrell and his business, and I've already talked to the media," Marge interrupted. "That Vern from the *Beacon* was here yesterday. You say you *used* to work for the *Beacon*. So, what are you doing here? Being nosy? I don't see how this is any of your business."

Lydia took a deep breath and stepped back. "You're right, it's not any of my business. But, after hearing what happened to your husband and remembering that I had picked up his business card around the time he went missing, it frankly stunned me. It isn't tattered and doesn't look like it blew in from someplace else. It appears that it was just dropped or something. I thought you might be interested, but I realize now that I've intruded, and I am so very sorry."

Marge stared at Lydia for several seconds. Then, her expression softened and her eyes welled up. "Oh, it's not your fault, honey. I guess I can see how you would think this is odd. I don't know what to tell you. Darrell managed a lot of properties, and I never knew much about them. I've searched my brain since he went missing and I can't make any sense of this. He'd been edgy for several weeks, but nothing that indicated he was suicidal or anything. I just don't understand it. I feared something terrible had happened, but when they found him in the river with damage to his head, I was shocked. What was he doing by the river, anyway? This almost sounds like a mob hit or something crazy like that. I'm trying to stay strong for my family. I have two sons and three grandchildren who have been traumatized by what has happened. Darrell was a good man. A wonderful husband and father. He loved those grandkids."

Suicide? Mob hit? There had been no suggestion of either possibility in the news reports. *This poor woman has been through hell,* Lydia thought.

"Darrell liked to hike and backpack, and he knew how to take care of himself," Marge went on. "He never would have been walking near the river in dress shoes, which is what he was wearing." Her face was angry, and she had a determined look in her eyes. "As I said, he'd seemed anxious. Couldn't sleep. Drinking a little more. And, he was getting home later than usual. He was obviously upset about something but wouldn't talk to me about it. Every time I asked, he would wave it off like it was nothing and tell me I was exaggerating. But believe you me, he was not fine. And, I guess we can now see that I wasn't exaggerating."

Lydia felt a lump in her throat seeing the woman so distraught. "Did he ever mention anything about having business over near Jorgentown?"

Marge's eyes searched for an answer. "No, dear. Not that I recall."

"I can't begin to imagine how horrifying this must be for you and your family," Lydia said. "It's hard enough to lose your husband, but under these circumstances it makes it much worse. Again, I am terribly sorry for your loss. Let me give you my phone number. Please feel free to call if you need anything at all. I would love to bring dinner over sometime. My husband is a fabulous cook." Lydia took a wrinkled scrap of paper from her purse, scribbled down her name and number, and handed it to Marge.

"Oh, that is so kind of you. We have wonderful friends and neighbors, and my freezer and fridge are full. The funeral is Friday and we have family coming into town, so we have a lot of support. But thank you very much."

"I will keep you in my prayers," Lydia said, backing away from the door.

"Thank you again."

As the door closed, Lydia nearly ran to her car and sat for a moment, thinking about what Marge had said. *It's all very strange.*

Then, her cell phone rang. It was Pete. "You're not gonna like this," he said. "Vern Livingston from the *Beacon* is at the club. He heard about the fifty K and wants a comment. I'm out of my element here, so I'm punting this to you. Sorry."

Damnit! "I'll be there in forty-five minutes."

She turned on the engine, spun the car around, and took off around the corner. She didn't notice a black SUV following close behind.

Working the Grapevine

LYDIA SPED into the Meadow Glen parking lot, her hands slippery with sweat on the steering wheel. She'd managed to keep her composure driving back from Marge Baker's house, furious but not surprised that word of the $50,000 had gotten out. Cops gossip just like everyone else. Vern had been a police reporter for more than forty years and had developed excellent sources who fed him tips all the time. He was practically a cop himself, with two police radios in his bedroom and three at the office.

She turned off the engine and took a deep breath before getting out of the car. She walked quickly, marching past the Sugar Shack and tennis courts where Grant and his assistants, Max Driver and Amy Blankenship, were running a tennis clinic for about thirty kids. Amy, still humiliated from getting caught in her sex romp with Sam, turned her back the minute she spotted Lydia. Brad and Tad were hitting balls on Court 6. On an empty court, the unsupervised Murphy boys were playing with sticks and throwing rocks. Jennifer was nowhere in sight.

The club was not overly crowded. But there, in the middle of the covered patio stood Vern—heavyset and unshaven with thinning gray hair, thick Coke-bottle glasses, a button-down blue striped shirt accented with a garish red and yellow paisley tie, and brown Oxfords.

"There she is," Vern called out in his raspy voice, teeth yellowed from years of cigarettes and strong coffee. "So, *this* is what you gave up your career for? To work at a frickin' rundown pool club? I thought you wanted to stay home and raise your kids."

Lydia's stomach knotted up. *Yep, this is what I gave up my career for.* "Hi to you too, Vern. It has its moments. And the kids are a full-time job, too. How have you been? How are things at the newspaper? What can I do for you?" She couldn't help but notice Jules pretending to busy herself in the Sugar Shack while eavesdropping on the conversation.

"Oh, same circus, different clowns. Waiting for the next round of layoffs. Anyway, I got wind of a potential story. Fifty thousand bucks in a bag here at Meadow Glen. Nobody's claimed it. What can you tell me?"

Lydia recalled that Vern liked to venture off the beaten path of murder and mayhem and chase down stories on the quirky side. This one was right up his alley.

"What have you heard from your sources?" Lydia figured she would play to Vern's need to always be the authority on everything. Plus, as every reporter knows: it's always better to be on the questioning, not the answering, end of an interview.

"Not much. That's why I'm here. Just that this big wad of cash was found near the trash can. Can I see the spot?" Vern's flippant demeanor had quickly pivoted to all-business.

Lydia led him around to the back. "The bag with the cash was found under the dumpster which, as you can see, is positioned right next to the fence that runs along the sidewalk. Anyone could have thrown it over the fence. We waited a few weeks to see if anybody claimed it, then turned it over to the police. End of story."

"Any thoughts on where this came from?" Vern asked. "You gotta wonder who would toss this kind of money over the fence."

"Your guess is as good as mine. Maybe money from a drug deal that went awry? What do you think?"

"No idea. But it's pretty bizarre. You don't just find fifty K in cash lying around. Plus, it would take some effort to place it *under* the trash bin. If someone tossed it, it would have landed on top of the bin. See?"

"I get your point, but this trash bin gets rolled around a lot. For example, the bag could have been thrown back here one night when the trash was out on the curb to be picked up, and then the dumpster rolled over it when it was pushed back. Nobody would have noticed."

"Hmm. Strange. We'll probably just do a brief on this for now, but I'll keep digging." Lydia sensed Vern's irritation that there weren't enough details to write a full-blown story. By four o'clock in the afternoon, Vern typically had as many as ten stories he was pitching to the City Desk, with room for only two or three at best. One day, he became so frustrated at the Desk's lack of interest, he stood up and shouted, "There's a fire on the freeway! Do we care?" That prompted a list of more than fifty "Vern-isms" titled "Fire on the Freeway…" that circulated around the newsroom.

He thinks this story is too juicy for a one-paragraph brief inside the Metro section, Lydia mused. *He'll be on this like white on rice.*

She took the opportunity to redirect the conversation to gain some information for herself. "I would think you'd be up to your eyeballs on the story about that guy's body washing up in the river. What's the latest on that?"

"Not a lot to go on at this point, but there's definitely a story there. Off the record, I'm hearing he may have been onto something. He apparently had made an appointment with the cops right before Memorial Day, but never showed up. Have no idea what it was about. He had no record and, except for three reports of burglaries over the past twenty years at properties he managed, never had any substantive contact with law enforcement."

Lydia froze at the revelation of a pending appointment with the police around Memorial Day, the date when everything about this puzzling summer was seeming to converge. "Were there signs of foul play or a struggle?"

"Yeah, there was a severe blow to the back of his head."

Whoa! He either fell backward and hit his head or was attacked from behind.

"My guess is that's what killed him, but we'll know more when we hopefully get some autopsy results in a few weeks," Vern said as he put the reporter's notebook in his back pocket, signaling the end of the interview.

"Sorry I can't help you any more with the story, Vern. I think this is just a fluke. Good luck with your brief."

"Yeah, well, call me if you hear anything," he replied. "Somebody out there has gotta be looking for their money in a bad way."

Buzzkill

LUNCHTIME HAD come and gone, and Lydia was starving, dehydrated, and getting a headache. The temperature was heating up, and with all the moisture from several days of rain it was very humid. She bought a bottled water and candy bar from the Sugar Shack and strolled over to Pete's office.

"Well?" he asked. "Are you going to be on the front page?"

"No, Vern didn't get much from me. Of course, I didn't tell him about all the weird stuff that's been going on around here. Hopefully, they'll run a brief and we'll be finished with this—at least as far as the *Beacon* is concerned." Lydia updated Pete on what Vern had related and about her visit with Marge Baker. "The poor woman is so distraught and confused about what happened to her husband. In my heart of hearts, I know there's something fishy going on with all this. We'll probably never know the whole story, and it will haunt me for years to come."

Then, in a more upbeat tone as she finished the candy bar and tossed the wrapper in the trash, she remarked, "The good news is, the money is gone and we're over the hump this season. Once the kids go back to school, this place will be a ghost town except for weekends. Then we can--"

A series of loud screams from the tennis courts ended their conversation. Lydia and Pete walked out of the office to see the kids, Grant, and the other tennis coaches running frantically off the courts, waving their arms. One little girl fell in the rush; an older boy picked her up and carried her as he ran. Lydia knew it would be only a matter of seconds before the startled child began crying.

The bees were back.

"Oh my God," Lydia yelled, now seeing the large swarm following the fleeing crowd, then extending their attack to the playground and patio, where a fresh snow-cone spill was rapidly melting. On closer look, she realized these weren't bees—they were wasps! Within minutes, the patio was swarming with the insects, stinging virtually everyone. Kids were screaming and crying as mothers raced over and, in some cases, picked up their children and threw them into the pool. Brad and Tad smartly had exited through the gates to the parking lot.

Lydia saw Chip near the deep end playing cards with some other kids, having skipped the tennis clinic and seemingly oblivious to the chaos that was unfolding. She looked around for Geoff and Andy and thankfully saw that they weren't there. *Geoff ditched the clinic too, and I don't care.*

In his office, Pete reached up to the shelf, pulled down a bag hand-lettered with BEE STINGS, and took out a tube of cream. He ran over to one of the kids and squeezed some cream onto a welt that was forming. "Here, I'll do this while you take care of the wasps," Lydia said, taking the tube. Pete then took a can from the bag and aimed it at a swarm of the insects, which fell one after another as they were sprayed.

Grant, his face and arms swelling up with red bumps, confronted Lydia with, "What the hell! I thought you had taken care of this problem. This is bullshit!"

"I know—" Suddenly Lydia felt a sharp sensation in her left arm and realized she, too, had become a victim. "We had two nests last summer and thought we had gotten rid of them."

"Well, obviously you didn't," Grant yelled, scratching his stings. "Look at all these kids, not to mention the assistants and me. As long as that disgusting snack bar is in business, we'll never get rid of this problem." He stormed off, leaving the screaming, crying children and incensed parents behind.

Then, a woman shrieked. "Call 911. My daughter is allergic and she's swelling up." Next to the woman was a young girl in a striped swimsuit gasping as she struggled to catch her breath. Another parent ran over with an EpiPen. "I'm a nurse, and this is a child's dose of epinephrine," she said, jamming the pen into the girl's thigh. In less than a minute, the girl's breathing stabilized.

Pete called for the paramedics and began calmly and compassionately going from person to person, checking them for stings and welts even as his own arm swelled up.

Lydia saw that in addition to the wasp attacks, there were kids injured from falling. She got some antibiotic cream and Band-Aids from the first aid kit in Pete's office and handed them to Max Driver to apply.

Shortly, a firetruck arrived from the station located a few blocks from Meadow Glen. After surveying the situation, the EMTs called for another unit and set up what amounted to a triage operation, treating the injuries and administering doses of antihistamine. The victims included the Murphy kids who, Lydia recalled, had been playing and throwing rocks on one of the tennis courts. A hysterical Jennifer rushed over from the pool to demand treatment for her howling children. Patients experiencing serious reactions were loaded into ambulances and taken to the hospital.

As the wasps dispersed, Lydia went over to the court where the Murphy boys had been playing. A few of the insects were still flying about in a frenzy, but a closer look revealed the remains of a wasp nest hanging from the roof of the water station. Putting two and two together, she concluded that the kids had dislodged the nest with their rocks and sticks, causing the angry swarm.

Her arm swelling up from the wasp sting, Lydia asked Pete to call an insect control company to come as soon as possible to rid the club of any other nests or beehives. *This will cost a fortune,* she thought. *Not to mention all the money we're going to have to pay out for doctor and ER visits, treatment, and ambulance/paramedic services. We'll probably get sued!*

As the paramedics left, Lydia was heartened that no one had unleashed any vitriol — yet. She knew that once the immediacy of the situation lifted, her inbox would explode with complaints from irate members. *Maybe we should have kept that fifty thousand dollars.*

A series of loud whistles and Pete yelling for everyone to vacate the pool brought her back to reality. Seeing what had happened, Lydia started laughing. She turned to Pete and said, "Good, now we can just close the club and go home."

Once again, someone had pooped in the pool.

Foiled Again

L YDIA LISTENED to the blades of the ceiling fan spin. It was three a.m. Bill was snoring lightly, and Stacie was sprawled out on the floor next to the bed. After the dreadful events of the previous day, Lydia had gone home and found the boys engrossed in their iPads. She called Bill, told him what had happened, then took an antihistamine and went to bed.

The fan was now clicking every eleven seconds.

Wide awake, with no chance of going back to sleep, Lydia went downstairs, made the coffee, and took a deep cleansing breath before opening her laptop. As expected, there were at least twenty-five e-mails from members, furious over what had happened.

Five were from parents of children who were allergic: "Do you realize how serious this could have been?" said one. "This is completely unacceptable. I'll expect the club to cover all our medical expenses."

From Jennifer Murphy: "This is insane! And you yell at my kids for just being boys! We've already contacted our lawyer." *Of course, it was your kids who set off the whole episode in the first place.*

And last, but not least, a complaint from Art Gilchrist, the arrogant captain of the 4.0 Men's team: "We showed up for our matches last night and found yet another mess on the tennis courts and the gates locked. We had to play at the park, which was a major hassle. The entire team is livid!"

Lydia texted Pete with a recap of the feedback. The weather was supposed to be nice, so the club would be busy. She also composed an e-mail to Mike Patterson on what had transpired with the wasps along with a question regarding club liability for the incident and if the board would be covered by D&O insurance.

With the house still quiet, Lydia made some eggs and toast. On cue, a still orange-and-purple-footed Stacie showed up in the kitchen to wrangle a few scraps. Lydia got down on the floor and hugged the dog. "I want your life," she said. After receiving her own helping of eggs, Stacie, carrying

Pink, went back upstairs to take over Lydia's side of the bed next to Bill.

A warm shower did wonders in washing away the previous day, although Lydia's arm still hurt from the wasp sting. Then, she roused a very irritable Geoff for swim practice.

Bill got up and joined Lydia in the kitchen. "That's a nasty one," he said, inspecting her swollen arm.

Suddenly overcome with emotion, Lydia began sobbing. "I'm so sorry I committed us to this horrible summer," she wept. Bill put his arms around her, and in a welcome expression of sympathy said, "I know. But you're almost two-thirds there, and hopefully the worst is over. Soon, this will be a blip on the radar."

Later, with Bill and Geoff gone and Andy still in bed, she checked her e-mail and found Mike's response. "Usually a wasp nest would be considered an act of God but given that we have had problems in the past and know it to be an ongoing situation, we could be liable." Lydia's heart sank. "However, our insurance should cover us," he continued. "To be on the safe side, we should offer to pay any out-of-pocket medical expenses that won't be covered by our insurance."

She took another deep breath as she typed a blast e-mail to the members, apologizing for the incident and advising anyone incurring medical expenses to send the bills, with receipts, to her.

Before it got too hot, Lydia took a walk through the neighborhood to decompress, leaving a disappointed Stacie home with Andy — and the dog door in. Nearing the club, she saw the pest control truck and several people attired in white coveralls and headgear with masks removing the wasp nests.

She rounded the corner onto Franklin Street, observing the slow, steady pool leak. Dwarfed by all the other problems at Meadow Glen, this one was almost comical, a realization that was confirmed by what she saw next. There, between the club and Claire Hoskins' house, was the blue sedan!

Lydia stopped in her tracks, hoping whoever was in the car didn't see her. She ran back to the club and told Pete, interrupting him as he talked with the pest control technicians. "Hey, sorry to butt in but the blue sedan is parked behind the club on Franklin Street. I don't think they saw me."

With no hesitation, Pete, Lydia in pursuit, took off out the front gate in hopes of finally catching the driver. "Did you happen to get a license plate number?" he hollered back to her.

"Oh geez, no I didn't. I guess I was so surprised, I turned and ran without thinking. Sorry!" As the two of them neared Claire's house, they saw that the car had already pulled away and was well down the block.

"Damnit, these guys are wily," an out-of-breath and frustrated Pete said. "I guess the good news is, it wasn't in front of my house. Or the club. What the hell is the deal with that car?"

High Stakes

WALKING TO the club for the final regular season swim meet, Lydia once again saw Deni Morales drop off Chip, then speed away. She felt sorry for the boy, who hailed her with a friendly "Hi, Mrs. P. I'm late for warm-ups," as he sprinted to the pool. *How did such a cold, neglectful woman produce such a nice kid?*

Lydia did not have any volunteer duties, but she had arrived early enough to snag a secluded spot for watching the meet. After picking up her doughnut, she settled herself in a chair near the baby pool and pulled out her iPad to read the paper. She observed Lawrence strutting around his small tent, giving orders to the coaches and timers.

There was no sign of Ernestine and her daughters.

After watching Geoff swim his first two events, she could tell that a week of no practice had slowed his times a bit. Chip's freestyle had improved immensely, although not enough to qualify for the League Meet.

"Next year you'll make it," Lydia told Chip after his race.

"Thanks, Mrs. P."

Periodically, she glanced over at the Meadow Glen tent where Chip was holding court with fifteen or so kids engaged in a card game. *This kid should be a dealer in Vegas!*

After nearly five hours, the meet ended with yet another Meadow Glen loss. Lydia watched Lawrence angrily throwing stopwatches, clipboards, and other meet paraphernalia into a plastic box. She decided to get out while the getting was good.

"I'm going home," Lydia called out to Geoff as the coaches began dissembling the tent.

"Hold up, Mom." Geoff stuffed his goggles into his swim bag and caught up to her. He didn't look happy. "Uh, can I borrow seventy-five dollars?"

"What? Why? What have you done with your allowance? I hope you haven't blown it on worthless crap and junk food."

"No, I haven't. I just need it for something. I'll pay you back in a couple of weeks," he said, refusing to make eye contact.

Lydia stopped. "Geoff, what do you need the money for? Please tell me. I won't get mad at you."

He stared at the ground for a minute, then looked up at her, his eyes welling with tears. "I lost it to Chip in a poker game and I need to pay him back by tomorrow or he'll charge me interest."

Lydia felt her knees go weak. "Oh no. How did this happen?"

"Chip was teaching us to play poker, and we all had to put in ten dollars. After four games, I ran out of money so Chip said he would pay for me. But I kept losing. Chip says I have to pay him back."

The image of Chip sitting next to Frank Fair on the Fourth of July popped into her head. *Those guys have schooled him on how to be a card shark, and now he's running a gambling ring in the swim team tent.* "Let me guess. You're not the only person who owes money to Chip, right?"

"Probably not."

I can't believe this, Lydia thought, trying to figure out how to handle the situation while anticipating the complaints from parents she knew would come in. She observed Chip on the patio playing cards with two of the guards.

"Mom, please just give me the money, and I promise I'll never do it again."

"No, honey," she said calmly. "This goes way beyond you. We can't have this kind of stuff going on. Tell Chip if he wants his money, he'll have to get it from me. I'm not mad at you, but you got taken. Now, do you want to handle this with Chip, or do you want me to talk with him?"

"I'll do it," he said begrudgingly, shuffling over to the patio as Lydia went home.

An hour later, an upbeat, somewhat cocky Chip rang the doorbell. "Hi, Mrs. P. Geoff said if I came over you would pay me the money he owes me."

This kid is Eddie Haskell, Lydia thought, recalling the smarmy, sneaky, 1950s TV character from *Leave It to Beaver.* "Yes, that's right, Chip. And here's the good news: I'm going to pay you a hundred dollars—more than what Geoff owes you. But here's the bad news: You are not to collect any more money from the other kids. Do you understand? You took advantage of all these kids, and that was wrong. Do not ever do this again. If I hear any reports or complaints from anyone about you asking for money—and

I will hear about it, trust me — I will have to contact your parents and you won't ever be allowed to come here again. Got it? You know, I'm the president of this club, which means I kind of run it. So, you don't want to mess with me."

"Okay." Chip, somewhat humbled by the dressing-down, took five $20 bills and left.

Geoff had witnessed the entire exchange from the top of the stairs.

"I hope you learned a lesson from this," Lydia told him. "And, yes, I do expect you to pay back your portion — seventy-five bucks."

TWO DAYS later, Lydia and Geoff, Susan Adams and her son Nick, and Arleen Schneider with her two daughters piled into Susan's van to head for the first day of the two-day League Meet being hosted at another club. *Thank God we didn't have to host this year,* Lydia thought.

Bill, who was tied up at work, would join Lydia for the second day. Lydia had planned on lounging in a beach chair in the shade with a book for most of the six-hour meet, getting up to watch Geoff and the other kids swim their events. Her anticipated relaxation was spoiled by a group of people from another club who had gotten wind of the recent shenanigans at Meadow Glen.

"Hey Lydia, we hear you're rolling in dough over there," said one, obviously referring to the money.

Another: "Hey, what's the *buzz* at Meadow Glen?" recalling the recent wasp incident.

"Ignore those jerks," Susan counseled her.

The catty comments were incessant. Lydia laughed off the remarks at first, then tried to take Susan's advice, pulling down her floppy hat as tight as she could and hiding behind her book. Eventually, she moved to a spot farther from the pool. But the ribbing had gotten to her. After reading the same paragraph three times, she finally gave in to her worries about the $50,000, the strange sedan, Darrell Baker, funds the club would need to settle claims from the wasp incident, Chip's gambling ring, the tennis court light petitions. *I've got to get with Rex.*

She was saved from a further downward spiral by a loud commotion at the pool. Recognizing the voice, Lydia stood up and moved closer to view the exchange. Betsy Broadhurst, adorned with her stopwatches, was arguing with two timers and the starter about Erica's place in the hundred-meter freestyle event. Evidently, Erica had lost first place by less than half a second, but Betsy was insisting that the winning swimmer should be disqualified for an illegal start. After a loud and lengthy argument with no change in the results, Betsy stormed off, an embarrassed Erica following. Lydia hightailed it back to her chair.

Geoff took third place in two events and his medley relay team placed fifth, much to the disgust of Lawrence. When the day's events were over, Lydia made a run for Susan's van.

The next day, the jokes had fortunately subsided as she and Bill watched Geoff compete in two more individual events and the freestyle relay. A week later at the State Meet, in a town an hour away, he took tenth place in one event and twelfth in another. *We're done.* Lydia was ecstatic. *Bring on August.*

August

Wrong Number

LYDIA WAS having a hard time focusing as she tried to compose an agenda for the final regular board meeting of the season. There were the usual Swim and Tennis committee reports, Amanda's final details on the Lobster Boil, and the Sugar Shack financials. *What else?* Both the wasp and the FunFro disasters would involve contentious discussions. Lydia anticipated Warren going nuts over the money for the iced drink cleanup, removal of the wasp nests, and expenditures to placate angry members literally stung by the most recent mishap of the summer. Of course, he would blame Pete for everything. Lydia had already received three invoices from members to cover medical expenses. And then the petition. *Rex absolutely needs to have those signatures. George Bishop will have a capital improvements report, but any short-term projects will probably be wiped out by the wasp settlements....*

The vibration of Lydia's phone brought a welcome distraction. Frantically, she rifled through the papers littering her desk and finally found it under a notebook. The number was unfamiliar, but she had learned over the summer that it was better to take the call than risk getting a voicemail from an irate club member that would need to be returned.

"Hello Mrs. Phillips?" a tired voice on the other end asked.

"Yes, what is it?" Lydia responded brusquely. Typically, when she got a call asking for "Mrs. Phillips," it was a telemarketer.

"Um, this is Marge Baker. You came to my home a few weeks ago to tell me you had found a business card belonging to my husband."

Lydia froze, and at the same time her voice softened. "Yes, of course. And please, call me Lydia. How are you doing, Marge? I've thought about you many times since we spoke."

"We had the funeral, which was lovely and very well attended. Darrell knew a lot of people through his work, and of course we have many friends and neighbors and a big extended family. And, we've been dealing with all the logistics—cancelling credit cards, closing bank accounts, association memberships. Fortunately, my sons are handling the winding down of Darrell's business. Most of his clients heard what happened, but we've had to pay final bills, notify the Secretary of State's office and the IRS. Lots of details and loose ends.

"Anyway, I've thought a lot about that business card you found, and I now agree there is definitely something strange about that. I don't ever remember Darrell talking about managing any properties way over on your side of town. But it turns out he kept a list of his clients on an Excel spreadsheet, and they were all over the metro area. My son Keith found a printed copy under a stack of papers when he was cleaning out the office. I don't know if any of these properties are in the vicinity of your home, but I have to admit that it does seem strange that Darrell's card would be floating around in a residential neighborhood. I'm very troubled by all this, and now with the police saying he probably was killed by the blow to his head and that it may not have been an accident, I'm having to face the possibility that my husband was murdered. I just don't understand why anyone would want to hurt Darrell." Her voice broke, and she began crying. Lydia felt for the woman, imagining that crying episodes happened often.

"I've even thought he may have been having an affair, though we had a good marriage. At least I thought we did. Maybe he got caught by the husband or something," Marge said between sobs. "Nothing makes sense anymore. I wish I could resolve this whole thing so I can move on. Anyway, I was wondering if you would mind looking at this list to see if anything rings a bell on your side of town. I just don't have it in me to track down all these places." By now, Marge was attempting to compose herself.

"Of course!" Lydia was ecstatic at the opportunity to view the list. "Have you shown it to anyone else?" Her first thought was Vern at the *Beacon*.

"No, I looked at it for the first time this morning. Do you think I should give it to the police?"

You're telling me the police don't even have this? Lydia was shocked they hadn't already combed through Darrell's computer and files. "That would probably be a good idea at some point, but let me run over later this morning and give it a look. I can be there in an hour or so. And Marge, I want to say again how sorry I am for your loss and for what you are going through," Lydia offered.

"Thank you, dear. I'll look forward to seeing you."

Lydia rushed upstairs, jumped in the shower, threw on a skirt and blouse, and put on some makeup. She scribbled off a note for the kids, who were registering for their high school classes. On the way to Marge's, she stopped at a bakery and picked up a sour cream coffee cake. Forty minutes later, she pulled up in front of the Baker house. The lawn had recently been mowed, and the plants watered. *Those boys are looking out for their mom.*

The street was quiet and empty—except for a black SUV across the street.

Marge came to the door wearing a pair of Bermuda shorts and a freshly ironed blouse. Her hair was pulled back in a French twist, and she was wearing makeup in an effort to hide the puffiness around her eyes. Lydia could tell she wasn't getting a lot of sleep. She also had lost some weight.

"Thank you so much," she said, taking the coffee cake. "I don't have much of an appetite these days, but this looks delicious." After offering Lydia an iced tea, the two women went into Darrell's office, a dark paneled room with an antique rolltop desk, an overstuffed chair, and two big filing cabinets undoubtably full of thirty years of documents. There were photos from happier times on the bookshelf—the kids, vacation photos of the family on a beach, and one of Marge and Darrell. She recognized that photo had provided the headshot of Darrell for the media.

"When he wasn't out at the properties, Darrell spent most of his waking hours in this office," Marge said, picking up the thick Excel printout.

The multi-page document listed forty or fifty commercial properties, each with the name of the property, address, owner name, and contact information. Other details, including the number of floors, number of spaces, occupancy, and cost per square foot also were noted. "I see he's got some e-mail addresses here. Have you gone through those?" Lydia asked.

"Yes we have, but Darrell was old-school. He preferred speaking directly with people, and so conducted most of his business on the phone and met with tenants and brokers or owners to write up contracts. We found a few e-mails, mainly about maintenance issues. The kids gave him a smartphone last year for Christmas, which he resisted at first but then began to use more and more. Of course, it's probably at the bottom of the river now…

"Enough of that. Let's sit down and have a piece of that coffee cake," she said, leading Lydia into a cheerful sunroom overlooking a large patio and yard with big shade trees.

"You mentioned Darrell's behavior had changed shortly before this happened, and that he might have been having an affair," Lydia said. "Do you really think that's what was going on? Were there any actual signs he was having an affair? Was he staying out late at night or not coming home?"

"Well, of course sometimes he did have to work late meeting with tenants or taking care of problems. But he always came home. I just can't come up with any explanation of why someone would kill my husband. I've gone over so many scenarios in my head to see if I've missed something. We were planning to go on a cruise next spring, and he seemed excited about it. He was around on the weekends as usual, and we would typically go out for dinner at least one of those nights. The only thing odd was, as I've said, he'd seemed preoccupied and uptight. I'd never seen him like that. Darrell never discussed his work with me. He didn't want it to permeate our lives any more than it already did. I mean, he worked out of the house and basically had to be on call twenty-four/seven. He and another property manager would cover for each other so we could take an occasional vacation, but otherwise the business pretty much consumed his life. I think his colleague is hoping to take over most, if not all, of the properties."

"Do you have the name of his colleague?" Lydia asked.

"His was name is Dale," Marge said. "My sons have been dealing with him."

AN HOUR LATER, Lydia was on her way home, the spreadsheet in her purse. Despite her eagerness to look more closely at Darrell Baker's property list, she made time for a conversation with the boys on what classes they would be taking. Andy, the more diligent of the two, had signed up for a fairly heavy load that included honors geometry and honors English. Geoff, Mr. Personality, had enrolled in theater, choir, and no honors classes.

Later, she closed her office door and settled into the comfortable club chair. Scanning through the spreadsheet, she read the names of commercial properties throughout the area, only a few of which she recognized. Not one was located anywhere near her part of town.

Then she stopped. About three-quarters of the way into the document a very familiar name jumped out: WLR RE Ventures. *Warren Reinhart! Had he known Darrell Baker?* In the righthand margin of the page, on the same line as WLR, was the handwritten name of another company, BSG

Investments, and then two initials and a number: BG 6784876. *A phone number?*

The property owned by Warren's company was called Pershing Plaza, 1571 Steele Street. Lydia looked up the address and saw that it was in a neighborhood near downtown. *Nowhere near here.* A recent article indicated the area was experiencing a turnaround with young professionals and couples moving in. She recalled the news story that Warren had purchased the Eastside Center back in June. *Wow. He's buying up everything.*

Then she logged onto the county assessor website and plugged in the address of Pershing Plaza on the business property address link. Sure enough, there it was. But the property had been sold in April and listed WLR Real Estate Ventures LLC as the grantor, or seller, and MetMe Properties as the buyer at a sale price of $19.5 million. *So, who is BSG Investments?* A deeper search on the assessor site revealed that WLR had purchased the property two years earlier for $15 million. *Interesting. Warren made a decent profit but might have done even better if he'd held onto it a few more years.*

She did a business search on BSG Investments on the Secretary of State's website. Nothing. Next, she searched MetMe Properties on the same site and again came up with nothing. Then, she did a general Google search of BSG with no luck.

Assuming the apparent phone number was local, she called it using the most common area code in the metro area. But she got that familiar and annoying signal and recording: *I'm sorry, your call cannot be completed as dialed.* She tried the other metro area codes and got the same message. And the same response using the two additional area codes for the state. She checked the printout again. *This must be a phone number.* Frustrated, Lydia put the document aside and turned her to attention back to the task that had started her day: the board meeting agenda. She finished it up and e-mailed it.

The dinner table discussion that night was all about the boys' first semester of high school that would start next week. The classes they were taking, the sports they'd signed up for — tennis for Geoff, cross-country for Andy — their first Homecoming. Lydia tried to be engaged, but her mind was a million miles away.

Field Trip

A T THE FIRST hint of dawn, Lydia quietly got out of bed. Since Stacie was already stirring, Lydia put the leash on her and the two ventured out for a walk. The sun was rising, but the streetlights were still on. She passed the Adamses' house, which was pitch dark, then rounded the corner and came up on Claire Hoskins' place, which was ablaze with lights. Looking in the kitchen window, she saw Claire on the phone. *She's probably rounding up HOA votes against the tennis light petition!* Lydia's stomach churned.

Walking up Franklin Street, she saw the ever-present trickle from the pool, then turned the corner toward the Meadow Glen entrance. Seeing that the gate was ajar, she guessed Pete was already on the premises. As they entered the club grounds, Stacie became very excited and began whining at the prospect of another wild romp at her home away from home.

The light was on in the office; Pete was doing paperwork. Now that the teachers were back in school, he came in early, took care of any overnight issues, and refilled the pool, which would be managed by Sam until the school day ended. Then, Pete would come back and close.

"Hey, how goes it?" Lydia asked. Stacie was barking and pulling on the leash as she watched the ducks swimming across the pool.

"Good. My lazy days of summer are over with school starting, but I think we've got things under control. Except for weekends, this place will be pretty dead for most of the day. Swim and tennis lessons are over, so Sam should be fine."

"You'll be at the meeting tomorrow night?" Lydia reminded him, warning that Warren was sure to blow up over the cleanup, extermination, and medical expenses associated with the FunFro machine and wasp incidents. Then she told him about her visit with Marge Baker and the list of commercial properties, including one owned by Warren's company.

"Really! That's interesting. I wonder if Warren knew Darrell Baker."

"I wondered the same. Next to WLR, the name of another company was jotted down along with some initials and what looks like a phone number but no area code. I tried calling, using all the local and state area codes, but came up with nothing. Ever heard of BSG Investments?"

"Hmm. Don't think so. Sounds like another mystery in a summer of mysterious happenings. I've got to get going. I'll see you tomorrow."

Lydia, dragging a reluctant Stacie, headed home and fixed coffee and a light breakfast before greeting Bill. The boys were still in bed. With just two precious days left of their summer vacation, she decided to let them sleep in and do what they wanted.

"What's on tap for you today?" Bill was particularly upbeat. "You've only got about a month left as Madame President."

"Nothing much. Maybe try to track down that phone number." Bill also had found the connection of Darrell Baker to Warren's company interesting when Lydia showed him the spreadsheet with the strange phone number. But he said it was unlikely Warren knew Darrell. "I'm sure his secretary or an underling hired Darrell. Warren would never get involved in something that mundane."

He also tried to encourage Lydia to drop the whole affair and not try to track down BSG Investments. "What are you going to do? Call every area code in the country?"

That's exactly what she intended to do. And pay a visit to the property itself, a plan she chose not to share with her husband.

AFTER BILL left for the office, Lydia took a quick shower, scrawled a note to the boys, made sure the dog door was in, and set out for Pershing Plaza. Traffic was heavy—rush hour. It took about an hour to get to the neighborhood, one of the oldest in the city. The strip center that had been owned by Warren's company took up half a block between an alley and a busy street. A parking lot faced the street, and behind that stood a row of connected, 1960s-era buildings—a hair salon, appliance repair shop, a liquor store. The only place that looked busy was a coffee shop. *I can always use another shot of caffeine,* she thought, opening the heavy glass door.

Lydia was shown to a small table by the window and ordered a coffee. When the waitress returned, she asked, "Is the owner or manager here?"

"Uh, yes. Is anything wrong?" The server's brow was furrowed in concern.

"Oh no, everything's fine. I'm trying to track down the property manager for this strip center. I assume whoever manages the restaurant would have that information."

"I'll check."

The waitress returned with a middle-aged, heavyset woman wearing a hairnet and a filthy apron. *Guess she's the cook too,* Lydia surmised.

"What can I help you with? You want the name of the property manager?"

"Yes, if possible."

"Can I ask why you're looking?"

"Um—" Lydia was irritated that she had failed to come up with a good story. "I'm looking for a property manager for a building I own, and an associate of mine said he was very good."

"Well, it depends on which manager you mean," the woman said. "We had one for a long time, but he drowned in the river two months ago. We have a new one, but I haven't had any dealings with him."

"Oh, yes, I heard about Mr. Baker's death. What a tragedy. I'm looking for the new one who I believe was a colleague of Mr. Baker."

"Hold on." The woman went back to the kitchen and returned with a greasy business card. "That's the only one I have, so can you copy the info and leave the card? I've got to get back to work."

"Thank you so much." Lydia used a napkin to scribble down the name and contact information for Dale Richards, DR Property Management. She swilled down the coffee and left five dollars and the business card on the table. On a drive through the neighborhood, she observed that many residences and businesses were being spruced up and remodeled.

It was after noon by the time she got home. The boys were gone, but Stacie happily rose from a nap to greet her. She fixed a peanut butter sandwich, left a message for the property manager, and promptly dozed off on the couch. The buzz of her phone jolted her awake.

"This is Dale Richards returning your call. What can I do for you?"

"Oh, hello. Thanks so much for calling back. Really appreciate it. I'll try to make this as short and simple as I can. I got your name from the manager of the coffee shop at Pershing Plaza. I'm looking for some information. I've been in touch with Darrell Baker's widow, Marge. I guess you're the man who would cover for Darrell when he was out of town. Marge thought you had probably taken over most, if not all, of his properties following his tragic death. And by the way, I am so sorry for the loss of your longtime business associate and friend."

"Thank you. Yes, Darrell and I knew each other for many years, and his death, not to mention the circumstances surrounding it, was quite a shock. I'm still reeling from it. And yes, I have taken over management of Pershing Plaza."

"I live in Jorgentown, and earlier this summer came across a business card of Darrell's just lying on the lawn of a nearby residence—which both Marge and I find quite odd since there are no retail establishments in the vicinity of my house."

"Jorgentown?" Dale paused. "Boy, I haven't been over there for a long time. I don't think Darrell had any properties in that part of town, but I'd need to check."

"Actually, Marge gave me a printed list of all the properties Darrell managed, and I haven't seen anything even close to my side of town," Lydia said. "However, I did notice that Pershing Plaza was owned previously by an acquaintance of mine. I see it was sold in April. Can you tell me anything about the new owner, MetMe Properties?"

"No ma'am, I can't give out any information like that."

Of course, you can't. What an idiot I am, Lydia chided herself. "I completely understand," she acknowledged. She decided to take a different approach, telling Dale what *she* knew. "I checked the county assessor's office, and the records show that WLR Real Estate Ventures sold the property in April for 4.5 million dollars in profit. I would think that with the neighborhood experiencing an upswing, a better move would have been to hold onto it for a few more years, increase the rent, and let it appreciate even more. And make a bigger profit."

"Why are you so interested?" Before Lydia could answer, Dale asked, "You say you're a friend of the previous owner?" She sensed a wariness in his voice.

"Oh no, not a friend. I've just happened to cross paths with him."

"Well, what I can tell you is that the property sold quite suddenly and at a bargain, in my opinion. Darrell hadn't even known it was on the market, and he told me it was valued at more than a million dollars over the actual sale price. He just got a call one day from the new owners—or someone representing them—notifying him the shopping center had been sold."

"And you can't tell me anything at all about the new owner? Not even where they're located?"

"No, I'm sorry. It's likely more than one individual, a consortium.

Ownership of these places often involves multiple investors with someone designated as the managing partner. In fact, I remember Darrell saying that an investor with the previous owner hadn't even known about the sale. He stopped by one day to look over the establishment, got Darrell's contact info, and called him. Darrell had to inform this guy he no longer had any stake in the place."

It took Lydia a moment to process what Dale had just told her. "So you're saying that this person, an investor when WLR owned the center, didn't even know it had been sold? That seems odd. Wouldn't he have received a payout?"

"You would think so. But these arrangements can be complex. It probably takes awhile to pay off all the investors."

"Are you familiar with a company called BSG Investments?" Lydia asked.

"No, doesn't ring a bell."

IT WAS mid-afternoon by the time Lydia ended the call. Thinking about what Dale had said, she came to the realization that MetMe Properties was irrelevant, the least important piece in the puzzling sale of Pershing Plaza. She looked at the strange number on Darrell's printout. *I guess I'll track this down the old-fashioned way.* She pulled up a U.S. map on the Internet and devised a circular pattern for making the calls, using Chicago as a starting point. First, she would call the number on the spreadsheet using area codes from the first tier of states—Illinois, Kentucky, Missouri, Iowa, Wisconsin, and Indiana—then fan out to the next tier of states. *How many can I get done in an hour?*

Not many, it turned out. Geoff and Andy came home on their bikes. "Mom! We literally have no food. We had to ride to the deli for lunch," Andy said, giving her a look that really said, *What the hell?* "And by the way, Geoff owes me eight bucks!"

"Oh guys, I'm so sorry." Lydia realized she hadn't done a major grocery run for over a week. She handed Andy twenty dollars and started a list, which turned out to be quite lengthy, and got in the car. Two hours later, she was back with several bags—and an earful of "suggestions" from Ernestine Knutsen-Askeland, who also had been grocery shopping.

"When are the people coming to get rid of the wasp nests at the club?" Ernestine had queried. "I think you're supposed to do it at night. You need to notify the members and the neighbors and provide a list of the chemicals they're using. They must be approved pesticides that aren't harmful to people or the ecosystem. You know, the Sugar Shack is probably attracting the bugs," she said in a hushed voice. "Maybe the board should consider getting rid of it."

Where have you been, Ernestine? "We've already taken care of everything, Ernestine," Lydia responded. "Pete got an eco-friendly company out right away, and I can tell you with utmost certainty that there are no more wasps or bees at Meadow Glen. I need to get going."

After putting all the groceries away, Lydia checked her phone and saw a text from Rex: "180 sigs. 20 more 2 go. These will be toughest." With the HOA meeting less than three weeks away, Lydia realized this was probably going to get nasty and go down to the wire.

Thunder and Lightning

DARK CLOUDS were forming as Lydia walked into the club, a metaphor for the impending board meeting, she figured. The late summer evening tennis leagues had started, and one of the men's teams was hosting a match. Players from both teams were warming up on the courts. Other than that, the club was empty. Grant was there and turned his back at spotting Lydia. The team captain scowled at her.

Guess I'm not exactly on everyone's Christmas card list.

Pete had arranged several tables in the corner behind the diving board for the meeting. Lawrence, Mike, Rex, and Amanda—wearing a tight blue tank top, white shorts, and spiked sandals—were already there. Lawrence was finishing up the first can of a six-pack of Stella Artois. Jules had arrived wearing sunglasses, her gray hair pulled back in a braid and her T-shirt splattered with multiple stains from a day in the Sugar Shack.

"Hey, everyone." Lydia passed out the agenda. A few minutes later, Liz, Mary, George, and Bud, bringing guacamole, chips, and a vegetable tray with dip, showed up. Last to arrive was Ron Gutierrez, the website manager. But no Warren. "Good, we have a quorum. Let's get started." Since the tennis light petition was first on the agenda under old business, she was hoping to get through that item before Warren made an appearance.

Then she saw him crossing the patio wearing a designer suit and his Cole Haan shoes. He had removed his tie. As he approached the group, Lydia found herself staring at him, wondering if he had in fact known Darrell Baker, and how he'd reacted to the news of Darrell's untimely death.

As Lydia called the meeting to order, Warren sat down, pulled out his phone, and began texting. He seemed agitated and distracted.

"Okay, Rex, where do we stand on the petition?" Lydia began the meeting. At that, Warren's head popped up.

"We've now got one hundred and eighty signatures. There are several residences where we have not made contact with the homeowners. Most of these folks are non-members. This weekend, my team and I are going to hit it hard and hope to wrap this up—"

"Your *team*?" Warren interrupted.

"Yep. Amanda and I and a few of the tennis players. And, I'm going to suggest we host a little gathering here one weeknight for these non-member signers. People can bring the kids to swim—"

Lydia braced herself.

"Oh no you're not!" Warren bellowed. "We've already discussed this. We're not going to use the club for political purposes. And we're sure as hell not going to invite in the neighborhood riffraff to bribe them into signing something that won't benefit them one bit."

"Oh get over it, Warren." Rex, his face reddened, was furious, something Lydia had never seen from the usually good-natured ad exec. "Just because you don't want to get involved in this issue doesn't mean we can't attempt to get others to support it. It's in the club's best interest to get this petition through for a whole bunch of reasons. You seem to be working against us. And by the way, these people are *not* riffraff. Many of them could be future members. And here's a news flash, Warren: most of us live in this neighborhood, and we're not riffraff either."

"We never should have spent the money to install those lights in the first place," Warren said, dismissing Rex's comments. "It was against the HOA covenants and it was irresponsible."

"I don't recall you objecting when this first came up last year," Rex replied.

Liz, her hair pulled back in a tight ponytail, jumped into the conversation. "With an invitation from Amanda, I'm sure most of these people will be thrilled to sign," she said, grinning broadly. Amanda's face lit up. *She doesn't get that Liz was referring to her scant, sexy attire, not her clout*, Lydia thought. *At least she's an equal opportunity offender.*

The lengthy discussion finally ended with the board voting nine to one to take all measures, including hosting the party for non-members, to get the petition through. Lydia was happy to see that people were finally waking up to the gravity of the matter. Warren, the lone No vote, sulked. His mood seemed to match the darkening sky.

Then, a bolt of lightning struck followed by a large clap of thunder and rain mixed with the hail of a summer storm.

"Girls' bathroom," Lydia yelled, as the board members grabbed their

belongings, snacks, and drinks and made a run for it. As the group sprinted for the bathroom, more than a dozen angry, soaked male tennis players
congregated under the covered patio, their tennis matches rained out.

Mike arranged some bathroom benches in a circle as rain and hail
pummeled the building. While the bathroom provided good cover from
the storm, it smelled and there was trash all over the floor. Pete had not
yet cleaned it, and Lydia could tell it was time for the drains and toilets to
be snaked again.

"This is nice," Warren said sarcastically, sneering at Pete.

Ignoring him, Lydia continued. "I know you're all aware of the FunFro
machine breakdown and wasp attack last month. The FunFro vendor covered the cost of replacing the machine, and we had to pay the five-hundred-dollar insurance deductible for the cleanup. As for the wasp incident,
I'm going to let Mike update the board on that."

Mike explained that the club had been billed nine hundred dollars for
the removal of two wasp nests. He also stressed the need to reimburse
members' medical costs as a goodwill gesture and to avoid potential
lawsuits.

Before he could go on, Warren began his tirade, uttering a string of
criticisms about the cost of both events and assigning blame. "We've already paid out close to fifteen hundred dollars for these disasters, and
I haven't even received the medical bills yet. As for the drink machine,
where were you?" he demanded, looking at a befuddled Jules as she
stuffed a guacamole-covered chip into her mouth. "If you'd been monitoring the equipment properly, this never would have happened. We should
take the expenses out of your pay."

"The machine probably broke early in the morning. How was I to—"

"Oh, spare me the excuses," Warren said, then directed his diatribe
to Pete. "We had wasp nests all over the place and you did nothing. You
should bear responsibility for all of this," he shouted, waving his arms.
"The bathrooms stink, the equipment doesn't work, the place is infested
with bugs. What exactly *do* you do, Pete?"

"I did—and do—take complete responsibility," Pete said. Lydia could
tell he was working hard to keep his composure. "I called the pest control
company immediately, and all the nests have been removed. I can say with
certainty that the property has been completely rid of all bees and wasps,
so we're starting from ground zero. We hadn't seen any evidence of bees
or wasps earlier in the season, so we assumed the measures we took last

year had worked. Next year—"

"There may not be a next year for you," Warren interrupted again. "You've shirked your responsibility—"

At that, Pete stood up and faced Warren directly. "Look Warren, you have every right to ask questions and hold me accountable, but you have no right to speak to me in that unprofessional tone of voice or make repeated snide comments," he asserted, finally reaching his limit. "The fact is, this place has a lot of infrastructure problems, and I'm doing my best to manage them. I know you don't like me, but you'll never find anyone as competent and dedicated as I am in running this place. Besides, I've brought in several member families, which translates to revenue. But, if you and the other board members are unhappy, then fine, I'll walk right now and you guys can run the place yourselves," he added, gathering up his papers.

Lawrence, now on his third beer, started to interject, but Lydia cut him off. "No! That is not going to happen," she said, her voice knife-edged. "Pete has taken full responsibility on a host of issues and challenges this summer. Furthermore, this is not the time to discuss his contract. We will visit that at the end of the meeting. Warren, your repeated attacks on Pete and other staff and board members need to stop right now or I will entertain a motion to have you removed. And that goes for you too, Lawrence. Now, is there a motion to authorize funds to cover out-of-pocket medical expenses from the wasp incident?"

George Bishop made the motion, with Mike seconding. Following a brief discussion, the vote was eight to two in favor.

"Jules? Anything on the Sugar Shack?"

"Uh, I think we did pretty well," she said, looking nervously at Warren. "Things were really busy in July. I'm sure we made a profit."

"Actually, after all expenses including salaries for the kids, the Sugar Shack made a net profit of twenty-five dollars in July," Pete said, passing the report to a somewhat sheepish Warren. Jules stared at the floor.

"Warren, do you have any more financials for us?" Lydia asked.

"I'll have a more detailed report, including the snack bar, for the annual meeting on Labor Day," he said, passing out a one-page summary of the July income and expenses. "But I've got a question." He glared at Lydia. "What's this receipt for a new grill and padlock from this Goldfarb guy? Are we now in the business of purchasing amenities for individual members?"

"No, Warren, this is a reimbursement for the kosher grill that the Jewish members purchased last year." She proceeded to relate the story of how another member had used the grill inappropriately, violating a key tenet of Jewish law. "Since the grill was taken from the back, we need to provide a lock to keep it secure."

"Oh, for God's sake. If you can't eat off the grills the club provides, you shouldn't join in the first place. The next thing you know we'll have to furnish grills for vegetarians, or the gluten-free people, and the lactose-intolerant crowd."

"As usual Warren, you're being ridiculous and taking this to an extreme," Lydia responded. The board voted nine to one to authorize the purchase.

Furious, Warren then said, "The bigger question is, where's the money?"

Lydia stared at him, searching for a clue. "What money?"

"The fifty thousand dollars that was found on our property. No one has claimed it, so we're entitled to keep it. Should be invested."

"The police have the money, Warren," Mike answered. "Don't you remember? We voted to turn the money over to the authorities at our last meeting. It was the absolute right thing to do. The police have analyzed the bag and money for fingerprints and are continuing to investigate. I've called them twice now, and they still don't have any leads."

"Which means they should return the money to us," Warren argued. "That money is just sitting there, doing no one any good. I told you it was a mistake to turn it over to the cops. In fact, it's outrageous!"

"Why are you so obsessed with that money?" Mary asked. "It's not like *you* lost it."

"I have a fiduciary responsibility to do what's best for this club. Giving the cops fifty thousand dollars of found money, after making a thorough effort to track down whoever lost it, was a completely irresponsible thing to do."

"Well, it's a done deal, Warren and we're not getting it back," Lydia said. "So, just drop it."

Warren turned his attention to his phone.

With those items addressed, the meeting continued with reports from the Swim and Tennis chairs, both reporting record numbers of participants.

"Let's move on to Social."

Amanda, holding a plastic glass of white wine, reported on the upcoming Lobster Boil, the last bash of the season before Labor Day. "We got a great deal on lobsters this year; they arrive Saturday morning. We have sixty people coming. Guests will be providing coleslaw, cornbread, potatoes, apps, and desserts."

The agenda had come to new business, and Lydia took a deep breath before bringing up the latest bylaw issue. "We've already discussed the need to clarify the definition of family, but we also need to address another matter that has arisen." She related the story of Chip Morales and the conversation with his mother, Deni, about dropping him off all day, every day.

"Yes, that is definitely a problem," Liz said. "We're not a babysitting service."

"Hold on," a still-agitated Warren said. "Morales is Mexican. Are these people even legal?"

"Of course they're legal, Warren," Lydia said. "Mitchell Morales is a bank executive."

"So what? His wife could be one of those Dreamers. Is the kid even his biological child? Where was he born?"

George Bishop broke the awkward silence. "Oh, c'mon, Warren. How racist can you get? You immediately assume that because this family has a Latino surname they're here illegally? Give me a break."

"I couldn't agree more," Ron Gutierrez echoed. "Not only is it racist, it's ridiculous. This country is full of legal, law-abiding citizens with Latino surnames. Like me."

"Well, these days you just never know. There are also millions of illegals in this country. And as for the definition of family, we have—"

"These are issues we'll be looking at in the off-season." Irritated at Warren's bluster, Mike Patterson shut him down. "Lydia was just bringing this up for informational purposes. I think it's now time to discuss Pete's contract."

That's was Pete's cue to exit the meeting. "I'll be in my office doing nothing and letting the club go to hell," he said, directing a snide look at Warren.

Once Pete was gone, Lydia began by saying, "I think Pete continues to do a great job for us, and I would like to renew his contract for another season. Mike and I have discussed this, and we are in complete agreement. Pete is here morning, noon, and night, the members like him, he is professional, and—"

"I think we can do better," Warren said.

"Really? How so, Warren?" Lydia asked.

"I think we can get someone a lot cheaper and more willing to take direction. We've given this guy way too much power and leeway, and instead of the board telling him what to do, he's telling us—"

"Agree. This guy thinks he can do whatever he wants," Lawrence chimed in, opening another beer.

"Wait a minute. We said we wanted a strong, take-charge manager when we hired Pete," Bud Wright noted. "We wanted someone to take responsibility and run the place so we could get away from all the micromanaging by board members that has plagued Meadow Glen for years."

The discussion lasted for twenty minutes, with Pete having the board's overwhelming support. Sensing that sentiment, Lydia asked for a motion to renew the contract with a ten percent raise. The motion passed eight to two with Warren and Lawrence dissenting. Defeated once again, Warren picked up his briefcase and stormed out of the club. As that was the last item on the agenda, the meeting was adjourned.

Lydia stopped by Pete's office to tell him the contract had been renewed with the raise, and high-five him for standing up to Warren. The rain had stopped and left the air refreshingly cool.

"After all this, do you even want to come back next year?" she asked.

"After this crazy season, I'm not making any commitments," he said. Especially if that blue sedan keeps coming around."

"Still?"

"Yep. Saw it early this morning on the back side of the club. It was too far away for me to see the plate number, and of course it took off before I could get closer. At least it's no longer casing my house."

Disturbed at hearing the car was still in the vicinity, Lydia asked, "Why would the car be over there? There aren't that many houses. Just Claire Hos— Wait a minute! Could Claire Hoskins be behind this? Remember, we saw the sedan near her house several days ago. Maybe she's so desperate, she has spies working for her."

Pete seemed doubtful. "Why would the car have been watching my house? Is she that crazy?"

"Yeah, Claire has always been a strange bird and will go to any length to win a fight. I'm sure she figures you're in favor of the lights. Could be, she's trying to cover all her bases and find out who has signed the petition, then get them to change their minds. She's probably had that car surveilling all the board members' houses. I'm going to ask Rex to set up that party."

"Any Tuesday or Thursday would work best."

Lydia felt the all-too-familiar knot return to her stomach. *This all could fall apart.*

Cracking the Code

A S THE CEILING fan clicked and Bill snored, Lydia tossed and turned, this time over the petition. While dealing with all the other Meadow Glen crises, she had left Rex in charge of the tennis court light petition, letting him take his time gathering signatures.

Now, certain that Claire was mounting a potent challenge, she recognized that an all-hands-on-deck effort was needed to fend off the lawsuit. After coming home from the meeting, she had fired off an urgent e-mail: "Rex, I think Claire is ramping up her efforts to submarine the petition, so we need to get this thing locked in. Please contact these last residents ASAP. Set up an evening party for a Tuesday or Thursday in the next week or so. Let me know so I can alert Pete. Include kids. Amanda can arrange the food and drinks. We can talk about it."

She copied Mike and Liz. She dozed off after midnight and was awakened by an impatient Stacie at five. Her cue to get up. Bill was snoring lightly.

Twenty minutes later, Lydia was sipping a cup of strong coffee and surveying the mess on her desk, with Stacie curled up in the middle of the floor. Mike had responded favorably to her e-mail late the previous night, but nothing from Rex yet. Liz, she knew, wouldn't respond. If she didn't hear anything from Rex soon, she would call him. The petition was now consuming her thoughts, raising her anxiety level to about a nine, she figured. *If we get sued, all this hard work and stress will have been for nothing, and it could shut down the club for good. And I'll be the one responsible.*

As a distraction, she decided to clean up her desk, tossing old receipts into the shredder, putting papers and memos she no longer needed into the recycling basket, and making piles of documents that required her attention. She completed a cross-country booster club form for Andy, wrote a check, and placed it in an envelope.

Then she spied the printout from Marge Baker. It seemed like weeks since she had started her area code blitz, when in fact it had been just a couple of days. Her desire to track down the strange phone number paled in light of the other issues on her plate. *Oh, what the hell. I've got to get my mind on something, or I'll just sit here and worry.*

As she picked up the printout, the paper clip came off and the pages scattered over her office floor. *Damnit.* She bent down to pick up the pages and began ordering them. It was then she noticed a handwritten three-digit number, 309, on the left edge of the page after the one listing WLR and BSG Investments with the seemingly phantom phone number. *What does this mean? This doesn't relate to anything,* she thought, frowning as she studied the digits.

It was close to seven when Bill came downstairs. "Where are the boys?" he asked.

"In bed, I guess. Why?"

"Lydia, it's the first day of school."

"Oh, right." She tore up the stairs and banged loudly on both boys' doors. "Get up, guys. First day of high school. I'll fix you some breakfast."

"Mom, we don't need to be there until eight-thirty. We don't have first-period classes. We told you," an annoyed and sleepy Geoff responded.

"Uh, I know. But it's good to start the day off right with a hearty breakfast," she said, wondering how two freshmen had managed to score such a desirable schedule.

By the time the boys came downstairs wearing their backpacks, Lydia had breakfast ready. "Okay, here's some juice, milk, toast, scrambled eggs, and choice of cereals. I also have banana nut muffins."

To her satisfaction, both kids and Bill ate a hearty breakfast then headed out the front door. The high school was less than a mile away, so the boys could walk. Standing on the porch in her robe, Lydia suddenly reached out and hugged her sons. "I can't believe you guys are in high school," she said. "You know we love you, and we're so proud of you."

"Ditto on that," Bill chimed in, joining in the group hug. Stacie, holding Pink, watched from the doorway.

After all three were gone she returned to the kitchen, her anxiety somewhat alleviated. With her appetite back, she sat down for a leisurely breakfast herself. And more coffee.

Her phone dinged. It was a text from Rex, responding to her e-mail. "On it. Amanda and I and whoever else will head out 2nite to get sigs. Will keep U posted. Don't worry. We'll get 'em."

Feeling much better, Lydia cleaned up the kitchen, got dressed, and settled herself in her office. *What was I doing? Oh yeah, that funny number on the printout: 309. 309?* Lydia stared at the number. Comparing the digits to the number on the previous page, she was sure the handwriting and ink were the same. Then, staring at the numbers side by side, she had an epiphany. *It's all one number.* It appeared that as Darrell had written down the digits, he had written across two pages. Put together, the full number now read 6784876 309. *Wait a minute. That must be the phone number for BSG Investments; 678 is the area code! 678-487-6309.* She did a Google search on 678. Atlanta, Georgia. Then, she picked up her cell phone and tapped in the numbers.

"HELLO?" A male voice answered after four rings.

Lydia tensed up, realizing she hadn't rehearsed her spiel. She'd figured the call would go to voicemail or a receptionist would answer.

"Uh, hello. I'm trying to reach BSG Investments."

"This is BSG. Who's calling, please?"

She took a deep breath. "Hi. My name is Lydia Phillips. You don't know me, but I came across the name of your company and this phone number in some paperwork from the office of Darrell Baker, a commercial property manager who passed away recently. I am helping Mr. Baker's widow."

"Okay. Let me think a minute. You found my phone number where?" he asked after a long pause.

"In some paperwork belonging to Darrell Baker, the property manager for Pershing Plaza, in which you apparently were an investor."

"Yes, I remember Mr. Baker. You say he died? That's too bad; I'm sorry to hear that. What can I do for you?"

"What's your name again?" Lydia knew he hadn't provided it.

"Ben Gregorie."

Ben Gregorie. BG. The initials in the margin. "I don't quite know how to explain this, so I'll just go for it," Lydia began. "I'll warn you, this may sound a bit crazy. Darrell Baker died under very suspicious circumstances. His body was found washed up in a local river. He had been reported missing around Memorial Day, and the body was recovered several weeks later after a week of intense rainfall. Apparently, he'd received a severe blow to the back of his head, which may be the actual cause of death. So, the police are investigating the possibility of foul play."

Silence. Then, "That does sound very serious and tragic, but why are you calling me? I met the guy once and only for a few minutes. Do I need to hire a criminal lawyer?"

"Oh no, no, no." Sensing where his mind was going, Lydia tried to slow down and speak in a way that sounded reassuring. "We're just trying to put the pieces of this puzzle together. I got involved when I saw the TV news report about Darrell's body being recovered. After hearing the story, I remembered that I had found a business card of his in a nearby yard, which is strange because there are no commercial shopping establishments within five miles of my home. I've had a few conversations with his widow, who is extremely upset. She gave me a spreadsheet with all the commercial properties he managed, and Pershing Plaza was one of them. That's where I found your number.

"I've also heard Darrell had scheduled a meeting with the police shortly before he went missing, and never showed up." Lydia's heart was pounding as she tried to say as much as she could before Ben hung up on her. "A friend and colleague of Darrell's took over many of his properties, including Pershing Plaza. Interestingly, that property had been owned by an acquaintance of mine, who apparently sold it quite suddenly—"

"Whoa. Please slow down, ma'am. This is getting a little complicated. First off, what are you? Some kind of PI or police detective? How did you track down all this information?"

"Coincidence, mostly. As I said, it started with finding Darrell's business card and then connecting with his widow and business colleague after he died. Also, a reporter I used to work with at the local newspaper gave me some information off the record."

"You're a reporter?"

"Used to be. Now I do volunteer work."

"And you say you know the previous owner of the property?"

"Yes, Warren Reinhart of WLR Real Estate Ventures. We belong to the same summer club. He's the club treasurer and I'm the board president."

"Good God! This is getting better and better!"

"I'm assuming you were an investor with WLR Real Estate Ventures. Do you have any idea why your name and phone number would be on a printout of properties that Darrell Baker managed?"

Silence again. "You know, I'm very uncomfortable with all this. I don't know you, and before we continue this conversation any further, I need to speak with my attorney. I need to process all this. Now let me get this straight. You're saying you found Darrell Baker's business card near your house. Then, after his body was found, you tracked down his wife. And it just so happens you know Warren Reinhart. And oh by the way, you're with the media. Un-fucking-believable."

"I know the story sounds crazy. And I completely understand your hesitance to speak with me. If I were in your shoes, I'd want to speak with an attorney, too. Can I call you tomorrow?"

"Give me a week."

Lydia disconnected the call, sat back in her chair, and thought about the significance of what she had just learned. *He didn't deny knowing Warren. And he confirmed that he met with Darrell Baker. This is getting creepier by the day.*

Seeing Red

LYDIA PUT the finishing touches on the coleslaw she'd been assigned to take to the Lobster Boil, which amounted to taking the store-bought salad out of the plastic container and arranging it in a fancy ceramic bowl. This would be the sixth year in a row she and Bill would attend the annual soiree, and she felt the event was getting a bit tired. Guests would play the usual ice-breaker games, then watch the lobsters race across the grass before being plunged into vats of boiling water. As much as she loved lobster, she thought it cruel to force the creatures to perform before being sent to their deaths. *I wonder if they feel anything.*

"Do we have to go to this?" Bill had asked. "I'm still recovering from the Steak Night fiasco when Stacie crashed the party."

"Yes Bill, we have to go," she responded sympathetically. "We can skip it next year. You can survive one more Meadow Glen party. How bad can it be?" Lydia knew there was no good answer.

Since her conversation with Ben Gregorie, she'd found herself thinking of little else. She had told Bill about the call, but he didn't quite share her excitement. "You know, this could be just a series of random occurrences that have no connection to each other," he'd said.

"Oh come on, Bill. How bizarre is it that I find Darrell Baker's business card just down the street around the time he went missing, when there would be no reason for him to be in this part of town? And that he managed a property that was owned by Warren's company? And that Warren abruptly sold that property and apparently didn't bother telling his investors? Not to mention finding fifty thousand dollars under the dumpster."

"Why would Warren selling his strip center have anything to do with Darrell Baker's death? Warren probably had Baker's card in his briefcase, and it fell out in the club parking lot and blew down the street. What's so strange about that? This guy Gregorie, whoever he is, isn't going to want to talk to you, anyway. He's in Atlanta and probably doesn't want to get involved. You need to drop this. We've got bigger things going on in our lives."

Lydia decided not to pursue the debate, but it all kept swirling around in her head. Weird coincidences, she knew, are the key to a fruitful police investigation and the way many great news stories begin. *It will be good to go out tonight and get my mind off all this,* she rationalized.

After checking twice to make sure Stacie was in the house and her door closed, Lydia and Bill walked over to the club with the salad and a bottle of wine, hoping to miss the games and the lobster race. The boys were each at a friend's house, so no one was home to inadvertently let the dog out.

The mid-August sun was lower and the days shorter, but the summertime temperatures had not abated much. Lydia had chosen wisely for the hot and humid evening — a strappy pink and white sundress and sandals.

As they entered the club grounds, she could tell this was a different crowd than they were used to. Neither the Schneiders nor the Adamses were there. Many of the guests were new or younger members Lydia had met but didn't know well. She noticed Amanda, attired in a tight-fitting lime green sundress with matching spiked-heel sandals, was at the check-in table standing next to a beaming Rex. *Where does she get these outfits?*

"We got eight more signatures," Rex proudly reported. "Twelve to go."

"Great, Rex. Keep them coming." Lydia felt some satisfaction but knew the next two weeks would be critical. *This will go down to the wire.* A few other board members, including Mary Cramer, Bud Wright, and George Bishop, also were there, as were Betsy Broadhurst and her husband.

The covered patio was appropriately decorated with strings of white lights hung across the ceiling, and netting and seashells on the wall. Tables of four, each with a votive, were covered in blue- and red-checkered tablecloths. Next to each table was a can with a plastic liner for the lobster shells. Three big lobster pots and burners were on a picnic table near the pool.

Lydia made her way to the buffet table where the last of the appetizers were being shoved aside to make room for salads, corn bread, boiled potatoes, and two Crock-Pots with melted butter that guests could pour into small plastic cups for their lobster. She found a spot for her coleslaw, then helped herself to a glass of Sauvignon Blanc. As Bill chatted with George, she looked around for a table.

Because they had arrived late, there were only a few seats left, which meant they probably would be sitting next to people they didn't know very well. Surveying the crowd, her eyes fixed on a small crowd gathered near the lobster pots. *Oh no.* There, standing next to a woman with a long, grayish-blonde ponytail, large, dangling seashell earrings, and wearing a wrinkled yellow linen sundress, was Lawrence Haskell. *Lawrence has a date?* His heavily tattooed arms bulging under a short-sleeved white shirt tucked into tight black shorts, he was, uncharacteristically, drinking a glass of red wine. *I guess he's trying to impress the woman.*

Panicked that she and Bill would be stuck sitting with either Lawrence and his date or, God forbid, the Broadhursts, who likely would still be whining that Erica had been cheated out of first place at the League Meet, Lydia frantically searched the patio for two vacant seats. She found them at a table occupied by two people who weren't socializing with anyone. The gay couple: Vince Albright and Roger Morey.

"Hello, Vince and Roger, right? Lydia Phillips. Are these seats taken?"

"No. Please join us, Lydia."

"Thank you so much. We'd love to. I'll let my husband know—"

Suddenly, she felt a tap on her shoulder. "Lydia, a word please." She turned to see an agitated Lawrence, full wineglass in hand, motioning her away from the patio to speak in private.

"Hi, Lawrence. What's up? You've taken things up a notch by substituting wine for your usual beer. What's the occasion?" Lydia asked, hoping to lighten his demeanor.

He ignored the question. "What are we doing about resolving this *situation?*" he asked, gesturing toward Vince and Roger then taking a large gulp of wine.

"What *situation*, Lawrence?" Lydia decided to make him say it.

"The situation with this gay couple. It came up way back in June, and then we never discussed it again. I thought Mike was going to look into this."

"Well Lawrence, I guess you weren't listening at the last board meeting, but it will be addressed along with some other bylaw matters over the winter. Plus, it's been a crazy season, and we've had more pressing issues to deal with. I get a lot of complaints from members, and not one of them has been about these guys. They are very nice people, and I personally think we should leave it alone for now and resolve it by updating the bylaws."

"I disagree. These guys are in violation of our rules, and we are leaving ourselves open to a court case. Mike was supposed to deal with this, and he conveniently dropped it," Lawrence said, emptying his wineglass.

"I think we run an even bigger risk if we exclude them now," Lydia argued. "Lawsuits. Publicity. Besides, social mores on this issue are changing rapidly, and I'd rather err on the side of progress than convention. Anyway, given that we have only about a month until the club closes for the season, what exactly do you want to do, Lawrence?"

"Right now, I want to get a refill on my wine. Stay put. I'll be right back."

Amused, Lydia watched him sway slightly as he zigzagged for the bar on the far side of the patio. She noticed his date was standing by herself holding a glass of white wine as the first plates of lobster were being carried over to the buffet table.

Returning with his wine glass filled to the rim, Lawrence, his voice rising, said, "I'm no lawyer, but it boils down to how this club defines a *couple* and how we define a *family*." He raised his finger to within an inch of Lydia's face.

Stepping back, she looked him straight in the eye. "Keep your voice down and don't you *ever* put your finger in my face again!" she said sternly, her jaw clenched. "This is absolutely not the place to discuss this, Lawrence. People are here to have a good time, and no one but you is bothered by Vince and Roger being here. You will *not* make a scene. This conversation is over."

Bill, seeing Lawrence jabbing his finger at Lydia, swiftly came to the rescue. "No shop talk, you two. How are you, Lawrence?"

"I've been better," he sneered, abruptly turning to once again refill his glass at the bar. Lydia observed that in the course of their last brief exchange, he had swilled down a full glass of wine. *I guess that's what happens when a habitual beer-drinker switches to wine. Does he not understand the concept of sipping?*

"What's with him?" asked Bill.

"I'll fill you in later. He's probably already consumed at least a full bottle of wine since he got here," she whispered, taking his arm and guiding him toward their table. "We're sitting with some newer members, people you haven't met."

"Those guys? Where are their wives?"

"They're a couple. The one on the left, Vince, has been a single member of the club for a few years, but this year his partner, Roger, joined him. They have two kids, including a seven-year-old son who was on the swim team this year."

"What? You mean—"

"Yes, they're gay, Bill. This is the couple I told you about at the beginning of the summer. They're very nice."

Bill stared at her. "I'm sure they're fine, Lydia. I'm not homophobic. I can be a big boy and make conversation."

Bill was, indeed, charming. "Bill Phillips," he said, extending his hand. "Welcome. Is this your first Lobster Boil?"

"Yes, in fact it is," Vince responded. "I joined the club myself a few years ago and didn't get involved or socialize much. Then this year, Roger decided to join me. We're getting married in December."

Lydia couldn't believe what she had just heard. *End of story,* she thought, feeling herself relax. *They'll be legally married, so we can check that one off the list.*

"That's great. Congratulations," Bill offered. Looking over at Lydia, he said, "What say we get some chow?"

All four got up and ambled over to the buffet table. Standing in line, Lydia heard Lawrence's voice booming over the chatter and music. Glancing over at his table, she saw that he and his friend were sitting with Betsy and Rick Broadhurst. "Yeah, I still hold the butterfly record at my high school," he bragged with a laugh. "A few kids have come close, but no one's beaten me yet." *Oh God.*

Once seated, their plates filled with lobster and all the trimmings, Vince asked, "What do you do, Bill?"

"I'm an accountant," he said with a mouthful of coleslaw.

"Corporate?"

"I have my own firm. I would say my clientele is about sixty percent individual and forty percent business. What about you?"

"We're both in criminal justice. I work for—"

He was interrupted by a woman standing at their table, looking at Lydia. "Hey you two, long time no see."

"Bonnie!" Lydia stood up and gave Rex Simons' wife a warm hug. "Yes, it's been way too long. How are you? You've been in West Texas all summer, right?"

"Yes, I'm afraid so. Things are really hot down there—in more ways than one. Business is booming. I know you think the weather here is oppressive, but it's nothing compared to Midland, Texas. Anyway, I was supposed to get in tomorrow night but managed to get a flight out today, so thought I'd surprise Rex. I see I'm a little underdressed; I came directly from the airport. Where is himself anyway?"

Never much of a fashion plate, Bonnie was wearing a pair of khaki shorts, a golf shirt with what looked like a faded spot of ketchup, and Birkenstock sandals. Her long, straight gray hair was tucked behind her ears and, as was typical, she wore little makeup.

"It's great to see you," Lydia said, looking around for Rex, who was nowhere in sight. Nor was Amanda for that matter. "Uh, I know he's here somewhere. Probably helping with the cooking. There's a ton of food, so please grab a plate and help yourself to some wine. There's no way I can finish this lobster. Split it with me. Bill, can you find a chair for Bonnie?"

"Oh, no worries. I'm allergic to shellfish."

While Bonnie waited in line, Lydia searched around frantically for Rex. Bill appeared with a chair from the pool deck and wedged it between his and Lydia's seats. *Where is Rex? And where is that crazy Amanda?*

After Bonnie sat down with a plate overflowing with coleslaw, potatoes, and cornbread, Lydia introduced her to Vince and Roger. "This is Rex Simons' wife, Bonnie. Rex is a board member who heads up our Tennis operations. Bonnie is an oil geologist who has been gone most of the summer."

"Oh, yes. We met Rex a couple of weeks ago when he stopped by the house with the petition," Roger said. Before Lydia could ask the obvious question, he said, "We signed it."

"Oh, thank you so much. So glad to hear that. This has been a real battle, and Rex is doing a great job." She glanced over at Bonnie, who was wolfing down her dinner.

"Nice to meet you," she said between mouthfuls. "I haven't eaten since early this morning, and I'm starving. This is all delicious."

The table's attention suddenly turned to a commotion near the bar. Focusing her eyes on the far end of the patio, Lydia felt a wave of anxiety. Staggering near his table was an extremely drunk Lawrence, who had tipped over several bottles of wine. As glass shattered and wine spilled, Lawrence stood, oddly staring at the mess with his hand over his mouth. Suddenly he lurched, then spewed a stream of red, projectile vomit all over the bar and onto two nearby tables. Screaming guests stood up and ran from the porch onto the grass. One woman, who had been directly in Lawrence's line of fire, promptly jumped into the pool. Several made a beeline for the bathrooms, hands over their mouths to avoid adding to the repulsive mess.

Horrified, Lydia stood up and made her way to the scene as she heard Bill, still seated, laughing. A virtual red river with the contents of Lawrence's stomach—undigested chunks of lobster, cabbage, and other unidentified matter—was now oozing across the patio. Lawrence, meanwhile, had found a way to stagger over to the cooking area where he continued to retch into an empty lobster pot as his date looked on helplessly. The area reeked.

Lydia grabbed a napkin to cover her mouth and nose, appalled at what she was witnessing. "Oh no. This is a disaster. Oh my God, what are we going to do?"

Bill and George took her aside. "The first thing we need to do is allow everyone who wants to leave, get out of here," Bill said, stifling a laugh. "Then, get Lawrence out of here." Bill approached Lawrence and gingerly pulled the car keys out of his pocket. He had stopped, or at least paused, hurling, but he was so drunk it was unclear whether he even knew what had happened.

Surveying the scene, Lydia observed women crying, their nice sundresses either stained with vomit or soaked from the pool. She could hear sounds of retching from the women's bathroom, which Lydia knew would be a mess for Pete to clean up. Someone then grabbed the vomit-tainted lobster pot and dumped it in the baby pool. *Oh no,* Lydia thought. *Now both pools will need to be shocked and cleaned.* Bill, on the other hand, was still laughing at the spectacle. Lydia failed to see the humor.

By now, Lawrence had passed out on the lawn while his shell-shocked date stood alone. Lydia went to her, took her arm, and pulled her off to the side. Then the woman began sobbing uncontrollably. "I'm so sorry this happened," she managed to say. "I know Lawrence is not used to drinking wine, and I think he just had too much. I tried to get him to slow down, but he wouldn't listen. I am so embarrassed."

"This isn't your fault," Lydia said, guiding her toward the club entrance. "You had no control over this. Believe me, I know Lawrence, and no one can tell him anything. Let's get you on your way. With time, you'll look back on this and laugh." *Actually, this will scar you for life!*

Meanwhile, Bill and George had picked up Lawrence. They carried him to the parking lot, put him in the backseat of his car, rolled down the windows, and handed the car keys to his date. By now, guests were hurrying to their cars to leave the party.

"You okay to drive?" Bill asked the woman.

"Yes, I'm fine. I'm not much of a drinker. I only had one glass of wine. My son can help me get him out of the car."

What on earth are you doing with a guy like Lawrence? Lydia couldn't help but wonder as the woman drove away, Lawrence slumped in the backseat.

With Lawrence gone, the trio walked back into the club. Bill was still chuckling. "What's so funny about this, Bill?"

"You gotta laugh," he said. "Someday, you'll see the humor."

Still annoyed at her husband, Lydia was gratified to see that the other board members had stayed to help put things back in order and hose down the patio. As had Vince and Roger, who were already moving tables out of the way. About twenty other people were still there, several of them in the pool trying to wash themselves of the disgusting spew. The stench was horrendous. Mary, holding a napkin over her face, was clearing off the buffet table, which still had some whole lobsters, potatoes, and salads. "What a shame to waste all this food," she said.

Just as she heard a cell phone ring, Lydia noticed Bonnie over by the Sugar Shack making a call. It was easy to locate the intended recipient. There, on the check-in table, was Rex's phone ringing and lighting up with "Bonnie" on the screen. *Bonnie is trying to call him, and he's nowhere in sight.*

By now, Bill had taken charge of the situation. "Okay, let's get the rest of the tables onto the grass and bag up the food scraps. Does anybody know how to turn on the floodlights?"

Lydia had no idea. She heard Rex's cell phone go silent, then saw it light up again with "Missed Call and Voicemail" on the screen.

"The switch for the floodlights is over on the side of the building. I'll get it," said Bud, disappearing around the corner. Suddenly, the patio lit up, as did the far end of the pool. Now, the full extent of Lawrence's damage was visible, and it was much worse than Lydia had realized. *We'll have to demo the patio.*

Looking out over the pool, Lydia noticed that the remaining guests had turned their attention to the deep end, which had been dark for most of the evening but now was illuminated under the floodlight. There, in full *flagrante delicto*, their bodies intertwined, were Rex and Amanda, both completely naked, on the diving board! Lydia put her hand over her mouth and joined the chorus of gasps that was quickly turning to laughter. Rex was straddling the diving board with Amanda on his lap, facing him with her legs wrapped around his lower torso. "Oh my God, they're doing it!" one woman exclaimed loudly.

"Hey, get a lounge chair," a man yelled out.

Apparently, Rex and Amanda had been so enraptured with each other, they not only had missed dinner, but Lawrence's performance as well. People stopped cleaning, and many gravitated toward the pool to get a better view. The noisy scene became silent. Suddenly aware that they had been caught in the act, both Rex and Amanda jumped into the pool and swam to the side where their clothes, clumsily removed in a fit of passion, were strewn.

As Lydia continued gawking at the scene, she became aware of someone standing next to her. *Bonnie!* Lydia froze, not wanting to confront her.

"Well, this isn't the first time Rex has pulled this," Bonnie said, her eyes welling up with tears. "I had a feeling something was going on. I can never reach him at home, and he rarely calls. But this time, he's really outdone himself by humiliating me in front of all these people."

By now, Rex and Amanda were out of the pool, both in their underwear. Rex was able to put on his shorts and shirt, but Amanda was having no luck squeezing her wet body into the tight lime green dress. Walking along the fence to avoid being seen, Rex made his way to the patio, running smack-dab into his wife. Lydia slowly backed away as she saw Rex's face turn white.

"Bonnie! What are you doing here? I thought you were coming tomorr—"

"I wanted to surprise you, Rex. But clearly, I'm the one surprised. Along with all these other people. Who's the slut this time?"

"Bonnie, I can explain. This was a fluke, a one-time thing. We both had some wine, and things got out of hand," he lied.

At that, Bonnie swung her right hand back and slugged her wayward husband in the face so hard, he reeled back onto the grass. In a voice loud enough to be heard by everyone, she shouted, "Don't insult me with your bullshit lies, you asshole. And don't come home tonight. We're done." She stormed off.

Without looking at Lydia, Rex got up, picked up his phone and car keys and headed to the parking lot, oblivious to the wreckage on the patio and leaving Amanda to fend for herself. Lydia saw she was still over near the deep end of the pool trying to get her dress back on.

"What are you doing, Lydia?" Bill abruptly ended the sad, but comical, distraction.

"Did you see Rex and Amanda on the diving board?"

"Hard to miss. But I've been a little busy cleaning up Lawrence's mess. You need to call Pete and tell him he's probably going to have to close the club grounds and pool tomorrow. Also, isn't there some stuff we can use to clean up the barf?"

I see you're not laughing anymore, she thought. "Right. On it." She called Pete; thankfully, he answered.

"Don't tell me. You found another fifty K?" he asked before Lydia could speak.

"No, but you aren't going to believe what just happened," she said, giving him the sordid details. "Bill thinks there's some stuff we can use to dry up the mess."

"Yeah, there are a number of absorbents that are effective. I don't have any at the club, and we'll never find anything open this late on Saturday night. But I know we keep a container at the high school. Sit tight."

Forty minutes later, Pete showed up with two packages of the compound, which he promptly spread over the drying piles of vomit. Once it was coagulated enough to dispose of, he, Vince, and Roger shoveled it into trash bags. Surveying both pools, Pete agreed they would need to be vacuumed and shocked with chlorine and other chemicals to sanitize the water after being contaminated. "No way we can open this pool tomorrow," he said. "It will take at least a day to get the patio completely clean. We'll have to power-wash it, for sure. The trash will reek, but not much we can do about that. As for any debris on the grass, let's hope the birds get it."

Lydia gagged at the thought. "I'll alert Ron Gutierrez to put out a blast e-mail that the pool and patio are closed tomorrow," she said. "The tennis courts should be fine."

Mary had found the whiteboard easel and markers to post a "Pool and Grounds Closed" sign at the main entrance.

By eleven-thirty, the situation was at least stable. The food had been bagged and put in the dumpster and the lobster pots cleaned with disinfectant soap. Mary put the leftover lobsters and potatoes into plastic bags and volunteered to keep them in her freezer until she could put them in the trash. The rented tables and chairs were folded up and stacked, along with the tablecloths and silverware, to be picked up by the party rental company. The bathrooms were cleaned up as best they could, save for one toilet in the women's bathroom that had overflowed.

"I'll arrange to have the drains and toilets snaked," Bud offered.

"Thank you, all of you, for staying to clean up this mess," Lydia said.

Looking around, she realized Amanda had skulked out in the midst of the cleanup.

After arriving home, she and Bill took showers, then sat out on the deck to decompress after what had been an entertaining, albeit disgusting, roller coaster of an evening.

"Rex and Amanda on the diving board, huh?" Bill said. Lydia related the scene with Bonnie, and Amanda's struggle to get dressed. "I can say with certainty that she got out of that dress a lot faster than she got back into it."

"You'd better tell Pete to clean off the diving board too," Bill added. Looking at each other, they both burst out laughing.

"How about a drink to finish off this memorable evening?" he asked.

"Sure. Anything but red wine."

Remnants

PETE UNLOCKED the gate early Sunday after finding an open equipment rental store that had a power washer. The main pool had been chemically shocked and the vacuum had been running all night, but larger debris floating in the deep end would need to be fished out with a net. The baby pool also would need cleaning and vacuuming. The patio still smelled. Wearing thick rubber gloves and a mask, Pete filled a bucket with bleach and water and began scrubbing and picking up small pieces of glass and food that had been missed the night before. An hour later, he hooked up the power washer and started hosing off the concrete. By ten-thirty, the patio was clean, save for a faint red stain, and the stench almost gone. Next, he turned his attention to the pool.

Lydia arrived at the club around noon after a great night's sleep followed by Bill's breakfast of French toast and fresh fruit. She'd called Susan Adams to recount the events of the previous evening and invite the family for dinner — since their regular Sunday night barbecue at the club had effectively been cancelled.

"Oh my God, I wish we'd been there," Susan had said, howling with laughter.

"No, it was beyond disgusting. Be glad you missed it."

"Are you kidding? The entertainment value would have more than made up for that. Barf fest meets sex orgy. I love it! Did anyone get any video?"

"I'll ask around."

Walking into the club, Lydia was amazed to see how much progress Pete had made on the cleanup. "Wow, the patio looks great. I didn't know you were going to show up so early."

"That's why you guys pay me the big bucks." She was glad to see he still had a sense of humor, even as he pulled chunks of undigested food from the pool with the long-handled net. "Lawrence will never live this down," he said. "I'll bet we won't have any more problems with him."

"Well, Lawrence isn't the only board member who shamed himself last night." Lydia filled him in on Rex and Amanda's not-so-private tryst and Bonnie's surprise arrival and decking of her husband.

"Oh geez." Pete laughed so hard tears ran down his face. "It's been pretty obvious those two have had a thing all summer. You think Rex's wife is going to divorce him?"

"She might as well. She's never home, and they really have nothing in common now that their kids are grown and out of the house. I just hope Rex sees the tennis light petition through. We've only got a few weeks until the neighborhood HOA meeting and less than a month until the club meeting on Labor Day. We have *got* to get this put to bed. I want to be able to stand before the membership and tell them this issue has been resolved once and for all. I cannot wait to close this place up for the summer. By the way, I'm going to put the final edits on your contract this week and will bring it over one night for you to sign. I assume you're still game?"

"Yeah, I'll give it another go. Except for last night, we've been on a roll the last few weeks, knock on wood. No pool jumpers, no poop in the pool, no bags of money, no break-ins that I know of. Piece of cake. We'll see where things stand this time next year. I mean, how bad can it be? Of course, then it won't be your problem, right?"

"You got it. So glad you're willing to hang in there at least another year. You have done such a great job. We've come a long way in the last few years, thanks in large part to you. I know there are always challenges—like obnoxious board members puking on the patio. But let's face it, this year has been over the top with one bizarre crisis after another, from the money to the blue sedan casing you, me and God knows who else, along with a few other strange goings-on. Next year should be much smoother."

Realizing she hadn't talked to Pete since school started, she updated him on how she had tracked down BSG Investments and her phone conversation with Ben Gregorie. "He said to call him back in a week, so I'm going to take him up on that."

"You're quite the sleuth," Pete said. "What are you hoping to find out?"

"I don't know. Bill thinks I'm nuts, and he may be right. But these loose ends are driving me crazy. There are too many strange events converging in one crazy summer. I still have a feeling these things are somehow all connected."

SUMMER CLUB | 191

THAT NIGHT, Lydia was pleasantly surprised to get a text from Rex saying he wanted to have the party for the last of the petition-signers a week from Tuesday, and to please alert Pete. "I'll take care of the invites, food, liquor, everything," he said, as though nothing had happened.

Good. He's changing the conversation and moving on. Probably trying to redeem himself for his bad behavior, Lydia thought as she texted Pete with the date.

A Secret Arrangement

L YDIA HAD breakfast on the table when Bill and the boys came down at seven-thirty. The family engaged in a lively conversation about school, Geoff's first high school tennis match, and Andy's upcoming cross-country meet. After the boys left, Bill strangely hung around longer than usual to read the *Wall Street Journal*, making Lydia antsy.

"Don't you need to be at the office?"

"No, I don't have my first meeting until ten. You trying to get rid of me?" He looked up from the paper and grinned.

"No, no. It's just that usually you're out of here by eight-thirty at the latest."

It had been exactly one week since the phone call with Ben Gregorie. Lydia busied herself cleaning up the kitchen, anxiously wondering what she might learn from a second call, which she planned to make as soon as she was alone in the house.

Finally, Bill stood up from the table. "Okay, I'm outta here. What are you up to today?"

"Nothing really," she fibbed. "Trying to get my ducks in a row for these upcoming meetings. Geoff's tennis match is at four, so I'll go to that. In a few weeks, I'll be done with all my responsibilities at Meadow Glen. We should celebrate."

"I'm for that. Maybe dinner on the diving board?" He kissed her good-bye, headed for the garage, and was gone in less than a minute.

Lydia raced to her office, where her phone had been charging since last night. *Good. No text messages, e-mails, or voicemails.*

She sat back in her chair, took a deep breath, and started to call Ben's number. Her phone rang before she could complete the call.

"Hello, this is Ben Gregorie. Is this the woman I spoke with last week? I'm sorry, I don't remember the name."

"Yes, this is Lydia Phillips." She couldn't believe he'd called back. "And yes, I did contact you last week. Thank you so much for getting back to me. I was just about to call you."

"Well, looks like I beat you to the punch."

"Yes, you certainly did." Feeling an acute sense of anticipation, Lydia thought it a good sign that Ben had called her. In fact, she was so taken aback she failed to even consider how he had gotten her phone number.

"I had your number on my Recent Calls list," he said, "so figured I would give it a try. I've had some time to think about what you told me and speak to my attorney. Your call really shook me up."

"Really? How so?"

"Tell you what. Rather than go into this on the phone, would it be possible to meet in person? As it happens, I'm going to be in your neck of the woods later this week. I'll be staying downtown at the Majestic Hotel. Probably fly in Wednesday night. I have some things to attend to on Thursday, but could we meet for lunch Friday?"

Lydia checked her calendar and saw that it was clear. "Yes, I can do that. What brings you to town?"

"You'll find out when we meet. I'll call you Friday morning to finalize the time and details. By the way, I'll be bringing my attorney."

LYDIA WAS so excited when she disconnected the call, her hands were shaking. *Deep breaths, deep breaths. Obviously, he's got something big to tell me if he's bringing his attorney. Maybe I should bring someone.*

She started to call her board colleague Mike Patterson, then thought better of it. *Mike doesn't even know about this Darrell Baker situation.*

Bill, Lydia knew, had a list of legal contacts as long as his arm, but would be livid that she had continued to pursue matters. *I guess I'll go alone. I'm sure it'll be fine.*

Friday was only a few days away but seemed like an eternity. Needing a distraction, she made a list of things to do. She pulled up Pete's contract on her computer and made some changes to reflect that he would remain as manager for another season with the pay raise the board had approved. Then, she started on the agenda for the annual Labor Day membership meeting open to all Meadow Glen members—*update and hopefully announce resolution on the tennis court lights and lawsuit, the treasurer's report, reports from the committee chairs, long-range planning and capital improvements, renewal of Pete's contract...*

Full of nervous energy, she then went on a cleaning spree, starting with the boys' rooms. Andy's room was relatively clean, but Geoff's was a mess with dirty dishes under the bed, half-full plastic cups, and a huge pile of dirty, smelly clothes. The cleaning blitz took all morning. Satisfied the upstairs was presentable, she made herself a sandwich and took out some steaks for dinner.

As she was leaving to go to Geoff's tennis match, her phone rang. It was Marge Baker.

"Hi, Marge, how are you doing? How are things going?" Lydia felt bad she hadn't been in touch.

"Okay, I guess. I don't have much new to report, but I did want to tell you that the police came by again this morning. This is the third time. They took Darrell's computer and business files. My son said it was okay. I went ahead and printed off another copy of that property list and gave it to them."

"Oh, good," said Lydia, her stomach tightening slightly. "I'm sure they want to be thorough." *It's about time they started delving into his business. Better late than never.*

"Were you able to get any information from the list?" Marge sounded hopeful, but frustrated.

Lydia considered telling Marge about her pending meeting with Ben but thought better of it. *I don't know anything at this point. Saying something now will either upset her or give her false hope.*

"Nothing important. I did speak to Darrell's friend Dale Richards, who couldn't reveal much about the properties or their owners. The police should have much better luck tracking down that information, and hopefully we'll have some answers soon." *But what the police don't have is the printout with Darrell's handwritten notes revealing Ben Gregorie's phone number,* she reflected, feeling especially smug that she was one step ahead of both the police and Vern. "I so appreciate your call, Marge. Let's keep in touch. My plate is pretty full through Labor Day, but after that I would like to take you to lunch."

"Oh, that is so nice of you. I would love to do that. I'll look forward to hearing from you."

GEOFF'S FIRST freshman tennis match ended in a tiebreaker, with Geoff and his partner finally eking out a win. The family celebrated at dinner — steaks with Bill's rich bearnaise sauce, smashed potatoes, vegetables from the garden, and leftover cherry pie and ice cream from Sunday night. Lydia was thankful for the distraction as she tried not to think about her upcoming meeting with Ben.

Keeping Bill from suspecting anything would be a challenge.

Downtown Rendezvous

IT WAS finally Friday, and Lydia was in and out of the shower by six-thirty, much to Bill's surprise. "What's got you up and at 'em so early?"

"Lots of little things, and I've got some things to do this morning so wanted to get this out of the way," she said, quickly going downstairs before Bill could quiz her any further. "And I want to make sure the boys get breakfast," she called out. "If I have time, I'll take Stacie for a walk. Andy has an orthodontist appointment this afternoon."

By eight o'clock, all three were gone. Knowing that sitting and waiting for the call from Ben would be nothing short of torture, Lydia put the leash on Stacie and ventured out the garage with her phone in her pocket. The club was locked and empty, save for one of the ladies' tennis teams practicing on Courts 1 and 2 in advance of a league match later in the morning.

Rounding the corner, she saw the ever-present trickle of water from the pool as she approached Claire Hoskins' house — where Warren's BMW was parked! Pretending to pick up after Stacie, Lydia bent down out of their view and gazed into the lit-up kitchen where Warren and Claire were having what looked like a heated discussion. Claire was doing the talking, and her arms were gesturing wildly. *They're probably doing some last-minute petition strategizing. This is getting uglier by the day.*

She quickly moved on, but before her anxiety level could rise, her phone rang. "Good morning, Lydia. Hope you're doing well." It was Ben Gregorie. "How does eleven-thirty sound for lunch at my hotel."

"Great. Looking forward to meeting you. Do I need to bring anything?"

"No, just have the front desk ring me when you get here. I'll be doing most of the talking."

BUILT IN the late 1880s, the Majestic Hotel was a downtown landmark that had been dwarfed by skyscrapers constructed over the last several decades. Throughout its storied history, the hotel had hosted a long list of famous

names, from U.S. presidents to rock stars. The fifteen-story red brick struc-
ture on the corner of Broadway and Spruce Street featured an atrium that
went from the ground floor to the ceiling and a grand staircase with an or-
nate wrought-iron railing where every Christmas season twenty privileged
young women made their debut in front of the city's movers and shakers.

Along the perimeter of the lobby was a high-end dress shop, a florist,
a candy store, an upscale coffee shop, and an overpriced, white-tablecloth
steakhouse that also served Sunday brunch on weekends. In the lobby,
walls of dark wood wainscoting and gold and ecru wallpaper coordinated well with the lush diamond-patterned carpet of red, gold, and green.
Scattered throughout the lobby were potted plants, overstuffed sofas and
leather chairs, and tables with lamps. The area was further illuminated by
gold sconces.

Traffic was heavy, and it had taken Lydia over an hour to drive downtown. At one point, she ended up virtually parked in an exit lane until a
black SUV slowed down and signaled for her to get over. She parked in
the underground garage and rode the elevator up to the lobby. "Hello, I'm
here to see Ben Gregorie," she told the woman at the front desk. "My name
is Lydia Phillips."

"Yes, of course." A polite, but severe-looking woman picked up the
phone. "Mr. Gregorie, Ms. Phillips is here. Thank you." Turning to Lydia
she said, "He'll be right down. Please, make yourself comfortable."

Lydia planted herself in a leather chair and observed people reading
the newspaper or on their iPads and drinking coffee or iced tea. Shortly,
a medium-height, attractive man with salt-and-pepper hair — dressed in a
long-sleeved dark blue collared shirt, khaki slacks, and what looked like
Gucci loafers — got off the elevator and approached her. Lydia guessed
him to be in his mid-sixties.

"Lydia?"

"Yes, Ben?"

"Nice to meet you," he said, extending his hand. "Thanks for coming
down. I hope this isn't too inconvenient."

"Oh, not at all. It's been awhile since I've been downtown, and it's
always fun to come to the Majestic," she said, wondering where they were
going to have lunch. *I'm starving.*

"I thought we'd have lunch in my suite where it's more private. I took
the liberty of ordering a couple of salads and some sandwiches. Does that
sound okay?"

No, not okay. I don't even know you, Lydia thought, wishing she had brought someone with her after all. "Yes, of course, that sounds very nice. Thank you so much."

Ben's suite on the eighth floor was quite spacious, with a large sitting room that opened onto a balcony. A dark red sofa with multi-print accent pillows was flanked by upholstered off-white chairs with pillows matching the sofa. A small table was set with three place settings. The bedroom was off to the left.

As they entered the suite, another man in a suit and tie stood and extended his hand. Short and somewhat stocky, the man had a receding hairline and looked to be around fifty. "Hello, Mrs. Phillips. I'm Walter Barnes, Mr. Gregorie's attorney. Please, have a seat," he said, motioning to one of the chairs.

"Thank you. Please, call me Lydia," she said, trying to conceal the uneasiness she felt at being in a hotel room with two strange men. *I am for sure outnumbered.*

"Of course," he said, smiling. "Ben filled me in on your phone conversation last week. That's quite an interesting story. We definitely want to talk to you, and perhaps we can enlighten you as well. However before we get started, I have a non-disclosure form for you to sign. Since this conversation will contain some very sensitive information, we need to ensure that everything said here is kept confidential. Obviously, things discussed between myself and Ben are covered by attorney-client privilege. But now that you are a part of the discussion, it is imperative that nothing Ben says be repeated outside this room. Are you comfortable with that?"

"Um, I guess so," Lydia said, wondering what "sensitive" meant. "I have to say that I understand your concern, but I wasn't expecting this. I had considered bringing my own attorney, but obviously did not. What about my protection? Will anything I say today also be kept confidential?"

"Absolutely." Walter smiled. "This is a document that both you and Ben will sign. That means everything either of you says during this meeting must be kept confidential. That also means you won't be able to take any notes. Okay?"

"That's fine."

Walter then opened a manila folder with a two-page document. "This first page contains a lot of boilerplate legalese. The second page explains that today's discussion is completely private, and that neither of the parties—Ben or you—can reveal to anyone what was discussed. Just print your name on this line at the top, and then sign at the bottom of the second page."

"All right. As long as nobody is breaking any laws," Lydia said, taking the pen. She noticed that Ben had already printed his name and signed the document.

"This is a very standard form used frequently for situations like this," Walter assured her. "We are not doing anything illegal."

As Lydia finished signing, there was a knock at the door.

"Room service." A hotel waiter wheeled in a cart draped with a white tablecloth and several covered dishes. He went to work arranging the plates on the table, removing the covers to reveal chicken salad, a spinach salad with strawberries and pecans, hummus and vegetables, three sand-wiches — ham and cheese, tuna salad, and roast beef — chips, and a plate of assorted pastries. On the bottom shelf of the cart were pitchers of iced tea, ice water, lemonade, and a variety of sodas. Lydia chose an iced tea.

"Shall we?" said Ben, motioning to the table.

Lydia sat down and took a big sip of tea. "Thank you, this looks love-ly." She had completely lost her appetite.

Power Lunch

A S BEN and Walter each polished off a whole sandwich, several helpings of salad, and multiple cookies, Lydia managed to get down about a third of a sandwich, a few spoons of spinach salad, some chips, and a brownie. The conversation was superficial—kids, interests, careers. Lydia learned that Ben was semi-retired and had spent thirty-plus years as a principal at an investment firm. He had two daughters, one of whom was to be married in a month. Ben was particularly interested in Lydia's career as a journalist and that she had chosen to give it up to stay home with the boys. *And yet, here I am in a downtown hotel room with this guy and his lawyer.*

"Now that we've been fortified with food, why don't we get down to business," Ben said, motioning to the sofa where Lydia dutifully sat, eager to hear what was sure to be an interesting story. "First, a little background," he began. "For the past several years, I've been engaged in what I like to call 'alternative investments,' meaning investments outside the traditional real estate and bond and equity markets. Basically, I'm looking for avenues of income in start-up companies or more complex commercial real estate ventures.

"Five years ago, a brokerage firm in Atlanta that specialized in these types of investments approached me with an opportunity to put some money in a company that buys and manages commercial real estate properties, mainly small shopping centers in lower-income, often gentrifying or transitioning, areas. Each of these properties is set up as a limited liability company. I would buy a membership interest in one of these LLCs and receive a minimum annual return, with payments to be made quarterly. Additionally, I would profit from the appreciation of the property if and when it was sold. I studied the numbers of several of these LLCs, and they all looked great.

"So, I invested 150,000 dollars in 2939 LLC, which owns and manages a strip center in Baltimore. The balance sheet showed assets of more than twenty-five million and cash amounting to half a million dollars. The broker handled all the paperwork. Mind you, I am only one investor in this deal. There could be as many as ten or fifteen other investors, and I have no idea who they are," he said, getting up to pour a glass of iced tea.

"Three years later, my investment had appreciated by about 22,000 dollars, or fifteen percent. So, I invested more money, ranging from 200,000 to 400,000 dollars, in three additional LLCs around the country. By now, the company was also offering promissory notes to be paid back over an eighteen-month period at interest rates of ten to thirteen percent, with interest-only payments for the first six months and then twelve months of principal and interest. My guess is the company wanted to raise more funds and boost cash flow. So, in addition to my membership interests in these LLCs, I purchased some promissory notes, bringing my total investment at this point to about two million dollars. Depending on the amount of each investment and the property, I figured to make anywhere from fifteen to twenty percent annually. One of those properties was Pershing Plaza, into which I invested 350,000 dollars. That was eighteen months ago."

So that's how Ben got involved in that property, Lydia realized.

"For the first six months, I received regular quarterly payments in separate checks for each of these membership investments. Then, the payments started coming more sporadically. One quarter, I would receive payments for two of the four investments. The next quarter, I would receive payments for one or both of the other properties. Essentially, I was receiving half the money I should have. For the promissory notes, I received regular interest payments for the first six months, as specified. But when it came time for the principal to kick in, the payments trickled in, eventually stopping.

"I contacted the brokerage firm that got me into these deals, and they said they would look into it. A week later, I received a letter from the firm stating that due to a variety of reasons — severe weather, an unusually high number of vacancies, and expensive repairs required at some of the locations — there had been a temporary downturn in income, but that the situation was correcting itself and that I would be paid the full amounts with additional interest. The letter also referenced a clause in the contracts indicating that payments could be interrupted due to 'extreme circumstances.' Of course I understand that any investment carries some degree of risk, so I wasn't overly concerned.

"Three months later, things had not improved—they had gotten worse," Ben continued. "One quarter, I received no money at all, and another quarter I received a payment for only one of the properties. I again contacted the brokerage firm, asking to be put in touch directly with the company managing these LLCs. They refused, saying they couldn't give out that information. But I pushed hard, and after repeated calls and letters threatening legal action from Walter here, they finally relented and gave me the name and phone number of what is basically the holding company for all these LLCs. That company is WLR Real Estate Ventures."

Lydia sat very still, laser-focused on what Ben was telling her.

"After several attempts, I finally got hold of Warren Reinhart, who I presumed to be the owner of this firm. The first thing out of his mouth was a question: 'How did you get this number?' When I told him, he became quite curt, clearly wanting to cut the conversation short."

Lydia was forming a mental image of an irritable, defensive Warren sweating profusely.

"Reinhart told me the situation involving these particular properties had amounted to a 'perfect storm' of problems that came all at once, and that they had never experienced anything like this. He said they expected to have things resolved within six months. He also explained that the biggest source of the problems concerned Pershing Plaza here in town, where several tenants had moved out and where a host of issues—including poor wiring and a sewer backup, neither of which was covered by insurance—were being rectified. He also said his company had discovered that the property manager at that site had done an extremely poor job keeping on top of maintenance issues, which was why so many tenants had not renewed their leases."

Darrell Baker. Lydia couldn't believe what she was hearing.

"I asked him where things stood, and he said they had done all the repairs and were in the process of hiring a new property manager to get the establishments rented. That was in January."

Lydia searched her memory for an impression of Pershing Plaza. The coffee shop, she remembered, was dated but clean, and had seemed busy the day she was there.

"By now, I was several years into these investments, and my estimated income was less than half of what it should have been. Furthermore, I'm still not receiving all the payments."

"What about the firm in Atlanta that put you in touch with Warren's company?" Lydia asked.

"Interestingly, they're no longer in business. According to the Georgia Secretary of State's website, the company, TRBD Strategies, was officially closed at the end of February and we haven't been able to track down the principal owner—yet. Eventually, we'll find him.

"Anyway, in early May I decided to take a look at the situation for myself," Ben went on. "We have a place in the Michigan U.P., and I usually go up every spring to get it open for the summer. So, I decided to take an extra day and check out the Pershing Plaza property since it's on the way. I expected to see a half-vacant strip center, but nothing could have been further from the truth. I visited every single establishment and learned that all the tenants had been there at least five years and that there had not been a sewer backup or any electrical problems. And that the property manager was great."

As Ben paused to take a sip of tea, Lydia sat shocked, her mouth gaping. "I don't understand this," she managed to say. "Was Warren just lying to you?" The memory of him pulling into the parking lot at Meadow Glen in his brand-new BMW was now vivid in her mind. *The newspaper pictures of him and Celia at the gala. The fancy new house. The country club...*

"It appears that way. But, there's more. After speaking with these tenants, I asked for the name and number of the property manager—Darrell Baker. I called him, told him who I was, and that I wanted to meet with him. He came right over. Seemed like a good guy. Been in the property management business a long time. When I told him about my conversation with Warren, he seemed upset and got quite angry. He told me that nothing Warren had said was true. He took particular offense at Warren's claim that he had done a poor job, indicating he had never been accused of such a thing. Then came the kicker."

Recalling her conversation with Dale Richards, Lydia knew what was coming.

"Baker told me that Pershing Plaza had been sold in April for 19.5 million dollars. Now, it was my turn to be stunned."

"He just sold it right out from under you," Lydia exclaimed. "Is there anything you can do?"

"Well, in fact, Walter and I flew up here yesterday to file a civil suit against WLR for fraud and for defaulting on the payments. We've also learned by checking county sales records that WLR purchased Pershing Plaza for fifteen million less than three years ago. So, he made a tidy profit of 4.5 million, to which I am entitled a cut as an investor."

"What about all the other properties?" Lydia could feel her heart pounding.

"Since those situations initially didn't appear to be as egregious as Pershing Plaza, we attempted to work out settlements with WLR. But they've been unresponsive, so we're in the process of preparing similar suits over properties in Little Rock, Pittsburgh, and the one in Baltimore. I haven't received any rental income from the Baltimore property for a good six months. And, it looks like the one in Pittsburgh may have already been sold when we made the investment!"

"Seriously? How can somebody even do that?"

"Oh, you'd be surprised at what people can get away with. I have no idea if Warren has partners. And, of course we don't know what, if anything, the other investors in these properties have done." Lydia tried to remember if she had ever heard of Warren having a business associate.

"So, there you have it," Ben said. "I had pretty much resigned myself to thinking this was just another run-of-the-mill fraud case, but when you told me on the phone about Darrell Baker washing up in the river and that he'd planned to go to the police about something, that sent me to a dark place. I don't want to jump to conclusions, but there are too many weird coincidences here."

Exactly what I said to Bill. Lydia found herself having a difficult time processing all the information. "I just can't believe this," she kept repeating. Then she remembered the $50,000 and Warren's ongoing obsession with taking control of it. *Surely these incidents are connected somehow. Should I tell them?*

Her indecision was interrupted by her phone vibrating with a text from Andy. "Mom, what up? Don't I have an ortho appt?"

Oh shit. It was going on three o'clock. She would never make it home in time. "Excuse me, Ben. I need to deal with a text from my son."

Even though her hands were shaking, Lydia managed to type out a text. "Sorry, honey. Held up. I'll resked."

"You know I got xcused from X-ctry practice for this!" he replied.

As she sat on the sofa, Lydia thought better of looping Ben in with what she knew. *It's my turn to process, and I'm not going to share anything at this point.* Abruptly, she stood and extended her hand to Ben, who stood up as well. "I'm afraid I need to get going. I've got some issues at home I need to attend to, and I want to beat the rush hour traffic. Thank you so much for lunch and for sharing all this with me. This has been quite enlightening, and you've given me a lot to think about. This is mind-boggling. I will certainly keep you posted if anything more comes up on my end. Good luck with your cases and have a safe trip back to Atlanta."

"Wait a minute. What about Darrell Baker?" Ben asked, indicating his disappointment at giving Lydia a lot of information while receiving nothing in return. "Have there been any developments on his death? I was hoping you could shed some light on that. It's keeping me awake at night."

Welcome to my world. "The investigation is still going on, but I don't think the authorities have come up with any leads yet. I do know they've seized all of Darrell's files. We'll see where that goes. As I said, I'll keep you posted."

"Okay. Well, thanks for coming downtown to hear my story. Remember, we have an agreement to not reveal anything we've discussed in light of our lawsuit against WLR." Ben's piercing blue-gray eyes made clear his expectations for Lydia's silence.

"Yes, I understand. I won't even tell my husband."

Too Many Coincidences

N THE PARKING garage, Lydia was able to focus her thoughts enough to phone the orthodontist and reschedule Andy's appointment. With her head spinning from what Ben had revealed, it took several minutes to find her car, which was sandwiched between a minivan and a black SUV. By the time she pulled onto the freeway, too preoccupied to notice that the SUV had followed her, it was rush hour with stop-and-go traffic. Actually, she was glad. *Sitting here in this traffic jam will give me time to sort through all this and decompress a little. When I get home, I can't let on that anything is amiss; I need to act as normal as possible.*

Dead-stopped, she texted Andy. "hey, honey I resked for mon. sorry. caught d'town in traffic."

Lydia took a deep breath and mulled over what she had learned. *So, Warren finds investors to put up money to buy these strip centers. Then he doesn't pay them. Cheats them. Makes up lies about why they aren't seeing any returns. That cock-and-bull story about Darrell Baker as an excuse for not paying. Then he sells the places out from under the investors. So, where's the money? Is this embezzlement? Or is Warren so sideways on these properties that he's floating money? Regardless, how can he justify spending all this money on what is a very lavish lifestyle? Does Celia know what's going on? And what about Darrell? Did he know something? This is way bigger than Meadow Glen. Oh God, what have I gotten myself into?*

She couldn't imagine living on the edge financially. Being married to a CPA, they had always tried to live within their means, and would never spend money they didn't have. *Warren must be in debt up to his eyeballs for the millions he owes his investors. I can't begin to understand how stressful that would be. No wonder he's such an unpleasant ass.*

It was after five by the time Lydia pulled into the driveway. Thankfully, Bill wasn't home yet. Trying to explain where she'd been all day would have been difficult.

"I'm home," she called out, opening the door to a very happy Stacie looking for some much-needed attention.

"Hi, Mom." Geoff was lying on the family room couch watching TV. "What's for dinner? I'm starving."

Realizing that neither she nor Bill had made any plans to feed the family, she thought a minute. "Well, it's Friday. How about we go out for dinner? What else are you guys up to tonight?"

"Football game, I guess. At least that's what I'm doing."

"Tell you what. Why don't you guys order a pizza and go to the game, and Dad and I will go out?"

"Sounds good. Some guy came by for you."

"Who?"

"I dunno. He had these stupid sunglasses on. I think his name was Max or something. He left a big folder for you. It's on the dining room table."

Rex. She raced into the dining room and opened the large manila envelope. There they were. Five pages of petitions with 203 signatures from throughout the neighborhood. *Thank God.* Lydia felt a wave of relief.

On top was a scrawled note. "Lydia. Here are the petitions, signed, sealed, and delivered. We shouldn't have any problems now. In return for their signatures, I promised ten families an evening at the pool next Tuesday, around 5:00. Probably be about thirty people, including kids. Let's hope the weather's decent."

Lydia was ecstatic as she texted the date and guest count to Pete. Moreover, she was impressed at how Rex had taken charge of the entire situation. *He's straightened up since his trip to the woodshed,* she thought, wondering where things stood with Bonnie. Barring any unforeseen issues, the tennis court light controversy would be settled in a couple of weeks. *Of course, Claire could make some last-minute play to derail this thing.* Lydia frowned as worry clouded her euphoria.

"What are you scowling at?" Bill had walked in.

"That's great news," he said after she updated him on the petition status. "Congratulations. And don't worry about Claire. There is nothing she can do at this point. Just relax. Let's go out tonight."

"That was my plan." Lydia gave Geoff some money for the pizza and yelled goodbye to Andy, whom she had not seen or spoken to since she got home. "You guys have fun tonight and be safe."

Dinner at a nearby Italian restaurant was enjoyable. The wine relaxed Lydia and stimulated her appetite. But the conversation was superficial as her thoughts kept drifting back to the meeting with Ben Gregorie. She also resigned herself to accepting that she had hit a dead end — at least for now. *It's over. I've done everything I can do. I can't talk to anybody about what I know. Not Bill. Not Marge Baker. Not Pete. And in a couple of weeks, the club will be closed for the season. I won't have anything to worry about. Or anything to do.*

LYDIA GOT a taste of what that was going to be like as the weekend crawled by with no Meadow Glen issues to deal with. Without saying it, she was starting to feel a letdown coming after a year of nonstop activity. And something she had not felt for a long, long time. Boredom. *I'm going to have to find something to fill the void.* Between grocery shopping and doing the laundry, she looked for excuses to get out of the house. Saturday afternoon she stopped by the club and found Sam and two guards on duty with only a handful of swimmers. The tennis courts were empty — except for Brad and Tad on Court 2.

Then she decided to take a field trip over to the country club area to get a look at Warren's house, which she had never actually seen. She Googled the address — 11 Cottage Lane — and plugged it into her GPS. As she entered the exclusive neighborhood, the road narrowed to a single lane shaded by huge maples and ash trees on lots that covered an acre or more. Rounding the corner onto Cottage Lane, she saw that the homes were bigger and farther apart as the road continued to meander. *Cottage Lane is not an apt name for this street,* she mused, studying the addresses. *Let's see. Number three, number nine, number ten...* There it was — a sprawling, two-story stone mansion with turrets on both sides, a sweeping, manicured lawn, lush gardens, and a circular driveway. Warren's car was parked in the driveway, and two of the four garage doors were open to reveal a red Mercedes convertible and a white Lexus. She parked across the street and stared at the property, wondering if Warren was even aware he was being sued for millions of dollars.

Then her mind wandered to Darrell Baker. *There are too many weird coincidences here,* Lydia recalled Ben saying. Lydia wished she could find out the status of the police investigation. Then it occurred to her there was indeed someone who might know. *I'll call the Beacon-News Monday and see what Vern knows.*

Confident she had a next step in place, Lydia started the car and made a U-turn to head back home, oblivious to the black SUV parked down the street.

A Soufflé of Possibilities

ONDAY MORNING was overcast and cool, a sure sign that fall was on the way with the boys in school and Bill back on schedule. Lydia had risen early to get the coffee started and breakfast going in a timely fashion, loading up the kitchen table with an assortment of cereals, store-bought muffins, bread, orange juice, fruit, yogurt, and milk.

"Geez, Mom. You never made a big deal about breakfast before," Andy said.

"I know, honey. I just want to make sure you guys get off to a good start now that you're in high school. That old adage about breakfast being the most important meal of the day is true," she said, as Stacie parked herself under the table, her tail wagging in anticipation of getting a few crumbs.

Orchestrating breakfast herself also made things go much faster than having the boys and Bill scrounge around in the pantry for something to eat. Her main objective was to have everyone, especially Bill, out of the house no later than eight o'clock. This morning, the timing was critical. Recalling that Vern typically had his first round of calls finished around eight-thirty, Lydia knew she would have a small window to connect with him on the phone before things got too busy with any breaking news.

As all three exited through the garage, Stacie furtively climbed onto a kitchen chair to help herself to a muffin. Unaware of the dog's transgression, Lydia settled herself in her office club chair and thought a minute about how she planned to approach things. She had already decided to start the conversation by asking for any leads on the $50,000 — a legitimate question. Then, she would broach the subject of Darrell Baker. She called the main number of the paper and asked to be connected to Vern's phone.

"Police desk." Vern picked up on the first ring.

"Hi, Vern. It's Lydia Phillips. Got a minute?"

After a long pause, Vern answered with more than a trace of sarcasm. "What? Slow day at the swim club? I know. A soufflé fell and you want me to write it up."

Ha-ha. "No, nothing like that, Vern. I just had a quick question—"

"Found any more money bags?"

"No. But, in fact that's why I'm calling. It's been over a month since we turned the money over to the police, and I was wondering if you had heard anything. Do the cops have any leads?"

"Why don't you ask them?"

"We have. They keep telling us there's nothing new. Besides, with your sources, I know you have an inside track on just about everything that goes on so I figured I would call you directly and avoid the runaround." Lydia was banking on a flattery-will-get-you-everywhere approach.

It worked. Vern dropped the snide rhetoric, saying, "I don't have anything concrete, but I can tell you they've ruled out drug money."

"Really? What made them reach that conclusion?"

"Fingerprints don't match those of any known perps. None of the undercover cops in vice have heard anything from their sources. Fifty thousand bucks would be a fairly significant drug deal, and losing that amount would be big news on the street. Nobody has come around Meadow Glen looking for the money. Have they?"

"No, not that I know of. So, where do they go from here?"

Another long pause. "Why all the questions, Lydia?"

She had expected this question. "The club members are asking about it. Obviously, they're upset that a crime may have been committed. This is a family environment, and the incident shook some people up." She embellished. "As board president, I feel it's my responsibility to keep the members apprised of any information when it comes to something like this. We have our annual meeting in a few weeks, and I'd like to be able to provide some answers."

"Okay, well as I said, they don't think it's drug-related. Which means it's probably stolen money. Maybe embezzlement."

"Embezzlement? Why that?" Lydia's thoughts turned to Warren.

"One, there haven't been any bank robberies lately. Two, people typically don't keep that amount of cash lying around. The next logical place to look is business fraud."

"Do they have any leads?"

"My guess is they do, but I haven't gotten wind of any—yet."

"Well, if you can, please keep me in the loop." Now to the real reason she called.

"Hey, on another note, what's the latest on the guy who washed up in the river? I'm sure that's keeping everyone busy."

"Oh, Darrell Baker. Nothing we didn't already know in terms of forensics. The authorities have determined he was dead before he landed in the river, so we're talking murder. Severe blunt force trauma to the back of the head. No evidence of any toxins in his system and no known association with any criminals. I guess you haven't been reading my stories."

"Uh—oh yes, I have. I thought that since I had you on the phone, I would ask. I have a lot going on these days, so don't always remember the details."

"The cops are now combing through all his business files, both paper and online. They've interviewed the wife three times. She's a mess. Thinks he was having an affair. Could be. My sources at the cop shop think it had something to do with his business."

Lydia's stomach churned. "And what was it he did? I can't remember," she asked, playing dumb.

"Commercial property manager. He managed a slew of properties all over town. They're gonna need to investigate all those places, so this will take some time."

"What would a commercial property manager do to get himself killed and dumped in the river?"

"Oh, a lot of things. He could have evicted a tenant who then retaliated. He could have gotten crosswise with a property owner. For all we know, he was skimming money off the top. A few extra bucks for the girlfriend, if there was one. That's not unheard of with these property managers. They get access to the owners' bank accounts and can pretty much do whatever they want."

Vern had raised a scenario Lydia hadn't considered. *Maybe Darrell embezzled the fifty thousand dollars! Then he got killed by someone who later dumped the bag of cash over the fence and planned to return to retrieve it.* Lydia remembered Marge had told her that she and Darrell were planning a cruise next year. Yet, from everything she had heard, Darrell didn't seem the type to embezzle money.

"Have there been any reports of stolen money by any of the property owners?"

"No, at least not that I've heard. This also could be a simple case of the guy being in the wrong place at the wrong time. He got mugged and his assailant dumped him in the river. End of story. Happens all the time."

"Hmm…interesting." *But nobody knows that I found Darrell Baker's business card down the street. You also don't know that Warren Reinhart owned a property that Darrell managed, and is being sued by an investor in that property.* "Well, good chatting with you, Vern. Let me know if you hear anything about the money," Lydia said. Disconnecting the call, she reminded herself how jaded Vern could be when talking about a crime. Even when it involved murder.

Let There Be Lights

A FTER PROCESSING her conversation with Vern, Lydia had forced herself to put aside any thoughts of the now-confirmed murder of Darrell Baker to focus on the party for the last of the petition-signers. She was looking forward to putting to rest once and for all the controversy surrounding the tennis court lights.

With Pete's new contract, she walked over to the club late in the afternoon. The skies were clear and the temperature warm. Perfect. New age music was playing in the background. A glassy-eyed Jules was perched on a stool behind the snack bar counter, and upon seeing Lydia immediately put on sunglasses. At this point, Lydia didn't care. "Hi, Jules, how's it going?" *Why are we even keeping this junk food shack open at this point?* she wondered, observing that aside from the tennis players and Fred Lyons doing his midday laps, the club was virtually empty most weekdays now that school was back in session.

"Fine," she answered curtly.

Then Lydia saw Rex straightening up the patio and putting plastic cloths on the picnic tables, one covered with paper plates, utensils, bags of chips, dips, a vegetable tray, fruit platter, and chicken wings. Two card tables with beer and wine and plastic cups were set up near the back, and two big ice buckets were filled with assorted soft drinks, juices, and water.

Party planner Amanda—Rex's erstwhile flame and diving board companion—was nowhere in sight.

"Hey, Rex, how are you? This all looks great. You've done a fabulous job." Lydia had already decided to behave as though the diving board sex incident never happened.

Rex turned around, his face nearly covered by a pair of huge sunglasses intended to disguise what was left of the black eye Bonnie had given him ten days earlier. Lydia could see a bluish yellow bruise on the right side of his face.

"Hi, Lydia. Thanks. I think we've got things in pretty good shape. I've got pizzas coming at five." Rex was pleasant, but not his usual jovial self. *He seems very subdued.* Lydia was tempted to ask how things were at home, then thought better of it.

"Rex, we could not have done this without you. On behalf of the entire board, I want to thank you for seeing this through. Have you heard any rumblings from Claire Hoskins? I just have this sinking feeling she's going to try to torpedo this."

"Not a word. We've got the signatures, and I don't think we're going to have any more problems from her."

"Good to hear," Lydia said as she went to find Pete, who was in his office working on the schedule for the remainder of the season and the final Labor Day bash.

"Hi, Pete. Thanks for being here tonight. I've got your contract."

"Hey," he greeted her, looking up from his laptop and reaching for a pen to sign the document. "Things are under control. I have two guards coming for the party. I'll close up, and then you probably won't see much of me until Labor Day weekend. Sam will be covering the shifts. I've got back-to-school night tomorrow and I already have some conferences scheduled with the helicopters," he said, referring to the micromanaging parents who ruled the roost at Roosevelt High.

"Watch it. I could be one of those parents when my stint at this place is over," Lydia said, happy for the back-to-school night reminder.

"Please tell me that isn't so."

At five o'clock, right on time, several families filed into the club as the pizzas were being delivered. By now, Liz had shown up and was helping Rex greet the adults with their kids, some as young as two, in swimsuits and armed with an assortment of pool toys. Lydia wondered how many of them could swim. *The guards are going to have their hands full. Good thing there's two of them.*

As Lydia moved toward the entrance to greet the guests, she noticed several showing Rex and Liz a bright orange 8½-by-11-inch piece of paper. "Hello and welcome," she said, suddenly sensing a problem as the group was obviously involved in a confrontation.

"Take a look at this," Rex said, holding up one of the papers showing a message in bold black words:

BEFORE YOU SIGN THE PETITION GET ALL THE FACTS

Then in smaller type:

Lights on the tennis courts at Meadow Glen Swim and Tennis Club are strictly prohibited by your Homeowners Association.

If you signed the petition, you have put you and your families at risk of being sued in District Court. You could lose your home.

Demand that your name(s) be removed now — until you hear both sides of the issue and get the truth.

Attend the HOA meeting 7 p.m. Aug. 30, Roosevelt High School auditorium

Lydia's heart sank but she was not surprised. *So this is what Claire had up her sleeve.* After reading the flyer, she forced a smile and introduced herself to the guests. "I am so sorry about this notice you all received. I can assure you, nothing could be further from the truth. The fact is—"

"Excuse me, ma'am. At this point, I don't know who to believe," a visibly angry man said. "I signed your petition last week, and then yesterday found this paper—from whom I don't know—stuck in the door handle of my front door. Now, I'm beginning to think we were bribed. 'Just sign the petition and you'll get a free night at the pool.' This doesn't smell right to me."

"I agree," said a middle-aged woman wearing a bright orange bathing suit. "We don't need to get involved in some legal controversy. This lighting issue sounds like a problem for your club, not the neighborhood. How do we un-sign this thing?"

"No one is going to sue you," Lydia responded authoritatively, feeling her face grow hot and red. "More than two hundred residents have signed this petition, and that represents a two-thirds majority of the neighborhood. I am one of those people, and I am *not* going to be sued. But, tell you what. Let me put in a call to our attorney and see if he can come by to walk you all through this. Enjoy the pool and dinner we have for you. Please don't leave yet."

Lydia called Mike Patterson's cell. It went right to voicemail. *Damnit.* She called the home number and got Mike's wife on the phone. "Jane, I desperately need to get hold of Mike. We have a problem at the club. Do you know where I can reach him?"

"He's out back. Let me get him." Lydia heard her open the back door and call out, "Mike, it's Lydia. Sounds like another crisis at Meadow Glen."

"Hey, Lydia, what's going on?" Mike was out of breath, having run in from outside. "On my way," he said after getting a brief rundown of the situation.

Ten minutes later, he walked into the club. By now, most of the guests had ventured over to the tables, helping themselves to appetizers, pizza, and drinks, or were in the pool. Lydia rounded them up.

"Everyone, our attorney has arrived. Please gather around here on the patio so he can explain exactly what is going on with this petition."

"Hello, and thank you very much for coming," Mike said, holding one of the flyers. "I understand you all received one of these at your homes in the last few days, and I can certainly understand your concerns. I'm Mike Patterson. I've been a member of this club for twelve years and am currently the board president-elect. I am also an attorney and I'm extremely familiar with this issue. Finally, I'm a resident of the neighborhood and I signed this petition along with a majority of the homeowners. Including you."

He continued. "Earlier this year, Meadow Glen petitioned your HOA to ask for a change in the covenants in order to install lights on our tennis courts. Historically, these covenants have prohibited the installation of any tennis court lights. However, with nearly forty years of tree growth and state-of-the-art technology, the lights we're installing are considerably more neighbor-friendly. They are designed to shine down only on the courts, so are much less obtrusive than previous lighting designs. They also can be put on a timer and programmed to be switched off no later than ten at night.

"If I can turn your attention to Courts 1 and 2 over there, you'll see that we already have installed lights on those courts. Since those courts are not visible to any residences, we felt we were safe to install the lights under the provisions of the covenants. We still believe that to be the case, but going forward with any additional lighting we want to make absolutely certain we are legitimate and have the blessing of the HOA. This petition drive was launched to ask the HOA residents to approve a simple update to the covenants to permit these very unobtrusive lights."

The guests listened intently as Mike went on. "However, there is one resident who is adamantly opposed to the installation of these lights, even though they in no way impact her property. She has been quite vocal and aggressive in opposing this measure and has, in fact, filed a lawsuit. That's what made it imperative for the club to go the petition route and get the HOA's explicit approval. I feel certain she is behind these flyers which, by the way, are unsigned and provide no contact information. On the other hand, our process has been very transparent."

"But anybody can file a lawsuit and even if it's not legitimate, we would still have to hire attorneys to defend ourselves," one man said. "Who's going to pay for that?"

"I can guarantee that you will not be sued. There is no law or regulation against signing a petition," Mike responded. "This amounts to freedom of speech which, last I heard, is still protected under the U.S. Constitution. And, like most contests in our country, majority rules. We have a clear majority here. Feel free to ask any questions. Also, I will pass around some business cards. Please don't hesitate to contact me free of charge for more information on this."

Liz stepped up. "And by the way folks, any improvements to this facility ultimately boost all our property values—*even yours.*" Lydia cringed. "So in the long run, you'll benefit from these lights whether you're a member of this club or not."

Lydia, visibly grateful for Mike's clear and reassuring words, almost wept out of relief. A few people spoke privately with Mike, then dispersed throughout the grounds as the late afternoon sun reflected off the pool. It turned out to be a fun night after all, and everyone seemed to have a good time. The guards gave some of the kids a free swim lesson, and two couples even danced under the patio lights. Lydia introduced several people to Pete, who graciously gave them a tour of the club. *Maybe we'll get some new members out of this.*

As the sun set, the party began breaking up. Almost all the food and drinks had been consumed. Rex, after a few beers, seemed more relaxed. "I think we've got this one in the bag, but we absolutely need to show up for the HOA meeting," he said.

As Lydia helped him clean up, he finally removed the sunglasses to reveal a still-black eye ringed with yellow. *Wow, Bonnie really decked him.*

"I guess I can't hide this thing forever," Rex sighed. "She was pretty pissed at me."

"What's going to happen with you two?" Lydia couldn't resist asking.

"Oh, nothing. She's back in Texas and probably won't be home for another four or five weeks. We've been through tough times before. Life goes on. The kids will be here for Christmas."

Amazing.

Lydia was back home by nine-thirty. Later, she and Bill sat on the deck and had a celebratory glass of wine while she related what had transpired. It was one of the few times this summer the two of them had really relaxed in their backyard. "You know, winning this battle against Claire feels so great. I've always been intimidated by her, but now—"

Then her phone buzzed. It was a text from Pete.

Bad Moon Rising

SINCE IT was a school night, Pete had let the guards go home as soon as the last of the partygoers left the club. He arranged the deck chairs, hosed off the patio, and cleaned the bathrooms. Turning off the lights, he noticed the sky was black as the moon hid behind a cloud. He made his way to the front gate, and by ten-thirty was pulling out of the parking lot when he phoned Shelly. "Hey, I'll be home in twenty minutes."

Halfway home, however, he noticed that his briefcase wasn't on the passenger seat, where he usually put it. *Shit.* He pulled over and took a flashlight from the glove compartment to search the backseat and trunk with no luck. Angry, he slammed the trunk door down, then made a U-turn to drive back to the club. He pulled into the parking lot and grabbed the flashlight to illuminate the sidewalk.

At the gate, Pete aimed the flashlight at the lock and was startled to see that it was unlocked! *Are you kidding me? How did that happen?* Troubled, he tried to recall how he had exited the club. *Was I in such a rush that I forgot to do something that's second nature? Was it too dark? How could I leave my briefcase and not lock up the club on the same night?*

He decided to let it go and quickly walked to his office. He unlocked the door and there, on his desk, was the briefcase. But as he locked the office back up, he became aware of a dim light coming from the back of the building near the boiler room and trash dumpster. He turned off the flashlight and peeked around the corner. The light was more intense, and he heard low voices engaged in conversation. Then, the smell of cigarette smoke.

"Who's there?" Pete called out. Silence. He turned his flashlight back on and slowly walked toward the boiler room where three men, all wearing baseball caps and long-sleeved shirts, were holding lit-up mobile phones. Two of the men were squat and heavyset with beards. One was smoking.

"What the hell?" Pete asked. "Who are you and what the fuck are you doing back here? How did you get in here? I'm calling the police." He started to pull out his phone to call 911 when one of the heavyset men quickly descended on him and grabbed the device.

"What the—?" Pete gripped the flashlight and shined it directly into the man's eyes, blinding him enough to force him to turn away and drop the phone. "Get away from me, you piece of shit," he said, picking up his phone.

"Nothing to worry about here, Pete. These guys are with me, and we're just conducting a little business. We'll be out of here in a few minutes. You can go on home now." Pete recognized the voice, but in the shadows had a hard time seeing the face of the speaker, who was clearly in charge of whatever was going on.

Walking closer to the dumpster, he pointed his flashlight toward the man's face. Warren Reinhart!

Furious, Pete confronted him with a raised voice. "Warren, what the hell are you doing here at this hour? You're not supposed to be back in this area at all. And who are these guys? If either of them lays a hand on me again, I will press assault charges against all three of you."

"Oh, don't be so dramatic. Remember, Pete, I'm a board member and I have the authority to go anywhere and do anything I want in this place. There is nothing in the bylaws that prohibits me from being in this part of the club. Furthermore, I don't answer to you, you pretentious little asshole. You answer to me. Now get out."

"No! I'm not leaving until I get a straight answer from you. Now, what's going on here?" Pete continued to shine his light onto Warren's face, where beads of sweat were forming on his forehead.

"None of your fucking business. Once more, get out," Warren said as he took a few steps forward, forcing Pete to back up and illuminate a broader section of the area with the flashlight.

Suddenly, Pete stopped. There, on the concrete, were three black bags exactly like the one he had found earlier in the summer containing the $50,000. He shined the light on the bags, then directed it back to Warren, his mind rapidly coming to the realization of what he was seeing.

"What's this, Warren? What's in these bags?" He bent down to pick up one and was grabbed from behind by the two stocky men, causing the flashlight to fall from his hands.

"Get your hands off me, you jerks."

"Tie him up and gag him," Warren instructed the men as he picked up the flashlight. And grab his phone."

Pete struggled, but he was no match for the two thugs. They pulled his phone from his pocket, tied his wrists, and sat him down against the wall of the clubhouse. Then, they bound his feet and placed a strip of duct tape across his mouth.

"You should have left when you had the chance," Warren said. "Now you're in a world of hurt and as far as I'm concerned, you'll never see the light of day." Then he bent down, grabbed Pete's right hand, and ordered, "Unlock your phone."

Pete formed a fist with his hand and shook his head, refusing to cooperate. But one of Warren's lackeys forced open Pete's fist and pressed his forefinger onto the fingerprint reader on his phone. After a few tries, the device unlocked.

"Give it to me," Warren ordered. He scrolled through Pete's list of contacts, finally stopping at Lydia's number. Tapping on the message icon, he sent a text. "Hey. Have something important to show you at the club. Can you come over right now?"

"This is working out perfectly," Warren said, grinning. "I've been trying to figure out how to deal with what have become a couple of nagging problems. Now, I can kill two birds with one stone."

Dodging a Bullet

"HMM, THAT'S odd. Wonder what's going on," Lydia said, showing Pete's text to Bill.

"You've got to be kidding me. It's after eleven o'clock. Can't this wait until tomorrow?" Bill was annoyed.

Lydia called Pete's number. It rang six times before going to voicemail. "He's not answering. It must be something important for him to want me to come over at this hour. Hope he's okay." She sent a text: "Coming over now," then put the phone in her pocket.

"I'm sure everything is fine, but I know I can't talk you out of this," a resigned Bill said. "Stacie and I will walk you down to the club and then I want you to call or text me when you get inside. Ask Pete to drive you home. Take a flashlight."

Bill put the leash on an excited Stacie, who led the way down the sidewalk. He watched as Lydia kept going toward the gate. Even with the streetlights it was quite dark, making it hard to see. "Remember, call me when you get in and make contact with Pete. I'll wait up for you," he called out as Stacie whined.

"Got it."

When she neared the entrance, Lydia tried calling Pete again. Still no answer. She put the phone in her pocket as she turned on the flashlight, barely making out a shadow near the gate. "Hey Pete, what's up? You've got me worried here. At least very curious." She felt a hand firmly grab her arm. "Pete?"

"I'm a friend of Pete's," the man said, pushing her into the club grounds. "I'll take you to him."

"What's wrong? What's happened?" Lydia asked. "Is Pete okay? You don't look like a friend of his. What's going on here? And let go of my arm; you're hurting me." The man was silent. By now, her eyes had adjusted enough to make out that he was short and muscular with a dark beard. He smelled of garlic and sweat. Lydia sensed he hadn't showered in at least a few days.

"You'll find out soon enough," the man responded, gripping her arm even harder and pushing her, causing her to stumble and drop her flashlight.

"Let go of me," Lydia demanded. "I can walk by myself."

The man didn't answer but kept pushing her along the patio toward the pool. As they rounded the corner of the office, Lydia could see a faint light. "Pete?" she called out. "What's going on?"

"Hello Lydia," said a voice that was not Pete's. Then another man turned on a flashlight to illuminate the speaker's face.

"Warren!" Lydia was shocked. "What are you doing here? And where's Pete? Did you two get into it?"

"You could say that," Warren said, shining the light to reveal a bound and gagged Pete propped up against the building, his eyes showing both sadness and fear.

"Oh my God." Lydia began shaking. "Warren, what's happened here?" She started to go toward Pete, but the first man held her back. "Warren! I'm demanding to know what is going on. And who are these guys? This is totally unacceptable — and probably criminal."

"Let her go, Mac," Warren instructed his subordinate. "Well, per usual, Pete stuck his nose into something he shouldn't have, so I've had to get control of the situation."

"What situation? Pete texted me a few minutes ago that there was a problem, and obviously there is. This is appalling. Untie him right now before I call the police."

"Actually Lydia, I'm the one who sent that text. And as for calling the police, that's one thing that *won't* be happening tonight. Here's the deal. As I said, Pete stuck his nose into something that was none of his business. And that's a problem I now need to fix. As it turns out, you've been sticking your nose into matters that aren't any of *your* business either. And that's also a problem. We've been watching you, Lydia. Following you. Keeping tabs on you. We know where you've been and who you've been talking to. Now, I'm going to take care of both of you once and for all."

Lydia's mind was a blur as multiple images began racing through her head. Marge Baker. The shopping center. Warren's mansion. The Majestic Hotel. Searching for the way out she knew was not there, her eyes found the concrete where the powerful flashlight revealed several familiar black cases scattered near the dumpster. *Money bags.* Her mind went to the

$50,000, then to Darrell Baker and Ben Gregorie. *Oh no. Please let this be a bad dream.*

Lydia grew terrified as the dire reality of what was happening began to engulf her. "Warren, please. Please. I'm begging you, please let us go. I have no idea what you're talking about." She started sobbing, then let out a bloodcurdling scream, prompting Mac to put his clammy, smelly hand over her mouth. She gagged.

"Tie her up," Warren instructed the man. "Right next to her boyfriend here. And prop that flashlight on the dumpster so we can see." As Mac shoved her hard against the cement, Lydia felt a sharp pain rip through her right shoulder. "Warren, you can't just leave us here," Lydia said, her adrenaline pumping as the disgusting man tied her hands.

Warren laughed. "Oh, don't worry. I'm not going to leave you here. You'll be long gone before anyone knows you're missing."

"Long gone where?" Lydia asked, feeling her phone vibrate in her pocket. She remembered she was supposed to call Bill when she got into the club grounds. *Please be Bill. No, I am not okay.* "You think you can get rid of us without anyone knowing?" Lydia was grasping at straws, hoping to reason with him.

"Oh, that's the easy part." Warren was on a roll now. "Everyone knows you and Pete have been having an affair all summer. You're always over here, flirting with him, hanging out in his office. I saw all the texts from you on his phone. Every day. This is a no-brainer. You'll leave a note for that loser husband of yours, he'll leave one for his wife, and the two of you will ride off into the sunset. Nobody will be surprised."

As Mac taped her mouth shut, Lydia felt her phone vibrate again. *Please, Bill.* She looked at Pete, whose eyes said *I'm sorry.* No longer able to even communicate with Warren, Lydia suddenly was overcome with nausea. She breathed as deeply as she could to avoid vomiting.

Warren reached for his own phone and walked back toward the boiler room. She could hear his muffled voice but couldn't make out what he was saying. Moments later, she heard a squeaking noise as the iron gate next to the dumpster was pushed open. Then Warren began barking orders at the two men. "Hector, pick up these bags and get rid of the cigarette butts and any other trash. Mac, go lock the main entrance and bring the car around to this gate so we can move everything out."

As Warren tossed Mac the keys, Lydia thought she heard someone else speaking in a low voice near Pete's office. She craned her neck to hear but couldn't make out any words. A faint light appeared in the same area, but it was quickly extinguished just as Mac turned the corner to go to the front gate. Then she heard what sounded like a thump, again near the office. She looked at Pete. His eyes were wide, indicating he had heard what she had. Her eyes moved beyond Pete to Warren, who was on his phone again while the other man, Hector, swept the area with a broom.

"We're ready to go," she heard Warren say into the phone. "Once you get here, we'll get these packages wrapped up and delivered."

Packages? Does he mean Pete and me? Lydia, now almost numb from the reality of what was happening, became vaguely aware of a light out of her right peripheral vision. She turned her head slightly to see someone standing about ten feet away. Bill! He was using his lit cell phone to show his face. *Thank God!* He nodded and gave her a thumbs-up before extinguishing the light and shrinking back into the shadows.

She looked over and saw that Pete also had seen Bill. *What happened to Mac?* A noise turned their attention back to the gate. Someone else had arrived at the party.

"Where's the car?" a woman asked. "I want to get this taken care of as fast as possible." The voice sounded familiar, but Lydia couldn't identify it.

"It's up the street. I sent Mac to get it. He should be here any minute. I'll go check."

"No, you stay put," she ordered. "Where are our friends?"

"Over here," Warren said, guiding the woman over to where Lydia and Pete were tied up.

"Well, looky here."

Lydia looked up but couldn't quite see the woman's face as Warren was blocking the glow from the flashlight. But when Warren turned slightly, Lydia was able to distinctly recognize the speaker—Claire Hoskins!

Lydia looked over at Pete, who was equally shocked and confused at what they were witnessing. *Claire is in cahoots with Warren. And she's the one in charge!*

Dressed in a long-sleeved dark shirt and tight black yoga pants, Claire loomed over Lydia, a broad grin expanding her already bulbous face. She had no makeup on, and her hair was piled on top of her head in a sloppily put-together coil. She bent down and ripped the tape off Lydia's mouth, leaving her able to talk—but speechless.

"So, how are you two lovebirds doing this evening?" Claire asked, her voice dripping with sarcasm. "Nice night for a swim, wouldn't you say?"

A swim? Are you going to throw us in the pool? "Claire, I don't—"

"Shut up, Lydia. You know, your mouth has always been your biggest problem. That, and wanting to be in charge of everything and butt your nose into everybody's business. You should have stayed working at the newspaper."

Yes, I should have.

"Warren!" Claire barked. "Where the hell is that car? I want to get out of here. I hope those two idiots of yours got weights and duct tape to seal the bags this time. We don't need any more evidence surfacing in the river."

The river. They're going to kill us and dump us in the river, Lydia realized, her thoughts turning to Darrell Baker. *This is what happened to him! He figured it out and they killed him.*

"I'm checking now," Warren replied, exiting the gate.

At that, Claire reached behind her back and pulled a gun out of her pants, aiming it straight at Lydia's head. She screamed.

"No! Claire—" *Bill?* Her heart was in her throat.

Thankfully, Claire's attention was broken by what sounded like a loud commotion out on the sidewalk. Claire looked back briefly, then refocused her eyes on Lydia. "I can't wait any longer." She again aimed the gun and prepared to pull the trigger. Lydia shrieked for Bill.

Suddenly Claire flew forward, her head landing with full force on the concrete, the gun sliding out of her hand.

And there, sprawled on top of Claire, was Stacie!

The dog looked over at Lydia, but amazingly stayed where she was to keep Claire down. Seeing what had just transpired, Hector ran toward Claire, desperately searching for the gun, but Bill got there first. As Hector tripped over Claire, falling to the ground, Bill kicked the gun out of Hector's reach, then grabbed it. Pointing the weapon at the thug, Bill ordered him to lie flat.

With Hector on the ground and Stacie atop a seemingly unconscious Claire, Bill went to Lydia and removed the rest of the dangling duct tape from her mouth. She sobbed with relief.

"It's okay, honey. The police are on their way. Good girl, Stacie."

"Bill, there's another guy—"

"I know. I got him with a baseball bat."

"Thank God you got here in time."

"Well, I got to thinking that Pete's text had seemed fishy," he said, as he untied Lydia's feet and hands with his left hand, continuing to point the gun at Hector. "He would never text you if something were *really* wrong. He would call. Then, when you didn't call and I couldn't reach you, I got concerned. So, I grabbed Andy's bat and came over. I was about to deck Claire, but then Stacie attacked her."

Still holding the gun, he turned his attention to Pete. "You okay?" he asked, pulling the tape from his mouth.

"A raging headache, but I'll take it over the alternative."

Now hearing sirens, Lydia started to get up, but was hindered by the excruciating pain in her shoulder. She let out a wail. Bill put the gun down to help her, giving Hector the opportunity to move in and grab for it. Bill kicked the gun away again and Pete jumped Hector, pinning him to the ground. With the two men struggling, Stacie, growling fiercely, moved off the unconscious Claire and started tearing at Hector's shirt collar. Bill reached for the gun. Then Lydia looked up to see Warren, his shirt in tatters and arm bleeding, stagger back in. Stacie ran toward him to finish what she had started. She leaped on his chest, forcing him to fall backward.

As Lydia watched the events unfold, she heard footsteps. Then, "FBI. Everybody, freeze." Two armed men wearing vests and baseball caps entered the area. Both were holding what appeared to be high-capacity guns, with additional guns strapped across their chests. Stacie turned her attention to the two agents and began barking ferociously.

"Stacie, it's okay. Sit!" Bill ordered. The dog obediently stopped in her tracks and went to Lydia. Pete and Bill both held their hands up. "Over against the fence, please," said one of the agents, motioning with his weapon. Pete and Bill dutifully lined up, their hands still in the air. Stacie, her fur up, hovered over Lydia and growled softly.

"I'm Bill Phillips. I'm the one who called this in. These people were going to kill this man and my wife, who is injured and can't move." By now, other law enforcement authorities had descended on the scene. The place was crawling with cops and FBI agents.

With Mac, Claire, and now Warren all incapacitated, only Hector was lucid. His eyes were wide with fear. As one of the FBI agents handcuffed him, reading him his rights, the other bent down to assist Lydia. He looked somewhat familiar, but the poor lighting and the bill of his cap made it difficult to see his full face.

"Hey Lydia, where are you hurt?"

What? You know my name? As a confused Lydia squinted her eyes to try to identify the man, he removed his cap. *Vince Albright!*

"Vince? I can't believe this. You're an FBI agent?"

"Yep, that's right. And over there you'll recognize my partner in crime and life, Special Agent Roger Morey."

Her eyes darting back and forth between the two men, Lydia was once again speechless.

"Where are you hurt, Lydia?" Vince asked again.

"My shoulder. It hurts to move. I can't get up."

"Okay, we'll call an ambulance."

By now, both Pete and Bill had been allowed to move about. Pete called Shelly, while Bill went to Lydia, holding her gently so as not to hurt her shoulder. "Help is on the way. It's all going to be okay," he said. Stacie put her head in Lydia's lap, licking her arm profusely and whining.

Another wave of nausea overtook Lydia as she felt the familiar signs of a migraine. Beads of perspiration began dripping down her face, and she shivered. Her shoulder throbbed. She felt dizzy.

Sirens. Getting louder. Floodlights. Lots of people here. Fred Lyons. Fred Lyons? Is it Adult Swim? Stacie licking. Bill's mouth is moving but I can't hear him. Where are the boys?

Then, darkness.

A Big Break

THE VEHICLE was moving fast. Lydia, awakened by the siren, was lying down, an oxygen mask over her face and an IV in her arm. Her shoulder throbbed. The ambulance was very dim, with only a small light overhead, and red lights were flashing. A woman with a stethoscope was taking her pulse and telling her to take deep breaths. She finally saw Bill seated next to her. He squeezed her hand.

"What's going on, Bill? What am I doing here? What time is it?"

"It's about one a.m. We're in an ambulance, going to the hospital to have your shoulder fixed. Do you remember anything that happened?"

An image of Claire Hoskins popped into her head. She quickly dismissed it, only to see Warren's face. He was wearing a baseball cap. She saw Pete tied up and gagged. Stacie lying on top of Claire, then licking her own arm. Vince Albright. Fred Lyons. "Yes, I remember something terrible happened at the club. Where are the boys?" she asked. "And Stacie? Is Pete okay? I keep thinking I saw Fred Lyons."

"The boys are fine. Everyone is home in bed, including Stacie. And the dog door is in. Everybody's safe. And yes, Fred Lyons was there."

"I'll never get mad again about you guys leaving Stacie's door open," she managed to mumble.

The ambulance stopped under a sign with **EMERGENCY** in big red letters. The woman and a man wheeled her out of the vehicle and into the emergency room. While Bill stayed behind to take care of the insurance and fill out paperwork, Lydia was taken into a curtained area with a bed and monitors. As a nurse helped her get undressed, she cried out in pain.

"I know it hurts," the nurse said. "We're going to get you down to X-ray as soon as possible to see what's going on with that shoulder. I'm giving you a shot to ease the pain." Lydia felt a slight prick in her arm; the pain subsided quickly. She dozed off.

Sometime later, a tall man in a white uniform wheeled her bed into a big elevator and took her into a room with subdued lighting.

"Lydia Phillips?" a woman asked.

"Yes." Lydia was more relaxed now and her shoulder didn't hurt much at all.

"Hi, Mrs. Phillips. Looks like you've had a shoulder injury. We're going to take several pictures from various angles to determine the extent of the damage. This may be a bit uncomfortable."

The process was indeed painful. Lydia winced several times. By the time they were finished, any relief from the painkiller had worn off. Back in her ER cubicle, the nurse gave her another shot. By then, Bill was there.

"Try to get some rest while we wait," he said. "They seem very busy tonight, and this could take awhile."

Lydia woke to the sound of someone flinging open the curtain. The pain had come back. Bill, who had been asleep in a chair, stood to shake hands.

"Hello, I'm Dr. Yang. I'm the orthopedic surgeon on call. I've looked at your X-rays. You've got quite a serious injury here. Can you explain what happened?" His demeanor was cold and very matter-of-fact. He looked over at Bill who, without getting into the gory details, explained that Lydia had found herself in the middle of an incident where she had been pushed hard to the ground, hurting her shoulder.

The doctor looked at Lydia, who nodded in agreement. She then realized the doctor suspected that Bill had done this to her. "That's right, Doctor, my husband's account is accurate. There was an altercation at our swim club last night, and I happened to be in the wrong place at the wrong time. There were several law enforcement agents there, as well as another witness, who can attest to that."

"All right. In that case we'll corroborate everything with the police report."

"And the FBI," noted a visibly furious Bill.

"Now, let's take a look at these X-rays." He put the film up to a lighted box. "As you can see, your humerus bone has broken off the shoulder and shattered. This will require surgery, and we'll need to do it sooner than later. We will place two five-inch pins to hold the bone in place. Then in about six weeks, assuming the healing process has progressed like we hope it will, we'll remove the pins. You'll need significant physical therapy."

"Oh no," Lydia replied. Sickened by what she was hearing and seeing, she began to cry. "I can't believe this."

"I guess we could get a second opinion," Bill offered.

"You can certainly do that, but the longer you put off the surgery, the less successful it will be in terms of long-term outcome, including range of motion," Dr. Yang said.

"Just do it then," Lydia said. "I want to get this over with and move on."

TWO DAYS later she was back home, her right arm in a shoulder immobilizer, propped on the couch in the family room. Stacie and Pink were constantly at her side. Sleep amounted to frequent short naps, as her movement was restricted and she could only lie on her back, which was uncomfortable; any sleep she did get was fitful at best.

Lydia tried hard to put together what had happened. She remembered arriving at the club and being led to the back by a strange man, seeing Pete tied up, and then being pushed to the ground. She knew Bill had been there and called the police but couldn't tell if she actually remembered that or because Bill had told her. She recalled seeing Claire and Warren. The faces of Fred Lyons, Vince Albright, and Roger Morey ran through her mind. And, of course, she vividly remembered Stacie's head in her lap.

But nothing else. She did, however, often wake up in a cold sweat after a recurring nightmare of a gun being pointed at her head. She had no appetite. Taking a shower was an ordeal, and her hair was a mess despite Bill's best efforts at styling. At his insistence, she scheduled a session with a psychologist after Labor Day.

The story of what had happened at Meadow Glen was all over TV and in the newspaper. It seemed the club had been used as a drop-off location for an embezzling scheme that ultimately involved millions of dollars from crooked real estate scams. The story noted that a bag containing $50,000 had been found on the premises earlier in the summer. Warren Reinhart, owner of a local real estate investment firm doing business all over the country, and Claire Hoskins, a well-known tax attorney, had been arrested and charged with multiple counts of fraud, embezzlement, and SEC violations, along with aggravated assault. Both were members of Meadow Glen. Additionally, some thirty civil lawsuits had been filed against WLR Real Estate Ventures. Two other men, Hector Cooley and Mac O'Neal, also had been arrested as accessories to the crimes.

Both Warren and Claire remained hospitalized, recovering from injuries sustained in the melee. A woman not connected to the crimes had suffered minor injuries, the article noted. *Funny what the medical profession considers a minor injury,* Lydia thought, popping another Tylenol.

Unable to recall many details of that fateful night, Lydia grew increasingly frustrated trying to piece together all the loose ends. She still couldn't fathom Claire and Warren in business together. *How did a bright, successful woman like Claire end up in a scam with a not-so-smart guy like Warren? What's the backstory here?*

After a few days, the story died down—as they always do. But Lydia knew it had just scratched the surface, leaving too many unanswered questions. For one thing, how did the authorities connect the dots about the real estate scam? And while she was relieved her name had not been mentioned in the coverage, neither had Darrell Baker's. That case, it seemed, had been long forgotten.

No, this story was far from over.

Provisions and a Pot-Pot

THE HOUSE smelled like a funeral parlor. As news of Lydia's injury got out, bouquets and plants arrived daily, and a parade of friends and neighbors brought enough food to keep the Phillips family well fed for weeks. The refrigerator and freezer were bulging with casseroles, salads, cakes and pies, a roasted turkey, soups, and fruit baskets.

"Well, have you learned your lesson?" asked Susan Adams, one of the first to pay a visit and bring a casserole. "Take this as a sign to never volunteer for anything again. You were safer covering drive-by shootings and drug busts."

Lydia rolled her eyes.

Bill, who was working from home, took charge of the household with help from the boys, who loved that the larder was stocked to the brim. "Wow, we've never had this much food in the house," Geoff remarked, causing Lydia to cringe. *Maybe if I'd paid more attention to feeding my kids, I wouldn't be in this position.*

Less than a week after surgery, Lydia began venturing beyond her perch on the couch, taking two to three walks a day. She had started physical therapy, supplementing it with at-home exercises, a regimen that was difficult, painful, and exhausting. Between frequent naps, she spent a lot of time icing her shoulder. When he wasn't in the kitchen, Bill waited on Lydia, delivering fresh bags of ice at all hours, and took care of some overdue chores around the house. "Fixed the ceiling fan!" he announced one morning, coming down the stairs.

Once she started feeling a little better, however, Lydia began to fret about what *wasn't* getting done. With just a little more than a week until Labor Day, she started panicking. *Just because I broke my arm, doesn't mean I can put Meadow Glen on hold. I'm still responsible,* she thought, her Type A personality winning out over sound judgment. Despite Bill's strong objections, she managed, albeit painfully, to send out a blast e-mail to the board calling for a special meeting. The response was immediate, and less than twenty-four hours later, the entire board —minus Warren, Lawrence, and Amanda—showed up, most of them bringing food.

The house was a mess, the couch exhibiting a noticeable sag and the coffee table littered with large rubber bands and other exercise implements, coffee mugs, glasses, magazines, and plates. The kitchen was full of dirty dishes as Geoff, who was on cleanup duty that night, hadn't gotten around to it.

The group gathered around the spacious dining room table in the main floor's only clean room, furnished with antiques, a massive, deep blue and red oriental rug, and a bay window with plantation shutters. Several watercolor landscapes had been hung strategically on the blue-and-white-wallpapered walls.

"You know, I have a great hairdresser who is just the best at short, easy-to-manage haircuts," Liz offered, looking at Lydia's disheveled mop. "And he does wonders with color and covering up gray roots."

Gritting her teeth and forcing a smile, Lydia responded, "Thank you, Liz. I'll put that on my to-do list."

After giving her sketchy account of what had happened that fateful night, she called the meeting to order. Things were amazingly under control.

"Given what has transpired, Claire Hoskins' lawsuit is obviously moot," Mike Patterson announced. He and Rex had turned the signed petitions over to the HOA and received the official go-ahead to install the remaining lights. "We'll be able to report to the membership that this issue has been resolved."

"Mike and Rex, thank you so much for shepherding that through," Lydia said. "It looks like our agenda for the annual meeting on Labor Day will be to deliver that good news and give the usual committee reports. And for the first time in many years, we can give a positive long-range planning report," she said, looking at George Bishop.

"Yep. We should be able to move forward with the overdue painting and landscape projects and, of course, proceed with the lights on the remaining tennis courts and throughout the grounds."

"Ron, I'll send the agenda to you to post on the website, which also will include a call for new board members," Mike added, directing his attention to the website manager. "We'll obviously need a new treasurer. And a new Swim chair. Lawrence Haskell resigned." Unable to stifle a smile, Lydia recalled she had neither seen nor heard anything about Lawrence since his public upchucking.

"What about the Labor Day barbecue?" she asked.

"I'll check with Amanda but as I recall, the caterer was set up weeks ago," Mike said.

As Lydia was about to adjourn the meeting, Ron Gutierrez raised his hand. "Uh, you probably haven't checked the website lately, but there are more than thirty, I'll say, 'comments' from members asking about the recent incident. Most of these people are quite upset and want an explanation as to how all this could have happened. Some are threatening to drop their memberships."

Great. "Well Ron, I obviously can't type very well, so I'm not able to respond to these people. And there's not much more to add beyond what's been in the news. What do you think we should do?"

"I can take a stab at a brief board statement, run it by you, and post it. Also, maybe it would be nice to comp everyone's lunch as a gesture of appreciation for their patience over this whole mess and since the club had to be closed for a few days while the police investigated."

"That's a great idea. I think we should do it," Lydia said. The board unanimously agreed. "By the way," she added, "if Pete hadn't confronted these guys, this never would have been discovered. He deserves a lot of the credit. We need to make sure we recognize that in the statement."

"Got it."

With things finally under control, Lydia felt much better; even her shoulder didn't seem to throb as much.

Ron had a draft of the board's statement for her to review the next day, and within a few hours it was posted:

To Members of Meadow Glen Swim and Tennis Club

As you no doubt have heard from TV and newspaper accounts, an unfortunate incident occurred recently at the club involving two members, who have been arrested and charged with several financial crimes. We are confident that law enforcement authorities will be diligent in pursuing this case. We also believe those same members were responsible for a matter that occurred earlier this summer when a black bag containing $50,000 in cash was found on the grounds.

We understand events of this nature are very unsettling, and we sincerely hope you will be patient in the coming months as the

investigation and judicial process continue. **Additionally, we owe a huge debt of gratitude to our manager, Pete Merrick, who uncovered these illegal activities while working off-hours at the club.**

We encourage everyone to attend our annual Membership Meeting at 11:30 a.m. on Labor Day, where we will present any updated information and where you will have the opportunity to ask questions. We also will report on other club activities, including our vision for the coming year and beyond, and elect new board members. Please send an e-mail to Mike Patterson if you are interested in joining the board.

In appreciation of your support, the club is hosting a picnic lunch on Labor Day <u>FREE OF CHARGE.</u> Please RSVP using the attached form, or by signing up at the Sugar Shack.

Thank you again, and we look forward to seeing you on Labor Day.

Sincerely,

The Meadow Glen Board of Directors

THE NOTICE prompted another round of visitors to the house—among them Jules, who appeared unannounced on the doorstep one afternoon wearing a long red-and-yellow cotton shift and dangling peace symbol earrings, with her hair neatly pulled back in a braid. Lydia detected the faint odor of marijuana and incense as Jules, who seemed to have finally gotten over her summer-long malaise, entered the front hall. She even brought a gift, which was beautifully wrapped in sunflower print paper and tied with a purple bow.

"Lydia, I wanted to give you one of my pot-pots—with a special surprise inside," Jules said, helping Lydia carefully remove the paper and open the box to reveal a small, deep blue ceramic jar with yellow and white flowers painted on it.

Lydia was overwhelmed. "Oh, Jules, how nice of you. Thank you so much. This means a lot to me. It's lovely, and I will treasure it." Looking inside, she saw a baggie containing some candies and a small vial.

"These will ease your pain, help you sleep, and relax you," Jules advised. "They are very safe. Take one candy at a time, and I would wait at least four to six hours before taking another one—depending on how you feel. It takes a while for the edibles to kick in, but they last longer. Same for the oil. Put a drop under your tongue at night and you'll sleep like a baby."

"I will definitely keep that in mind." Brushing away some of the litter on the couch, Lydia motioned for her guest to sit down. "Jules, I'm hoping we can put this awful, miserable summer behind us. It's been very bizarre and stressful, and I am so sorry for suspecting you might have had something to do with that found money. Obviously, that was not the case at all. I know now you are not selling drugs. I am so very sorry."

Tears welled up in Jules's eyes, and she suddenly engulfed Lydia in a big bear hug, carefully avoiding her wounded shoulder. "Of course, I forgive you. I know I've been mad at you, but I don't want to be mad anymore. All that negative energy is so unhealthy. I've been out of sync all summer. We've known each other so long."

The two women talked, laughing about the club, the exploding FunFro machine, the mess, the sex-capades. Connecting the way they had years ago, Lydia recalled how bright and engaging Jules could be. She felt a wave of sympathy for this woman who had fallen on such hard times. "When I get out of this ridiculous sling, we're going out for drinks," Lydia announced, reaching for another hug.

As Jules was leaving, Ernestine, wearing a pair of wrinkled off-white linen slacks, a loose-fitting pink blouse, and yet another one of her big floppy hats, was coming up the steps carrying a large wooden bowl. Lydia, exhausted and her shoulder aching, took a deep breath.

"Lydia, how ahhr you?" she said in her feigned New England accent. "I've brought a big salad for your dinner tonight. It's all organic, lots of kale, spinach, antioxidants, and other good things conducive to healing. And here is the dressing, also organic. The salad should keep for a few days. May I come in?"

"Yes, of course, Ernestine. How thoughtful of you. Please, have a seat."

The woman looked apprehensively at the cluttered, sagging sofa, then sat down on the edge. Stacie eyed her suspiciously from across the room. "Do you think you'll ever get back full use of your arm?" Ernestine asked, her voice reduced to almost a whisper. "I just can't imagine... well, you know...being that way."

"Of course I'll have full use of my arm!" Lydia answered, unable to hide her annoyance at the question, which reflected Ernestine's penchant for always looking at the negative side of things. "I'm getting better every day and doing lots of PT. I should be in very good shape in a couple of months, and the doctor tells me I'll be back on the tennis court next year."

"That's so good to hear," she said breathlessly. "You know, I was thinking the club should install a state-of-the-art alarm system with wires at all the gates and detectors and cameras along the fence that would alert the police if someone breaks in. That way, anyone who even tries to get in at night would be spotted immediately, and we could avoid problems like this going forward."

Lydia steadied herself. "That's a great idea Ernestine, but it would be quite expensive and probably not a good investment for a three-month summer club. This was a highly unusual situation that has now been resolved. Plus, as a board member, Warren had a key. So, I don't see that in the cards."

"Oh, I disagree. I'm hearing that everyone is quite upset about what happened, and I think having a security system would go a long way to calming nerves. It may even attract new members, you know set us apart from the other clubs. People want to know they're safe, especially when it comes to their children. You can't be too careful this day and age."

Lydia chose not to argue. "Tell you what. I will bring your concerns up with Mike Patterson, the president-elect, and the new board can consider it."

Ernestine stayed another twenty minutes, mostly to talk about her daughters. "Gwen has been accepted into the gifted and talented program, and Claudia is taking all AP and honors classes. Most children can't take that kind of pressure, but she thrives on it. How are your boys doing this year?"

"They're fine. Taking mostly regular classes. You know, they're the only kids at Roosevelt High who aren't gifted."

"Oh!" Ernestine said, after several seconds of awkward silence. She quickly stood up to leave, car keys in hand. "Time for me to get going. The girls will be home any minute. Enjoy the salad."

There was no room in the refrigerator for Ernestine's salad bowl so Lydia left it on the counter, hoping someone would either get rid of the salad or put it in a plastic bag and forget about it. *There's no way Bill or the boys will eat one bite of this.* She pulled an icepack out of the freezer and plopped down on the couch, drifting off into a fitful sleep.

The doorbell jolted her awake. It was Pete, who she had not seen since the night of the incident, and Shelly. "I've been wanting to come by, but thought I'd give you some time to recover," he said. "Then when I saw the letter on the website, I figured you were back at it. By the way, thanks for the kudos. I know that was from you."

"Hey, you two. Thanks so much for coming over," Lydia said, giving Pete a hug, then reaching out to embrace Shelly who was holding a plate of cookies and a large vase with a colorful array of fresh flowers. "I know you've been inundated with food and flowers, but I wanted to do *something*," Shelly said.

"Thank you. The flowers are absolutely gorgeous. And cookies and brownies have become my favorite go-to snacks. I can eat them one-handed."

"How are you doing?" Pete asked, as he and Shelly followed Lydia to the kitchen with Stacie following close behind. Shelly bent down to scratch the dog's ears. "I hear you're quite the heroine," she said. Stacie wagged her tail and wiggled, lapping up the attention.

"I'm okay," Lydia said, not convincingly. "I'm doing a ton of PT and getting sleep when I can. It's pretty uncomfortable, and I'm learning how to be left-handed. It's very restricting. More importantly, how are *you* doing?" She thought Pete looked tired and thin.

"Fine, physically. But I'm having a rough time with the mental images," Pete said. "I'm not into guns, so the whole thing was really traumatic. I felt so bad when I saw that goon bring you to the back and tie you up. I don't think I've ever felt so useless. I'm going to see a shrink next week."

"There was nothing you could have done," Lydia reassured him, attempting to hide her angst at Pete's alarming revelation about guns. A reminder of her recurring dream fleetingly surfaced. "Please don't give it another thought. I'm going to get some psychotherapy too. I can't remember a lot of what happened, and Bill thinks I'm repressing some things."

"That's certainly understandable. It will probably take both of us awhile to get over this. Now I've got an inkling of what PTSD must be like."

Lydia stifled the urge to ask him if he was still planning on returning next summer. *Let's get the club closed and let some time pass.*

The two stayed for about half an hour. As they walked out the front door, Lydia's phone rang.

"Lydia. Got a minute? You and I need to talk." It was Vern Livingston from the *Beacon-News*.

A Star Is Born

"**V**ERN, NICE to hear from you. I've been reading your stories on what happened at our swim club. You've done a great job. What's up?" Lydia made an effort to sound especially upbeat, knowing that Vern was likely fishing for something.

"I was hoping you could tell me. I heard you had a pretty bad injury and had to have surgery. Sounds like you had a close call, with Claire Hoskins pointing a nine-millimeter handgun at your head. Good thing the Feds showed up in the nick of time. I heard your husband was there, too. How did you get mixed up in this thing anyway?"

Claire pointing a nine-millimeter at me? Oh God. Is that what happened? Lydia broke out into a cold sweat. "Uh, we happened to be at the club late that night, cleaning up after a little party, and found ourselves in the middle of this fiasco. To be honest, I can't remember much of what happened." Lydia thought it best not to go into the details of what she did remember, thinking Vern was taking notes. "What are you hearing?"

"The cops are still doing their investigation. Warren Reinhart got released from the hospital yesterday and is in jail. Claire Hoskins is still in a rehab facility. She has a very serious head injury."

"Not a lot of big developments, I guess. How did the police know about all these fraudulent real estate schemes?" *And what about poor Darrell Baker?* she thought, wondering if anyone had made that connection.

"That was the FBI. I don't have as many sources there, but apparently these two left a trail of bad deals all over the country, and the FBI has been tracking them for months. It will take awhile to unravel everything. Should be a great story when it all comes out, though.

"Anyway, I was wondering if you'd be willing to do an interview and talk about what happened from your perspective. You know how people love survival stories."

Lydia was stunned. "You want to interview *me*?" She thought a moment. *I guess I am the victim here.* "Well, as I said, there's a lot I don't remember, and at one point I blacked out. So I don't think I could give you much."

"What about your husband?"

"Bill? Oh, God no. He would never agree to be interviewed."

Just then, Stacie came trotting in from the backyard, her tail wagging as she spotted Lydia, and picked up Pink.

"You know, Vern, the real hero of this story is my dog. She's the one who stopped Warren in his tracks and knocked out Claire. She has a habit of jumping the fence and going over to the club, and that night she prevented Claire and Warren from carrying out whatever they had planned. So, she's really the story."

"Well, I can't exactly interview a dog," Vern quipped after a long pause.

"Yes, I know that, Vern, but I — or Bill and I — could give you the background of how Stacie intervened, and you could get some pictures. She's very photogenic, and people love dog stories. Of course, I would have to run it by Bill first."

"Okay, I'll pose it to the folks here. I don't do animal stories, so we'll probably just send a photog and an intern. I'll get back to you." He hung up the phone abruptly.

Grudgingly, Bill acquiesced to the story on Stacie — with the caveat that only Stacie would be photographed, and that the boys not be photographed or mentioned.

"We need to give him something or he'll keep bugging me," Lydia had argued in presenting the idea to Bill. "By the way, Vern said Claire pointed a gun at my head. Is that true?"

Bill hesitated. "Yes," he acknowledged. "I had inched my way along the fence and was about to hit her with the bat when Stacie intervened."

"Why didn't you tell me?"

"Since you've obviously blocked it, I was hoping you would remember that detail in therapy so a professional could help you."

"Okay, let's avoid any discussion of that with the paper," said Lydia, now glad that Bill had insisted she get some counseling. She also informed Pete of the interview.

"As long as I don't have to be there and my name's not mentioned, I don't care," Pete said.

THE FOLLOWING afternoon, a shy, twenty-something woman and photographer showed up at the house. Mindful of Liz's critique on her hair, Lydia had managed to get a hair appointment, and came home with a short cut that was easy for Bill to style. She also had gotten her roots dyed. She had to admit she looked ten years younger.

The boys had rushed home from school and put a red and white bandana on Stacie, who reveled in the attention and submitted to several poses for the camera. Bill and Lydia told the story of how the dog saved the day.

"It was really just a coincidence," Lydia said. "We'd had a little party up at the club that night. Our club manager, who stayed late to clean up, caught Warren Reinhart and his thugs bagging money they had allegedly embezzled from their real estate deals. These folks got hold of the manager's phone to text me to come to the club, and then tied up both of us. Then, Claire Hoskins showed up."

"And why did they want you to come to the club?"

"Uh, well, let me see—" Lydia desperately searched for a good explanation that would not reveal the fact that Warren had known she was snooping around and wanted to silence her. "I knew the manager had been there late, and I suppose these people wanted to scare me or silence me from saying anything in case he got injured or disappeared or something."

Before the confused-looking reporter could pursue the issue further, Bill picked up the narrative. "I got suspicious when I didn't hear from Lydia, so I went up to the club with a baseball bat, saw what was going on, and called the police. Our boys were in bed already, and in my rush to get out of the house, I forgot to close Stacie's door." Stacie's ears perked up at the mention of her name.

"Stacie hates to be left alone, and if her dog door is left open when we're gone, she goes out, jumps the fence, and bolts over to Meadow Glen," Lydia explained. "She's done it several times this summer. She's very comfortable there. Everybody knows her. She loves to swim in the pool and chase the resident ducks.

"Anyway, when she sensed I was in danger, she jumped Warren and attacked Claire, causing her to hit her head on the concrete. Then she stayed with me until I was taken to the hospital. She's a good girl and is very attached to everyone in the family, especially me." Stacie's tail thumped the carpet as she lay her head on Lydia's lap.

THE STORY ran the day before Labor Day, with Stacie's photo on the front page. The boys were ecstatic. Bill was relieved it was over.

"Oh, it wasn't that bad," Lydia chided him, picking up her vibrating phone.

"Hello, Mrs. Phillips?"

"Yes, this is Lydia. Who's calling?"

"This is Fred Lyons. I'm a member of Meadow Glen."

Fred Lyons. "Yes, of course, Fred," Lydia said, an image of his great white girth and goggles on his zinc oxide-covered face popping into her head. "I know who you are. You're our resident lap swimmer. And a very disciplined one, I might add."

"Yes, I guess so," he chuckled. "I'm calling because I read the story about your dog in the paper today. Quite an interesting account."

"Oh, thank you. She loved it. The newspaper initially wanted to interview me, but I'm a little foggy on everything that happened so I suggested we make it a more light-hearted feature focusing on Stacie."

"Stacie deserves a medal for probably saving your life," he said, "and I can certainly appreciate how you may have blocked out some of the details. That's not unusual in circumstances like this. You know, I was there that night. Perhaps I can fill in the gaps."

Thick as Thieves

THE DOORBELL rang promptly at four o'clock. Fred Lyons, whose imposing frame and bulging torso overwhelmed most of the doorway, looked out of place in khaki pants, a red-checked shirt, and running shoes. Lydia realized she had never seen him in street clothes. His bald head, freckled face, and arms were scarred from what looked like skin cancer removals. She guessed him to be around sixty.

Surprisingly, he was accompanied by Meadow Glen member and FBI Special Agent Vince Albright.

"Hello, Mrs. Phillips. Nice to see you. I brought Vince along to keep me honest and make sure I get all my facts straight."

"Hi, Fred. Please, call me Lydia," she said, confused as to how the two men even knew each other. "Vince, so good to see you. Fred, this is my husband, Bill. And this is Pete Merrick. I thought Pete might be interested in what you have to say since he was there that night. I hope you don't mind."

"Of course not," Fred said, shaking Bill's and Pete's hands.

"Hey, Vince," Bill said, extending his hand. "I have to say, seeing you that fateful night was sure a sight for sore eyes."

"Glad I was there to help," Vince said. "Since Roger and the kids are out of town, I was more than happy to tag along with Fred today. Looks like you're on the mend, Lydia."

"I'm getting there," she said, leading the group into the dining room, where Bill had put out a pitcher of lemonade, some waters, and two plates of cookies.

After exchanging pleasantries, Fred said, "Let's get down to the reason we're here. I imagine you all would like to piece together this puzzle of strange events. We're still conducting our investigation, but we can give you a pretty good summary of what has transpired at Meadow Glen over the summer. By the way, Warren Reinhart has been quite cooperative, basically implicating Claire Hoskins as the mastermind of the whole plot."

"Hold on," said Bill, looking at Fred. "*You're* involved in this? I thought you were just an innocent bystander who happened to be at the scene that night. You're CIA, right? How is this a CIA case?"

"FBI," Fred corrected him. "Soon to retire. This case came up about a year ago."

"As much as I dislike Claire, I never imagined she would stoop this low," Lydia said, now comprehending the connection between Fred and Vince. "But why the FBI?"

"Well, this is a white-collar crime case that involves a complex real estate scam, embezzlement, and securities fraud spanning across several states," Fred explained. "Therefore, it falls under our jurisdiction. In financial cases like this, we investigate and partner with other law enforcement agencies, including police departments, the Securities and Exchange Commission, and even the IRS. In this instance, there's a good chance a grand jury will be called."

Her thoughts turning to the meeting with Ben Gregorie and his lawsuit against Warren, Lydia realized she probably already knew a lot of the story. Bill, of course, had no knowledge of any of it—and knew nothing about that meeting. She hoped it would stay that way.

Vince began with some background. "Warren Reinhart has been on the radar of the Feds for years. He's been in repeated hot water with the IRS over failure to pay taxes but has managed to avoid formal tax evasion charges by using a number of tax loopholes. That's because he's had a good lawyer—Claire Hoskins."

"Aha," Pete said. "The plot thickens."

"Warren began dabbling in real estate investment deals more than fifteen years ago when he began buying homes in transitioning neighborhoods and flipping them," Vince said. "Then in 2008, the recession hit. That set him back big time. He sold commercial real estate for a few years then set up a company, WLR Real Estate Ventures, which purchased commercial real estate properties, primarily strip centers in gentrifying neighborhoods, by putting together groups of investors. His first deal involved the purchase of a retail establishment outside of Atlanta for eleven million dollars about nine years ago. That investment proved to be pretty successful. He sold it four years later for a profit—about three million—when prices started rising. Somewhere along the way, he came across a firm called TRBD Strategies, which procured investors for nontraditional investments. It turns out that the managing partner of that firm has had his own problems with the IRS and the SEC."

"Yeah, I'm familiar with that ilk from my years on Wall Street," Pete noted. "You've got to be careful with those guys. Often, they're not even licensed. They present themselves as above-board, but some of their clients can be on the shady side. What exactly did this firm do?"

"They would put together a slick, professional-looking prospectus with all kinds of charts and graphs, which they would then use to lure investors with the promise of huge returns," Fred explained. "For a fee, TRBD Strategies put investors in touch with companies like WLR Real Estate Ventures. Then, this firm would simply move on to the next deal without providing any oversight. They were just the middleman.

"Warren would take the investors' money in exchange for membership interests in various LLCs, which would then purchase commercial properties. The investors would profit from the stream of income generated by rents as the properties appreciated in value. When a property sold, presumably at a profit, the investors would see a big payday.

"The investors also were sold promissory notes with varying interest rates and durations, usually between twelve and eighteen months. The objective was to raise cash quickly," Fred said. "Typically, the first few months of payments would be interest-only, followed by a year or so of principal and interest. However, these notes are considered securities by the SEC and state securities agencies. People who sell them are required to be licensed and to register the notes. Warren did neither."

Exactly what Ben got involved in, Lydia thought. "What happened with this TRBD company?"

"It shut down months ago, and we haven't been able to locate the managing partner. He's basically disappeared into thin air. Eventually, we'll find him."

"This is brilliant," Bill said. "Warren made it simple for these people to get involved in what looked like risk-free passive income generators — PIGS."

"That's right," Vince said. "As the economy continued to improve, this firm in Atlanta set Warren up with a huge number of investors to purchase commercial properties all over the country. At one point, he had close to fifty properties, with investors paying his company more than five hundred million dollars. However, it appears that Warren may have gotten in over his head. About a year ago, investors in some of these deals began filing lawsuits because after the first six months or so, they weren't receiving the expected income and weren't being paid on the promissory notes. Either the payments fell short or didn't materialize at all due to some fabricated catastrophic event or sudden loss of rental income, which WLR promised it would make up. In more than a few instances, these properties were being sold without the investors even knowing it. And in some cases, WLR, with help from TRBD Strategies, even lured investors into real estate deals where the properties they were investing in had already been sold. They were buying—well, nothing. Pure fraud."

Lydia vividly recalled her meeting with Ben, and how his experience confirmed what Vince was now saying.

"Let me guess," Pete said. "Warren was floating money. He would acquire new properties with new investors' capital, then comingle that money with that of the other LLCs to keep the payments going to the older investors. When he ran out of money, he would either make up a story or, more likely, sell off a property and not tell the investors but continue to pay out at least some amount in monthly distributions while stringing the investors along. And, of course, skimming off the extra profit for himself."

"This sounds like a Ponzi scheme," Bill said. "He needed continued influxes of cash from new investors to keep paying the old ones."

"Pretty much," Pete said. "And no matter how much cash he took in, it was never enough."

"Exactly," Fred said. "When these lawsuits started cropping up, the SEC and various state agencies, along with the FBI, began watching Warren as he continued seeking new investors for properties, not informing them of his company's existing debt and losses. Interestingly, around this time Warren began making lavish purchases: an expensive new home, several new cars; he joined a country club and spent a lot of money on overseas trips, among other things."

Images of Warren's fancy mansion with its expansive lawn and gardens and the garage with the high-end Mercedes filled Lydia's head.

"The WLR books, which Warren willingly turned over to the authorities, indicate the company currently has a negative equity of close to two hundred and fifty million and about ninety million in unpaid, overdue promissory notes," Fred added.

Lydia was dumbfounded. "How could someone get to this point and live this way?"

"Oh, people extend themselves all the time," Pete responded. "They simply can't stop spending. This just happens to be an extreme example of it. People have a way of separating their personal lives from their professional ones. And, a lot of times they get away with it."

"So, where does Claire Hoskins come into the picture?" Bill asked.

"Good question," Fred said. "Based on Warren's past real estate dealings, which indicate he isn't the sharpest bulb in the box, we figured he had to be partnering with someone. You don't all of a sudden go from being a small-time residential real estate flipper to running an operation this complex and lucrative. So, about nine months ago we put a tail on him, and the destination he frequented most often was—"

"Meadow Glen Swim and Tennis Club," Pete exclaimed.

"You got it," Fred confirmed. "Which was quite strange, since for most of this time the club was closed. In addition, all the visits were at night. Since Meadow Glen is private property, we couldn't trespass, and we didn't have enough solid evidence to go on yet to obtain a search warrant or set up a sting.

"However, we had something almost as good. Coincidentally, Vince here, one of this FBI field office's best agents, is also a member of the club. So, we assigned him to do some digging, go through the directory to come up with some leads of potential business accomplices. And the most obvious one to surface was you, Pete."

"Me! How in the hell did you make that connection?"

"Well, you've got a strong financial background, worked on Wall Street, and would obviously have some knowledge of these types of investment arrangements," Vince pointed out. "Believe me, we did our homework. You were extremely successful as a portfolio manager. And as the club manager, you had complete access to the grounds. As did Warren, it turns out."

The keys. This was all starting to make sense to Lydia. "That's why Warren freaked out when we rekeyed the club and was so insistent on getting a new key so quickly. He was effectively locked out of his secret rendezvous spot."

"That would be my guess," Vince said. "And, based on our conversations with Warren, that was the purpose of the break-in at this house back in June."

Lydia had almost forgotten about the incident that had occurred on Steak Night.

"Warren absolutely needed a key," Vince said. "He had a two guys, Mac O'Neal and Hector Cooley, he used as bodyguards and to handle his more sordid dealings. He enlisted them to break into your house to find a key. Unfortunately, you interrupted them. Wasn't that around the time you found the money under the dumpster?"

"Yes! It was the next day," Lydia remembered.

"Wait a minute," Pete said. "I want to get back to me being the alleged accomplice. Was I close to being arrested?"

"We never got to that point, but we did surveil you," Vince said.

Pete thought a minute. "The blue sedan! That was you?"

"Yep, those were our guys. In fact, sometimes it was me behind the wheel. That's why we could never let you get close to the car. We had a tail on you for weeks but could never come up with anything. We'd watch your house at night, then follow you to Meadow Glen and back. You actually lead a pretty boring life."

"I guess that's a good thing."

"But I remember seeing that car in broad daylight, across the street from the club and near my house," Lydia said. "And then early one morning a few weeks ago, I saw it in front of Claire's house."

"We're getting to that part," Fred assured her. "After you found that money and turned it over to the police, we figured we were barking up the wrong tree with Pete, so we were back to square one. Meanwhile, Vince was still keeping his eyes and ears open. And by this time, his partner, FBI Special Agent Roger Morey, and their two kids began using the club. Roger is another one of our best agents. I'm sorry to say we'll be losing him, as he's starting law school this fall.

"Anyway, as we dug deeper into Warren's past tax problems, we were able to connect him to Claire. So, early last month we started keeping tabs on her. Over the past several weeks, Warren has frequented her place several times. These weren't social calls. Looking in the window, we saw them engaged in a number of what looked like heated discussions."

Lydia recalled seeing Warren and Claire having a very animated conversation in Claire's kitchen the morning she had met with Ben.

"After Warren confessed they were in cahoots, he gave us the background on how this whole real estate scam got started," Vince continued. "As I mentioned, Claire had helped Warren out with some tax issues several years ago. So, when Warren started up his commercial real estate investment business, she became one of his earliest and, it turns out, most prolific investors. According to Warren, she was the one who concocted the whole scam. It was her idea to issue the promissory notes and skim off cash from the get-go, funneling it to offshore bank accounts. Warren traveled to the Cayman Islands once every six to eight weeks. They figured they could each eventually make off with tens of millions of dollars, then simply declare the company bankrupt.

"Claire was adamant that there be no e-mails, phone exchanges or voicemails, and no local bank accounts in which to deposit the money. That way, nothing could be traced," Vince said. "That's why they used the club for their meetings, to distribute the money, and pay the two hired guns. Warren would send Claire a terse, obscure text when they needed to meet, which was about once or twice a month. She liked the club because it was proximate to her own home, and was a rundown, nondescript building that was closed most of the year. Plus, Warren had access. And, it was dark. Warren said that when the weather turned cold, he used his key to access the manager's office and even brought in a portable heater to have their meetings."

"That's why Claire was so fiercely opposed to the tennis court lights!" Lydia realized. "She didn't want anything done that might expose their secret hideout."

"Let me get this straight," Pete said. "Warren and Claire were using the club to meet and distribute their embezzled monies and therefore keep the operation separate from their offices and homes. Warren had access with his key, and Claire could walk over. But when we rekeyed the club, neither of them could get in. So that night back in June when he couldn't get into the club grounds, he just threw the money over the fence, hoping no one would find it. The next day, it got lodged under the trash dumpster when Sam rolled it back in from the curb."

Lydia completed the scenario. "Warren couldn't retrieve the money that morning because there was a swim meet going on, with a few hundred people on the grounds and the back area effectively blocked off." She recalled how Warren had strangely interrupted the meet, imploring Lydia to give him his key, then showed up at her house to again demand one. "Failing to get a key from me, he figured he would find one at our house the following night when we were out, then let himself into the club later, take the money, and run."

"Thanks to our amazing four-footed friend here, that plan never materialized," Bill said. "Lydia interrupted them when she went home to retrieve the leash after Stacie so unceremoniously crashed Steak Night." Stacie, who was napping next to Bill, sleepily raised her head, her tail wagging slightly.

"Of course, he would have had a hell of a time retrieving it from under the dumpster," Pete observed.

"At that point, it became quite obvious that as long as Meadow Glen was open for the summer — at least until the season started to wind down — it was a risky place for Warren and Claire to secretly meet," Fred said. "So, they resorted to meeting late at night or early in the morning at Claire's house, which we were able to document with our ongoing surveillance. That's when things really started to come together for us."

"It sounds like Warren has thrown Claire under the bus," Lydia noted. "Is that going to save him?"

"Yes and no," Fred responded. "In exchange for delivering Claire, he'll probably plead to a reduced charge like tax evasion or misappropriation of funds on the financial charges and be sentenced to a few years in prison. Since he was unconscious when Claire pulled her gun and threatened you, he probably can avoid an attempted murder charge. But he'll lose everything — his house, cars, jewelry — to make restitution to his victims once all these LLCs get sorted out, which could take years. He'll of course lose his real estate license and will never regain it. In other words, he is ruined — financially and personally."

Vince, however, suggested the stakes were even higher. "A ruined career is going to be the least of Warren's problems," he said. "There's been another development in the case. And it's much bigger than any financial misconduct or someone waving a gun around."

Nothing But the Truth

LYDIA STARED at the floor. Her shoulder was throbbing, but she hardly noticed as she digested Vince's jolting words about a new development. She had a pretty good idea where the story was going.

By now, it was going on dinnertime. Geoff came in from a tennis match. "I won," he announced, opening the refrigerator, oblivious to the group in the dining room. "When are we having dinner? I'm starving." Hearing the word "dinner," Stacie shot up and made a beeline for the kitchen.

"Good going, Geoff," Bill said. "How about we take a break and have something to eat?" he suggested, directing his attention to Fred and Pete. "Would either of you like a beer or a glass of wine?"

"Oh, I don't want to impose," Fred said. "Maybe we can pick this up another time."

"No, please stay," said Lydia. "We have enough food for an army. Bill, can you heat up one of those casseroles? Pete, why don't you call Shelly and have her come, too." Turning her attention to Geoff, she said, "That's great, honey. Congrats. Where's your brother?"

"I have no clue. Probably playing a video game."

"No, I was doing homework," Andy said, coming down the stairs.

"You're kidding. Homework on a weekend night? I'm impressed." Bill started clapping.

After Bill and the boys set the table and heated up food, the Phillips family, Fred, Vince, Pete, and Shelly gathered around the table to a dinner of chicken and broccoli casserole, French bread, and some of Ernestine's kale salad that Bill had managed to stuff into a plastic bag and refrigerate. It was not a hit. "What is this?" Andy asked. "It tastes like dirt. This is the worst crap I've ever eaten." Despite the rude assessment, Lydia couldn't chide him as she was having a hard time gagging it down herself. The boys were otherwise in good spirits and quite talkative, finding a receptive audience in Pete who engaged them in a challenging discussion about math theory. Stacie strategically planted herself under the table. And after two glasses of wine, Fred became quite jovial, regaling the group with FBI stories from his career.

"What's for dessert?" Andy asked.

"Here's an idea," Bill said. "If you guys can do KP duty, I'll give you ten bucks to go get some ice cream. Just be home by eleven."

The boys quickly cleared the table, loaded the dishwasher, and made their exit.

"Now, where were we?" Bill said, opening another bottle of wine. "This has been a fascinating story, and I can't wait to hear the final chapter. What's this new development?"

"Actually, your wife is the one who can enlighten us on that," Fred replied. "She's been one step ahead of us, so I'll defer to her."

Feeling her face redden, Lydia once again looked at the floor. She managed a sideways glance at Bill who sat motionless, staring at her.

"What are you talking about?" she asked nervously. The room was silent.

"Darrell Baker," Fred said gently. "You've known for some time there was a connection between his death and Warren, right?"

Resigned that her surreptitious investigation had been exposed, Lydia recounted how she'd picked up Darrell's business card near the club early in the summer, then coincidentally found it in the pocket of some pants the night Darrell's body washed up in the river. And how she had tracked down and visited Marge Baker, who gave her the printout of the properties Darrell had managed, discovering Warren had been Darrell's client for Pershing Plaza. How she'd visited the shopping center and subsequently contacted the new property manager, Dale Richards. How it had been Darrell who informed one of the Pershing Plaza investors that the property had been sold without his knowledge. And finally, how she had found that investor, Ben Gregorie, from the phone number that Darrell had scrawled on the printout.

"You gotta be kidding me," Bill said, throwing down a napkin, then pouring himself a large glass of wine. "I thought you were going to drop all that."

"Well, I didn't, Bill. I couldn't exactly ignore something that fell into my lap." As Bill sulked, Fred took the story further. "But then you actually met with Gregorie who, we've just learned, has filed a civil suit against WLR Real Estate Ventures."

"You didn't!" Bill blurted out.

"Yes, Bill, I'm afraid I did. I am so sorry."

"I specifically asked you to drop the idea of pursuing Ben Gregorie. Now, it turns out, you met this guy by yourself? He could have been a crook too, and worse! He and Warren could have been in it together. Damnit, Lydia—"

"I can see I've opened up a can of worms here," Fred said, standing up to leave. "Maybe now isn't the time to discuss this."

"No, please stay Fred," Lydia said. "We might as well get this all out in the open. Bill, we can talk about this later. It was Ben's idea to meet when he came into town to file the lawsuit. Based on what he told me, I became convinced that Darrell's death was connected to Warren's company. By the way, I had to sign a non-disclosure document stating that I wouldn't reveal anything from my meeting with Ben—even to my husband. That's why I didn't tell you, Bill. Now that I've told everyone, I hope I don't get sued too."

"Don't worry about that. This was all going to come out anyway," Fred assured her. "Because after going through Darrell's business files, we came to the same conclusion. Learning that Darrell had managed Pershing Plaza for Warren's company proved to be a big break in the case for us. We then spoke with Dale Richards, and he corroborated that Darrell had met with one of Pershing Plaza's investors—Ben Gregorie, it turns out—and informed him that the property had been secretly sold.

"Yesterday, we had a face-to-face with Warren, who broke down in tears and confessed when he realized we had him. Warren explained that Darrell, after learning of the Pershing Plaza sale and then meeting with Gregorie, followed him to one of his late-night rendezvous with Claire at Meadow Glen. He confronted them and threatened to call the police. We've since verified that Darrell had in fact scheduled a meeting with the police the next day, but of course never showed up."

"That's when he must have dropped his business card near the club," Lydia surmised.

"Probably so," Vince agreed. "Warren said it was Claire who hit Darrell over the head with a wrench lying near the boiler room. He insisted that Claire had not meant to kill Darrell, but when they realized he was dead, she instructed Mac and Hector to dump the body in the river."

"So what happens now?" Bill asked sharply, still visibly angry that Lydia had stepped up her involvement behind his back.

"We're rechecking the evidence, including the wrenches from Meadow

Glen, to test for DNA and fingerprints in the hope that we can definitively connect these folks to Darrell's murder. Then, we'll probably charge Claire with second-degree murder and Warren as an accessory. Warren may think his confession will get him off that charge, but he'll likely spend several years in prison."

The room was silent for a long time.

"I guess that's better than the death penalty," Pete said. "The crazy thing is, they almost got away with it."

"And here all this time poor Marge Baker has been worried her husband was having an affair and was killed by the jealous husband," Lydia lamented. "But I have a question. How did you figure out my involvement? Were you tailing me too?"

"No, we were tailing the people who were tailing you," Vince said, chuckling.

"What? What are you talking about?"

"In addition to keeping tabs on Warren and Claire, we began following Mac and Hector, who drove a black SUV. About six weeks ago, we tracked that vehicle to Marge Baker's house. And lo and behold, your car was there too. Warren confirmed that after Darrell was killed, Mac and Hector began watching the Baker house to see who was coming and going. However, as we continued to follow the SUV, it became clear their favorite surveillance target was you, Lydia. By the middle of August, wherever you went, the SUV followed, including downtown to the Majestic Hotel. It wasn't hard to figure out who you were meeting with that day."

"Oh my God," Lydia said, astonished at what she was hearing. "Now that I think about it, I do remember seeing a black SUV a lot but stupidly wasn't paying attention."

"You had no reason to believe someone was following you," Vince noted. "And black SUVs are very common."

IT WAS JUST after ten by the time Fred, Vince, Pete, and Shelly said good night. As the door closed behind them, Lydia braced herself for Bill to unleash his wrath.

She turned to face him. "Bill, I am so sorry this got so out of control. You were right, I shouldn't have gotten involved. Then, things escalated to a point where I couldn't tell you anything."

"It's one thing to go behind my back, but it's another to almost get yourself killed. That's ultimately what happened here. You went nosing around, even after I asked you not to, and look what happened." He gestured to her broken shoulder.

"I know. I just couldn't help myself. I deeply regret what I've done and have learned a lesson. I've never kept anything from you, and never will again. Please, can we move beyond this?" she pleaded, her eyes welling up with tears.

He looked at her for several seconds. "Yes, we'll get beyond this," he sighed, putting his arms around her. "I knew what I was getting into when I married you, so I guess I shouldn't be surprised. As much as your dogged determination frustrates me, it's one of the reasons I love you. But good God, this has been a nightmare—in a nightmare of a summer."

"One more day, Bill. One more day."

Labor Day

The Last Hurrah

ONE MORE day at the club. One final meeting. One last day of summer fun. It was six a.m.; the house was quiet. Even Stacie wasn't stirring yet. The sun was starting to peek through the shutters, making a fragmented pattern of light. Having mastered the coffeemaker with her left hand, Lydia poured herself a large mug and heated up a muffin in the microwave. She turned on the TV, flipping through the channels and finally stopping at the Home Shopping Network, where a woman was selling silver jewelry.

Bill came downstairs dressed to play tennis in the Labor Day Round Robin and carrying a bag with towels and sunblock. "Do you want me to take this over and snag a table?" he asked, turning his attention to fixing Stacie's breakfast.

"No, thanks. I'll go over around nine and bring the towels. I need to make sure everything is set up for the meeting and lunch." This would be her first visit to the club since that awful night, and Lydia had to admit she was feeling apprehensive. Having a few tasks would make it easier, she figured.

"Since this is your last tango in Paris, I won't try to talk you out of it," Bill said, kissing her goodbye.

But there was something she needed to do first.

MARGE BAKER sounded groggy when she picked up the phone. "Marge, it's Lydia Phillips. Did I wake you? I just realized it's a little early for a holiday."

"No, I was awake, dear. Taking my time getting up. I was going to call you this week. I read about what happened and how your dog saved your life. What a terrible experience that must have been."

"It was, but I am on the mend. If a broken shoulder is the worst thing that happens to me, I'll consider myself very lucky. Anyway, I wanted to call because I have some information that I think you'll be glad to hear. I can't give you any details, but I want you to know that Darrell was definitely not having an affair. In fact, he died trying to do the right thing, and you should be very proud of him."

Silence as Marge processed the information. "Thank God. And thank you so much for calling. I can't tell you what a relief it is to hear that." Lydia could hear her voice breaking. "These last few months have been the worst of my life. First, losing my husband, then not knowing why. How did you find out?"

"As I said, I can't tell you. But the authorities will be in touch very soon to give you a full, official account of what happened. And once I'm out of this ridiculous shoulder immobilizer and can drive, we'll go out for that lunch."

"Thank you so much, Lydia. I'll look forward to that. I feel so much better knowing an end to all this is in sight."

Pleased that she had at least brought some closure for Marge, Lydia scrawled a barely legible note for the boys saying she and Bill were at the club.

THERE WERE six doubles matches underway on the tennis courts and another dozen or so players on the patio waiting their turn. She saw that Bill was paired with Jennifer Murphy on Court 2. *Ugh. I wonder if she's cheating. Bill won't stand for that.*

"Lydia, how are you? How's your shoulder?" Grant had never been so friendly. Several tennis players also stopped to ask how she was doing and hear the details about her harrowing experience.

Jules was busy opening the Sugar Shack, the faint, familiar odor of marijuana wafting onto the patio. She came around the corner and gave Lydia a big hug. "Have you tried any of the goodies I brought you?" she asked.

"Not yet, Jules. I've actually been sleeping a little better. I know it's there when I need it." As she proceeded toward the pool, Lydia felt her hands get clammy and her breathing pick up, remembering how Warren's hit man had escorted her into the club that terrible night.

A long table was set up along the back of the patio, and the catering company was arranging plates, silverware, and chafing dishes under the supervision of Amanda Wilson, uncharacteristically dressed in a pair of

Bermuda shorts, T-shirt, and flip-flops.

"Amanda. We missed you at the meeting last week."

"Hi, Lydia," she said, not making eye contact. "Yeah, sorry I couldn't make it. By the way, I'm resigning from the board. With my busy schedule, I don't have time for this." Gone was the gushiness. Lydia guessed Amanda, humiliated by her diving board romp with Rex, just wanted out.

"Sorry to hear that. You've done a nice job." Lydia made her way past another set of tables arranged in a semicircle for the board to conduct the annual meeting. A long cord connected a microphone to an outlet on the patio.

Pete was in his office, enjoying a moment of quiet before the pool opened.

"Hey," Lydia said, poking her head in.

"Hey, how's it going? Last day. Can't say I'm sorry after what we've been through this season. You recover from the meeting last night?"

"Yes, things seem to be okay. Bill and I talked it out."

Reading her mind, he smiled and said, "Don't worry. I'll be back next year. You can announce it."

Lydia found a table in the shade, propped her arm on the pile of towels, and breathed a sigh of relief knowing that the season was ending, and Pete would be back. Looking around, she saw the ducks taking their morning swim before the pool became crowded with children and pool toys. The ducklings, however, were nowhere in sight, a sure sign they had left the nest to make their own way in the world.

An older man wearing white shorts, a blue and white shirt, and white hat, and carrying a tennis bag, quickly skulked to the corner of the pool deck. This time it was Al Flood in disguise to get in early and claim the coveted poker table.

She dozed off but was awakened by a shrill whistle signaling the opening of the pool for the last time this summer. As people began pouring in, she realized she had never seen the club so crowded. No doubt some members were interested in seeing the scene of the crime and hearing the latest gossip, while others were lured by the free lunch. With the tennis matches over, the courts were filling up with kids and couples. The grass area was crowded with people spreading out their towels as all the tables had been taken. Bud Wright and several other men wheeled the grills out for the barbecue.

At eleven-thirty, the whistle sounded again. Lydia's cue to start the meeting. By now, the other board members had gathered around the table, with Rex and Amanda occupying the far-end seats, staying as far away as possible from each other. She took the microphone and called the meeting to order. Loud cheers emanated from the crowd, then a standing ovation— a response that nearly moved her to tears.

"Thank you all for being here and for your participation and support this summer," she began. "It has been a strange season, to be sure, but I feel this summer marks a turning point for Meadow Glen. I am happy to announce we have a waitlist of fifteen people and are positioned to create a new beginning for our beloved club. Thanks to Rex Simons, we have received permission from the neighborhood HOA to finish installing lights on the courts and around the club. The lawsuit is behind us." The news was met with another huge burst of clapping.

"Please give a round of applause for our amazing manager, Pete Merrick. We could not have gotten through this summer without him. I am thrilled to announce Pete will be back next year." Once again, the crowd erupted into loud cheers and whistles.

"I also want to thank my fellow board members, who have been so supportive and done a fabulous job. I especially want to thank Mike Patterson, who is so valuable to this club. He will do a great job next year as your president." More clapping.

"And finally, a special thanks to my wonderful husband, Bill, and my sons, Andy and Geoff, who this past year have put up with things you can't begin to imagine."

"What about Stacie?" someone in the crowd shouted.

Lydia's throat tightened at the thought of her beloved dog's unconditional love and loyalty. "And yes, Stacie," she said, making eye contact with Bill, who was standing off to the side with a wiggling and whining Stacie on a leash. Bill let her go, and she ran from person to person, reveling in the attention, before running to Lydia. As the dog licked her face and the applause continued, Lydia managed to say, "Stacie, you have made a lasting impression on Meadow Glen. I love you, little girl." Bill then took the leash and walked her back home.

THE MEETING lasted just forty-five minutes. After the requisite committee reports, George Bishop presented the long-range planning report, indicating that lights would be installed on the remaining courts and throughout the grounds, and landscaping and painting would be done next spring. "Then, we'll look into remodeling the bathrooms and updating the plumbing," he said as another cheer erupted.

Cheers? What? No complaints? Lydia thought, recalling last year's contentious meeting over everything from the lights to the snack bar offerings. "Before we elect new board members, is there any new business?" she asked, expecting a huge number of raised hands. But only one person came forward. It was Vince Albright. "In light of what happened over the summer, what about adding some security cameras throughout the club grounds?"

More applause, as several members expressed support for the idea.

"I think that's definitely worth looking into," Lydia said. "However, since I'm stepping down, I would now like to turn the meeting over to our president-elect, Mike Patterson. It will be Mike's board that will address this issue."

"I agree, that's a great idea," Mike echoed. "And Vince, if you'd be willing, I'd like to nominate you as an at-large board member responsible for safety and security."

Vince was roundly supported, along with two nominations from the floor, including a new treasurer.

It's over, Lydia thought as Mike adjourned the meeting.

PETE CRANKED the music back up, and burgers began sizzling on the grills. Watching the queue of people going through the buffet line, Lydia sensed that everyone was embracing the festive mood even as the rituals of summer at Meadow Glen carried on: Nancy Brown practicing her forehand on the backboard. Grant giving a private lesson to a young new female member. Little girls squealing as Fred Lyons donned his swim cap and applied zinc oxide. Ernestine in a big floppy hat slathering her daughters, both buried in books, with sunblock. Betsy Broadhurst timing Erica. Brad and Tad on Court 2.

In the corner, the four poker players were already deep into their game—and their cocktails—with Chip squeezed in next to Bob Mackie. Spying Lydia, he waved and came running over to her table, friendly as ever. "Hi, Mrs. P. Here's your money back."

"Chip! Thank you very much," a surprised Lydia responded. "I appreciate that."

By now, a smiling Deni had approached. "I found the money in his room and forced him to confess where it came from," she said. "We're making sure everyone he took money from gets it back. How's your arm?"

"Much better, Deni, thank you. And thanks for having Chip return the money. That's very nice of you. So glad to see you here," Lydia said, wondering how someone who had been so unpleasant was now nice as pie.

"When we heard about the free picnic lunch, we decided we'd give it a try."

Whatever it takes. "Enjoy yourself."

Lydia couldn't believe how well the day was progressing. *People actually seem...happy.*

And the playground? No tantrums, but there were the Murphy boys throwing rocks and having a peeing contest on the slide. She smiled. *Some things never change.*

Lydia returned to the table; soon, Bill and the boys appeared with plates piled with food.

A long whistle signaled Adult Swim. Fred Lyons waved to Lydia, then eased into the lap lane. Geoff and Andy joined a group of boys tossing around a football.

"So, Madame ex-President, how does it feel to be just one of the masses?" Bill asked.

Lydia started to answer but was distracted by a commotion erupting near the Sugar Shack. She looked over to see Stacie grabbing a hot dog off a frightened toddler's plate. An interruption to the pleasant ambience that had so far defined the day. Bill rushed over to intervene.

The dog door. Lydia searched the crowd and locked eyes with Geoff. He raised his shoulders and shrugged in an it-wasn't-me response, then bolted.

As Bill attempted to corner Stacie, the crowd erupted into yet another round of applause and began chanting, "Stace the Great."

A few minutes later, the commotion had died down and Stacie was sitting amongst ten or twelve young girls, happily having her fur brushed as she licked their plates.

"You asked me how it feels to be just a regular member," Lydia said when Bill returned to the table. "I'm feeling good. Really looking forward to opening a new chapter. Don't worry, it won't involve any volunteer work!" Smiling as she watched a bee hover over her potato salad, she added, "I can't wait for next summer."

Afterall...how bad could it be?

Acknowledgments

The stories in this book are just that—stories. But the inspiration for them comes from real experiences and real people who either knowingly or unwittingly made it all possible. I would especially like to thank my wonderful son, Zach, without whom there would be no tale to tell; and my husband, Bob, an amazing writer and storyteller whose sense of humor and insight have been invaluable. I also want to give a huge thanks to Frank Harper, Miriam Whitney, Susan Kudla, Mary Chedsey, George Chedsey, Dave Price, Jo Fukaye, Stephanie Greenberg, Jane Swanson, Mark Swanson, Beth Samuelson, Joan White, and Barb Cleveland. And of course, Ginnie and Bob.

CPSIA information can be obtained
at www.ICGtesting.com
Printed in the USA
FSHW010754030221
78144FS